DELIVERY

DELIVERY

a novel by

BETTY JANE HEGERAT

OOLICHAN BOOKS

LANTZVILLE, BRITISH COLUMBIA, CANADA

2009

Library and Archives Canada Cataloguing in Publication

Hegerat, Betty Jane, 1948-

Delivery / Betty Jane Hegerat.

ISBN 978-0-88982-257-3

I. Title.

PS8615.E325D44 2009   C813'.6   C2009-904757-8

We gratefully acknowledge the financial support of the Canada
Council for the Arts, the British Columbia Arts Council through
the BC Ministry of Tourism, Culture, and the Arts, and the
Government of Canada through the Book Publishing Industry
Development Program, for our publishing activities.

Published by
Oolichan Books
P.O. Box 10, Lantzville
British Columbia, Canada
V0R 2H0

Printed in Canada

1

The ferry connects to the dock with a thud, and Lynn opens her eyes. Thick ocean smell has filled the car, settled cold on the back of her throat. She swallows hard, presses her palms into the seat and raises herself slightly. Her thighs feel as though they have grafted to her jeans.

Every muscle aches. Lynn is tempted to get out, stretch, stand in the wind for five minutes before she drives off the boat, onto the island. But without the motion of the sea or the car, the baby in the back seat will squall. She's been awake since they boarded the ferry, but mercifully quiet.

Lynn turns, leans into the back of the car and peers into the laundry basket. Through the criss-cross of seatbelts strapping her bed tightly in place, Beegee's dark eyes shine up at Lynn. She's found her thumb, the steady *suck-suck-click* soothing her for the moment.

Lynn strokes Beegee's cheek with the tips of her fingers, whispers to her. "So, Baby Girl. Just a few more minutes. And so far, we're doing fine." Well, maybe not fine, but better than she could have imagined if she'd ever dared to imagine this journey. Calgary to Quadra Island, non-stop except for two naps in the car in deserted campground parking lots. A family trip that always involved a leisurely two days with a stopover in the Okanagan. Lynn and Beegee have done it in slightly more than twenty-four hours.

Lynn starts the car and follows the truck ahead of her onto solid ground. The stars outshine the few lights in the village ahead. The air rushing in the open window is surprisingly soft for October. But then Lynn's never been to Quadra at this time of year. Their trips were always in August, just before Jack and the kids went back to school, and they always ended, it seemed, in rain. Lynn's memories of the drive home are hung with grey drizzle, the swish of windshield wipers, and her children, Marty and Heather, wrapped in blankets in the back seat.

She licks her lips, and finally reaches for the bottle of water in the beverage holder between the seats. She's been desperately thirsty since she drove off the first ferry that brought her from the mainland to Nanaimo, but wanted to avoid a bathroom stop. She never took Marty and Heather into public toilets when they were babies. And she's terrified of exposing Beegee. Even worse, though, is the thought of leaving her alone in the car. This Lynn cannot do. So many things she's forgotten about babies, and what she can and cannot bear to do.

As though she's tuned in to Lynn's thoughts, the baby begins the preliminary snuffles and squeaks that will escalate in minutes. Beegee seems to have inherited both her style and intensity from her mother, Heather.

"Shhhhh." Lynn turns her head to see a small arm waving. It looks as though Beegee has wriggled free of the blanket cocoon, but there's no point in stopping now. They'll be at Einar's cabin in minutes.

Lynn drives up the hill from the ferry, past the pub where Jack and Einar spent a ritual boys' night out at the end of each holiday, letting memory be her guide. She's glad Einar is away. Her thoughts, somewhere around Banff, when she finally admitted where she was headed, were of the cabin and solitude. She imagined how empty the space would seem without Jack, just when she thought she'd become accustomed to his absence. When she finally stopped to phone Einar, she hoped if she admitted to some kind of personal emergency, he might excuse himself and go elsewhere as he had during the summers when he had so graciously given them the use of his cabin. Otherwise, here he'd be, along with her. And Beegee.

Over the phone, Lynn didn't mention the baby to Einar. She could barely find the words to explain that she was coming. "If that's okay," she said. "If it's not any trouble. I just need to get away, and I can't think of anywhere else."

"Of course it's okay," he said. "When are you leaving?"

"Actually, I've already left." She paused, swallowed. She was afraid the spasm in her throat would turn to a sob or a bark of hysterical laughter. "I'm at Lake Louise, Einar. I'll explain when I get there, okay? How long do you think it will take?"

"You're not driving straight through?" he said. "That's a torture test reserved only for fools like me. Stop somewhere for the night, Lynn. Don't drive in the dark."

Sleep? In the past three weeks, most nights she'd spent more time staring at the bedroom ceiling and tiptoeing down the hall to peek in at Heather and Beegee than sleeping. "Yes," she said. "I'll stop." This was what he wanted to hear.

There was a silence so long she thought they might have been disconnected, and then finally he spoke again. "You caught me on the way out the door. I promised to install some cabinets for a friend in Sidney this weekend. But maybe I should stay."

"No, Einar, I'll be fine. Really. Do your work and I'll be there when you get back. Like the old days," she said. Likely, he'd assumed that her need to get away had to do with the divorce. Best to leave it at that.

"All right then, make yourself at home. Drive safe, and I'll see you Sunday night or early Monday." Just the sound of his big voice calmed her a little. "The key's under the same rock where you always found it."

And that was that. She shouldn't be surprised. Einar never questioned, never judged, in fact never seemed fazed by anything. Nothing was urgent, nothing required explanation. This, Jack said, was one of the things he admired most about Einar. This, Lynn thought long ago, was probably why Einar was no longer married.

Her sense of time is muddled. It was yesterday, Friday, when she called; today is Saturday. He'll be home tomorrow or the next day. For now, all she needs is the key.

She realizes that she has no idea which rock Einar was talking about. It was Jack who invariably retrieved the key from its hiding spot. She and the kids waited on the carpet of needles at the front door, arms stretched to the ceiling of cedar to rid themselves of all the kinks from the long drive. She grips the wheel tighter. If she's made it this far, she can meet the small challenge of getting into the cabin. Even in the dark, she has the sense that nothing significant has changed.

Nothing but the fact that Lynn is in charge. And instead of her long-ago Marty and Heather, flushed with heat and boredom at the journey's end, she has Heather's daughter warming for a rousing concert that could wake the whole island. The adrenaline that's kept Lynn's foot on the gas pedal, hands on the wheel, is running low.

She slows at a crossroads. Not here. The next corner. Any minute now she'll have to turn and drive deeper into the island. She clicks on the high beams, and two deer bound across the road into the thick forest. Now the left turn. After the log house there should be another driveway, a sign with Einar's name burned into the wood. When her headlights play across the piece of driftwood, Lynn cranks the wheel fast, and the car rolls down the tunnel of driveway, dark trees arching overhead. Lynn remembers that arriving at Einar Haugland's cabin always made her feel like she was being swallowed.

The car coasts to a stop in front of a pile of firewood and Lynn's hands slip off the wheel, her shoulders sagging. She opens the car door, then yanks it shut when a shadow flings itself from the front step. The dog flies at the car, a volley of guttural barks chasing him. Lynn cracks the window just far enough to call softly.

"Hey, Loki. What a good boy for keeping watch."

The bark turns to a growl, to a whine, a final puzzled woof, then his jaw relaxes and his tongue lolls. Lynn rolls the window all the way down and lets Loki sniff her hand. She opens the door and crouches on the damp bed of needles. "Looking pretty spry!" she says. Einar has had Loki as long as Lynn can remember. Or maybe, Heather once suggested, he kept getting new dogs and calling them Loki. Loki looks from Lynn to the car where all is quiet, at least to Lynn's ears. When she opens the back door, Beegee's small hand is waving, sleeper-clad feet pedaling. Loki presses close and tries to scramble into the car.

"Oh, dog." Lynn pushes his muzzle away from the basket. "You won't believe what I've gone and done."

She lifts the baby out of damp bedding, and stands beside the car, holding her close. "We made it," she whispers. "Now what do we do?"

Lynn has not been allowed to either ask or answer this question. She didn't need to be told by the social worker at the adoption agency that the decision of what to do with Beegee was Heather's. Even when Heather came by with a questionnaire she was to fill out, all the reasons for keeping the baby on one side of the page, the reasons for giving her away on the other, even when Heather left the keeping side totally blank, Lynn didn't push. Although she did ask why only half the assignment was done. What about the other side of the page?

"Not going there," Heather said. "I've made up my mind."

Today is Saturday. By now Heather will have discovered that Lynn and Beegee are missing. Lynn clings tightly to the baby, and takes deep breaths to control the tremor that begins whenever she thinks about Heather. She hopes that Heather is not alone. When Heather's distraught she calls Lynn. Who would she call this time? Probably Marty first, then Jack. At least a half dozen times on the trip Lynn has slowed at a town, intending to find a phone, to call Heather, to assure her that Beegee is fine. But then what? Explain what she's done? She hasn't explained it adequately to herself, in spite of the monologue that's been going on in her head for a night and a day. All it would take, she's sure, is the sound of Heather's crying to convince her to get back into the car, turn around, and go home. And there's the problem. Beegee has another home waiting, and Lynn cannot bear to think about that. Or about how Heather will have to explain to Carmen and to Donna and Grant that her baby is missing, kidnapped by her mother. Madness that no one mentioned in the family history?

For now, Lynn won't think about any of it. She will change her granddaughter's diaper, feed her another bottle of her mother's milk, and rock her to sleep. They have arrived. There is no urgency. Lynn has all the time she needs. She's taking a leave from trying to sort out her own life, from all the boring temporary jobs with which she's filled her time since Jack left.

Poor Beegee is soaked, and so is her blanket. Lynn reaches into the basket for the towel she folded for a mattress. She wraps it around Beegee, kisses the top of her head. One thing at a time. First she'll address the problem of the key. The dog looks up at her with pathetically confident eyes. "Right," Lynn says, and pats Loki's head. "You're a big help. But you'll be good company."

She anchors the baby to her chest with one hand, and crouches in the light of the dim bulb over the front door. The rocks at the foot of the step all look the same, none more or less permanent or mysterious than any other. Finally, she stands and flips moss-covered logs with her foot, then lifts pieces of driftwood and seashells that line the front step. The baby is strangely content, but Lynn's eyes can't help searching for bats in the flickering shadows. With Loki at her side, she rounds the corner to the rear of the cabin and has to stop while her eyes adjust to even darker night. She knows from previous visits, from Marty and Heather climbing into the cabin through every possible portal, that the waist-high bedroom window slides easily and makes a joke of the well-hidden key. But of course, there is the watchdog.

She hesitates, considers going back to the car, locking the baby in the back seat once again while she completes this mission. Oddly, this patch of ground, the faithful dog, feels safer to her than the lonely car. She takes off her jacket and fashions yet another bed for Beegee. "Loki, stay. Watch. I'll be back in one minute flat."

Hands to the soft old wood of the window frame, she raises it with no effort at all, and shakes her head. But who is she to chide Einar for his lack of security? She refuses to use the alarm system in her own house. She hoists herself onto the windowsill with her forearms, kicks against the wall, and wriggles through head first. A soft landing on Einar's neatly made bed, a dash to the kitchen door and she's back into the night. When she returns, panting, Loki is curled around the jacket, ears pricked.

"Good boy. You're hired." She carries Beegee to the car, hooks the picnic cooler with its precious baggies of breast milk over her shoulder, grabs the box of Pampers, and gulps down one more lungful of moist air before she enters the cabin.

The dog follows Lynn into the kitchen, his toenails clicking on worn linoleum. Moonlight streams through skylights. Even without electricity the inside of the cabin seems lighter than the yard with its canopy of cedar. Lynn pauses to put heel to toe and pry her feet out of her running shoes. She wriggles her toes inside sweaty socks, then pads across the room to the bathroom, and turns on the light. In the sudden brightness, she blinks and shades Beegee's eyes with her hand. She shakes a towel from the neat pile on the back of the toilet, spreads it on the floor and unwinds the baby's damp layers. This time there is no preliminary warm-up. Seconds after Beegee is unwrapped, her siren wail sends Loki flying to the kitchen.

Now that they're cloistered within the thick walls of the cabin, Lynn can close her ears to the crying. She moves slowly, sponging every inch of the baby, tossing Einar's facecloth into the tub when she's done, lobbing the disposable diaper into the plastic garbage can under the sink. There'll be time enough tomorrow to deal with it all.

"Shhhh," she whispers over and over, patting the soft skin dry, taping a clean diaper neatly around that ridiculously tiny bottom. She shakes out another towel and swaddles Beegee, just her howling red face exposed now, black hair sweaty against her scalp, the top of her head pulsing. "Shhh." Lynn stands, rocks and sways her way to the kitchen. She unzips the cooler bag, takes out a slushy sleeve of milk and with one hand manages to slip it into the plastic tube and fix a nipple on top. By the time she's warmed the milk in a cup of water and settled into the rocking chair, Beegee is frantic. Hungry, and furious that another plastic nipple is being forced between her lips, she arches her back and swings her head side to side, refusing the bottle.

When Heather worried about Beegee's switching from breast to bottle, Carmen, the social worker, assured her it would be just a matter of a day or so, no major trauma. But that it would get harder the longer Heather procrastinated. The unspoken, of course, was that there would have been no problem if Heather hadn't insisted on taking Beegee home and letting her nurse in the first place. Against Carmen's advice. Lynn could have told Carmen that her advice was probably what swayed Heather. Push in one direction, Heather moves in the other.

Heather sobbing in her bedroom in Calgary with her breasts as hard as granite. And Donna, the would-be adoptive mother? What is she doing now in her pretty house with the soft pink nursery? Such a mess, and now it's even worse, and Lynn knows it's her fault.

Loki slinks across the room and drops, whining at Lynn's feet. Head cocked, as though asking what it is, exactly, that Lynn has gone and done.

This is what amazes and terrifies Lynn. She's stolen Heather's baby. Grabbed her and run. "How will you feel if Heather places the baby?" Carmen asked Lynn months ago. If she'd felt more comfortable with Carmen, Lynn would have put her hand on the woman's wrist and said, "I will want to grab her, and run as fast as I can. But don't worry. I'm not known for acting on impulse." She would have believed it herself.

She sets the bottle on the floor beside the chair, slides

her hand under the small body and holds Beegee at arm's length. The baby's head would fit neatly into the palm of her grandpa's hand. Lynn has a vivid flashback to Jack holding Heather just so when she was brand new. But never Marty. They were so nervous with Marty. Lynn's arms were so awkward when he was placed into them for the first time that Jack jumped up and immediately took the baby himself. When she asked him later, why, he said, "I was afraid you'd drop him, and they'd change their minds and not give him back."

Lynn shakes her head, trying to focus on the baby she's holding. As she feared right up to Beegee's birth, she finds it impossible to untangle this baby from the memories of her two. She brings Beegee's face close to her own. "Little girl! Get over it. Same food, different package. It's the best I can do for now." Tomorrow. Surely by tomorrow Beegee will accept that there is only one way to get her mother's milk. Tonight she's red with rage.

Lynn sways and croons, teasing the baby's lips with the bottle. How many times, watching Heather nurse her baby, has Lynn felt the tingling in her own nipples? Eyes closed, she rocks and tries to imagine Beegee nursing peacefully in her arms. When she looks down, milk is dripping from the stout yellow nipple, running from Beegee's chin into the folds of her neck. Sad little face searching for warm skin and finding plastic and her grandma's wrinkled shirt.

Lynn exhales. Why not? She can at least provide the skin. With her free hand, she tugs at the buttons until her shirt gapes, slides a bra strap far enough to liberate her breast and snuggles Beegee's reddened face against her side. As though twenty years have fallen away, Lynn's fingers gently guide her nipple toward the open mouth and Beegee latches on. Such ferocity in those first sucks that Lynn gasps and holds her breath. She can feel the pull deep in her belly; tears rush to her eyes. But now what? No matter how hard Beegee sucks, or how right this feels, these breasts are dry. Lynn flattens the squat nipple of the Playtex nurser between her fingers, and wriggles it into Beegee's mouth. When the suction around her own nipple breaks, she slips it free, then holds the baby's chin firmly with her thumb, a finger on each side of the mouth until it fastens around the plastic. Beegee's eyes fly open and meet Lynn's. "Yes," Lynn whispers. "We can do this." She clasps the baby's face even closer to her breast, and as the milk flows from the bottle, Beegee growing softer, sleepier in her arms, Lynn can think only of Heather. The infant Heather, nursing with the same wild hunger at her breast, and the new-mother Heather gazing intently at Beegee each time she fed.

Lynn puts her head back and stares into the dark beams of the ceiling. The cabin is exactly as she reconstructed it in her mind after the phone call to Einar, down to every shabby detail, every leftover shadow of the dozen or so years of visits. By morning, the walls will be closing in, and she will need to stand outside and look for a window through the trees. What other destination could she have chosen? How dismal is it that she had no where else to go?

Finally, Beegee's jaw has gone slack. The nipple falls from her lips, milk runs out the sides of her mouth and she gives a deep shuddering sigh. With the corner of her shirt, Lynn blots up the excess milk and pats the white blister on the baby's upper lip.

She takes care not to jostle her on the way to the bed. She sits on the edge and wriggles out of her jeans, swings her legs up under the covers, her back against the wall. When she stretches to pull up the quilt, Beegee whimpers and releases a barrage of farts that brings a curious Loki to the side of the bed.

She reaches over and pats the dog's head. "Competition,"

she tells him, almost managing a smile. She remembers Einar proudly proclaiming Loki the island's champion farter. Marty, holding his nose, Heather trying to out-fart the dog. Loki's been well-mannered since they came inside. Or Lynn has been too tired to notice. Or this is a different Loki.

With the baby still nestled in the crook of her arm, she curls on her side and closes her eyes. Finally she will sleep. She feels a gentle stir of air as Loki circles three times before he settles on the rug beside the bed.

In the night, Lynn wakens to the sound of dripping rain. The sheets are clammy, with a faint tinge of male musk. Lynn turns her face to Beegee's soft hair. The primal newborn smell, growing fainter day by day, still takes Lynn back twenty years. She's sure she inhales a memory of Heather from this child. Even farther back, Lynn knows she carries the memory of Marty's newborn scent even though she only held him for a fleeting few seconds before he was whisked away. Two weeks later, when she finally pressed her nose to his skin once more, the smell was lost.

All she wants is sleep, a few more hours of forgetfulness, but her brain has returned to the road, remembering every curve and stop, reversing all the way back to Calgary. When sleep finally returns, she dreams she's never left, never gone farther than the car, baby and laundry basket in her arms. There she sits waiting for Heather to come to her senses. To realize that asking a woman to deliver her granddaughter to the permanent care of strangers is too much. In the dream, Lynn chooses fight instead of flight and is on her way back to the house when she wakens again, her heart banging against her breastbone. Loki stands beside the bed, watching her across the towel-bundled baby.

"Oh jeez." Lynn takes a deep breath then another. "I

think I was going into the house to shake some sense into her, Loki," she whispers.

When Heather veered from her plan of giving the baby to Donna and Grant the day she left the hospital, she insisted that it was only for a week or so. The baby was barely a day old, so vulnerable, so in need of her mother's milk, that Heather couldn't bear to tear her away from her breast quite yet. But in a week, she would switch Beegee from breast to bottle. She, herself, because she wouldn't entrust the job to anyone else. Then she needed one more week, and into the third week, Lynn began to breathe easier, to talk about buying a few things. Offering small encouragement, and yet afraid that Heather would seize on it. Terrified for her daughter should she choose to be a mother, and even more frightened that she'd give the baby up when she seemed to have no idea what this would mean. Through it all, Lynn pressed her fingernails into the palms of her hands, and curled her tongue against the roof of her mouth to keep from blurting out all that she should have been allowed to say. And couldn't say, because they swore, she and Jack, that they would never talk again, not even between the two of them, about those two weeks after Marty's birth.

Lynn tried to ask Jack, just months ago when they found out Heather was pregnant, if he thought they would have let the adoption go ahead if they'd known Marty was already safe in the arms of his new family for those two weeks rather in the limbo of a foster home. "This has nothing to do with Marty," was all he would say, "nothing at all."

"Fine," she said, "you go ahead and believe that if you can." Lynn knew that for her, Heather's dilemma had everything to do with her own history, and she also knew the danger that Heather would move in exactly the opposite direction from anything Lynn suggested. So much at stake, and all she could offer was a tiny lounging seat so Heather could put the baby down occasionally. A sling for carrying Beegee close to her breasts but freeing her hands to read a book, or to study. On Friday morning, she had suggested a stroller so Heather could take the baby into the sunshine.

Heather was sitting sideways on the sofa holding Beegee, staring out the window. Lynn, in her chair on the other side of the room, had been mesmerized too by the flaming leaves of the mountain ash in the front yard. Such a glorious autumn, and she'd barely left the house. Suddenly Heather stood up and flew down the hall to her room. She was back in seconds without Beegee. "No! We are not buying furniture. How many times do I have to tell you I'm not keeping her?"

Lynn put down the book she'd been trying to read. "Heather," she said, straining to keep her voice steady, "it's okay to change your mind."

Heather stood there in the hallway, arms folded, feet planted in the immoveable stance that had been her signature posture since she pulled herself to standing when she was barely seven months old. "I'm phoning Carmen."

Lynn felt as though the roof had lifted and a funnel cloud roared above them. "Heather, no! Not that fast. It's Friday, and it's late in the day. Carmen's probably left the office by now." Lynn knew Carmen was always at the end of her phone, always ready for urgent action. Heather swooped down on the coffee table and grabbed the phone. She punched numbers, her cheeks flaming into two bright circles. She was barefoot, wearing a pair of badly-stretched black leggings she'd matched with baggy sweaters and men's shirts through the last weeks of her pregnancy. Back and forth she paced, then threw the phone onto the sofa.

"No, I do not want to talk to her supervisor! Her recording says she's away for the weekend, leave a message or call her freakin' supervisor if it's an emergency." She picked up one of Beegee's receiving blankets by the corners, shook it out with a snap and began to fold it, smoothing the edges as though she was packing for an urgent trip.

Lynn didn't dare move. "Heather, slow down," she said. "Don't be in such a rush. This feels dangerous."

Heather clutched the neat square to her chest as though she thought Lynn was going to snatch it from her. "I'm going to phone Donna and Grant and tell them you're bringing the baby. You'll take her for me, won't you? I can't wait for Carmen to get back, and I don't want some stranger carrying Beegee away."

Lynn's head had begun to shake as soon as Heather mentioned Donna and Grant. Ever since Heather brought Beegee home, Lynn had not allowed herself to think about those hapless hopeful people and the anguish they must be suffering as they waited for the baby.

"Oh no. No. Do not ask me to do this, Heather."

But within minutes, the phone call was made, Heather so abrupt, Lynn wondered what on earth Grant must be thinking. Surely he'd call back any minute and tell Heather to wait until Carmen was back. But when the phone did ring again and it was Grant, he only wanted to let Heather know about road construction so she could tell Lynn which alternate route to take. Heather rushed around the house with Lynn at her heels, pleading with her to stop.

"What about switching her to a bottle? You said you were going to do that before you gave her up."

"They can do it. Carmen said it won't take more than a day or two."

"But it will. Heather, sit down. We need to talk."

Heather clamped her lips tight, and shook her head. She filled the insulated bag with frozen milk, and stuffed Pampers and a couple of receiving blankets into the diaper bag. She pawed through the pile of papers, all the information about adoption that had been sitting on the end of the coffee table for months, and found Donna and Grant's address. She copied it in big black letters for Lynn, but stopped halfway through the directions on how to get there.

"You'll find it," she said. "It's not hard."

Perhaps she knew that Lynn had already driven by the house three times, imagined herself parking across the street, stalking, watching for a glimpse of the baby, little girl, teenager, for the next eighteen years?

Finally, Heather scooped up the baby, who was still sleeping more peacefully than she had in days, and deposited her in Lynn's arms. Then with her hands on her mother's shoulders she pushed her toward the door. "Go! Please, Mom, just do this for me. Otherwise, I have to go by myself."

Mom. Under any other circumstances, Heather's spontaneous defaulting to "mom" would have galvanized Lynn into helping her. But this time, Lynn knew as surely as she'd known anything in her life that what her daughter was asking was not going to be a help. Before Heather could change her mind and say she was coming along, Lynn walked out the door. But she did not, she reminds herself in this chilly bedroom, promise Heather that she was going to follow those orders.

As Heather slammed her bedroom door, Lynn walked stolidly across the kitchen, clutching Beegee to her shoulder with one arm, the bag full of milk and the diaper bag on the other. There was a basket of clean laundry at the basement door. Lynn kicked out all but a couple of towels, dropped the two bags into the basket and scrunched down to hoist the whole load under her arm. All so fluid, she was sure she knew what she was doing.

Outside, instead of heading for Heather's car with the baby seat—the car they'd used the two times they'd gone out with Beegee, both times to the doctor's office—Lynn went straight to her own car. She spent so long securing the basket in the back seat, she was sure Heather would come out and ask her what on earth she was doing. She hoped that Heather would, so that she could talk her into the passenger seat, and drive round and round the neighbourhood explaining to her why she needed to stop and listen to her tears. Then her fear that Heather would indeed come out and pluck Beegee away into her own car and make that trip to Donna and Grant herself overtook all caution and Lynn backed the car into the alley. She slowed before she pulled onto the busier street, and turned to look at the baby in the basket, so snug and secure. Then on to the next corner, where, instead of turning right to make her way to the northern suburb of the city where Donna and Grant were undoubtedly standing at the window waiting, Lynn pointed her car west, straight into the blazing sunset. She didn't know exactly where she was going when she left the city behind—not until Canmore, when the memories of so many other car trips with Jack and the kids crowded through the muddle in her head. At least she can claim that this crime was not premeditated.

The dog watches for another minute or two, then whimpers and drops back to his spot beside the bed.

Finally, Lynn drifts off again, dreaming miles of twisty highway and that she's driving blind with the baby clutched to her shoulder with one hand and the other like a vise on the wheel, waiting for the crash.

Each time she floats up out of the nightmare, her arm clenched around the baby, she has to remind herself that this is Beegee, Heather's baby. Not Marty. Her breath comes in gasps, trying to catch up with her galloping heart; she's astonished that Beegee sleeps on. The gentle dripping lulls Lynn back to sleep.

2

Heather kicks at the tangled sheets. Her breasts are so hard and hot, she can't bear it any longer even though she wants to stay asleep. For like about a month? Why does Carmen insist that it's better for her to stay away for a month? She has no intention of screwing up Donna and Grant's *bonding*. But she knows babies change quickly. In a month it'll be like looking at some strange kid. She won't recognize her own baby. Maybe that will be a good thing.

When she turns over to crawl out of bed, the flab on her belly rolls under her like an old boot. Jelly belly, leaky breasts, dripping eyes. She sits up and pounds the sheet. Okay. This she can fix. A good solid month at the gym and she should be able to get her old body back. Keep busy. That's what Carmen told her. Keep your mind off the baby and on the road ahead. Yuck. Support group stuff. She was a total failure in support group.

Jack offered to pay for a weekend in Las Vegas if she could find someone to go with her. The only person she can think of is Marty. How sad is that, to want to go to Vegas with your brother? But he's the only one who wouldn't be either all *rah rah* and trying to cheer her up, or else gooey-eyed and *oh poor you*, like some of her friends.

Everyone has suggestions about how she can get through the next ten days. As though it will be over then. That's the problem. The minute she heard Beegee crying in the delivery room, Heather knew it wasn't going to be over anytime soon. Such a big voice. Heather couldn't wait to hold her baby girl and look at every inch of her. Why didn't anyone tell her about all this hormonal crap? Well okay, so they did, but they didn't tell her it would be this bad.

She sits up, swings her feet to the floor and pulls them up fast. The hardwood is icy cold. The only heat in the room seems to be radiating from her chest. The front of her nightgown is so drenched with milk, she should be steaming. The dripping started as soon as she sat up, yesterday's leakage adding a sour smell to the mess. She drops a pillow on the floor and snuggles her feet into it, not wanting to stand too quickly. Like some kind of invalid, she still feels queasy when she gets up too fast.

The only sound is the hum of a computer. She's now holed up in the spare bedroom in the condo her dad, Jack, shares with his new wife, Rhea. The room also happens to be the office they share. Jack, all ruddy-cheeked and rubbing his hands together loves the cold, but skinny Rhea must wear a parka to work in here, whatever work it is that she does at home. Heather's never gotten that straight. Her brother, Marty, probably knows but Heather hasn't bothered to listen or to ask questions, because she really couldn't care less. She's made it clear to Jack that she doesn't need a stepmother. She's twenty years old and the mother she has will do.

Heather needs to talk to her mom. What time is it anyway? Her head's so full of sticky questions, she feels like she's been drugged. Why hasn't Lynn come over here and found her, told her how things worked out? She doesn't want to hear that Beegee woke up crying, but then Lynn probably didn't stick around long enough for that part. Heather covers her face with her hands and blows out a long breath. Guilt, yeah, that's what this is, on top of feeling like she's bloody well just ripped out her heart. Guilt because she knows this is something she had no right to ask of her mother. Didn't even ask, just assumed. She will not start crying again. Will not. If she waited until Monday, until Ms Social Worker was back and able to take the baby away, she would have lost her nerve. She was sitting there, watching the leaves fall off the trees, trying to figure out how to tell Lynn that she was at the freakin' end of her rope. If she was turning Beegee over to the adopting people, which she was, then she had to do it now, but she couldn't. But she had to. Back. Forward. Back. Then Lynn gave her the perfect opening with all that talk about the cute things they should buy and *blah blah blah* go walking in the sunshine.

Heather almost chickened out when she saw the horror on Lynn's face after she stuffed Beegee into her arms. But by then, Heather was such a basket case, it was either shove them out the door or fall apart for good. Okay, she admits she's actually considered changing her mind. At least a dozen times. But never for more than a minute, and then she was back on track again. Just waiting for the right time, and the clock got stuck. Now it's ticking.

There's a phone beside the computer. And a clock. It's two in the morning. She knows she's been here longer than one night. Remembers Jack knocking on the door with toast and coffee. That must have been yesterday. Did she eat? The room is tickety-boo tidy, no dirty cups or plates. She doesn't remember another pill, but it seems she's been sleeping, for…more than twenty-four hours. How is that possible?

Jack's probably screening calls and even if Lynn phoned,

he wouldn't wake Heather. She needs to call her mom. But at two in the morning? With luck, Lynn is finally asleep too. Everyone gets to sleep now. Everyone goes back to their routine lives. And what does that mean for Lynn, who almost seems to be in the same space as Heather—trying to figure out what to do with the rest of her life. For the short time she and Beegee had been at home with Lynn, she hadn't gone to work at all. Heather had only realized this after a couple of days. They were having lunch.

"Hey, you're not working now," she said. "What happened to the real estate job?"

"You're a few jobs behind. And you make it sound far more important than it was. I answered the phones, Heather. I'm a temp. Nothing more. And I've told the temp agency to put me on hold." She looked at Heather while she trailed her spoon through the bowl of soup in front of her. "Looks like soon we're both going to have to decide what we want to be when we grow up."

Heather's not sure if Lynn needs to work—she thinks there's a bit of money inherited from her grandparents and Lynn doesn't spend much. She's told Heather that when she graduated from high school she wanted a career that would take her to some third world country on a humanitarian mission. Romantic stuff, she said, for which she realized later she was about as well suited as she would have been as a trapeze artist. Bad balance, fear of heights, and sheer wimpishness when it comes to creature comforts. Also a tendency to become terribly depressed over the state of the world. After Marty and Heather were in school, Lynn thought about going back to university but instead worked part-time at a variety of different jobs, most of them in schools.

Heather thought one of Lynn's awesome moments, jobwise, was when she applied to be a mailman. Letter carrier, she insisted, but Jack kept ragging about how she didn't need to be a mailman when he was able to get her any job she wanted in the school system. Any job but teacher or principal, of course. Unfortunately, Lynn caved, even though Heather was cheering from the sidelines.

Heather licks her lips and reaches for the ever-present glass of water, but it's not there. Of course not. It's Lynn who keeps a glass of water with ice at Heather's elbow. Brings the breast pump as soon as Beegee's done sucking. Beegee. Like the corny rock group Jack made them listen to all those summer holidays in the car. Geezer music, Calgary to the island. Trust Lynn to come up with that name for Baby Girl, but the funny thing is, it suits the little twerp.

Better than Belinda, but Heather's managed to keep her mouth shut on how she feels about that name. She's hoping that if she can think of Beegee as Belinda, it will be easier to think of her as Donna and Grant's baby. Easier. How many times, from how many pathetic voices, has she heard that it won't be easy? She's not some needy fifteen-year-old who wants to hang onto her baby like it's a teddy bear. The choice was easy. Be a single mom, or give the baby away and get on with life. She planned that the day after she signed the consent, she'd get up, shower, slide into pre-preg jeans and sweatshirt, go up to the university and sort out her courses for the winter semester. The next day she'd get up, shower, put on something sexy and find a job. Lynn has a friend who owns a secondhand bookstore, who'll hire her in a minute, or Jack can get her on as a teacher's aid somewhere. Gag. She'll have enough of books and teaching when she's finished her degree. What she's going to do is slither into the sports bar that's partly owned by one of Marty's old school pals and talk him into giving her a job. She's sure she can make more in tips in a couple of good nights than she can make in a week's wages at the dusty old bookstore. Easy. It all sounded so easy until she held Beegee.

All through the pregnancy, Heather imagined a baby with a kewpie doll mouth, long eyelashes curled on her cheeks while she slept, wispy spirals of black hair. Skin? She asked Winston what colour he thought their baby's skin would be.

"Heather, we're all mongrels. Who knows what colour this puppy is going to be?"

It didn't matter to her. Not at all. But as it turned out, it mattered to people who wanted to adopt babies that Winston, the father of this one, was black. Except Donna and Grant. Of all the profiles Heather looked at, photo albums and histories of about a dozen families, there were only two who felt right. Neither of them had kids. She wanted her baby to be a first child. She'd never liked little kids, and pictures of grinning four-year-old brothers and sisters only made her think that her baby would have to share the attention. Or that the jealous little sister would tiptoe into the nursery when Mommy wasn't looking and try to carry the baby down the stairs. Donna and Grant McDonald were actually her second choice, but they moved up when the first family waffled around too much when they heard about Winston. Heather decided she was no longer interested in them.

"These people, these McDonalds," Heather asked Carmen, "are they saying they'll accept a mixed baby because they're in a hurry, or do they have some creepy idea that it'll be exotic and make them more interesting?"

That wasn't the first time Carmen pursed her lips and took a deep breath before she answered Heather, but it was the first time she dropped the compassionate routine and got real. "No, they are not hiding either of those motives," she said. She sat back and folded her arms. "Heather, I like that you're honest and blunt, but please do not come on this confrontational when you meet these people, okay?"

Heather behaved herself, and she liked Donna and Grant. She liked that they seemed nervous about making a good impression, and that they sat snuggled close together as though they needed each other for support. They chose that same cosy place on the sofa all three times that she met with them at the adoption agency. She wondered if they noticed, in the meeting to which Lynn and Jack came as well, that Heather's parents ignored the other sofa and sat in chairs that were in opposite corners.

Heather liked everything about Donna and Grant, but the closer the time came to her due date, the less she wanted to see them. Carmen proposed that she'd call Donna and Grant as soon as Heather went into labour so they could come to the hospital immediately after the baby was born. It would be good for them to hold the baby within a few hours. Heather had done her reading. She couldn't help imagining Beegee waddling along behind like a duckling bonded to human parents.

"No," she said. She didn't care how tight anyone's lips pressed together over her stubbornness. "I'll let you know when it's time to call them."

The doctor put Beegee on Heather's chest right after she was born, and that kid stared right at her and scrunched up her face so she looked like one of the troll dolls Heather used to have lined-up on her bookcase. Forget skin colour. She was red. And sleep? Yeah, right. Beegee was all sweet and dozy for about two days, and from then on she wanted to suck non-stop and woke up instantly if Heather dared to put her down. But it was all the other parts of her, so perfect, that made it impossible for Heather to let go of her even when she was content. Seashell ears, round little feet and toes that begged to be sucked. And her fingernails—those just blew Heather away. She'd need to keep them trimmed, the public health nurse told her. Some people find it easier to just gently nibble them off, they're so soft, and it's so easy to cut too close with the clippers. Well, that job got assigned to Lynn. No way was Heather taking the chance of cutting off Beegee's fingers, and she wasn't going to nibble her nails off either.

Heather grabs a tissue from the box on the bedside table and blows her nose, surprised by the wetness on her cheeks. What is the matter with her? She knows having a baby makes you stupid for a while, but she has to get over this. That's all there is to it. Think about something else, she tells herself. Anything. About finding a job, about going back to school in January, about what she'll do later today, about tomorrow, about anything except Beegee. Okay, now stand up and walk across the room to the desk.

Two o'clock in the morning. What time is it in Jamaica? Ever since Winston buggered off back home, the scared rabbit, she's known exactly what time it is in Jamaica. Four in the morning Kingston time, when she called from her hospital bed a few hours after Beegee was born. "You have a daughter," she said, and then slammed the phone down. He probably thought she hung up in fury, but really, she was on the verge of saying, "and she looks just like you," but she knew the words would unstop another flood of those goddamn tears.

Winston was the lab guy in a chemistry course she had to take, and on the very first day she sat there with her arms folded, rolling her eyes at the stupid safety lecture. With a totally straight face, he told them they shouldn't "pipette" by mouth—like someone would actually try to suck chemicals up a tube with their lips? She was the last one to leave the room, still packing up her books, trying to figure out a way to drop the course when he came and leaned against the counter, arms folded.

"So, tall pretty girl, what don't you like about my lab so far?"

"Being treated like a moron, mainly," she said. She'd been so pissed about the waste of time, she'd stared into space and ignored the fact that the man was gorgeous. Black velvet eyes with ridiculously thick lashes. His lab coat hung loose around his hips but strained across wide shoulders.

Okay, so he was just doing his job. "Hey, sorry if I misbehaved. It seems to me all of this is just common sense," she said, and shrugged.

No smile in return. "Take it seriously," he said. "If it was such common sense we wouldn't need rules."

"Righto!" she chirped over her shoulder as she flounced out the door. "I'll make sure to wear my bio-hazard gear tomorrow."

For the next month, he paid her no attention at all. If she asked for help, he was brusque and never teased or joked the way he did with everyone else. One afternoon she lagged behind.

"I probably shouldn't do this," she said, "but when somebody doesn't like me it helps to know why." Actually, she didn't have any interest in flirting with him, but she was getting nervous about her grade in the course. Chemistry was not easy for her, and she needed all the help she could get. She wasn't going to settle for less than a B.

He looked at her for about a minute, his mouth opening as though he was going to say something, then closing right up. Cute, like a fish, she thought. Then he threw his head back and laughed. "Okay. You want to know why I stay away from you?"

She nodded.

"Don't be so scary! You scowl at your book, you snarl at your partner, you look like you're being tortured the whole time you're here. Don't you ever smile, girl?"

They went for coffee, and he made her smile, and he even made her laugh at herself. Then he told her he couldn't see her outside of class because of the student-teacher thing; not until December, when the semester ended. Like she was looking for a relationship with him? Of course she was. No one had ever made her feel this way. Okay, semester end would do.

He was such a stickler for rules, Winston. So afraid of losing his funding, being kicked out of the country. When Heather told Winston she was pregnant—he was the first one to know—he looked as though every drop of blood had whooshed out of his body. His face went all dusty grey, even his lips.

She was amazed he hadn't ask how that could have happened. Glad she didn't have to admit that she'd stopped taking her birth control pills after the first couple of weeks because they were making her fat. She really did intend to use something else, and meanwhile she'd counted on the condoms. She'd insisted on condoms—all that sex education about STDs wasn't wasted on her—and Winston was so agreeable to everything. So careful too, she couldn't believe they'd got caught.

"What are we going to do?" he asked. "Oh my." He held his head in his hands. They were standing in his messy kitchen. "What's this going to do to my student visa?"

"Settle down," Heather said. "Like I'm going to report you to the Dean of Grad Studies? I might have an abortion." She could see him exhale; he seemed so relieved. "But then again I might not."

"Heather, don't do this to me!"

"Do what? Seems to me I'm the one who's been done." She'd already imagined Jack reacting this way, like she'd planned this to cause him trouble and a whole lot of embarrassment, but she hadn't expected the same from Winston.

"No, no," he said, and pulled her down onto the sofa. "I didn't mean it that way. I mean don't tease me that way. Tell me what you're going to do."

"I don't know!"

"Well then, let's discuss this." He looked quite frantically around the little basement suite. "We could get married."

"Married?" She shook her head, and shoved a pile of clothes off the sofa to move farther away from him. "I do not want to be married. Not to anyone, so don't take it personally. God, Winston, that's not a solution."

"Why not? It would help me to get my permanent resident card." He had the decency to look embarrassed. "That's not the only reason, Heather. We could be fine together with a baby I think. Yes, fine."

"Well I think not," she said. "Especially not the baby part. If I don't have an abortion, I'll probably give it up for adoption."

Two weeks later, when she told Winston she was definitely giving the baby up, that she'd talked to an agency and they'd be in touch with him for information about his family, health, all that stuff, he panicked.

"Don't make a big decision now," he said. "You're going to feel so different after that baby's born."

"Nope. I will not."

"I do not get to have a say?" She'd been waiting for that question to come up. Until the social worker at the adoption agency asked if the baby's father was in favour of an adoption plan, Heather hadn't even considered giving Winston a vote. But apparently he did have that right.

"Yeah, actually you do, but I thought you wouldn't want to sign any legal documents. I wasn't planning to tell anyone your name. If you want it that way."

Heather has no idea what she would have done if he'd

come through at that moment and said he was staying, he'd sign, he'd be with her through all this mess.

Instead, he said he was going home as soon as the winter session ended in April. He'd be back in September before the baby was born and they'd make the final decision then. But it didn't work out quite that way.

Heather squeezes her elbows over her breasts and feels milk trickle into her belly button. "Sucks!" she says into the cold room. Maybe she should forget the breast feeding sooner instead of later. Somewhere she has a prescription for pills for drying up her milk. She'll look for it when she picks up her stuff today at Lynn's. She didn't exactly pack for this sleepover. Lynn and Beegee drove away and Heather cried. Cried and cried and cried, and when Lynn wasn't back an hour later, she was so afraid the tears were never going to end, she called Marty. She wanted her big brother to come and tell her to stop this and get her shit together. When she got Marty's voice mail, she called Jack. Must have scared him, the way she was blubbering and carrying on. He was at the door almost before she had time to realize that he wasn't on the other end of the phone anymore. He got a cloth from the bathroom, wiped the tears and snot from her face, sat her down on the couch. Picked up the breast pump and the roll of plastic bags. "Jesus H. Christ. I knew I shouldn't have left this to Lynn. You've been breastfeeding, haven't you?" Great deduction, Sherlock.

She shouldn't have called him, she thought. She should have known he'd blame Lynn. Imagining all this through Jack's eyes, she had to admit it had turned into a mess. But Jack wasn't any help. He hadn't been over since she came home, just phoned every night to see how she was doing, was she any closer to finalizing things. She wanted Lynn, not Jack, and she almost found the guts to tell him to go away again. That she'd be okay. But Lynn wasn't there, and Heather wasn't okay.

She snuffled and scrubbed her face with the cloth. "It wasn't Mom's idea."

Jack opened his mouth as though he was going to argue with her, but then closed it and shook his head. He had said surprisingly little all this time. Usually he was big on pros and cons and debits and credits and spreadsheets and whatever it took to make decisions complicated. It was up to Heather, was all he'd offered. Over and over again, he said it was up to her to know the kind of future she wanted and did it include being a single mother? He couldn't resist that, but then he always went on to tell her nobody else could know what was best for her.

She wondered if he'd even noticed that she'd said "Mom." Wondered herself, where it came from. At fourteen, she ditched the formality of "Mom" and "Dad" in favour of "Lynn" and "Jack." Testing. What liberated parents. After the first few looks of surprise, they never said a word. Even Marty picked it up. Lynn and Jack.

Jack opened the closet at the front door, took out her jacket, and hung it over her shoulders. "You're coming home with me. I can't imagine what's taking Lynn so long. You'd think by now she'd be willing to carry a cell phone." He whipped out his pen and scrawled a line on the notepad by the phone. "Anything you need to bring along?"

Heather threw her toothbrush, a nightgown, a clean t-shirt and the breast pump into a plastic bag, and let Jack hustle her out to the car. At the condo, he whisked her past Rhea and into the spare bedroom. A few minutes later he came back with a glass of milk and a capsule in his hand.

"Take this," he said. "It's a mild sleeping pill. One won't hurt you, and God knows, sleep is what you need."

Whether the pill was more than she needed, or her need

totally took over, she's been asleep for way too long. She stands, and plods across the room to the door, down the hall to the bathroom. Vaguely she remembers getting up at least twice to pee and let her breasts drip into the sink. The bathroom blinds her—huge mirrors reflecting glass shower doors, spangles of light bouncing off white tile. Black marble sink and counter, thick white towels that feel like velvet and don't absorb either milk or tears worth a damn.

She drags her nightgown over her head, folds a facecloth into a square as thick as a pillow and soaks it in hot water before she presses it to her breast. It's a wonder the boob doesn't just burst like a balloon, her skin is stretched that tight. She imagines her milk spraying the walls, the ceiling.

She left the pump in the bedroom. Never mind. Her nipples are bruised from the mean suction. She's been getting better at the manual technique. Yeah, won't that be a useful skill some day along with everything else she's learned in this adventure? She takes a deep breath, holds it. If she closes her eyes, she can imagine her fingers are Beegee's lips, and that gets the milk flowing instantly. Thumb above the nipple, two fingers below, press, roll. Exhale. A good rhythm, and the stream of milk hisses against the marble sink. When she bends slightly to keep from splashing too much, her tears drip too.

Why didn't anyone tell her how this would feel? Sad she could have handled. She was all prepared for sadness. Carmen told her she would grieve, but to remember that she hadn't really lost Beegee, that she could see her once or twice a year, watch her grow up. Heather could live with that, even though it messed with her head. But nobody told her how it would feel in her body. All she could do was curl up and bawl. She never acted this way. She and Jack were the tough ones. It was Marty who was the marshmallow. And

Lynn. Heather can't remember ever seeing her mom cry, but Lynn had a way of wearing sadness like an old coat.

Heather switches the hot compress to her other breast, goes through the same routine, expresses just enough milk to stop the throbbing, then rinses the milky puddle down the drain. How long will it last? As long as you keep pumping, her doctor said. She sponges her breasts, dries them, and opens the door.

She's only been here once before, the day Jack and Rhea got married and Marty told her she'd be a complete asshole if she refused to come for just one glass of champagne. The dark is disorienting, and it takes her a minute to find the light switch in the kitchen. She takes a glass from the cupboard, goes back to the bedroom, and sits on the edge of the bed, gritting her teeth when her hot breast settles into the cold plastic hand of the pump. The same wrench in her guts as when Beegee latches on. This time she empties both breasts completely, staring at the wall, at the map of the world that used to hang in Jack's downstairs office at home. It used to hang above his dad's desk, Jack's told them about a hundred times. There are reds pins stuck in all the countries Grandpa Bishop visited, some of them during the war. The yellow pins are Jack's. Jack says he and Rhea plan to travel; this is one of the things that attracted them to each other. Before she did whatever it is she does now, Rhea back-packed all over Asia. Jack keeps trying to get Heather to talk to Rhea about her travels. He's been pushing both Marty and Heather to "see the world" ever since they were big enough to look at the map. Marty's not interested at all, and at the moment, Heather's having a hard time imagining going back to her own apartment, never mind flying to Australia.

After she returns to the bathroom to mop all her leaking parts, wash her face, brush her teeth, put on a clean t-shirt, she tiptoes to the kitchen. She finds plastic sandwich bags, pours the milk into one, zips, and flings it onto a stack of Lean Cuisine in the freezer.

She pours a glass of orange juice and then another, shaking so violently by the time she gets the second to her lips that juice spills down the front of her shirt. On the black slate floor, it could be blood, just more of the post-birth blood she's been gushing for three weeks. She stares at it until the shaking stops. A quick swipe with a handful of paper towels. Her dad will stick to the floor in the morning when he wanders to the fridge for milk for his All Bran. If he still eats All Bran. Might be one of the many habits he tossed when he moved out of home.

Heather realizes that she can see her feet again. For almost two months, her belly blocked the view. She wets a paper towel, sits on the floor, washes between her toes. A few nights ago, she grudgingly let Lynn trim her toenails. Snarling and nasty about it, she sat nursing Beegee while Lynn knelt beside the footstool and carefully clipped each nail. But on the second foot, she snatched the file from her mother's hand and threw it across the room. "You don't have to do this!" she shouted. "What the fuck does it matter if I have pretty feet?"

Now she owes Lynn two apologies. She truly is sorry. Sorry for being a bitch about the pedicure. Sorry for making her mom do something so hard.

Maybe the gnawing in her gut is hunger and not just rage. Why is she so angry? Hormones? Yeah, that's the answer to everything. She finds a deli container of hummus in the fridge, but no pita bread in sight, not even a cracker, so she eats it with a spoon, then halves a kiwi fruit and sucks the green flesh from the skin. The house is quiet except for the purring of the fridge and the sound of a breeze licking the blinds on the bay window. Jack must have every window open. He and Lynn used to fight constantly over the temperature of the house. Windows and doors. Jack's habit of throwing windows open, and Lynn's forgetfulness over locking doors. Now he has it his own way. A security system and fresh air.

Heather would like to wrap herself in a blanket, sit on that window seat and breathe the night air. But she knows the alarm is set and even the screens shriek if they're touched. Jack installed a security system for Lynn before he moved out, but she never turns it on.

With a pitcher of water and a glass, Heather tiptoes back to the bedroom and the computer. Jack's credit card is on the desk. She knows this is the one he reserves for online purchases, the one with the small limit. She palms it, stares at it a minute, then walks to the bed where she slides it into the pocket of her jacket which is lying there. Blushing with the shame of it, but unable to resist. She's broke, and before Jack moved out they all had the use of this card. She'll re-pay everything eventually. Meanwhile, back to the computer.

It's been weeks since Heather checked her email, weeks since she talked to anyone but Lynn and baby Beegee, Jack, and Carmen, who phoned every day to find out if Heather was ready. Carmen will not be happy with the way this has gone. She wanted to be there with Heather when Beegee was handed over, and Grandma was not supposed to be part of the plan. Heather knows that her mom makes Carmen nervous. Funny, because Lynn never has that effect on anyone else. In fact, she usually blends right into the background.

Heather knows that Carmen is away for the weekend; she knew this even before she made the phone call asking her to pick up Beegee. She suspects that she's deliberately chosen to do this while Carmen is out of town. To cut Carmen out of the action. She has to punish someone. Irresponsible of her? She could at least have a left a phone message. But if she tries phoning again, it's just possible Carmen will answer. Better to send an email, let her know that everyone's wishes have come true, and Carmen can dash over with the papers on Monday morning.

She takes a deep breath. Yes, this is better. She can feel her head taking control in spite of the drowsiness. A few more hours of sleep and she really will be thinking clearly. In the morning, she's going home. First to Lynn's house to pack, then back to her apartment and her real life, up and out of all this emotional shit that's landed on her. She swallows. That hard taste at the back of her throat will go away. If only she can stay away from her mom. When Lynn's hurt, her eyes look bruised, and her skin gets pinched and white around her nose and mouth. Heather tries to imagine Lynn, driving up to Donna and Grant's house, unbuckling Beegee from the car seat, carrying her to the door. Will she have taken the baby, and then gone back for the bags? No, it's more like Lynn to try to carry it all in one trip, everything dangling from her arms, bumping against her hip. She'd be frowning and readjusting as she walked to the door. Maybe mumbling to Beegee while she walked. What would she be saying to Beegee? No matter how hard Heather tries, she can't get this picture clear in her mind.

Finally, she pounds out the message. She knows the p.s. reminding Carmen that she'll have to deliver Heather's milk for a few days will make the adopting parents crazy. But as long as Heather still has the power to change her mind, they won't argue. And they probably know that Heather will lose interest in pumping, and her milk will dry up without the hungry baby at her breast.

She runs the flat of her hand over the keyboard, hesitating over the "send". No, there isn't any need to send a message. She hits "delete" instead. They'll find her. There's that unsigned consent. She still has something everybody wants.

3

When Beegee begins to stir, Lynn slides from the bed and feels her way to the dark kitchen. Even though the light has gone from black to pearly grey in the chilly cabin, she needs the walls to find her way. It will take at least eight hours of sleep to restore her balance. The floor seems to slope, propelling her to the fridge for the milk, then to the microwave. Then it tilts to send her reeling back to the bedroom.

Curled on her side once again, she teases the latex nipple across the baby's lips. Beegee latches on, rhythmically begins to empty the plastic sleeve without opening her eyes. "Yes," Lynn whispers to the baby, and pulls her close. "Now you're catching on."

As always in this cabin, she feels the weight of silence. She remembers waking Jack on a night in this bed just to hear his voice. The dark ceiling seemed so close she was sure sound could not travel through the compressed air. She had gone deaf. The memory must be old, because Jack was patient. Whispered to her that her ears were fine, the air was fresh and cool and he was right there beside her.

She takes deep breaths. In the two years since Jack left, she has grown comfortable with the silence of her own home. Comfortable, too, with wandering their old haunts on her own. By the end of their marriage, there were so few places they regularly visited together. At the Farmer's Market on a Friday morning instead of Saturday, Lynn now enjoys being the one to choose a small sack of perfect apples, enjoys sitting alone with her curried chicken pie, watching the other shoppers. There are restaurants she'll avoid, because the ghosts of too many anniversaries and celebrations of Jack's promotions still lurk. But this cabin, this summer spot, is one place to which she never thought she'd return.

When Beegee finally whimpers and spits out the nipple, Lynn puts the bottle on the floor beside the bed. Loki looks up at her, head cocked, eyes gleaming in the dark room. "Good dog. You stay right here and keep watching." She tiptoes to the bathroom, but stops at the door, remembering Heather last week with her nose in one of the books from the pile on the coffee table.

"Research shows that infants who sleep on their stomachs have an increased risk of SIDS." Heather had slammed the book down and glared at Lynn as though she had just settled a whole roomful of doomed babies on their bellies.

"You survived," Lynn muttered.

She shakes her head and goes back to the bed. Why did she allow Heather to bully her? She never argued with her own mother over how to care for Marty when he was new. Her mom knew about babies, Lynn did not. It was as simple as that. Between her and her mom—and her dad as well—there was also the knowledge of how close she and Jack had come to letting go of Marty. Her parents were the only ones who knew, and Lynn had sworn she would do anything to thank them for keeping that secret. Now she wonders why her parents agreed, when they were so wise about everything else.

Beegee is sleeping peacefully on her stomach. Lynn will be ten feet away. Still, she eases the baby onto her side, props pillows around her. Feeling like a thief, she slowly opens the drawers of Einar's dresser until she finds a pile of under-shirts.

Her watch is on the edge of the bathroom sink. Six o'clock. Four hours of sleep. A record for Beegee. In the very early hours of yesterday morning, both of them slept in the car in a deserted picnic ground. Much later in the day, just a few miles out of Nanaimo, Lynn was struck with fatigue again, her foot like a stone on the accelerator. She pulled into a campground, parked beside a barrier that said the area was closed for the season and took Beegee out of her bas-ket. With the baby nestled inside her jacket, Lynn marched briskly up and down the short stretch of road, hoping the gulps of sharp air would revive her for the remaining two hours of the drive. When they got back into the car, Beegee was sound asleep, curled like a kitten against Lynn's chest, so she reclined the driver's seat, locked the doors and again the two of them slept.

With luck, the baby will last another fifteen minutes. Lynn turns on a slow trickle of water, then lets it thunder into the tub. Her t-shirt peels off like peach skin, the bra underneath crusty with the spilled milk that soaks everything when she holds the baby close for feeding. When her socks come off, she stares at her pale feet. Wrinkled, toes cramped, they look as though they walked the journey. One Mother's Day just a couple of years ago Marty and Heather had given her a gift certificate for a pedicure and manicure. The suggestion, she learned later, had come from Marty's girlfriend. The mani-cure was insignificant, but the pedicure—the soaking, filing away of years of tired skin, the massage of rich cream—put a sassy bounce in her step. She wore sandals through the cold wet month of May, through two spring blizzards, so she wouldn't lose sight of her blushing toes. When she gets home—which she has trouble imagining—she'll treat herself to a pedicure.

She steps into the tub, dips, then stands to suds herself from nose to toes with the lumpy bar of Zest before she stretches out. Head back, she floats under the dancing tree shadows on the skylight. And listens to the drip drip drip.

At nine o'clock, Lynn is pacing the kitchen, Beegee howling, Loki cowering under the table. When the door blows open, the dog flies across the room and skids to a stop.

A woman steps into the room shaking rain from the red hair that's looped back from her face and tied halfway down her back with a leather thong. Hannah. Lynn was well on her way, rushing toward this sanctuary, when she remembered that the bubble of privacy around Einar's cabin stretched only as far as the house next door. The last couple of summers they had spent on Quadra there had been neighbours. This woman, Hannah, and her husband and a gaggle of kids with whom Heather and Marty had run wild. Lynn had hoped she could stay well-hidden, that none of the neighbours would even know she was here.

Hannah's been talking since she came in the door, but Lynn can't hear a word of it over Beegee's screaming. She shakes her head until finally, Hannah shrugs out of her dripping green canvas jacket and hangs it on the back of the door. She wipes her battered sandals on the mat before she stomps across the room and peers down at Beegee in Lynn's arms, the baby's face red with howling. Lynn finds herself staring at Hannah's toes. Big brown Sasquatch feet poking out of sandals. This is what she remembers of Hannah. A leathery brown woman, loud and tough.

"Lynn, right? From Calgary?" Lynn nods, a little surprised that Hannah remembers her name, remembers her at all. Hannah is unforgettable, but Lynn has always felt ordinary in the extreme. A generic, middle-aged, brown-haired woman.

"Let me try," Hannah says, and before Lynn can object, she's scooped the damp bundle out of the cradle of Lynn's arms and into her own. Lynn is left standing, her empty arms suddenly cold from the draft in the room. Yes, this is the Hannah she remembers. The Hannah who pushed her way in front of Jack when he was building a fire because she didn't like the way he had the wood arranged. His method might have been fine in his Boy Scout days, she said, but didn't cut it on the beach.

Hannah shushes and sways, running a hand over the baby's fiery face. "Gas?"

Lynn shakes her head. "Hungry. But she won't take the bottle."

Hannah snorts. "Why would any kid want a bottle? How come you're not nursing? Are you sick?" For a confused few seconds, Lynn feels she should come up with a reason for bottle-feeding the baby, as though she has a choice.

"There's breast milk in the bottle," she says, not sure why she feels bound to explain, but carrying on anyway. She looks directly into Hannah's astonished face. "This is my daughter's baby, Heather's, and we're trying to switch from breast to bottle."

Hannah looks as though she's going to object, but seems to reconsider. "All right," she says, "I'll solve this problem for you. For now anyway." She drops into the chair, throws up the corner of her red plaid shirt and bares a breast. She presses the baby tight against her flesh and with a finger, teases Beegee's lips with a freckled brown nipple. Still the baby fusses and twists and draws her legs to her chest and wails. "Aw the poor tyke has nipple confusion something fierce. Why the heck does Heather want to switch her to a bottle?" She looks across the room to the bedroom door. "Where is Heather?"

"At home in Calgary." Lynn has had two days to come up with intricate lies to explain why she and Beegee are holed up in Einar's cabin, but there is simply nothing she can say that makes sense. "It's complicated."

"Uh huh." Hannah squints at her for another minute, then begins rocking and cooing and using two fingers to squirt milk onto the baby's lips. Beegee's cheeks, her chin, the front of her sleeper are soaked. Lynn wishes she could pull up a chair in front of Hannah, put her elbows on her knees, chin in her hands, and earnestly spill forth the whole story. Lynn has only three friends with whom she'd share this dilemma, but all of them have had their own troubles in the last year. She hasn't spoken to anyone about Heather in months. But Hannah is almost a stranger, and Lynn does not remember any sisterly vibrations between them.

Again, Hannah plays her nipple against the baby's clamped mouth and this time Beegee latches on, sucks, sputters and coughs. When Hannah lifts her almost to sitting, Beegee shudders audibly, gulps and swallows a few times, then seems to relax into slow, even sucking.

"How old is this kid?" With the tip of a finger, Hannah strokes the hand that has settled on her breast like a small brown butterfly. "Only a couple of weeks, I'd say."

"Three," Lynn says. She looks away to the window, almost expecting to see Heather striding toward the house. "Three weeks yesterday. We have enough milk to last until tomorrow. I'll buy formula today."

Hannah's head flies up and she looks like Lynn's just declared she's going to start filling the bottles with Pepsi. "Cow's milk is for calves," she says. "Formula is for sick kids or orphans. Kids who have no choice." She seems to take up so much space in this room. "You can't mess around like this with a new baby. She could stop feeding altogether. She's had three weeks of breast?" Lynn nods. "How long have you been trying to cram the bottle into her?"

Can it really only be two days? "Since Friday," Lynn says. She pulls out one of the kitchen chairs, lines it up to face the rocking chair at about arm's length. So that she can lean forward as soon as Beegee is done feeding and take her back into her own arms. She feels her mouth opening, closing, trying to find some words to explain this predicament of bottles and breasts, but what can she say except that she hasn't a clue what she's going to do next. "I'm hoping…"

"Heather and her breasts going to follow you out here?"

"Yes." Lynn nods and nods. Yes, that's what would be best, but it's not as though Heather is next door or up the street. Lynn and Beegee are at least a thousand kilometers from home.

Hannah rocks, the toe of her sandal creaking the linoleum with each push and the chair making a soft swish with each glide of the runners. Her face a wide blank, she watches Lynn, waiting. Finally she nods too. "Well, that would be best for this wee one, for sure." She lowers her voice. "Does Heather know where you are?" As though they're sharing a secret.

And so they are, Lynn thinks, because Einar's neighbour is the only person who knows that Beegee is here on Quadra Island. So tempting to lie, to say that Heather is on her way, that it's nothing more than a tag team holiday, badly planned. The muscles in her jaw twitch, and Lynn knows that no matter what she says, her face will give the lie away. She says nothing, just glances from Hannah's searching eyes to the window and back.

Hannah shrugs. "None of my business then. Why don't I feed her for you for a few days. Until…?"

Lynn is glad to be sitting, because the walls wobble, the

46

chair feels as though it's tilting beneath her. She's aware again of the pounding in her head that began midway through Beegee's howling this morning but seemed to abate when Hannah took the baby from her arms. What kind of offer is this, to nurse someone else's baby, and how can she decline when she knows it is the kindest, the best solution to Beegee's woes?

"What about your baby?" she says. She can't remember how many kids swarmed out in the yard those long ago afternoons, but it seemed Hannah was always pregnant or carrying a baby in a sling.

"My baby's two," Hannah says. "He only nurses when he's tired. The rest of the time he eats at the table with everyone else." Her face softens. "This one needs it more than he does. Lord but she's precious. Makes me want to have another one. Good thing Hank's away north." She tilts her head and studies the baby. "Nice colouring. Quite a bit darker than Heather, eh?" She looks pointedly at Lynn, who easily ignores this question. Donating her milk does not entitle Hannah to snoop into Beegee's parentage.

Lynn raises both hands to knead the back of her neck. Coffee would help the headache. She'd like the neighbour to leave now. She needs to return to the plan that was almost fully formed when Hannah came through the door. Consider getting back in the car and going home. But the woman has just rescued Lynn and Beegee from that growing necessity, and isn't Lynn the host here even though she's a guest herself and Hannah was not invited? "Would you like some coffee?" she asks.

"No thanks. And you shouldn't drink it either if that's the commercial crap Einar keeps buying." With a great swoop, a tucking in, and *shh, shhh, shhhhh*, she expertly switches Beegee to her other breast. "I gave him five pounds of organic coffee beans for building me a new bathroom cabinet, but every time I come over here he offers me that swill he buys at the grocery store."

The tarry-bottomed coffee pot is on the stove. Lynn will remember to ignore the can of Folger's on the counter and look for the organic fair-trade beans. She can almost smell the dark oily grounds she'll brew after Hannah leaves.

The only sound in the room is the creak of the chair. Hannah is focused on the baby, a smile playing around her lips. Occasionally she glances up at Lynn, who blinks and tries to think of something to say. Lynn doesn't remember ever being alone with Hannah, or having a conversation with her. There were always children, and men. Lynn could ask what Hannah's been up to in the last few years. After Hannah's shrugged and talked about the last baby, she'll ask what Lynn's been up to. Then they can talk about the divorce and the boring jobs Lynn's been doing while she tries to come up with a career plan. None of that is more appealing than silence.

If Lynn were here on a holiday, the weather would be the obvious place to start, but after a glance at the rain-streaked window, Lynn knows all there is to know. It's raining, it was probably raining before she arrived, it will continue to rain.

The baby's head lolls. Hannah lifts her gently away from her breast and lets the shirt drop over her rolls of flesh. "Listen, why don't I just take her home with me? You look like you could use some sleep."

Lynn shakes her head so violently she feels as though her eyes are knocking against her skull. Her arms reach into the gulf between the chairs. There are already too many people who want this baby. "No," she says. "You don't need to do that. We may be leaving soon."

Hannah's eyebrows wing up into the deep creases of her forehead. "Good God, you just got here! Where are you going now?"

Lynn sees herself through Hannah's eyes, a wild-eyed woman with a crying infant. "Nowhere else," she says, "but I may not stay. I may change my mind and go home." Still those eyes are boring into her. "Because of the feeding, and Heather…it's complicated."

"So you've said already." Hannah leans forward to settle Beegee into the crook of Lynn's arms. "Do what you gotta do, I guess." Now she sounds more like Einar than the strident woman Lynn remembers from weiner roasts on the beach, Hannah arguing with Jack about everything under the sun. Home schooling, organic farming, clear-cutting, Hannah surprising Jack and irritating him no end because she is as well-read and opinionated as he is.

"Call me if you need me." Hannah nods toward the fireplace, where Lynn notices for the first time that Einar has lain wood for a fire. "I'd put a match to that if I were you. It'll take out the chill."

When she thinks of being alone again, a fire crackling, Lynn thinks she may even nap with the baby. She, who can never sleep in the daytime because she fears developing a habit that feels aimless. Elderly. Even more now that she lives alone, she worries about growing into a strange old woman with no routine or purpose.

Hannah has a purpose. A gaggle of children are waiting for her to come home, and Lynn is pleased to see her button her jacket, walk to the door. Then Hannah turns around.

"Just tell me one thing, okay?" Hannah doesn't wait for Lynn to answer, probably knows that even one answer might be more than Lynn can manage. "The kid really is your granddaughter, right?"

"Yes." That she can say with a breath of relief.

"Okey dokey then. That's enough for me." She opens the door. "Einar will be back sometime tonight, I think." She flips up the hood of her jacket and steps into the rain.

Lynn shifts Beegee to her shoulder, and the baby produces a satisfied belch. They stand at the window while Hannah disappears into the trees. Lynn looks sideways at the dusky cheek, rests her own against it. "Just what we needed—a wet nurse. The problem is, little girl, this one is even bossier than your mom. So do we stay here, or go home and face some very loud music?"

4

Heather would love a robe like the one Rhea's wearing when she wanders into the kitchen. Cream-coloured satin with flared sleeves, a deep vee in the front. Her new breasts would look fantastic in that rig, at least until they shrink back to normal size.

"Nice robe," she says.

"Birthday present from your dad." Rhea looks embarrassed, like Heather isn't supposed to know Jack buys her lingerie.

"Really? Never would have guessed that," Heather says. Must be why Jack's credit card was on the desk beside the computer. Ordering online from Victoria's Secret?

The robe, she thinks, would look better on Lynn. Her mom has exactly the right peachy colouring. Heather doubts that Jack ever bought lingerie for Lynn. She remembers books, gardening tools, kitchen gadgets, and oh yeah, every Christmas a bottle of the same perfume Lynn's worn for years. She makes a mental note to buy something pretty for her mom, to say thanks for the past three weeks. That'll surprise her. Maybe a sweater. While she's at it, she'll order one for herself.

Heather's never seen Rhea without make-up, and once she's out of here, she hopes this-way-too-personal kind of encounter won't happen again. White white skin next to deep burgundy hair does not work—maybe Rhea's not as young as everyone thinks she is. Would it make a difference if Jack had left Lynn for someone over forty? Fortunately, Jack wanders in before Heather and Rhea have to try and make conversation. He looks even worse than Rhea.

"Jeez, Jack, you look horrible. Go back to bed." Her dad's face is ashen. Scary. "What's wrong?"

He stands there, blinking. "Just tired," he says.

This is the same look on his face as the day Heather told him she was pregnant. He went even greyer when she said she had no intention of having an abortion. In fact, she was on the verge of making an appointment, and if he'd just hugged her and handed her the cash, she might have done it. But instead, he recovered enough to deliver a lecture on why abortion was the reasonable option. A simple procedure, he said, and that was what tipped her. Sure, Jack. Nothing to it.

Jack takes orange juice out of the fridge and swirls the pitcher before he pours three glasses, hands one to Heather.

"Thanks, but I was looking for coffee. Did Lynn call?"

"We're out of coffee beans," Rhea says. "Are you going out, Jack? Or will I?"

Jack runs his hand over the stubble on his chin. Heather hopes he'll tell Rhea to go shopping. He shouldn't be going anywhere except back to bed. Maybe to the medi-centre.

Lynn would be trying to coax him out to the car by now. Even if she and Jack were in one of their lethal silences, she would notice that her husband looked like death.

"No," he says, "no, I don't think I'll run this morning. I'm going to sit a while, look at the paper."

"What day is this?" Heather looks around the kitchen for a calendar, even though she can't imagine what help that would be. She lost track of time on September twelfth, the day Beegee was born.

"Sunday," Jack says. "October third." His cheeks might be pinking up a shade, but his lips still have the scary look of clay.

"Are you feeling better?" he asks Heather. "You woke up, then went back to sleep so often I was getting worried." He steps forward, puts his arm around her. He smells faintly of nighttime. Of sex with Rhea.

"Has Lynn called?" Heather asks again.

"Not yet," he says. She shoves his arm away. "She's probably as exhausted as you are. Sleeping it off."

"Didn't you try to phone her? Jeez, Jack." She feels that twist of guilt in her chest again. Has she tried to call her mom?

"I thought about phoning your adopting people. Maybe you should do that, Heather. Just reassure yourself that the baby's fine."

Heather's been thinking about calling Donna and Grant since she got up, but she promised Carmen she wouldn't. At least not for ten days after she signs the papers. If she wanted to get in touch, or if she wanted in some miraculous turnaround to change her mind, she's supposed to phone Carmen. Let her make the call. But the papers aren't signed yet. "No, I don't want to talk to them."

Rhea is pretending to be engrossed in the magazine she picked up at the first mention of Lynn. Sitting legs crossed at the kitchen table, she sips her juice, manicured fingers flipping pages. The few times Heather saw Rhea during her pregnancy, Rhea looked everywhere except at Heather's belly. "How are you feeling?" she said each time but with such phony-sounding sympathy it was like Heather was faking an illness.

"I want to go home," Heather says. "Will you drive me to Lynn's to make sure she's okay? I'm going to pack up and go back to my place later."

"Of course I will." Jack moves away from Heather, puts his hand on Rhea's silky sleeve. "I'll get coffee on the way back."

As soon as she steps inside, Jack at her heels, Heather knows the house is empty. The air feels cold, unused, not a whiff of anyone there in at least a day.

"She's not here," she says.

"Lynn!" Jack's big voice booms through the silence. "Maybe she's asleep."

Not anymore, Heather thinks, if that was even a possibility. "Lynn never sleeps in the daytime." You'd think he'd remember a few things about his wife?

Everything is exactly as they left it. The nest of quilts in the living room still has the imprint of her baby's body, and when Heather looks at it, she can feel the weight of Beegee in the crook of her left arm. There's an empty Pampers box on the floor, and the sleeper Beegee was wearing before they dressed her in the Peter Rabbit outfit dangles from the edge of the coffee table like a rag doll. Lynn is not here. By now she would have whisked away all these baby reminders. By now she should have come looking for Heather.

In the kitchen, the table is set with bowls and spoons. There's clotted soup in the pot on the stove. Lynn kept shoving milky foods at Heather. She made cream of broccoli soup on Friday, but Heather didn't want it. All that morning she'd been choked with the idea that if she didn't give Beegee to Donna and Grant right then, she wouldn't be able to do it at all. Then Lynn with that damn shopping list of things they'd need.

For two days she's been rewinding, replaying Friday afternoon and the argument with Lynn. She never gets beyond the slamming of the doors, Heather on her way into her bedroom, Lynn on the way to the car with Beegee in her arms. And where is Lynn now that she's "placed" Beegee with Donna and Grant? Where does this vocabulary come from? Relinquish, place, revoke, finalize? What does it have to do with breasts and diapers and little fingers with nails like tissue paper? She clamps her elbows over her breasts when she feels the tingle in her nipples. How long before she can stop thinking about babies? There is no room in her life for a baby. That's the way it is.

Heather watches Jack open the back door and step outside. He expects to find Lynn out there raking leaves? Heather shakes her head and walks down the hall. All dim and quiet in the bedrooms too.

At the closed bathroom door, the sick feeling that has been lapping at her since the middle of the night rises even higher in her throat. Maybe Marty was right when he worried about Lynn being on her own after Jack left. Two years ago Heather blew off his idea that they take turns checking in. She worried that her mom would be lonely, but she never thought Lynn was unbalanced. And besides, she'd offered to move home and Lynn had snubbed her. About a week before Beegee was born, Heather told Marty she was keeping the possibility of going home with Lynn in the back of her mind, and he did a one-eighty turn on her. "You and the baby?" he asked.

"Just for a few days. I think I might need a bit more time." She had a niggling feeling that she wouldn't be able to hold things together the day the baby was born. Already she'd begun to blubber at the stupidest things. She might need some time to get herself organized and back on track so she could do this properly. She expected him to say it was a good idea. Good for her and good for Lynn. She was sure Marty didn't have a clue what was good for Beegee. He'd been telling her all along, "Just go with your gut, kid. I think that's all you can do."

She couldn't believe how mean he was about it. "Fuck it, Heather!" he said. "You've been saying since you found out you were pregnant that you're giving it up. Mom looks like she's going to melt down whenever anyone mentions the baby. You need this? She needs it? If you need more time to make up your mind, at least go home to your own place and try it out."

"I'm not trying it out! I just want time with my baby." She didn't admit to him that she was terrified of being alone with a baby. The only place she could imagine going was to her old bedroom at home.

When Beegee was four days old Marty came over with a humongous pink teddy bear, his old attitude in place. "What happened?" he asked her quietly when Lynn was out of the room.

"I guess you could say my gut told me to bring her home."

"So now you're keeping her?" He looked around the living room, the house they'd grown up in, and frowned.

"Of course not," she said. "Why does everybody think I'm not going to be able to do this adoption? Relax. It's only for a week or so."

So it was more than a week, but at least now she's let go.

She pushes the bathroom door with her foot and exhales when there is nothing on the floor but the mess of towels from Beegee's last bath.

Back in the living room, Jack has folded the quilts and is sitting on the sofa looking through a pile of mail on the table. "You don't live here anymore," Heather says. "I can't believe you're doing that." He squints at her as though he has no idea what she's talking about. When he crosses his legs, he topples the stack of library books between the sofa and Lynn's chair.

Heather goes back to the kitchen and picks up the phone, working her way through the call display. Click click click back to Friday. Grant McDonald. Grant called back, she remembers vaguely. About detours. But the phone says he phoned five times on Friday. Repeat calls from someone at a "private number" on Friday night. Three calls from Jack late Friday night. He didn't lie, she realizes, just didn't answer her question. He did call. Many times. There's his number on Saturday as well. And Private Number trying again and again.

There's a sound like the opening of a door in Heather's head. The private number is Carmen's cell. She's sure of it. Carmen has been phoning frantically because Donna and Grant are frantic. Heather's mind has stalled whenever she tried to imagine Beegee with her new mother. Not just because she couldn't bear to look, but because that image would not focus. Maybe the reason is that Beegee is not in Donna's arms.

Lynn. What have you done? Heather braces herself against the wall with one hand. When Jack walks into the room, she tries to look casual. She doesn't want him to figure this out. Not until she's absolutely sure.

"You did phone," she says. "Your number's on the call display."

"Of course I did. I care about your mom, Heather. This has been much harder on her than you realize." He runs his hands over his face and looks around the kitchen. "It could be she was here, asleep when I called, but she went out this morning."

57

He takes the phone from Heather's hand, sits down at the table. "I tried calling Marion yesterday, but I kept getting her answering machine. I thought Lynn might have gone to her place. Or to Jean or Bernie. Do we have Bernie's number?"

"Marion's in Toronto," Heather says. "Her granddaughter has cancer." She wonders if Lynn has told him this, or if the split between them extended through the friends too. She always thought it was strange that her mom and dad didn't have couples as friends. Jack had his friends, and Lynn had hers. Lynn only has three. Three women she grew up with in that little town that's disappeared from the map. They get together a couple of times a year, but Marion's the one Lynn sees more often.

Heather tries to imagine Lynn at either Jean's house or Bernie's apartment. Heather doubts Lynn has talked with Jean or Bernie since Beegee was born. It's been like Heather and Beegee and Lynn are marooned on an island. But if she was desperate? Where else would she go?

Heather needs to call Carmen, but first she has to get rid of Jack. He'll do something drastic like call the police. What if something terrible happened to Lynn and Beegee on the way to Donna and Grant's? What if this isn't Lynn's fault at all? Heather needs Marty. Marty will tell her to stop worrying. Tell her maybe Lynn's done something wildly stupid, but she'll be back any minute. Heather presses her hands to her sides to keep from shaking.

"Yeah," she says, "she's probably at Bernie's. I'll find her. Why don't you go home, and I'll call you as soon as I track her down." She takes the phone out of his hand. "I'm going to phone Donna and Grant, and I really want to be alone for a while. I'm okay now." He squints at her. "Honest, Jack," she says, and this time she puts her arm around him. "You look like you need sleep as much as I did. Go home."

"All right. But call as soon as you find out anything. Anything. And come back to my place when you finish whatever it is you need to do here."

Not likely, but she nods anyway. "Tell Rhea if she throws out the milk I left in the freezer I'll rip out her heart." Heather walks toward the front door, expecting him to follow. "I'm going to call Marty," she says. She realizes neither of them has considered the possibility that Lynn is with Marty, but surely Marty would have called Jack. He'd need to know Heather was okay once he heard she'd gone through with the adoption. Except she hasn't gone through with it. And maybe she's wrong in all of her worrying. Maybe Carmen's only calling to find out how she's doing. Without Beegee. And to get her to sign the papers. The only way to find out is to call Carmen. She gives Jack a gentle shove. "I can handle this, Jack."

"Do you have your cell?"

She shakes her head. Hasn't a clue when or where she last saw her phone. She's been trying to avoid phones, tired of everyone asking how she's doing and what she's going to do next. She finally understands Lynn's attitude about cell phones. Why, her mom asked years ago, when she leaves the house for a bit of solitude, should she carry a device that makes her accessible to everyone and his cat?

Jack wraps another big hug around her and she knows that if it lasts any longer, she's going to cry. "Go already," she says, slipping out of his arms.

Heather opens the door, and when it closes behind Jack, she runs to the living room and throws herself onto the sofa, face pressed to the quilt, taking deep breaths, trying to reassure herself with the scent of her baby that everything is fine. How is this possible? Lynn running away? Everything fucked up, just when she thought it was over? Or maybe Lynn will be back any minute, but Beegee is gone for good.

How fine is that? Or the even more horrible possibility that something's happened to both her mother and her baby.

Heather finally pulls herself up on the sofa. She runs her hands through her hair, shudders at the thick smell of sweat that wafts from her t-shirt. She needs a shower. But first she needs to call Carmen. She needs to know how Beegee's doing with the bottle. After the first attempt to feed Beegee from a bottle, Heather gave up. The little twerp threw her head back and howled as though she was being tortured. "Can you blame her?" Lynn asked quietly, barely looking up from her book. With her finger marking her place, she finally gave Heather her attention. "It won't be quite as easy as Carmen suggested, but she will survive. If you want to make it easier for Donna and Grant, maybe you should stick with the bottle-feeding. Do you want me to try? She can smell you, and she's expecting your breast."

Heather declined Lynn's offer. She barely let Lynn hold the baby, because she was afraid Lynn would get too attached. Besides, making things easy for Donna and Grant hasn't counted much in Heather's plan and she doesn't mind admitting this. Sure, she chose them because they seemed like they'd be great parents, and it's too bad they can't have a kid of their own, but she figures they're the ones who get the prize in the end. They're the ones who get to call the shots after those ten days of everyone holding their breath are past.

Heather's told Carmen she wants the grandparents to get pictures every Christmas, but she's the only one who'll visit Beegee. Lynn closed her eyes and nodded when Heather told her this. "I had a feeling that's the way it would go. But for now I can't imagine sitting in their living room and visiting with my grandchild over a cup of tea, Heather, so it doesn't matter."

Heather goes back to the kitchen for the phone and calls Carmen. Voicemail is not what she expected. Not at all. She's imagined Carmen pacing, waiting for her to call. This is reassuring. Maybe all is well. Lynn spent the night in Bernie's spare room? She'll try to hang onto that possibility while she waits for Carmen to return her call.

In the shower, she lathers and rinses and lathers and rinses and sniffs her skin and her hair. No more scent of baby and mommy. Then she rubs herself dry, wraps a towel around her hair and pads naked back to her bedroom. Odd the phone hasn't rung. Now that she smells sweet, she'd like to put on something fresh. Anything other than an old shirt and the badly stretched leggings she's been wearing since Beegee was born. She kicks a pile of rumpled maternity tops across the floor, and burrows through old clothes in the dresser drawers and closet. Flings out stuff that goes back to junior high. Lynn doesn't throw anything away. Here's a black sweater that Heather loved in high school, but with these boobs it makes her look like a hooker. She hoists her breasts into a bra even though she hates wearing one. Helps to soak up the drips, and the way she bounces without it is obscene. There's nothing here to replace the leggings, so they'll have to do. Maybe she can borrow a top.

She stomps into Lynn's room and finds the pale yellow sweater her mother wore a couple of days ago and left folded on the end of the bed. Not Heather's best colour, she decides in front of the mirror, but the fit is good, the way the long sleeves cover all but her fingertips. Lynn always pushes the sleeves to her elbow, looking business-like in this sweater. Heather spreads her arms at her sides, hands slightly upraised, fingers peeking out.

Still strange, no call, but she'll give Carmen a little longer. In the kitchen, she rolls the cuffs past her wrists before she dumps the soup, washes the pot and re-fills it from the giant Tupperware bowl in the fridge. Soup is Lynn's specialty, recipes from her mother. Heather has no memory of her grandparents, just a shadowy sense of them from old pictures. Lynn's parents died within a year of each other, a long time ago.

The soup has just begun to steam when the phone rings.

"Heather, finally. I've been trying to reach you for two days."

"Yeah, well. Things got a little mixed up here. I'm sorry I didn't wait until you got back, but it seemed like now or never." She holds her breath.

"I don't understand." Carmen's trying to sound calm but she's obviously agitated as hell. "Where is Belinda? Grant called me on Friday night, and said you'd phoned late in the afternoon to say your mom was bringing Belinda within the hour, and then she never showed up."

Heather sits down at the table, and pushes aside the bowl, crackers, glass of water she's set out for herself. So Lynn has split. Taking Beegee with her. But where? And how is she going to tell Carmen? She hears the hiss of soup bubbling over onto the burner just seconds before she smells scorched milk. "Just a minute!" Leaving the phone, she dashes to the stove.

"Heather!" Carmen's squawk carries across the kitchen.

"I'm back." She holds the phone with her chin and wipes hot soup off her fingers with a tea towel. Too much. This is too much to deal with all at once. "Look, Carmen, can I call you back in about five minutes?" She clears her throat, tries to sound calm. "I was heating up some soup, and it boiled over and everything's such a mess. I need a few minutes. Or maybe you could come over tomorrow morning." The kitchen clock says it's three o'clock. Surely by morning Lynn will be back, and Heather can put Beegee in Carmen's arms and let her do her job.

"Why don't I call back in ten minutes," Carmen says. "Donna and Grant have been sitting there waiting and wondering and worrying themselves sick. Heather, it's okay if you changed your mind. But I need to know."

"I haven't changed my mind. It's just…something came up." Heather hears the in-drawing of breath, imagines Carmen closing her eyes and telling herself to take two more deep ones. "I should have called Donna and Grant. I'm sorry. Really. I won't do anything like that again."

Another silence. "That's good, Heather. Donna and Grant have been very patient, but you can't keep them waiting forever. How's Belinda?"

She really hates lying. Wants to fling up her arms, tell Carmen she doesn't have a clue how or where Baby Belinda is at this minute. But she can't. "She's growing a lot. Yeah, she's a lot different now than when they saw her at the hospital. Her skin's a little darker too." She's not sure why she says this. She has the feeling, Donna especially, even though she says skin colour isn't an issue, will be glad if the baby doesn't get too dark, if she looks pleasingly blended, rather than black. So far Beegee is a pretty shade of light brown. Or at least she was two days ago. Heather needs to hang up this phone before she says anything more at all. "So tomorrow, okay? Like noon, maybe?"

"Heather?" Carmen's voice is kind. "How are you doing?"

Heather presses the tea towel to her head. How is she doing? Fine, except for this fucking big lump the size of a baseball that's sitting in her throat.

"I'm okay," she says. "I'll call you tomorrow. Bye for now." She puts the phone down, and flings the towel across the kitchen.

She has to find Lynn. And soon. She has no idea how to do this. She needs to talk to Marty.

5

Lynn opens a sleeve of soda crackers and a can of sardines and eats it all, every crumb and every oily flake of fish. She finds the coffee beans, but no grinder, so decides to settle for tea. Cup in hand, she's on her way to the sofa when Beegee begins to fuss. All it takes is the lift to Lynn's shoulder to release another burp, and the baby goes soft with sleep. Lynn pulls the rocking chair close to the fire. She pushes with her toe—feet cosy now, the warm crackle of the fire the only sound as she imagines rocking her way back to Calgary.

From where she sits, she stares at the phone, wanting to call, but wanting desperately to stay hidden. She closes her eyes. If she could just rock her way back to a time before Beegee, and sit her girl down for a good long talk. Even though it wouldn't have made a whit of difference, she'd like to think she'd tried much harder. Heather, at twelve, rolled her eyes when Lynn wondered if there were things she needed to know, to talk about.

"Mom!" she said—this back in the days before she stopped acknowledging them as parents and opted for first names instead—"don't you remember signing the permission slip for those classes in grade five? I know all about sex, and I'm not going to do anything stupid. *Puleeze* don't embarrass yourself by talking about birth control."

Birth control? Lynn had hoped they could talk about abstinence, about a young woman's right to say no, about peer pressure. They'd had all the same talks with both kids about drugs and booze. Jack had talked with Marty about girls and sex. Lynn had been happy to leave that to him.

Marty wandered into the kitchen at the end of their short conversation. When Heather flounced out of the room, he wiped the mustard from the corner of his mouth with a knuckle and cleared his throat. At sixteen, he was already six feet tall and had inherited the lazy grin Lynn remembered so well from the young Jack she'd married. Whatever, she wondered, happened to Jack's smile? It was years since he'd grinned at her.

"I don't think you have to worry, at least for now, Mom," Marty said. "Honest. Scott and his friends are all scared of Heather." Scott was Marty's girlfriend's younger brother. "Besides," he mumbled, "nobody likes talking about sex with their mom." He blushed so fiercely the tops of his ear turned a hot pink.

Through junior high, Heather was scornful of every boy who paid her attention, and Lynn wondered if she might be gay. Had even mentioned this to Jack.

He put down his newspaper and shook his head. "No," he said with absolute conviction. "She doesn't suffer fools, and she has everything going for her—looks, brains, athletic ability, personality—so she knows she can be choosy. She's strong and in control of her life, Lynn. I think we've done a damn good job."

Lynn didn't think she'd had much to do with Heather's personality, nor that it was always an asset. Heather was prickly, argumentative enough that there'd been conferences with teachers over behaviour that bordered on disrespectful. But Heather's downright bluntness about everything going on in her life kept them in-the-know and reassured. Sometimes they heard way too much information, Lynn thought, about who was doing what in Heather's small circle of friends, but Heather herself seemed to be on the right track.

Lynn glances at the babe in her arms and wonders what personality is waiting to emerge from this little girl with the dusky skin and bright eyes. She sees Heather in the elegantly arched eyebrows, and suspects that Beegee will use them, as Heather does, to show utter disdain. The high forehead is Winston's. Beegee will have even tighter curls than Heather's wild mop but perhaps with the copper glint that shows up in Heather's hair in the summer sun. If she's lucky, she'll be tall and slim and move with the same grace as both her parents. Her skin is darker than Heather's, lighter by far than Winston's, but Lynn knows this may change.

Winston. The day Heather told Lynn about Winston, it was like some other girl, a stranger, had disguised herself as Heather. She dropped in unexpectedly after her classes one afternoon, let herself in with her key, and perched on the very edge of the sofa across from the chair in which Lynn was reading. The same places they claimed after Beegee was born and mother and baby came home with Lynn. Heather, who usually sprawled in the chairs at home, was almost vibrating. It was late fall. Her cheeks were pink from the wind, and she had a grin that made Lynn laugh out loud.

"What's up? Do you know how much you look like Marty with that big smile? Do that more often, Heather. It's awfully becoming."

Then, even more uncharacteristically, Heather giggled. "I met this man," she said. "Well actually I met him ages ago, but we went for coffee and I really really want to see him again."

"And you think that will happen?" Lynn felt herself mentally crossing fingers and toes that this radiance in her daughter's face would last.

"Uh huh. But not until the end of semester. He's my lab instructor for chem."

Lynn felt her own smile slide away, the fingers in her mind quickly uncross. So then he really was a man, not a boy or a "guy" as Heather would normally have referred to a new interest. A teacher with an interest in a student. She could imagine the look on Jack's face when he heard about this. But she would not be the one to tell him. Jack had moved out at the end of August.

"Don't look so bent out of shape, Lynn. He's a grad student. From Jamaica. And he's not that old. Probably about Marty's age." So much to process in so few sentences.

Lynn didn't meet Winston until the beginning of January. She was sick with the flu over Christmas, and the kids and Jack celebrated together at his apartment. Heather and Marty stopped by with presents, a deli container of chicken soup and litres and litres of ginger ale. She'd been feeling so miserable, and was so thankful for the company of her children, that after they left she became totally maudlin and wept for an hour. About a week later, Heather called to ask if she could bring Winston by for coffee. Lynn suggested they come for dinner instead. She wanted a reason to cook a proper meal, and she also wanted the chance to get a good long look at this man.

He was indeed a man, and Lynn could see why her daughter was smitten. So much so that she was as afraid as she was delighted for Heather. Not only was Winston ridiculously handsome, charming, but he also seemed totally at ease with Heather. She did not scare him. At least not until three months later, when she told him she was pregnant.

Which apparently had happened a few days before Heather came to tell Lynn.

"You're going to be really upset with me," Heather said, when she was barely through the door. Lynn just shook her head, sure that this had to do with the car, maybe a fender-bender, or money, possibly an overdrawn account, or a school problem, a failed assignment in one of the science courses Heather was agonizing over. "I almost sent an email instead of coming over." Heather sniffed and looked so close to tears, Lynn felt dread begin to grow in her chest.

"Just tell me," she said.

"I'm pregnant." Heather stood there, twisting her face this way and that the way she'd done when she was a very little girl, admitting to some misdemeanor. "And I know exactly what you're going to say. You're going to say, 'You never heard about birth control?'"

Lynn couldn't speak. She shook her head, reached for her daughter and sat down on the sofa to hold Heather while she sobbed. Through the gulps and the swallows, Heather said, "I really really really don't want to cry about this." She grabbed a handful of tissue from the box beside Lynn's reading chair, and blew her nose.

"Why not," Lynn said. She smoothed the tangle of hair back from Heather's forehead, quelling her own turmoil, trying to be calm when she felt like she'd just plunged through ice into six feet of water, she who was never a strong swimmer. "Sorry, kiddo, but I do have to ask. What were you using for birth control?"

"A condom. And the pill too, but I got all puffy and my skin broke out so I quit." Heather sounded so young, Lynn could hardly bear to listen. "Yeah, I know. Dumb."

"No." She patted Heather's cheek. "Bad luck. Exactly how pregnant are you?"

"About eight weeks. And yes, I know, it's still safe to have an abortion. I'm thinking about it."

"Good," Lynn said. "I'm glad. And Heather," she managed a smile in spite of the deep ache that had risen up her throat and would soon turn her lips to stone as well, "I'm really glad you didn't tell me this in an email."

Heather curled up on the sofa and went to sleep, Lynn sitting there beside her, unable to move, cursing this bad joke. About fifteen minutes later, Heather sat up, blew her nose again, announced that she was feeling better. She'd call Lynn in a day or two—and then she was gone.

Even though she was alone in the house, Lynn went into her bedroom to weep because there was nothing she could do. It was all up to Heather. Every difficult step of the way.

The fire settles into itself with a crackling release of sparks. An ember lands near Lynn's foot, but dies quickly, leaving just a wisp of ash. She leans forward, lifting the warm baby away from her chest and then settling her carefully on the other shoulder.

Winston and Heather. And now Beegee, but no Winston. Heather said he'd promised to be back in September, said it as though she believed it would be so, and all through September, every time the phone rang, Lynn saw her snap to attention. Now it's October and weeks since Heather has mentioned his name. Winston, Lynn has to assume, is no longer in the picture, if he ever really was, so far as the baby is concerned. And that leaves Heather a single mother.

"Is that what you want?" Jack asked Lynn the day after Beegee was born. Heather had called to tell him she was taking the baby home instead of handing her over to the adopting couple. As soon as Jack arrived at the hospital, Lynn left the room, but within minutes he found her in the hallway, practically wringing his hands in agitation. "She says she's taking the baby home. You really want Heather to shelve all her plans and be a single mother?"

"What I want doesn't matter," Lynn said. "She hasn't said she's keeping the baby, in fact she insists she's not. She just wants a bit of time with her." Lynn knew, as soon as Heather made her announcement, that Jack would be furious. For months Jack cautioned Lynn to stay out of Heather's way, let her make her own decision. As if it was even possible to sway Heather one way or the other. Though he himself hadn't even tried to appear neutral. Once Heather had decided against an abortion, he'd strenuously endorsed this adoption plan.

"But that's dangerous. It's a bad move." He pounded his fist into his palm, flinching as though he was punishing himself for Heather's actions.

"Why? Because she might decide she loves her baby and can't give her away after all?" She was so tired of Jack harping about Heather's future. As though there couldn't be a future with a baby.

"Because she's strong. She can handle this, so long as she doesn't let her emotions get the best of her."

"Unlike another young woman you knew?" She could hardly bite out the words she was so furious with him.

He snapped his head round to look back at Heather's room, then turned sideways so he could keep both Lynn and door in view. "We do not need to dredge up the past, Lynn."

It was strange to hear Jack whispering—Jack of the big confident voice—trying to get Lynn to do the same. Lynn would not tone down. "Aren't we supposed to learn from history? Especially when it involves decisions we've never regretted." Or at least she'd never regretted. But she couldn't say more, because the door was open and Heather might be listening. Jack surprised her by coming back later that evening with Rhea, to reassure Heather that no one would interfere with her decision. Whatever it turned out to be. This, Lynn was sure, was meant more as a caution to her than reassurance for Heather. Heather had already decided that no one was allowed to enter this discussion.

So Lynn has not been allowed to say anything to Heather in the three weeks they've been living together, tending the baby, watching her grow. Nothing about her own choice long ago, because of the promise she and Jack made to themselves. Nothing about Heather being a good mother. This, Lynn thinks, must be the point of what she's done. When she calls Heather, after she has apologized a hundred times, she will say that yes, of course, she knows that her stealing of the baby is inexcusable. Madness even. This is Heather's decision. But one mad person at least, believes Heather is as capable of looking after Beegee as she is of giving her away. And all Lynn asks is that Heather at least consider that option.

Lynn has turned Heather's reaction every which way in her mind. Heather will be furious with her. Will she be afraid for Beegee? Afraid that Lynn has gone so totally off her rocker that the baby is in danger? Lynn strokes the baby's cheek with the tips of her fingers. No. Heather will know in her gut that Beegee is safe with Lynn. Lynn will phone and reassure her, soon she will do that.

And Jack? What about Jack? It's occurred to her that she should phone him. Tell him not to call the police. But that's not likely anyway, because he would be afraid of turning up in the news. What would the parents of his students think? Jack will be furious, but Lynn will tell him that she has had hours to think and she knows for sure that he is wrong. That their decision twenty-four years ago does matter. It turns out Lynn is no more capable of quietly relinquishing her grand-daughter than she was of relinquishing her son. The decision isn't hers, but she can't stay quiet any longer. Whether or not they say anything to Marty and Heather, Lynn is convinced that at least she and Jack need to talk.

What will everyone think? Lynn pushes a little harder with her foot, the rocking chair finding its sweet rhythm. For once, she does not give a good goddamn what anyone thinks.

The baby begins to squirm and grunt, and Lynn feels the explosive filling of the diaper through the thin towel she's wrapped Beegee in, for want of a clean blanket.

"All right then. At least we know the answer to this problem. Time for a bath."

She spreads a towel in the bottom of the bathroom sink and fills it with warm water. Spreads another towel on the floor and undresses the baby.

With a trickle still running from the tap, she lowers Beegee into the warm water on the crook of her arm. Instantly, the thrashing limbs relax and dark eyes lock on Lynn's. "You," she says, gently sponging Beegee with a folded facecloth, "get brighter by the minute." She stares at the pink nub on the baby's stomach. "Your cord's finally dropped off." A quick glance at the diaper on the floor. "No, we are not going to look for it." Fortunately, Lynn can be sure that Heather will not want this souvenir.

This talking to Beegee is new. At home, it was Heather who murmured constantly, but always looked up resentfully if Lynn came too close, as though it was a private conference.

The baby seems to be listening. Lynn smiles at her, and begins to hum. Funny how those songs abide in a woman's head forever. *Hush bitty baby, don't you cry. Grandma's gonna sing you a lullaby.* She cups her hand under the fresh stream of the tap and tips Beegee back, spilling warm water over the fluff of black hair.

Clean diaper, but the outfit Beegee wore on the journey—that special white velour Peter Rabbit sleeper chosen by Donna and Grant for the homecoming—is pee-stained from the waist down and the collar stiff with spit-up. In the damp cabin it will take days to dry. For now, another towel will have to do.

"Today we will go shopping," she says. Shopping. They need diapers, formula, and there must be somewhere on the island to buy baby clothes. She might have to load her credit card with hand-knitted, gift-shop baby clothes. Amazing, she thinks, how this child seems to have grown in the hours it took them to trek over the mountains. Under her chin there is the hint of softness, a plush swelling of fat. It's been days since Lynn even really looked at Beegee. Heather held the baby almost non-stop even while she slept, curled around her in bed at night, dozing on the sofa in the living room during the day with Beegee sprawled on her chest.

Lynn's arm is beginning to ache, and the water is cooling. In a quick swoop, she lowers the dripping baby to the towel on the floor, tapes another diaper in place, binds her snugly in another dry towel.

By the time Lynn carries Beegee into the kitchen, she is as limp as a sleeping kitten. The fire has burned down but the room is deliciously warm. Lynn nests Beegee into a knitted afghan on the worn plaid sofa. Probably made it himself, that old Norwegian who's providing their shelter. The kids almost exploded with embarrassment the first time they saw Einar sit down in his rocking chair and begin clicking away at a half-finished sock.

There are only a few pieces of wood left in the box by the fireplace. One more glance at Beegee, one more tuck of the blanket, and Lynn slips on her jacket and quietly opens the door. She almost trips over Loki who seems to be guarding them well. He looks up at her and whines. "Oh go on in."

She holds the door wider. "You're breaking my heart, you lovely animal."

The rain has stopped, but still the cedars stream. Lynn draws the scent of salt and evergreen deep into her lungs. Face to the road, she closes her eyes and imagines the other side of the island, the long finger of Rebecca Spit stretching into the sea, the black heads of harbour seals popping up here and there, and there again. One summer when Marty was about ten, they had to drag him away from the beach long after the sun went down because he could not take his eyes from the sea, waiting for the appearance of just one more sleek black head. Lynn was willing to stay there with him forever because this was the only place on the island where she had a clear view. Jack brushed away her complaints of suffocating claustrophobia as self-indulgence. Each year, she swore this would be the last vacation she spent on the island, and every year until Marty was eighteen, they came back. Then one more time, two years ago, she and Jack made the trip alone. And here she is again.

If she turns to face the cabin and the dense growth of cedar behind, the sound of the sea will be audible. Any minute the ferry will call its arrival. If Einar drove up now, while she is in this circle of calm, she feels sure she could convince him that all is well, that she has not lost her mind. Hannah has already blown away her dream of a few days of solitude, time alone with Beegee. Lynn realized this afternoon when she was lighting the fire, that she is curious to see Einar again. She's still not sure why Einar, always Jack's friend more than hers, is the one person she summoned up as someone she could trust in those moments when she streaked past the turn that would have taken her to Donna and Grant's house, and headed west. Or maybe it was just the memory of this lonely cabin that drew her here.

Branches stir beside the cabin, the whisper of feet. A child in a yellow plastic cape emerges from the trees, head down, muttering under its breath. The child finally looks up, then stops abruptly a few feet away, between Lynn and the door. A girl. Braids spill from under the hood, the ends tied together under her chin and secured with a wooden barrette. She pulls her hands out of the stiff folds of the slicker, holds a pile of cotton out to Lynn.

"Mom sent nighties for your baby." But before Lynn can reach out to take the clothes, the girl slips them back under the rain cape. She grins, showing a gap where one front tooth is missing. The one beside it is barely a nub. "Can I see her?"

Lynn hesitates. Hannah was enough. She doesn't want anyone else to see Beegee, to know she's here. But how to say no to a little girl. Lynn tries to picture Beegee at this age with braids and a bright yellow coat. "Sure you can," she says. As soon as she opens the door, the child slips past and takes off her boots. When she spots Loki beside the couch—the silly dog grinning from the child to the baby on the sofa and back again—she tiptoes theatrically across the room.

"Awww," she whispers. "Can I hold her?"

Lynn imagines Heather's face at such a request from a strange, wet child. The girl is already shrugging off the cape. Underneath she's wearing a grey t-shirt and baggy shorts. Tall, like her mom, but all knobby elbows and knees. Maybe eight years old. Without waiting for an answer, she scoops up the baby, sits down and cradles her, fussing with the end of the towel. In Hannah's brood, everyone is likely expert in the art of baby tending. What a contrast with Heather, who actually trembled every time she picked up Beegee for the first five days. When she was growing up, Heather never showed an ounce of interest in babies. She laughed when Lynn suggested babysitting as a way to supplement her allowance, delivered flyers instead.

One afternoon not long ago, Lynn came quietly to the doorway of the living room and watched Heather playing with Beegee. She had the baby on her knees, naked except for her diaper, and leaned down to drop loud smacking kisses all over Beegee's chest. Then she took the baby's small hands in hers and clapped them together. "Yay, for kisses! Come on, smile!" When she looked up and saw Lynn, Heather quickly wrapped Beegee in her receiving blanket and stood up.

"Looks like fun," Lynn said. "Don't let me interrupt."

"That was enough." Heather glared at her. "I don't even like babies."

Lynn couldn't help herself. She burst out laughing. "Neither did I, kiddo, except for my own. Mother Nature's little joke." Which only made Heather scowl all the more.

Clearly the little visitor does like babies. When Beegee begins to sputter, Hannah's daughter stands up and walks stolidly to the rocking chair. Within seconds, the baby is still again, the only sound in the room the creaking of the floor. Finally the child looks up at Lynn.

"Don't worry. I won't wake her up. I know how to keep babies happy." The braids form an inverted heart under her chin.

"Good," Lynn says, "because this one is a bit fussy."

The girl snorts. "I know. We could hear her crabbing all the way to our house." She looks down at the bundle in her arms. "This is a girl, right?" As though, if she were holding a boy, she might have second thoughts. Lynn nods. "What's her name?"

"Beegee," Lynn says. Then, "We call her bee gee. For Bonnie Gale. What's your name?" Bonnie Gale. Lynn has no idea where the Gale came from, but Bonnie was the name she had chosen for Heather. Unfortunately, it was a name Jack hated. He wanted Candace. They compromised on Heather.

"Destiny."

Six summers ago, that last time they were all here together, Heather was a grouchy fourteen-year-old. Marty was eighteen and drove out for a few days with one of his friends. This was the little girl who'd toddled around trying to keep up with the teenagers because her younger brothers ran off and left her and her mom was busy with a new baby. Lynn remembers Hannah on her front step, new baby nursing on one breast, Destiny on the other.

"I can stay and babysit," Destiny tells her. "In case you want to have a nap or something."

"Thanks," Lynn says, "but I don't need a nap." She can't drag her eyes away from this child holding Beegee, much less leave them alone together.

"You could just sit on the couch and read," Destiny says. "You don't have to talk to me." She wriggles a little in the chair, shifts Beegee to her other arm. "I mean you can if you want to, but my mom said not to bother you."

Lynn sits sideways on the couch, facing Destiny and Beegee. "You were barely more than a baby yourself, the last time I saw you." The little girl nods solemnly, as though she remembers that visit as well.

"How come you didn't come back for a long time?" Destiny asks. "Were you too busy?"

Lynn can't help but smile at the child. "I guess that's what happened."

Busy? She wonders what excuse Jack gave Einar when they finally stopped coming to Quadra. Heather was barely two the first time they made the trip. Jack and Einar met at university. Jack a whiz-kid who helped Einar, the mature student who was struggling with an education degree because he wanted to teach woodworking in high schools. He

77

and Jack ended up teaching in the same school in Calgary for a couple of years and then Einar's second marriage fell apart and he left for the west coast. Lynn doesn't remember ever meeting the second wife, or the first one. But she does remember Jack telling her about the bitterness of the first divorce, and the three children who moved somewhere far south, down in the States with their mother. It was always just Jack and Einar drinking beer and studying at the kitchen table. Then the standing invitation from Einar to come enjoy his little cabin in the woods on their vacations.

Destiny stands up, Beegee a little awkward in her arms now, the towel slipping. Lynn swings her legs to the floor, gets ready to grab the baby, but in seconds Destiny and baby are seated beside her. Beegee is waking up. One little snuffle, then another. Lynn hoped that the soporific heat of the fire would keep the baby under its spell for at least another half hour.

She looks at her watch. There won't be any shopping until Beegee is fed again. "I think she's hungry."

"Should I get my mom? She said to tell you she'll come down and feed the baby."

Lynn wonders what else Hannah has told Destiny about the baby next door and the woman who can't feed her. She shakes her head. "Tell her thanks, but we'll be fine."

Destiny's face closes up, no smile. She lays Beegee on her legs, binds the towel tight, and hands the baby to Lynn like a package. She hesitates. "Can I come back and see her again?" she asks.

"Sure," Lynn says. While Beegee begins to root, tossing her head side to side, the hiccups escalating, Destiny puts on her coat and boots and is gone before Lynn gets up to warm a bottle.

Two bags of milk remain after a feeding that takes over

an hour and leaves both Lynn and the baby sweaty with exhaustion even though the fire has long gone out. Now what? Lynn changes the diaper and unfolds one of the flannel nightgowns Destiny delivered. She runs her hand over the faded fabric, the bit of smocking at the top. Just like the nightgowns her mother bought for Marty. Piles of flannel nighties, hand-hemmed diapers, sleepers to grow into, and a ridiculous little sailor suit when he was six months old, barely able to sit for his first formal photo. She saved the nightgowns for Heather, but that wee girl kicked free of blankets, squawked when she was wrapped too tight and had to be dressed in footed sleepers to keep her warm.

Lynn slips Beegee's fists, the bent little arms, into the sleeves of the nightgown, ties the piece of bias tape at the back, then cradles the baby close to her face. She buries her nose in faded flannel. Hannah has stored these in cedar. They smell of forest.

Lynn wraps Beegee in yet another clean towel, the last in the stack. Where, she wonders, does Einar do laundry? She will need to wash these towels for him, remake the bed. Or maybe…maybe she needs to turn around and go home before he gets back. Just leave a note of thanks, and a clean cabin.

The towels that are still damp from Beegee's bath will dry on the back of a kitchen chair if she sets it close to the fireplace. She'll light another fire when she gets back from buying formula. She's known how to split kindling and build a decent fire since she was Destiny's age, and even though Jack insisted on being in charge of campfires as well as almost all the other practical tasks Lynn learned from her dad, she's sure she hasn't forgotten the skill.

So organized, she sits down at the table, Beegee against her shoulder, and makes a list. Diapers, formula, baby soap and shampoo, fruit, and ingredients for soup. There are chunks of frozen meat in brown wrappers in the ice-encrusted cavern in the top of Einar's fridge, but she won't eat his food. In fact, she will leave hearty soup in the freezer when she goes. She prints "Advil" at the bottom of the list. The headache is now concentrated above her right eye. When she comes back she will phone Heather.

Coat on, Beegee snug in her towel, Lynn opens the door, steps into the dusk, and sees Hannah coming down the driveway. She's carrying a woven bag in each hand, and clumps them down on the step in front of Lynn.

"Where are you going? I brought milk and some supper for you."

She brushes past Lynn, into the kitchen. One bag on the table, and the other she carries to the fridge. Lynn inhales one more deep breath of the mild damp, and follows Hannah back inside. "You didn't need to bring anything," she says. "I was on my way to the store." Hannah takes packages out of the freezer, rearranges, and then begins to pull baggie after frost-coated baggie from the carrier. Creamy-coloured reserves of milk, just like the ones Heather pumped and saved. She slams the freezer door shut, dusts her hands together.

"There you go. Enough breast milk to last at least a week."

"Are you sure you can spare all that?" Lynn asks.

"You'd choke if you saw the emergency supply of breast milk in my freezer. I never seem to need it, but just in case, you know? I've been pumping for years. The kids claim it dates all the way back to Sunny, and she's nineteen—don't worry, this is all fresh!"

Lynn fights back a wave of revulsion at the thought of warming Hannah's milk. Why would that disturb her more than warming milk from a cow? Or buying a milk substitute produced in a factory? Seeing Beegee at Hannah's breast only evokes envy, not distaste. Okay. She mentally crosses formula off her list. She makes a show of looking at her watch. "Thanks. And thanks for the supper. I'll have it when I get back."

Hannah digs into the other bag now, empties a plastic container into a pot from the shelf above the stove. "It's Sunday. The store closes at six. This is Quadra."

Campbell River is a ten-minute ferry ride away. Lynn stands in the doorway with the towel-bundled baby, imagining herself back in the car. There's time. So long as she can get there and back before Beegee needs another feeding.

"It's cold in here again," Hannah says. "Why did you let the fire go out?"

The cabin does feel chilly. Dark and damp as a cave, now that Lynn is back inside. Outside, gold light is filtering through the trees, dappling the wet ground with shadows, sparkling on the tips of branches. Inside, Hannah has the heat on under a battered saucepan. Hannah, with her big breasts full of milk and her generosity has saved Lynn a trip back to bright lights. As much as she does not want to be beholden to this woman, Lynn feels relieved.

The smell of tomato and garlic has begun to fill the room. Hannah the vegetarian. Hannah's husband, Einar told them years ago, often snuck down to share bacon and eggs, and the two oldest boys would eventually find them and sit like puppies until Einar set plates in front of them as well.

"What's wrong?" Hannah says.

Wrong? Lynn is sure Hannah doesn't need to ask the question. Here's a grandmother with a baby, a rapidly diminishing food supply until the generous neighbour shows up, and no plan other than the vague idea of going somewhere sometime to buy diapers. Hannah is watching the pot of soup, but her eyes may as well be on Lynn, she's so still.

"What about Heather," Hannah says at last. "When is

81

she coming out here?" She looks across at Lynn, lower lip caught between her teeth.

Lynn is about to cobble together an answer when Hannah interrupts. "She knows where you are, right?"

There is no way to answer without lying, so Lynn makes the simple declaration that's been her mantra for two days. "I'm going to call her," she says, and knows that she's already waited too long.

6

It takes Heather until well into the evening to track Marty, and he doesn't want to come over. He's meeting his latest woman and some of her friends at a martini bar. Martini bar? Normally, she would roll her eyes and say goodbye. Good luck. But she needs her brother. Needs him to tell her to chill out, everything will be fine. Beegee is safe—she's with Lynn, isn't she? Heather can't shake the thought that something terrible has happened to both of them.

"Dump her. There is no way you're going to last with someone who drinks martinis so you may as well save yourself time and money. Go pick up someone at a sports bar. But first come over here. I need to talk to you."

"No, you're gonna love Kaylee. Meet us down there."

"I can't meet you in a bar, you moron. The front of my shirt is soaked with milk every hour on the hour."

He groans. "Damn, Heather! I'm sorry. I forgot about you having to feed the baby." She imagines him hitting his forehead with his fist. "Of course you can't bring the baby to a bar. Hey, maybe Lynn would watch her for while."

What does Marty know about looking after a three-week-old baby? What did she know until three weeks ago? She cuts to the chase. "Lynn's not here. Neither is Beegee."

"What do you mean?"

"I mean they're missing."

"Since when? What's going on?"

She fights to keep from screaming. Hysteria is not the way to deal with Marty. Scares him spitless. "Since Friday."

"Holy shit! Have you called the cops? What about Dad?"

"Just come. I'll tell you about it when you get here. And don't bring any Krissy or Kylie or Karri with you."

For the next half hour she paces. The hall carpet is matted and grey down the middle. When she closes the drapes in the living room, there's a small puff of dust. Has this happened in the two years since Jack left? The house was never tidy enough to suit Jack, but it seemed clean. Now there's a creeping shabbiness. There are paint cans in the corner of the living room. Heather's surprised Jack didn't notice them. Heather offered to move back home when Jack split. She was living in university residence, and when she calculated the amount she could save from the monthly allowance Jack was giving her, it didn't seem like a bad idea at all. At least for a few months. But when she suggested coming home, Lynn totally surprised her.

"Why?" she said. "For the first time in my life I can do exactly what I want, when I want. I don't need a roommate, Heather."

Heather didn't ask permission to come home after Beegee was born. Where else would she go?

Back to the other question. Where has Lynn gone? Heather flips the address book in the kitchen open to Bernie's number. She's been putting this off because she's sure it's pointless, but mostly because she doesn't like Bernie. As long as Heather can remember the woman has been bossy and tactless. The conversation goes pretty much the way she expects it to after she asks Bernie if her mom is there, if she's heard from her at all today. She almost says "since yesterday" but that sounds so drastic she can't get the words out. Bernie will go ballistic if she hears Lynn is missing.

"Haven't talked to her in a couple of weeks," Bernie says, with a tone that suggests this is probably Heather's fault. "What makes you think she'd be here?"

Heather fumbles a bit, irritated that even though she steeled herself, Bernie still makes her feel like a ten-year-old. "I can't remember what she said. She went out...for the day and then there was something about tonight. I'll try the other couple of places she mentioned. Maybe she's at Jean's."

But she doesn't get off that easily. "Jean's in England. I don't blame Lynn for needing to get out. You're not planning on staying there indefinitely, are you? Heather, give the woman a break. She's barely got her feet under her from your dad leaving."

"Thanks for your help," Heather says. "I'll tell her to call you when she gets home."

She sits down and seethes. At Bernie, at herself for letting the woman get under her skin, but mostly at Lynn. Marty is taking a ridiculous length of time to get here. She wonders what he's told his date. If Kaylee will be scared off by a family that sounds straight out of the soaps. She turns on the television to break the silence, and tidies the living room. She gathers up the quilts and dumps them on the bed in her old room. Empties the pitcher of water and stacks it in the dishwasher with the soup pot and Friday's dishes.

She realizes that in the time she and Beegee have been here, she's been so absorbed by the baby she's barely noticed how this house feels, day by day, without her dad. Maybe it hasn't changed that much. It was always a quiet house, even more when Lynn and Jack were pissed off with each other because silence was the weapon of choice for both of them. They froze each other out, rather than shouting and storming out of the house the way the parents of one of Heather's best friends did. It seems ironic to Heather that her teenage friends were all envious because the Bishops were one of the few families around with two parents, the original parents. Angela's parents, the screaming door slammers, are still together. Heather and Marty have spent hours—at Heather's insistence, Marty dislikes talking about Lynn's and Jack's personal life, so Heather does all the talking—trying to figure out what happened.

When Heather was about ten years old, she went to a birthday skating party at a private club. When the girls were leaving the snack bar, Heather saw her dad and a woman she only glimpsed, going into the cosy-looking café across the hall. She wanted to rush over and find out why Jack and a strange woman had come looking for her, but the girls were in a hurry. And something else held her back. At supper that night she asked. "Hey, why were you guys at the Winter Club today?"

Lynn looked blank. "Not me, kiddo," Jack said. "I was at school grading papers all afternoon. What were you doing at the Winter Club?"

"Why do you ask?" Lynn said quietly, her eyes on Heather. She glanced at Jack. "She was at a skating party. If you'd been here for dinner last night, you would have heard about it."

Heather had a funny feeling in her stomach. "I saw somebody who looked like Daddy."

"Lucky guy!" Jack said with a laugh. "As good-looking as me and free to loaf around at a club on a Saturday afternoon." Heather didn't tell him there was a car in the parking lot that was a ringer for his as well.

Marty says he knew for years that Jack had other women.

Overheard arguments that made him clamp his hands over his ears and hide in his bedroom. When Grandpa Bishop died, it took Lynn hours to find Jack because he wasn't at school when she phoned and no one had any idea which "meeting" it was he'd signed out to attend. Marty also figures Lynn decided long ago that she'd live with the infidelity.

For at least five years, Jack and Lynn seemed to run on separate parallel tracks, rarely going anywhere together, but civil, available, and on rare occasions even affectionate. Heather remembers walking off the stage at her high school graduation, looking out into the audience to where she'd spotted her parents earlier, and seeing Jack's arm around Lynn, her head tilted toward him. She took it as a good sign a couple of years ago when they went off to Quadra all by themselves. Lynn never seemed happy on the holidays to the island, always anxious, she said, to be able to see beyond the trees again. But she was surprisingly cheerful about that trip. They were barely home again when Jack took Heather and Marty out for dinner and told them he was moving out. Better for both him and Lynn, he said, and then with this stupid smile he kept trying to hide, he told them about Rhea.

Not Rhea's fault that Jack split, Marty says, but he thinks she's the reason. After all the other women, Jack finally found someone important enough to make him want to leave. They're planning a trip to Europe. Heather has never seen her dad so excited as when he talks about the places he and Rhea are going to visit. "Can you imagine Lynn wanting to "do" Europe?" Marty asked Heather.

"Yes!" she said, out of fierce loyalty to her mom and because she doesn't think she'll ever feel kindly toward Rhea the way her brother does. Really, though, what she can imagine is Lynn in a villa in one of those romantic places in Italy or France. Shirley Valentine, like the play Lynn and

Heather saw a couple of years ago. Of course getting there would involve flying, which Lynn doesn't like.

She should probably take comfort in knowing that Lynn hasn't flown away somewhere with Beegee. Wherever they are, it must be within driving distance. She crushes the Pampers box and stuffs it in the garbage. Picks up the sleeper and holds it against her cheek. What will she do with this, and with the other tiny undershirts and sleepers that are still in a drawer in her room?

Finally, she flings the scrap of pink into the bathroom on top of the towels and scoops the whole mess into a laundry basket. The sleeper should be washed with pure soap—she's learned these things from Lynn—but it won't matter now, because that fabric is never going to touch Beegee's skin again.

The house is almost presentable when Marty shows up, phone in hand. "Okay, what's the deal?" he says, one big mitt clamping onto her shoulder with a brotherly squeeze.

She feels like resting her forehead on his chest. "Don't be too nice to me," she says, "or I'm going to start bawling again. I just spent two days in Jack's spare bedroom blubbering into the pillow. That's enough."

He looks so much like her, it's spooky. Everyone knows instantly that they're sibs. But neither of them, Heather's always thought, looks much like Jack or Lynn. Except for Jack's height. Marty's six-two, like Jack, and Heather's five-eleven. They've all towered over Lynn for years. Even though she's not exactly short herself.

"Sit down," Heather says, pointing to the kitchen table.

Marty takes the chair across from her. "Where's Lynn. And where's the baby?" He glances at his watch. "Short version please."

"Like this is simple?" God, to be like her brother with nothing on his mind but a hot date. She plants her elbows on the table, chin on her fists and stares at him. "So on Friday I decide that if I don't go through with this adoption it's not going to happen. I'm getting way too attached to the little poop. And Carmen is away, so I phone Donna and Grant and tell them their baby's on the way, and then I ask Lynn to take her over there."

"Jesus, Heather!" Marty pounds his fist on the table and she almost bites off her tongue with the shock to her jaw. When he throws his arms in the air, Heather's surprised his cell doesn't fly across the kitchen. "Do what you gotta do, but where the hell do you come off asking Lynn to do something you know is going to make her crazy?"

"Do I know that? Has she told me what she thinks I should do, or even what she's feeling?"

"No, probably not, because you told everyone months ago to butt out. You basically told everyone to piss off on the one hand but to make sure they stuck around to support you on the other." He exhales, reaches across and puts that hand on her shoulder again. "I know, it's the absolute shits and you don't need me yelling at you. Then what happened?"

"I packed up Beegee's stuff, and gave her to Lynn and she went out the door and I haven't heard from her since. Neither has anyone else."

"Including those adopting people?"

"Correct. I didn't realize she was gone because I went to Jack's on Friday night and didn't wake up until today."

"Well, did she seem distressed when she left? Like she might do something erratic?"

Heather shakes her head. "Would I have noticed? I don't even remember what she said. About any of it."

"What did Jack say?"

"He's worried. He phoned all day yesterday trying to find her, and he doesn't even know yet that she still has Beegee."

"What did he say about you asking Lynn to do that?"

"Nothing." She sits back in the chair and folds her arms. Wishes she felt as sure of herself as she's trying to appear. The interrogation is getting to her. "But that's not the point, right now. The question is where the hell did she go?"

"Yeah," he says, "that's the question all right. Did you try calling her friends?"

"Marion's in Toronto. Apparently Jean is in England, and Bernie says she hasn't heard from Lynn since right after Beegee was born. She was so sniffy with me about moving in here with the baby that we didn't talk."

He taps his fingers on the table, on the phone. "Maybe we'd better tell Jack."

"Not yet," she says, even though she's had the phone in her hand twice while she waited for Marty to arrive. Heather has this feeling in her gut that she'd better find Lynn herself, or at least try.

Marty leans back in the chair. "Look, maybe you need to wait. She's going to come back, Heather, surely we can assume that. What about the baby people?"

"They don't know. I mean they don't know she's still gone and has Beegee."

"Shit. So do you have any idea what she's doing?"

Back and forth they go, trying to get inside Lynn's head, but the truth is neither of them knows what their mother has been thinking about Heather's adoption plan. Did Lynn have some crazy idea about keeping Beegee herself? Making Heather keep her?

"I can't believe she wants me to be a mommy. Especially after she screwed up her own plans exactly that way." Oh jeez. Marty was the reason Lynn and Jack got married. She holds up her hands. "Sorry."

He shrugs. "Am I supposed to feel guilty? It's old news."

Right. That's Lynn's line. She won't talk about getting

pregnant when she was in university, or how she and Jack decided to get married right after Marty was born. Neither will Jack, except to insist that they would have stayed together anyway. Heather doubts anyone would even have figured it out if she hadn't asked Lynn, about ten years ago, which anniversary she and Jack were going out to celebrate. Lynn was busy rummaging around in a drawer, looking for pantyhose. "Fifteen," she'd said. And then she'd looked up like she'd just heard a gunshot. Well hey! Even at ten, Heather knew her brother wasn't supposed to be the same age as her parents' anniversary. But no big deal, Jack claimed later at suppertime when Heather brought it up again. It was the era of "free love" and Marty just happened to arrive a little earlier than they planned. Marty looked so embarrassed to hear their dad mention sex and his own name in the same sentence, he almost climbed under the table. Heather's always wondered why, if it was no big deal, Lynn and Jack kept their anniversary a secret. Not the date, but the number of years was never mentioned again. Not even after that big disclosure about Marty being illegit.

"Okay, so that's old news. But Lynn just ran away with Beegee and totally fucked up my plan, and that is news."

Marty gets that steely look in his eye that she hates.

"I know!" she says. "I fucked up all on my own. Big time. But you have to help me out here. What do I do?"

"How the hell did you let that happen, anyway?" Marty asks, but she can tell from the look on his face that he really doesn't want to hear the details.

"Condom," she says. "You might want to keep that mind."

He shakes his head, not nearly as sympathetic as Lynn who seemed to understand that Heather hadn't been as well-prepared as she should have been. Bad luck, she'd called it.

Marty is staring at Heather, not at her face but at her shirt, and she looks down at two saucer-sized circles of wet.

She is going to take those dry-up pills, she really is. But not until she finds Beegee. She stands up. "I need to pump some milk before I explode."

"Not in here you don't!" He practically kicks over the chair scrambling to his feet.

She remembers now that the couple of times Marty's been over since Beegee's birth, when she fed the baby he found an excuse to leave the room. Seeing as the kid nurses non-stop, most of the conversations they've had in the last few weeks were shouted between kitchen and living room. She grabs the pump from the counter by the sink. "It's a natural function. Get over it."

When Heather comes back to the kitchen with the cup of milk ten minutes later, Marty's still at the table. Playing a game on his cell phone.

She smacks him on the back of the head as she passes. "You're supposed to be thinking about where Lynn could have gone." Opens the fridge and stows the cup there. She's tempted to pour the milk down the drain. While she was pumping just now, she had the horrible feeling that Beegee would never get another drop of her milk. If she believed in premonitions, she'd be sure that both Beegee and Lynn were dead. Fortunately, she doesn't have any patience with that kind of crap. She sits down across from her brother.

"This is how I think, Heather." He doesn't even look up. "I don't stomp around throwing things." Finally he puts the phone down. "Have you checked Lynn's email? Maybe there's a clue there."

"How would I do that? Like I know Lynn's password? I'm not in the habit of snooping, Martin." She knows she sounds prissy, but she actually likes to make him squirm. One of the biggest fights she and Marty ever had when they were both still living at home was over his snooping through her messages. He'd seen her at the mall with a couple of her friends who went Goth for about a month, and was afraid she was hooking up with the dark side. He never did tell her what he planned to do about it.

"Besides," Heather says, "Lynn couldn't have planned this via email because I sprang it on her. I seriously doubt she was sitting here plotting a kidnapping."

"Is it a kidnapping? Really? If it's the grandma?" He stands up and starts crashing around the kitchen. Marty always grazes his way through this house. He takes cheese out of the fridge, breaks off a chunk and stands there gnawing on it, an apple in his other hand, looking at her thoughtfully. "You know, Heather, you're looking good. I think having the baby gave you kind of a…"

"Voluptuous?" she says. "Is that the word you're looking for."

"No! Healthy. Sort of softer around the edges, and good colour. Yeah, that's part of it. You have good colour. Like you've been out in the sun."

Both she and Marty do have Lynn's fair skin. They burn if they even look out the window on a hot day. She's pleased with the compliment. For months she's looked in the mirror and wanted the fat, splotchy-looking stranger to go away, but right now she wishes this laid-back brother would go away and be replaced by one who takes her problem seriously. "You're not concerned at all? You think I should sit here and wait for Lynn to wander back? Say, when Beegee's ready to start school?"

"Of course not. And of course I'm worried. But I'm not the RCMP, Heather. Do you want to call the police or not? How about phoning the relatives? Ask if anyone's heard from her?" He waves the suggestion away as soon as he's made it. He knows as well as Heather does that the aunts, uncles, cousins Lynn never sees except at funerals are not people she'd even call in an emergency, never mind if she's done something totally insane.

"Forget airlines. At least we know she didn't fly anywhere. How far can you drive in two days?"

He shrugs. "Depends on whether or not you stop to sleep. I guess a baby would slow you down." He takes a major chomp out of the apple, juice spraying. Two more bites and he lobs the core across the room into the garbage can.

Heather has to keep from rolling her eyes or he'll get ticked off and be of no help at all, but really! "You know, you could be right. So if she's moving slowly, how far could she have gone? Do you think we should call the hospitals? What if they were in an accident?"

"By now the police would have been here. Even if she wasn't carrying ID, they'd trace the car to this address." He raises his hands. "I don't know, Heather. But I'm really sure you don't have to worry. This is Lynn. Mom. She can't be far away. And she's basically a sensible person." He checks his phone. Reading a text message. "I have to go."

"Marty, she stole my baby."

He taps the phone against the palm of his hand, and looks as though he's trying to work out a very hard math question. Finally he sits down. "Maybe we should think closer to home. Maybe she's holed up in a hotel or something? Maybe she thought you needed more time to—I don't know."

"You're the practical one." She feels like screaming. She does not scream at her brother. Not at anyone. "So tell me. If you were Lynn, where would you go?"

Again, he frowns and shakes his head. "I don't know." He chews his lip. She has the same nervous habit. She's amazed her mouth isn't ragged and bleeding after the past three weeks. But lip-chewing isn't getting her anywhere.

She's tempted to phone Marion in Toronto, but she hates to worry the woman when she's already strung out over

her granddaughter's cancer. Marion's been out there helping with the other kids so her daughter can take the little
girl back and forth to treatments. Heather remembers her
mom's face when she told her all this.

"Horrible enough to see her granddaughter so sick," Lynn
said, "but then there's her daughter too, and what she's going through."

No, Heather's sure Lynn wouldn't have bothered Marion
with this small problem of her own granddaughter.

Who else? She thinks back to the couples Lynn and Jack
used to see occasionally, for the theatre, or for dinner, mainly colleagues of Jack's. No one she can imagine Lynn keeping
in touch with, now that Jack's gone. The only one they saw
regularly, or at least once a year until they stopped going
on family vacations, is her dad's old pal, Einar, out there
on the island. Heather's memories of summer have those
west coast trips embedded in them. The whale-watching trip
with Lynn seasick the whole time, days and days playing
Monopoly and Sorry because the rain kept pouring down,
the musty-smelling mattress on the bedroom floor and Lynn
and Jack and Mr. Haugland—when did he ask them to call
him Einar?—talking quietly in the next room. Sunny days
traipsing next door to round up the wild kids who lived
there, the walk to the store for Popsicles, the air buzzing
with heat. But Lynn always complained about going to the
island. The place gave her the heebie jeebies, so closed in and
dark. She said she was a prairie girl, she needed to be able to
see farther than beyond the next tree.

Heather reaches for the address book, opens it to "H"
and stares at his name. She drums her fingers on the phone
number. "Quadra," she says. Marty stares at her as though
she's mentioned Jupiter.

"What? To Mr. Haugland's place?" She shrugs. Marty

laughs, bats the very idea out of the air with his hand. "Come on, Heather. Why would she go there?"

"Why is she going anywhere? There or to the prairies." And they are back to the beginning again. She realizes Marty is not going to be of any help tonight.

"Okay," she says. "Go to your Martini Girl. Call me when you get home. I'm not going to bed. I've been sleeping for two days."

After he leaves, Heather returns to the table, to the address book. Einar Haugland. He was always away for part of the time they were at his cabin, but when he was around, she remembers her mom laughing with him, sitting on the front step with a drink in her hand, relaxed. Yeah, Einar was someone with whom Lynn seemed at ease, not distant the way she was with most people she only knew casually. But would she consider him her friend, not just Jack's? Quadra is so far away, surely she wouldn't think of going there?

There's no one else to try. The worst that can happen is that Mr. Haugland will think she's nuts for calling, but he's so laid back she doesn't think he'd make that kind of judgment. Wonder about it, maybe. Tell Jack that she phoned? Why would that matter? Heather keys in Einar's phone number and holds her breath. She lets it ring about ten times before she hangs up. Okay, so much for that shot in the dark.

She sits a long time at the table, staring at the phone book. She should call Jack. She will, or soon enough Jack will call her. Quadra. That cabin tucked under the wet trees is so vivid in her mind she can smell it. Why would Lynn go there? Because it's closed in, a hiding place?

When there's no answer at Einar's number on the next try, Heather walks down the hall to her bedroom, that room full of junk that Lynn would never throw away. She drags a shoe box out of the closet. The boxes from Marty's size thirteen basketball shoes were recycled to hold photos and old cards

96

and receipts all over this house. This one is crammed with letters from Heather's elementary school penpal in England, an autograph book, a Xena Warrior Princess address book. Xena's photo has been obscenely altered. Marty?

What was their last name, those neighbours on Quadra? Sunny was the girl two years younger than Heather. She promised to write if Heather wrote to her, but never answered any of Heather's letters. Heather suspects she'll have erased Sunny's address. She was unforgiving when she was fifteen. But there it is under "S". Complete with phone number.

A male answers. "Sunny's not here," he says. "I don't know where she is." From the attitude in his voice, the note of couldn't-care-less, Heather guesses this is the boy just a little younger than Sunny. There were a bunch of boys, and Sunny and a baby sister.

"Actually, I'm trying to get hold of Einar Haugland. Do you know if he's around today?" She can hear a television in the background, and from the long silence she figures that is where this kid's attention is, not on her question.

"I dunno," he says. "Why don't you call back and ask my mom. She should be here later." Heather remembers the mom as a big, bossy woman who made Sunny look after the little kids for hours every day.

"Yeah, okay," she says, "I'll try later. Hey, you don't happen to know if there's someone visiting Einar?"

"Hang on." She can hear him talking with someone. Finally he's back. "Yeah, my little sister says there's company at Einar's. Some woman and a kid."

"Like a kid kid or a baby?" she asks. "Is she driving a blue car?"

"Just a minute." He sounds like this is a huge effort. Again, the muffled conversation. "Really small kid. I don't know about the car."

97

Heather puts the phone down as carefully as she'd put down a sleeping baby. Oh my God. All the way to Quadra? What is Lynn doing? She's sure it's Lynn. It has to be. And what is Heather supposed to do now?

She goes back to the window, looks at her old car sitting in the driveway. Keep phoning until Lynn finally answers? Shout at her to come back? What if she refuses? Call the police and report a kidnapping? She begins to pace, suddenly hungry, and in need of something she can do. Pack?

Heather phones the pizza place in the strip mall at the corner and orders a large Spicy Italian, then sits down at the computer while she waits for her food to be delivered. Mapquest. Calgary to Quadra Island. Sixteen hours and seventeen minutes, 1219 kilometres. The woman with the baby made good time.

Maybe she won't call Jack. Instead, she phones Marty. There's a babble of voices, laughter. Three times she has to tell him she was right before he finally gets it.

"Just a minute." The sound is muffled as though he has the phone in his pocket. When he speaks again, he's clear. Outside, probably. "Quadra?" he says. "I don't get it. Why?"

"Why not?"

"Come on, Heather, you don't know for sure."

"It's her."

Long pause on his end. "Well, maybe," he says slowly, "but you're not thinking of going all the way out there? Keep phoning. If she's there, she's bound to answer eventually. Or Einar will."

After the first two calls Heather's been reluctant to try again, vaguely thinking that if Lynn knows her cover's blown she might go somewhere else. But she doesn't want to tell Marty this, it sounds silly, like they're in some dumb movie. And she has this funny feeling something else is holding her back as well. At least driving to Quadra will feel like she's doing something. Like she's back in motion again. She should let Carmen know…something. Before she leaves? No, she'll call Carmen as soon as she's got Beegee.

She rubs her eyes. "I have to go. I can't sit here any longer without going out of my mind. If Lynn was whacked enough to take off like she did, do you think she's going to come right back just because I yell at her?"

"You could try not yelling."

"I'm going, Marty."

"Then I'll come with you," he says. "How about we leave tomorrow night? I have to be around for a meeting that'll likely go all day."

"Nope. I'm out of here as soon as it gets light."

"In your car? How long has it been since you've had any service done on that old beater, Heather?"

"It'll be fine. If I'm old enough to give away a baby, I'm old enough to drive across the mountains." She doesn't tell him she's stolen Jack's credit card and if she needs help along the way, she'll charge it. Or if the car breaks down altogether, rent another car at his expense and abandon hers.

"Have you told Jack?" Marty asks.

"I'll call him…or you call him."

"Heather!"

"I'll call him." She hates lying to Marty.

"Have you got your cell?"

"I'll call you when I get there. My cell's at home and I don't know where the charger is anyway." Also, if she doesn't have her phone, Jack can't find her and tell her to come back. The doorbell rings. "I have to go," she says. "My food's here."

She eats half the pizza, puts the rest in the fridge as though someone will be around for leftovers. Then she locks the house and drives back to her apartment to pack some real clothes and sleep for another few hours before she leaves.

7

One more feeding, Beegee still fighting the bottle, another diaper change, only four diapers left. Too early to go to bed. Lynn wishes she had a book. She thinks longingly about the pile of library books at home, and her own solid chair with the good reading lamp. She's had enough rocking to last a lifetime.

She stares at the phone. Twice in the last two hours it's rung and twice she's ignored it. Possibly Einar, checking to see if she's here, but more likely someone wanting cabinets built. Next time she'll answer, take a message. If she's not busy with the baby. And soon she will make that call to Heather. She promises herself this. Promises Heather. Promises Beegee. Bonnie Gale.

A few hours after Heather gave birth, she announced that the adopting parents were going to call the baby Belinda Janice Marie. Janice and Marie for the grandmothers. Stroking a pouchy cheek with two fingers, she'd been alternately mesmerized by the baby and scowling at Lynn as though daring her to indulge in tears. Lynn, the real grandmother, left the room without comment. One of the nurses was out in the hall. She sighed when she saw Lynn's face. "I wish they still did it the old way," she said, "when we just whisked them away and that was that." Lynn shook her head. No! she wanted to scream, that was the cruelest way of all. But she didn't say anything, just clasped her hand over her mouth, stumbled onto the elevator, randomly stabbed at a floor number and then wound her way through a maze of corridors to an outside door propped open and guarded by an orderly sneaking a cigarette on the fire escape. He stepped aside and let her share his four square feet of solitude. After five minutes of staring at the stars, gulping the frosty night, she nodded, and then found her way back to Heather's room as unerringly as if she'd tied a string to the bed. Walked to the plastic bassinet and tapped the pink sticker that cheerfully declared: I am a girl! My name is BABY GIRL BISHOP.

"Her name for now," Lynn said, "is Bee Gee Bishop. Beegee."

And now, she's also Bonnie Gale.

Lynn allows herself, finally, to imagine Donna and Grant and the worry they must be going through. They will not be thinking of Beegee, a baby girl in Heather's arms, but of Belinda, *their baby*, disappeared. Missing and in the dubious care of a crazy woman.

When Lynn and Jack met the adopting parents after Heather had settled on them as the best choice, the couple's discomfort was almost palpable. Lynn was sympathetic. So much hanging in the balance for them, these people who'd been trying for ten years to have a baby of their own. Finally there was hope, and Lynn, looking at Heather through their eyes, thought they must be thrilled that she had chosen them. A girl so pretty, so bright, a girl from a good home, with good genes. Winston, of course, was a bit of a mystery, but a graduate student, an intelligent young man who, Heather assured them, had nothing in his family background that should cause anyone alarm. She'd quizzed him, she said, and though he wouldn't sign his name to anything, she made him answer all of the questions on the medical and social history.

So Donna and Grant got to meet with the grim-faced grandparents, the grandfather all business-like and giving them the first degree, and the grandmother looking as though she wanted to fly out the window, would rather be anywhere else. Carmen had assured Lynn that open adoption was the best for everyone, especially for grandparents who sometimes had more contact than the birthmother as the years went on. Because birthmothers—Lynn cringed every time Heather was referred to as a birthmother—went on to new stages of their lives and often needed less and less contact as time passed. Who were all these shadowy people, Lynn wanted to know, on whose experience Carmen was basing her stories? She had never been able to imagine herself moving on to a new stage of life without Marty. She's sure she would have been stalled forever, paralyzed by not knowing what had become of her son. Although that was Carmen's point, wasn't it, that with open adoption they would know. But move on?

Donna and Grant were quiet, considerate, patient with Jack's questions. Lynn found herself staring at them, and even though she knew she must be making them uncomfortable, she couldn't look away. They were in their early forties and could have passed for siblings. Both slightly shorter than average, a bit on the chubby side, fair-skinned brunettes. Donna's hair was cut in a style that Lynn would have liked herself, that sort of casual, do-nothing look that is the work of an expensive stylist. Both of them were professional engineers they said, and they'd been together since their university days, married for twelve years.

While Jack asked his multitude of questions, Lynn imagined these two people with a child, what fine and doting parents they'd be. She saw them with a little boy, brown-haired, their hands holding his while he raised his chubby legs and swung, squealing with delight. A child who looked like both of them, and not remotely like the son of a Jamaican father and an intense, tall, wild-haired Caucasian mother.

When everyone began to shift in the chairs, the visit obviously coming to an end, Carmen turned to Lynn. "Mrs. Bishop, is there anything you want to ask Donna and Grant? Or tell them about Heather?" She smiled. "Or maybe you want to save those stories about what she was like when she was a little girl and share them along the way." As though Lynn was going to be walking down the road with the happy little family. She shook her head.

"I can't think of anything," she said. "I'm sure you'll be fine parents, and I wish you all the best." All eyes focused on Lynn. She realized that what she'd just said sounded too final, dismissive, as though she never expected to see these people again. She attempted a smile. "I guess we'll work it out as you go along." There was an almost audible letting-go of breath in the room, a shaking of hands all around as though a deal was being sealed, and that was that. What can Donna and Grant be thinking, now that Heather seems to have reneged on the deal? Carmen is a bright woman. She will have prepared them for the possibility that Heather would change her mind, but how could she have prepared them for this melodrama?

Beegee is quietly content, but Lynn won't risk putting her down and starting another round of wailing. She wraps her in the thick cocoon of Einar's afghan and carries her onto the sloping verandah. The moon is so bright after the dim cabin, Lynn blinks and shades the baby's eyes.

She stands swaying, humming, remembering other nights

she'd sat out here under the trees. If she closes her eyes, she can see a young Marty and an even younger Heather asleep on a foam mattress on the bedroom floor, Jack fixing a gin and tonic to bring out into the night. The only place, the only time she craved the bite of gin, the sting on her lips from the twist of lemon he took care to curl around the rim of the glass. What would she have been imagining on such a night ten years ago? That she'd be back some day with her daughter's kidnapped baby? That Heather, pregnant at twenty, would decide her only option was to give her baby to strangers? That she, Lynn, would be forced to revisit the two weeks following Marty's birth, turn that decision inside out even though she has never doubted that it was the right one?

Drawn by the splash of moonlight on gravel, Lynn meanders toward the road, tempted to drive to the beach. Pack along some wine from Einar's stash in the kitchen. But this is not grandmotherly behaviour, to lean against a pile of driftwood, sucking on a bottle of cheap wine. And she would have to bring the baby along with her. For now, Beegee asleep in her arms, this patch of nighttime will do.

Lynn sits on a log at the top of the driveway, her back against the post that holds the mailbox. She tilts her head back and breathes, trying to relax, to ignore the tunnel of trees and the way it is beginning to close. Two days has always been her limit on the island. Two days and she needs to pace the shoreline, eyes fixed on the misty mainland. Imagine herself sailing over the mountains and landing, at last, back on the bald brown prairie.

Beegee will wake in another hour or two, but only long enough to latch onto the bottle, fill the empty ache in her stomach and go back to whatever babies dream about. When Marty was new, Lynn had held him for hours on end, watching him sleep. Every twitch of his lips, the mewing sounds, seemed precious. Heather, after a week of sleeping, her mouth bowed in a perpetual smile, woke up and howled for eight months. When Heather slept, Lynn was too exhausted to sit and gaze.

In spite of the damp, the night is mild. Lynn loosens the heavy blanket, and the baby frowns, wriggles, frees a hand from the swaddling. She sighs and begins to suck in her sleep. Lynn crooks her finger against the moist lips and instantly her knuckle is drawn in.

From here, Lynn can see lights twinkling through the trees at regular intervals down the road. The first set at Hannah's house. Imagining the bedtime ritual around six children, Lynn rests her head against the metal flap on the mailbox. The eldest of those children must be finished high school by now.

So caught up in her own story, Lynn hasn't asked for updates on Hannah's kids. Doesn't remember even asking about them. Do they do well in school? Are they involved in team sports? Music lessons? Is there a Brownie pack, or Boy Scout troop on the island? What about swimming lessons? All those things mothers talk about while they lean against the school wall waiting to walk their kindergarten children home, or while they trundle along on school field trips. Lynn wasn't close friends with the mothers of any of Marty or Heather's friends, but had a casual acquaintanceship with several. Car-pooling, checking the details of sleepovers and birthday parties, comparing notes on teachers. Does Hannah have those connections? Is that the kind of relationship they would have if Lynn was an island mom, if Beegee were her own child? Does she dare even imagine such a possibility? The first words out of Lynn's friend Bernice's mouth when she heard that Heather was pregnant were, "Now, don't you get stuck raising that kid. Do you know how often that happens to women our age? My God, Lynn!" At that point, Lynn had barely gotten beyond thinking about the pregnancy, about Heather and how she was coping, never mind imagining a baby in anyone's arms. Out of long habit, she'd argued with Bernie anyway.

"Why is that so wrong?" she asked. "Isn't that the way it works in other corners of the world? If a mother can't do the job, someone else in the family does? It's only if there is no family that it's left up to the rest of the village?" She held up her hand at the look of bug-eyed alarm on her friend's face. "Oh don't worry. We can be sure that's not going to be anywhere on Heather's list of possibilities."

In fact, it was not an idea Heather ever approached. She'd kept Beegee fiercely to herself these past weeks, barely letting Lynn be a grandmother, never mind mother-substitute. Why? Because she didn't think Lynn was capable? She didn't think it was fair to ask such a thing of her mother? Lynn wonders if this is something Carmen ever broached with Heather. What about your mother? Surely this is the first question anyone should ask. Lynn has a vague memory of the kind Mrs. McKinnon, the social worker from Marty's time, asking if someone else in the family could take the baby. She imagines her own reaction, although she doesn't remember it. Her mother take on a new baby? Everyone of that generation seemed elderly to Lynn. The social worker was probably Carmen's age, with young children of her own, but to Lynn she was an older woman. Lynn's mom had not been well, a series of vaguely alarming illnesses that led, just a year after Marty was born, to a definitive diagnosis of cancer.

Lynn watches approaching car lights fan through the dusk and is surprised that she doesn't instinctively run inside. Instead, she feels the log solid on the backs of her thighs, the tree shadows wrapped around her and the baby like a cloak. The car doesn't slow.

"Babe," she whispers to Beegee as the taillights disappear

around the next bend in the road, "we're invisible." Unaccountably she hears an echo of the words. A memory of Jack's voice in her ear. When? It must have been on one of the evenings when the kids were still too small to leave alone, except for a brief interlude at the end of the driveway.

Lynn looks down at the sleeping face of her granddaughter. She's wracked with this need to hold tight, and yet how could she even consider sliding back into motherhood when she's barely made the transformation from marriage to her single life?

The irony of choosing this place as a safe haven hits her now as though one of those stars high in the tops of the giant trees has come plummeting to earth. It was here, on that last visit two years ago, that she finally knew without a doubt that she and Jack were finished, even before Jack gave her his news. She runs her hand over the grey silk stretch of log beside her.

She was stunned when Jack suggested the trip to Quadra. It had been five years since they'd visited Einar, five years in which neither of them seemed interested in taking a vacation, particularly not together.

They were at the kitchen table on one of the first mornings of summer vacation, Jack in the baggy grey track suit he wore around the house, Lynn still in her nightgown, drinking coffee, hidden behind their respective sections of the Calgary Herald. Jack got up to pour another cup of coffee, and surprised Lynn by bringing the pot to the table and topping up her cup as well. When he sat down, he pushed the paper aside, folded his arms, leaned back in the chair.

"What do you say to a trip to the coast next month?"

Lynn put her cup down. Could she possibly have heard him correctly? "Why?" was all she could come up with.

"I think we need some time together. Away from home, and Quadra was always a good place, wasn't it?"

She looked at him for a long time before she answered, but couldn't find anything in his face except gentle concern. With a naïveté that was as strange as his suggestion, she thought he was showing genuine concern for their relationship, and an astonishing desire to mend it. Embarrassed by how eager she was to believe him, she pretended to hesitate, think hard about the trip before agreeing.

"I don't suppose you'd consider flying out and renting a car?" he asked.

Lynn was even willing, for a few minutes, to think about that alternative, but in the end she shook her head. Someday, she vowed, she would get over her ridiculous fear of flying, but not yet. Surprisingly, Jack didn't roll his eyes or chide her.

Einar was away when they arrived, and they never did see him because they left two days earlier than planned. On the fourth night they drove to Rebecca Spit, barbequed salmon they'd bought on the dock at Quathiaski Cove, and sat on the sand, their backs against a driftwood sculpture, drinking wine. A full moon rose up out of the ocean like a huge pink pearl. When the last of the bottle of Jack's favourite Chardonnay was poured, Lynn stretched her bare arms along the log, braced herself slightly.

"I've been thinking," she said, and was aware of Jack tensing beside her. "When Heather was looking at all those university catalogues in the winter, I got to thinking the time might be right for me to go back to school." Jack started to bluster a little and she put up her hand. "No, no. Hear me out. I don't want to finish an education degree. I took those courses so long ago they probably aren't worth credit anymore. I thought maybe a year in General Studies first to explore some of the things that interest me."

"Such as?" he asked, as though she had no interests at all, or at least not any he could imagine taking seriously. That tone of voice. The mood changing abruptly from an intimacy more tender than Lynn remembered in years, to the old pattern of habitual disagreement.

"French, maybe German," she said, "philosophy, religious studies. I used to think I was good at languages, and I'd like…" She stopped at the expression on his face. Jack was shaking his head, lips compressed, clearly not listening to the words.

"Your timing is unbelievably bad. Even if you were planning to take something productive, this is just not practical. Not now."

The damp seemed to have suddenly seeped up from the sand, cold fingers. Lynn's arms trembled. She grabbed her jacket from the log behind her and wrapped it tight around her chest. "How can it be so bad? Marty's finished and supporting himself. You told Heather there was no problem at all with her getting her own place, enough money in the educational fund to handle that."

"Tuition has gone up dramatically, in case you hadn't noticed."

How would she know that when Jack insisted on looking after all the accounting himself? Except that she opened the desk drawer and sifted through the statements herself every few months. Not because she needed to know what it cost to send her son to school, but because she'd made this a habit years ago. There had been a time when she'd considered leaving Jack, and she'd realized she had no idea what the two of them were worth together, and how that would be divided if they were to part. In the end, she'd decided that it was better for everyone if she stayed, but still she kept an eye on the pay stubs and the bills.

Jack stood up and put the cork back into the empty wine bottle, stowed it in the basket with his glass and stood waiting for Lynn to hand him hers. "Certainly there's enough in the RESP to get Heather through. But our investments are shaky, especially the Asian markets. It's not the time to be spending."

She flung the last drops of wine across the sand, and shoved the glass at him. "Then I'll sell the stocks from Mom and Dad. They've done well."

"When we could have used that money for a mortgage, you said it was staying in trust for Heather and Marty. A gift from your folks to them some day. You're going to spend it for your own entertainment?"

Entertainment. She was so angry she would have stomped away, except that he had the keys to the car and it was too long a walk back in the dark.

"Besides," he continued, smoothing the edges of his words a little, "why on earth do you need a university degree? I thought you loved the job in the school library. I'm sure we can find you another position like that."

"That was years ago. And I did not love the job. I just liked it better than supervising the lunchroom."

"Then find something you *do* like that won't take four years and a fortune in tuition."

She knew in that moment that her future was of no concern to Jack at all. As he stood there tapping his foot, looking impatiently in the direction of the car, the only thing that registered on his face when he glanced her way was indifference. She could do what she liked so long as it didn't cost him anything. No concern for the distress that must be obvious from her flushed cheeks and the inarticulate stammering as she tried one more time. "I need something, Jack, something that's my own now that…there's time and space."

"If you're telling me you're bored and discontented, this is hardly new," he said. "It's too late in the game, Lynn."

She'd known that all along, and she was furious with herself for being sucked into this ridiculous charade. This was his curtain call, she was sure of it.

They left for home at five o'clock the next morning, and seemed to have a tacit agreement that they were traveling non-stop. The car felt clogged with silence. At the first stop for gas, Lynn went into the washroom and when she came out Jack was in the passenger seat, folding his jacket into a pillow, eyes closed before she pulled onto the highway. After the next stop, he was back behind the wheel, and she slept. They were an hour away from home, just coming out of the mountains, the point at which Lynn usually relaxed, breathed easier, when Jack began to talk. It took him an hour to tell her all of the things that were wrong with their marriage, all of the reasons they should separate, precisely how he proposed to divide their property, when and how they should tell Marty and Heather. Lynn stared out the side window so long she was carsick by the time they drove into their garage. Couldn't answer even if she'd known what to say. She covered her mouth with her hand, dashed first for the bathroom, and then fell into bed.

In the morning she had only one question. "Why did we go all the way to Quadra for you to tell me you were leaving? That's the one thing you didn't cover in your address to the union yesterday. Or did you have some romantic notion that a moonlit beach could repair the damage?"

For the first time in all their years of marriage, Jack seemed unable to explain himself. Just sat there drinking his coffee, frowning into space. If Lynn had known that his relationship with Rhea was the catalyst for the separation, his muteness and the Quadra trip would have been all the more bizarre.

Lynn turns her head and looks back at the cabin. The dirty smudge of light from the kitchen window isn't inviting. Neither is the thought of the telephone call she's going to make. But it's getting late, and it's an hour later in Calgary.

Back inside, Lynn holds the phone to one ear, feels the tickle of Beegee's soft hair against the other. The phone rings and rings in her kitchen at home. She considers phoning Marty, or Jack. Whether either of them wants to or not, there are things she needs to discuss with Jack. But not until she's spoken with Heather. She'll try again first thing in the morning. Try Heather's apartment in case she's gone home. She's sure Heather has a cell phone, but she doesn't know the number.

In the night, Lynn hears the swish of truck tires down the soft carpet of driveway and then the rumble of Einar's voice outside.

"Company, Loki? The lady did get here after all?" The door *screaks* across the cedar threshold and the click of Loki's toenails follows Einar's quiet tread around the kitchen.

Lynn eases herself out of her curled position around Beegee, sits up and pulls a sweater over her nightgown. Which is actually Einar's shirt, but she doubts he'll notice. Not the kind of detail to which he pays attention.

She opens the bedroom door, closes it quietly behind her. He's sitting in the rocking chair taking off his boots. When he sees her, he kicks off the second boot and crosses the room in loping strides to lift her off the floor. His plaid jacket closes around her and she almost chokes on the scent of wood smoke and sweat. "Lynn! You're a bachelor's dream. A nightmare of a long drive, and then a warm woman comes wandering out of the bedroom. I think you must be a mirage."

Oh dear God, does he think she's come with romance on her mind? But when she glances up, there's only weariness in the lines beside his eyes, and a deep furrow of concern etched between his eyebrows. Lynn puts her cheek against his chest and hugs back so ferociously that Einar releases her, tilts her chin to look into her eyes. "Okay?"

She nods. "Yes. Glad to be here." She has a sudden flash to a summer night about ten years ago. Too many gin and tonics, Jack crashed on the couch, snoring. Einar, always the last one standing, appearing behind her in the kitchen where she was going through the motions of tidying up. His breath on the back of her neck, then his lips.

"Einar, no," she'd whispered, turning to face him.

"Aw, why?" he asked. "Just a little kiss." That smile, daring her. Then, he'd taken her hand and pulled her outside, under the sighing trees. She, not resisting a bit, until she glanced at the bedroom window behind which Heather and Marty were asleep.

"I can't," she said. "I don't, Einar. I just don't."

"Why?" he asked again. "You're a faithful woman, the good wife, we all know this. But a little kiss isn't anything, Lynn." His big hand cupped her chin, lifted her lips to his again. That time, she pulled away and went into the house.

He apologized in the morning. "Too much booze. I should know better." She nodded, and understood that neither of them would ever mention this to Jack.

She pulls away from Einar now, away from that memory. "Very glad to be here," she repeats.

"No gladder than I," he says. "I'm sorry I woke you. You want to go back to sleep? We can talk in the morning?"

She shakes her head. "No. I should move out of your bed." And take my baggage with me, she thinks, wondering if it would be possible to carry that bundle to the couch without Einar any the wiser before morning.

He waves away her words. "Why? I've slept in the back of the truck for two nights. The couch will feel fine."

She glances at the clock on the wall. It's just past midnight. She's only been asleep for an hour, and she knows she won't fall easily back into her dreams.

Einar has moved to the stove and is measuring heaping spoonfuls of coffee into the pot. Loki sprawls at his feet, nose resting on a grey work sock.

"Lord, Einar, won't that keep you awake?"

"Nah," he says, "nothing keeps me awake. You going to join me?" From the pocket of the jacket hanging beside the door, he produces a mickey of rye. "We'll add a splash of this to settle us down?"

Perfect. And a drop or two into the bottle of Hannah's breast milk to settle Beegee. As though she's heard her name and is thirsting for that bottle, Beegee lets out the first hiccups of what will soon be an outraged wail. Loki springs up from between Einar's feet and slinks to the door, looking alternately toward the bedroom door and pleadingly at Einar.

Einar turns puzzled to the window and pulls the curtain aside. "What the hell was that?"

Okay. No point in explaining first. Lynn holds up her hand, walks to the bedroom where the cry is climbing to a crescendo. She lifts the baby into the crook of her arm, back to the kitchen and plants herself in front of Einar.

"What the hell?" he says once more. He puts his face close to Beegee's as though he's thinking he might recognize her. "Where did you get this?"

"She's Heather's," Lynn says.

He can't seem to raise his eyes to Lynn's, but stares instead into Beegee's. She's stopped squawking for the moment, stunned probably by this huge hairy face looking down at her. "Heather? Heather's a kid!"

"No, Einar. Heather is twenty years old, and this is her baby."

He hesitates, then holds out his hands. Without any of

the resistance she felt with Hannah, Lynn passes him the baby. Legs drawn tight to her chest, Beegee fits into one of his hands, and he continues staring at her, shaking his head, finally smiling as though someone's just handed him a splendid surprise.

He lowers himself into the rocking chair, settles Beegee in the crook of his arm where she disappears into folds of red plaid. "Watch the coffee, eh. Smells like it's going to go over any minute."

When she's poured two mugs, she starts toward Einar but he waves her back. "No, no! I can't drink hot coffee when I'm holding a baby." Finally he looks up at Lynn. "Where's Heather?"

She pulls a wooden chair from the table and sits in front of him, hands tight around the mug of coffee. Beegee must feel his heartbeat, as steady as a hammer.

"Heather's at home. In Calgary." Her gulp is audible in the room. "She was going to give Beegee—that's what we call her—she was going to give her away. She picked these people through an adoption agency." Lynn tries to take a sip of the coffee, but it's too hot. "Then she decided she needed some time with the baby first, so she's been staying with me for three weeks. And then…what day is this?"

"Sunday, going on Monday," he says.

Lynn counts back. "Then it must have been Friday. Was it Friday I phoned?"

"Could be." He shrugs. "What happened on Friday?"

"She asked me to take the baby to the adopting people. I said I would, but I couldn't." Neither can she talk beyond that point. Her shoulders begin to shake, the most awful wrenching sobs issue from her throat. She sets the coffee on the floor, stands up, holds out her arms for Beegee. When Einar is slow to react, she goes down on her knees and lays her head on his knee like a child, tears streaming soundlessly now. Hand in her hair, Einar pats and croons, sounding astonishingly like Hannah when she was feeding Beegee.

"Cry, cry. We have all night." He touches her cheek and points at Beegee who is sound asleep. "Or at least until the little one wakes up."

When she's cried out, Lynn tries again to take Beegee from Einar, to tuck her back into the bed. "Not yet," he says. "But you can bring my coffee now. I'll be careful."

Slurping and rocking, he listens to her long story about Heather and Winston. About how both Lynn and Jack tried to convince Heather to have an abortion. She never planned to get married, Heather told them, and kids? That was an idea from another galaxy. But this way she'd at least have had the experience of pregnancy. Just another experience, then she'd get on with her life. Why was that surprising? It sounded so much like Heather that Lynn could have written the script. And Einar just nods his head, obviously remembering Heather well. Surely he must be asking all the same questions that have been shouting inside Lynn's own head, but he doesn't ask "why?" "now what?" "then what?" Which must be another reason her instincts brought her here.

He shifts, slightly raises the arm that's holding the baby, and pushes out of the chair with the other hand. "Maybe we can put her down now. What did you call her?"

"Beegee," Lynn says. "Short for Baby Girl, because I didn't like the name the adopting people were going to give her. But since we've been here I told Hannah's daughter that she's named Bonnie Gale."

Einar considers the sleeping face. "Beegee's good enough, I think."

Instead of taking Beegee back to bed, Lynn fashions a nest on one end of the couch while Einar brings the fire back to life, and then she and Einar sit together on the other end.

They ignore the dregs of coffee. Sip rye and water from jam jar glasses.

Lynn puts her head back, stretches her neck muscles, and sneaks a glance at Einar, wondering what he's thinking. About all of this. About her. When she turns, he's looking at her quizzically. She nods. "Yes, I know. I've made a terrible mess of this. It was hard enough for Heather before and now it's even worse."

He rakes his fingers through his beard. "Does Heather know you're here?"

"I've been trying to call her. There's no answer."

She still can't tell what's going on behind those bushy eyebrows. She's never found Einar so difficult to read. In fact his transparency is one of the things she's liked so much about him, but there is none of that tonight. And does she really want to hear that she's a meddling mother, seizing control of a situation to which she has no rights?

Einar looks as though he's having trouble getting words out. He opens his mouth, then closes it. Looks at her hard and shakes his head. "Lynn," he says finally, "what is it you want?"

She pulls a corner of the afghan that's hanging on the back of the sofa across her shoulder, her arm, and smooths the ridges of brown and green knitting. There are loose strands along the edges. Too many washings have begun to unravel the blanket, but it will probably hold together as long as Einar does. "What I want doesn't matter," she says. "This is Heather's decision. That's been made very clear to me."

He takes a drink, wipes his mouth with the back of his hand. "But maybe it does matter. It matters to you, anyway. How have you been, Lynn? I haven't even asked you yet. How are you getting along on your own?"

She fights with a lower lip that threatens to give away her exhaustion. She does not want Einar to think that she's come here battered from the divorce. "I'm all right. Maybe better off than I've been in years." Einar has to have known about Jack's women. It's come back to Lynn since the divorce that many people wondered why she put up with his infidelity for so long.

Einar props his big wooly feet on the coffee table. He holds the glass of rye in two hands, staring into it. "He's been a good friend to me, Lynn. Not much I can say here. But I'm glad you're doing fine."

Poor Einar. If it wasn't for this dilemma, Lynn would never have come here again. In the same way that Lynn's friends are not likely to ever have a conversation with Jack Bishop again, Einar is relegated to the crowd of people she will only see at formal occasions. The weddings of her children, perhaps. Funerals, God forbid. The friends are divided up like the furniture, the kitchen utensils, the music CDs, the bank accounts. And yet she has come here.

Lynn pulls the afghan over her legs. The damp presses in whenever the fire begins to fade. "You are his best friend, you know. He loved coming out here all those summers." She shakes her head and smiles at him. "Not me, though. I'd have given anything to stay in Victoria and have tea at the Empress."

He reaches for her hand, gives it a squeeze and then lets go too quickly, almost as though he's forgotten himself and taken a liberty. "Now that would have been a shame," he says. "I looked forward as much to seeing you as I did Jack. Alone, he would have been…something missing."

"He needed you, Einar." And now? When did Jack stop needing the steadying company of this old friend? There isn't anyone else with whom he's gone fishing, chopped firewood, sat up late into the night in conversation so slow that Lynn, half-asleep in the next room was sure they'd both dozed off. She tilts her head to look at Einar. "Have you seen Jack since we split up?"

"No," he says too quickly. Hesitates. "But he's coming out here in the spring, he says."

Spring break. And he won't be alone. "You've met Rhea?"

He shakes his head. "We go back a long way, Lynn. If it wasn't for Jack I would have flunked out of university, done something stupid when Beata took off with the kids. I was going to chuck it all, go up to Alaska, get a job crabbing. That was what my dad and my brothers did in Norway you know. Fishermen. My dad froze his hands so many times he ended up losing them. Jack convinced me to stick out the schooling." He drains his glass. "So then my short career as a teacher. I hated it, but still I proved to myself that I could be something more if I wanted to."

He doesn't need to explain or apologize for his loyalty. If Jack had told her any of this, about Einar wanting to run away to Alaska, she's forgotten. Or maybe was just too wrapped up in her own life to have paid attention. "I'm sorry," she says, "to have put you in an awkward position like this."

"Life is awkward, no? You need to go sleep, Lynn. And you need to figure out what to do. But morning is soon enough. You have everything you need for the baby?"

"I'll buy a few things tomorrow. Your neighbour came to our rescue." The bags of frozen milk seem too intimate to mention.

"Hannah? Oh she won't let you down. She could look after a whole village of babies on her own, that one."

Something missing in this picture, Lynn thinks. "Has Hank been gone for long?"

"He's back pretty regularly to see the kids."

"They're separated?" Lynn tries to remember the

conversations she had with Hannah, to recall what stupid things she might have said, assuming Hank was still around.

"He figures so, but as far as Hannah's concerned, he's just up island."

Lynn wonders what Einar's told Hannah about her and Jack in the years their paths crossed here. That Jack was up island, and Lynn kept pretending he was home in their bed? It seems likely that in front of the fire over their rye and water nightcaps, Jack has told Einar how difficult it is to live with Lynn. She knows she's not an easy person. All those years of passive resistance. She can't stand fighting—no one in her family ever raised their voices—so instead of objecting to Jack's bossiness, she ignored him and did things her own way. Instead of trying to talk him into compromising and finding things to do, places to visit for both of them, she went along with what he wanted to do and made them both miserable in the process.

"There's no way of knowing, is there, what goes on in other people's lives," Lynn says. "But you know what?" He looks at her, nodding ever so slightly, as though he knows what's coming, or is just willing to accept whatever she has to say as truth. "After all that time to think, all that insight into why Jack and I messed up, here we are with a new problem—a big one—and I haven't done a damn thing differently in the last seven months."

They sit there a long while, watching the sparks dance in the fireplace. He puts his arm around her, and she stays because she desperately needs that embrace.

"So," he says finally, "you screwed up. We all do that, but you need to phone Heather. And Jack."

She skips over Jack. For now. "I'll try Heather again first thing in the morning."

His big eyebrows collide. "You think she's sleeping if she doesn't know where her baby's gone? Come now, Lynn."

"First thing in the morning, Einar," she says stubbornly.

He squints at her, his jaw working. "Okay," he says. "First thing in the morning, I'll be gone. I have a job to finish down the road, but I'll be back by nighttime."

When she hears scratching at the door, Lynn gets up to let Loki in, and with the dog settled on the hearth, they are as complete a picture of tranquil domesticity as could be found, she thinks. Until Beegee's small stomach wakes her again. Lynn warms a sleeve of milk in the microwave, then moves quietly to the rocking chair with the baby. Einar, head back, snores, sawing the warm air in the living room. He hasn't stirred when she's done with feeding, changing and settling Beegee back into the big bed again. Neither does he wake when she covers him with an extra blanket from the bedroom closet.

She stands for a moment watching him sleep, imagining what it would be like to ease herself onto the couch beside him. To fit into the hollow made by the bend of his knees and the curl of his chest. She knows that she doesn't want Jack in her bed ever again, but she does miss a warm body. Not just any body will do, she's not desperate. And no, not Einar. In spite of the long-ago stolen kiss, and all the weeks on this island, they are no match. At least this is something she knows for sure. She has not come here for Einar.

She doesn't sleep as easily as Einar. She lies awake a long time, listening to the soughing of the wind in the trees.

8

Heather has been on the road since six o'clock this morning.
She's still reeling from the discovery that Lynn has gone all
the way to Quadra, the last place she would have expected
her mom to choose as a hiding spot. But then the idea of
Lynn running away with Beegee and hiding is so bizarre,
why not? Maybe Lynn's Plan B is to fly to China if she gets
wind that she's been found. Maybe she's talked to Marty
today, knows Heather is on the way, and she and Beegee are
about to hop a plane for Beijing. That would be the final
touch to this Lynn-gone-totally-nuts scene.

Every time Heather checks her rear view mirror, the
sight of Beegee's car seat makes her want to kill her mother.
Lynn has gone all the way to the island with Beegee…what?
Stowed on the back seat like a parcel?

She's hungry, and the junk food she grabbed when she
stopped to buy gas was a mistake. She ate so healthily while
she was pregnant, even a handful of dry-roasted peanuts and
a can of Coke has lost its appeal. She slows at Salmon Arm,
and finds a hole-in-the-wall restaurant that advertises Viet-

namese, Chinese, Western Food on the sign in the window. While she waits for her bowl of vermicelli with shrimp and bean sprouts, she stares out at the parking lot. She lost the sun about an hour ago. The clouds are so low and heavy it's almost dark at four in the afternoon.

She digs out her Mapquest printout and a pen and is poking holes in the paper when the waitress slides a bowl in front of her. The directions aren't making sense. The girl tilts her head and looks down at the page. "You lost?"

"Maybe," Heather says. "But I have a map in the car." She's better with visual cues than with written direction. She unwraps the paper sleeve of chopsticks. "How far to Vancouver from here? How many hours driving?"

The waitress shrugs. "Maybe four or five. My boyfriend claims he can do it in three and a half, but he claims a lot of other things too."

The girl looks Asian, but sounds like every other teenager. She's maybe sixteen or seventeen. A boy who looks even younger is waiting on another table. Heather wonders if the fast-driving boyfriend meets the approval of the woman in the kitchen who keeps poking her head out. Possibly the mother is as liberal as Jack and Lynn who didn't even raise an eyebrow when they met Winston.

"Are you going all the way tonight?" the waitress says.

Jeez, did someone contract people along the way to watch for her? When she stopped for gas in Revelstoke she got the same third degree from the kid who filled her tank and cleaned the windshield. And then from the cashier inside when she bought the map of B.C., just in case. Where you headed? Going all the way tonight?

Heather shakes her head, nods, shrugs, lets the waitress think whatever she wants as she walks away to take someone else's order. Setting up a surveillance network sounds like something Jack would do. But, she remembers, Jack doesn't know where she's gone. She feels a twinge. He'll be worrying. She should have called. By now, though, he'll have talked with Marty.

She works her way systematically through the bowl, eating first the shrimp and bits of pork, then the bean sprouts, and stopping, finally, halfway through the rice vermicelli. If she eats any more she'll need a nap. And the answer to everyone's question? Yes, she is going straight through tonight.

She pays for her dinner with Jack's credit card, and considers asking for a coffee to go, but remembers that she saw a Tim Horton's across the street. Better coffee, and maybe she'll pick up a couple of apple fritters for later when she starts to get hungry again. She seems to need feeding every two hours, just like Beegee. And until she gets to Quadra, she needs the sugar to stay mad at Lynn.

Fortunately the woman behind the counter at Tim's isn't the slightest bit interested in Heather or her journey. She hands her the bag of donuts and the paper cup without a word.

Back in the car, Heather unfolds the big map and spreads it on the passenger seat. Why is this confusing her? How hard can it be to just point the car west and end up at the ocean? Maybe it's because she was always a passenger on this trip, whining in the back seat, wishing it were over. She leans over the map and traces the highway with a stubby finger. She trimmed those nails last night. West to the water. Except, then what? Where to take the ferry? Sometimes they went to Victoria and hung out for a day to humour Lynn. Lynn would probably have been happy if they'd left her there to drink tea and wander around the shops for the whole two weeks.

When Heather shifts the map, the breast pump underneath slips onto the floor. Oh well. She's not going into the donut shop to wash the damn thing. She's going to have to pump so that she doesn't explode, but she's dumping the milk. By now Beegee's probably drinking coffee. All day Heather's been trying to do the math in her head—trying to estimate how many times she pumped extra milk after Beegee's feedings to put those bags in the freezer. She wanted to be sure there was enough for the first two or three days, enough so that at least Beegee would still be getting the same food. How many feedings were there in that insulated bag Lynn was supposed to be taking to Donna, how many feedings on the way to Quadra, how many since? No matter how she crunches the numbers, Lynn will have run out of breast milk. There are so many reasons to be furious with Lynn. So how to get to her as fast as possible?

Definitely the ferry to Nanaimo looks faster, and fast is what counts. Heather puts her hands on the wheel, takes two deep breaths and turns onto the highway. Today is Monday. Today she was supposed to appear in Carmen's office to sign the papers giving Belinda Janice Marie to Grant and Donna McDonald. Carmen will be phoning frantically once again. She should have called Carmen this morning. She should stop and call now. Then why can't she? Why does her foot get heavier on the gas every time she thinks about pulling over to find a phone?

Just outside the town limits, a guy is holding a sign: *Desperate! Vancouver! Please!* Desperate's kind of cute. She's tempted. Imagine the look on Jack's face if he knew. One of the teachers Jack worked with had a daughter who disappeared somewhere in the forest in B.C. They think she was hitchhiking. Just gone on some lonely stretch of highway. But this is different, isn't it? She's not the one thumbing. And Heather's always wondered if that girl was taken by a bear. She glances in the rearview mirror and catches sight of the baby seat again. Would she even consider this with Beegee in the car? Does she want someone to tell Beegee she was adopted because her mother was murdered by a lunatic hitchhiker? That her mother was a lunatic for stopping. Her foot hits the gas and she moves into the centre lane to give the guy a wide berth. Sorry. Some big truck driver's going to have to be the one.

One hand on the wheel, the other holding the coffee while she sips, she watches the hills roll out ahead of her and can't stop herself, no matter how hard she tries, and has been trying for hours, from thinking about Winston.

Heather hasn't told anyone, not even Marty, that Winston called a couple of days after she got home from the hospital. He'd been trying her apartment, he said, and finally realized she might be at Lynn's.

"Heather, I can't stop thinking about this. I'm so glad you didn't give her away. Come to Jamaica. Bring my baby girl and we'll stay for a year. Then we'll go back to Canada, to school."

Winston, she was sure, would be going to school forever. "What would be the point of all that?" she asked, looking down at the fussing baby in her arms. "Why would I come there?"

"So you can get to know my mom, and my sisters. Then we can leave the baby with them when we go back. My sisters have all left kids with my mother, one time or another. One more baby, no problem."

Heather almost hung up at that point. She'd had no idea Winston was insane!

"I don't have to come all the way to Jamaica to give my baby away. I found someone here who wants her."

"But then she's their baby, Heather, not ours. My mother is her grandmother."

That stopped Heather for a moment. She had a hard enough time acknowledging Lynn and Jack as Beegee's grandparents, knowing they were going to be out of the picture shortly. "Does your mother know about her?"

"Of course," he said. "She says please send a picture of the baby." His voice on the phone was so different from having Winston in front of her. He sounded much younger, unsure. "Okay," he said, "so come here for a while, and then when we go back we'll bring her with us and leave her with your mom while we go to school."

Heather was so glad Lynn had gone out for groceries and was not eavesdropping on this conversation. "My mother is too old to raise another baby!" Beegee was getting hungry, starting seriously to fuss. Heather was tempted to put the phone to the baby's small mouth and let her tell her father what she thought of his plan. "Winston," Heather said, "it would be a whole lot simpler if you just came back here yourself and talked to me in person."

"I can't," he said. "I didn't apply to the university to retain my position."

"Well let me know when you get your life sorted out," she said.

She hasn't heard from him since. But she does intend to call him after those ten days that she has, to revoke her consent, have passed. And when will that be? she wonders. She'd like to keep right on going, even if it means getting to Quadra in the small hours of the morning, except she knows the ferries don't run all night. She'll probably have to find a motel in Campbell River, if she makes it that far. Maybe Nanaimo is more reasonable. She'll need to have a decent sleep before she picks up Beegee, turns around, and heads back home again. Unless she leaves her car there, and insists that Lynn drive them back. Yeah, that's a better plan anyway. There's no way Lynn can refuse her that after all the trouble she's caused. She throws the empty coffee cup onto the floor. Why Quadra?

Most of what Heather remembers of Quadra is bikes and beaches. They hauled the bikes on top of the car, looking, Heather always thought, like some strange beast with deformed antlers. And in the back seat, she and Marty poking and taunting each other, and making fun of Jack's music.

No wonder she's going crazy talking to herself. She's just driven for eight hours without music. She's heard it so many times, she can turn it on in her head. Heather pounds on the steering wheel in time to the Bee Gees. *Stayin' alive.* Yeah.

9

Rain rain rain. Lynn swipes at the condensation and tries to look out to the road, but the outside of the window is streaming as well. She sets the coffee pot, the second one she's brewed today, back on the heat, waits until it gurgles, then pours a cup so thick and gritty she has to chew the last mouthful. Beegee is asleep, fed, bathed, and snug in a flannel nightgown. Mysteriously, there was a cache of cloth diapers and more nightgowns on the kitchen table this morning, and Lynn has been spared the trip to the store for Pampers. But for the rain, she would have gone anyway to get out of the cabin. She's found a tattered BC Ferries schedule tacked to the wall by the phone and has been keeping track all day of the departures, wondering each time one leaves, if she should be on the next.

She tidies the kitchen, sterilizes nipples for Beegee's bottles, dashes through the rain to carry the bag of dirty diapers out to the trash. While she putters, Lynn replays last night's conversation with Einar in her head. Wondering if she's said too much about her marriage. She's never talked with anyone about Jack's infidelity, not even to Marion, whom she's known since they were little girls, confiding their secret crushes on the boys in their class.

Jack Bishop was the kind of boy Lynn dreamed about when she was sixteen, a painfully shy girl, all skinny legs and long neck. The kind of boy who didn't exist in the small town where she grew up. Or if he had, he would have hung around other girls' lockers, and teased them and driven them home from school dances, and only ever talked to Lynn to ask to borrow homework. He was a "hunk" in the giggly lingo of her friends, a well-muscled, sandy-haired, confident boy with a sexy grin and a fast car. The kind of boy Lynn encountered when she went to Edmonton to university, but was still too timid to flirt with even when she had the chance.

One day in the Students' Union cafeteria, she was waiting in a cashier's line with chips and gravy, an apple, and a large coffee balanced on a tray on one hip, her pea jacket and a sociology text on the other. She felt a warm tickle on her neck. When she turned her head she was nose-to-nose to with one of those boys she'd dreamed about.

"Hey, you can smack me if I'm being fresh, but you smell exactly like the girl I've been looking for."

Instead of blushing and going stumble-tongued, as usual, Lynn gave him a sassy grin. "Tangy apple? Or eau de greasy gravy?" she said, the sort of snappy comeback she normally didn't think of until hours later.

That day, and for the next three months, she made Jack laugh, and felt like a girl in a movie. This was the boy, she decided, for whom she'd saved the virginity no one else had seriously pursued anyway.

Lynn wonders how Jack remembers that brief time in their life. The first part so sweet they could have been acting a sappy love story, and then the turmoil when they found out she was pregnant. She should have asked him the day he barged into the house right after Heather told him she was pregnant. Maybe if she'd invoked the memory of that tender-hearted boy and girl, they would have handled Heather's crisis far better. Jack has refused to see Heather's pregnancy as similar in any way to Lynn's pregnancy when she was also a mere twenty years old. Not open for discussion. Even though Lynn knows it has everything to do with how she feels.

Jack let himself into the house that day without ringing the bell first. "I thought," Lynn said from the floor in the living room where she was trying to follow a yoga video Heather had given her for her birthday, "that we agreed you would stop behaving as though you still live here." She stood up, all that lovely relaxation lost.

"How long have you known about Heather's condition?" he barked. He was truly unnerved. Keeping calm, modulating his voice was something he'd mastered as a teacher, administrator, father. Only as a husband did he occasionally allow his voice to give him away.

"Condition? You make it sound like asthma. Or arthritis. You mean the pregnancy?"

"Of course that's what I mean, Lynn! How did this happen?"

"The usual way, and you of all people should know that it does happen."

For a minute she thought he was going to say all the things she'd been thinking herself. About the unfairness of Heather being caught in the same net that had snared them. And what was the point of learning life lessons if you aren't allowed to transfer them to your children? And how could they possibly enter into a discussion with Heather about her plans unless they were totally honest about their own experience? As a matter of fact, anticipating Jack's visit, Lynn had been thinking about the best time, the best way for her and Jack to talk with Marty. But each time she got as far as imagining them all seated—Marty looking from one to the other with his head slightly tilted, one eyebrow cocked, curious, but patient as always—she backed right out of the fantasy.

"Sit down, Jack," she finally said. "Fuming isn't going to make things better, and if you're looking for someone to blame, go ahead and blame me and get it over with."

He finally sat down on the couch, exhaled, shook his head. "Why would I blame you? If anyone, I'm going to blame Winston." He stretched his legs out, and looked around the room as though he was wondering how he'd gotten there.

Lynn took her place at the other end of the couch. "He's certainly the most convenient one," she said. "Did you blame yourself when I was pregnant?"

"Lynn, let's not go back there at all. Please. We were different." He frowned. "How long has Heather known this guy? Two, three months? We had a relationship, we cared about each other."

"Jack?" Lynn stared at him. "We met in September, were sleeping together in October and November, and then you started seeing someone else and I didn't talk to you again until January when I bumped into you quite by accident."

He looked at her as though she was speaking another language. "I don't think so." Then his cell began to buzz somewhere deep in a pocket. He pulled it out, hesitated a minute, and walked out of the room to answer the call. When he came back he was all business. "I guess we remember things differently, which is another good reason not to dredge up the past. What did you tell Heather?"

"I told her that it's early enough that an abortion is probably the best solution."

He nodded. "Yes, I told her the same thing."

By the end of that short meeting, Lynn and Jack reached

a wobbly agreement to be supportive of whatever decision Heather made. To stay out of the way. But Lynn knew that was untenable for Jack. He'd never sat in the back seat in his life.

Again, the thought of Jack's reaction when he finds out Lynn has grabbed the wheel keeps her pacing. Finally, she picks up the phone and calls—first her own house, then Heather's apartment. Still no answer at either. Then she tries Marty and gets his voice mail. She leaves Einar's number, asks him to call. Finally holds her breath and dials Jack. She has to let someone know that Beegee is fine. So that Heather will know.

After the fourth ring, when she has her message at the ready, expecting the machine, a breathless female voice answers.

"Rhea," she says, "this is Lynn. Is Jack home?"

"No, but I'm so glad you called. Phone him on his cell. He's worried sick. Where are you?"

"Is he at school?" Lynn glances at the clock. It's five-thirty, an hour later in Alberta, but Jack often works late. Used to.

"He's gone to Heather's, looking for her. Do you need his number?" Rhea has a soft voice, the connection isn't great and Lynn has to strain a bit to hear her. "Is Belinda okay? There's nothing wrong is there?"

"No," Lynn tells her. "The baby's fine. I know Jack's cell number. But just tell him we're fine." Then she hangs up. Einar's number will be on the call display on Jack's phone. She has allowed herself to be found. Now Lynn urgently needs to talk with Heather first, so that when Jack calls she can tell him there's nothing to say. This is between Lynn and Heather. This is what she would like to say to him, but in her mind she's already forming the answers, the argument for when he calls.

She sits down and tries to read. Under woodworking and

fishing magazines in the bathroom, she's found half a dozen ancient issues of *National Geographic*. Left here by the former owner of the cabin? The faded address labels are unreadable except for a P.O Box on Quadra. Lynn tried to read an article on New Zealand this morning while Beegee slept. She's always thought she would like New Zealand. That she should go there some day.

She can't concentrate. The words wriggle and the lines tilt. Yesterday's headache has begun drilling her forehead over her right eye like a well-aimed knitting needle. She needs to eat. This wobbliness will go away after a decent meal. When she opened the fridge this morning, she discovered that Einar had brought food last night. There is a thick slab of bacon wrapped in brown butcher's paper, another dozen eggs, a jar of strawberry jam and on the counter a loaf of sliced white bread. So far, Lynn has had nothing but a slice of bread and jam.

She fries bacon and eggs, dawdles over the food as though she can slow time with this ponderous chewing. When she looks out the window, the rain has stopped and the step is steaming under the slanted rays. The sunset, if she could get to the beach, would be spectacular, she thinks. But she has business to attend to.

Again she calls Marty, and again she gets his voice asking her to leave a message. She wishes she knew how to send him text messages. Those he reads instantly, Heather claims. Lynn eyes the old rotary dial phone on the wall. Not likely you could text anything to anyone with this relic, even if she knew how.

She makes tea, one of the herbal varieties Hannah brought with supper last night. Tiptoes into the bedroom to check on Beegee who's been asleep for almost three hours. So long that Lynn is feeling the need to hold her again. She picks up the sleeping baby and the mug of tea, and goes outside. Half-hidden by overlapping boughs of cedar, Destiny is slumped on the bottom step, chin in hands, staring down at the wet bark at her feet. Lynn sits on the step above her with Beegee on her knees.

Finally, the little girl looks up. "Hey, Bonnie Gale." She leans sideways, her cheek brushing the baby's.

"What are you doing out here in the rain?" Lynn asks. "You should have come in." The child frowns. There's a cloud around her even though the sun's come out. "Was it you who brought me the diapers?"

Destiny shakes her head. "My mom."

"Tell her thanks. She saved me a trip to the store in the rain."

"She's busy. She's talking on the phone to Sunny. She kicked us all out of the house." She turns sideways and fiddles with Beegee's hair, trying to re-arrange the curls.

Sunny. Lynn has a flashback to a sullen blonde girl crouched, hiding behind the cabin with Heather. Of Hannah storming into the yard because Sunny has abandoned the younger kids in her own yard when she's supposed to be looking out for them. Of Lynn herself pointing out that Marty has been with those small kids all the while and he, in fact, is older than Sunny. How long ago was that? When Heather was about twelve? Sunny a bit younger? Heather was indignant that Sunny was "slave labour."

What is Sunny now, Lynn wonders, if Hannah has to speak privately with her? Where is she? And why the long face on her little sister at the mention of her name? "What's Sunny doing these days?" Lynn asks.

Destiny ducks her head, brushes her cheeks with the ends of her braids. She glances up and shrugs.

"Is she still at home?"

A quick shake of her head. "I'm not supposed to say." She looks at her wrist, at a watch with a red band and a cartoon face. Stands up. "I can go now. It's just about suppertime." She leans down and blows a kiss onto the end of Beegee's nose.

In that meeting with Donna and Grant, they had told Lynn and Jack about their extended families. Brothers and sisters who all have children, lots of cousins for their hoped-for Belinda or Jeremy —they've had names picked for years, they said. Lynn hopes there's a little girl cousin just like Destiny, who loves babies and kisses them and plays with their hair. Since she spoke with Rhea, Lynn has had such a strong sense of being pulled back to Calgary, to all those people waiting for Beegee.

Destiny waves, plods back up the path to her own house, and Lynn sits a minute longer, sad for the child who's just left, and mindful of the one in her arms. The baby's skin is tawny in this fading sunlight. She's begun to squirm a little and in a few minutes, she'll need attention. Well done, little girl, Lynn thinks. You've given me an entire afternoon to myself.

Lynn is back in the rocking chair, Beegee draining the bottle of Hannah's milk with gusto, when the phone rings. Long ago she was able to do most anything around the house with a baby on her arm, and she finds that dexterity is returning. She leans against the counter, baby in the crook of her elbow, hand steadying the bottle, grabs the phone with the other hand.

"Mom?"

"Marty." Lynn has to tense the arm holding the baby, she feels such sagging relief. "Finally."

"You're at Mr. Haugland's, right? We've been going nuts trying to figure out where you'd gone. Heather's been tearing her hair out. Jeez, Mom!"

"I know," she says. "This was a terrible thing to do, and I

am so so sorry, and I'll try to explain to Heather. But where is she? I can't find her."

Beegee's lost the nipple, and will be wailing in a second. Lynn clasps the phone with her chin and uses both hands to rearrange the baby and her bottle. She needs to tell Marty to hold on so she can drag a chair over. He's lowered his voice and she can barely hear him. Other voices behind him.

"I'm still at work," he says. "I can't really talk now. Heather's on her way out there. She left this morning, and you probably won't hear from her until she's at the door. She's driving."

"Alone?" Lynn has a flashback to those miles and miles of dark highway.

"I'm going to call you back in about an hour," he says. "Everything okay? Is the baby all right?"

"Baby is fine," Lynn says. "Yes, please call back."

Lynn sits down with her son's voice still in her head.

Marty has had little to say about Heather's pregnancy. When Lynn asked him how he felt after Heather told him this news, he shook his head. "Not something I would have predicted in about a trillion years," he said. "Were we even sure she liked men?"

"You'll talk to her if she needs someone, won't you?" Lynn asked. "She's not going to discuss this with your dad or me, we know that."

"Sure," he said, "but what do I know about having babies?"

"Almost as much as Heather does at this point," Lynn said. "Just listen when she's scared or sad."

"Of course," he said, "but Lynn, if Heather goes through with the adoption, it won't be the end of the world, right?"

She could hardly breathe, hearing him ask that question. Lynn has avoided talking with Marty about Heather's plans ever since, because she is afraid she will tell him that it will be the end of the world. Lynn had walked away when Marty

137

was a baby, and even though she got him back, she can't erase that image of a bundle so small he was barely a blink in a hospital nursery full of newborn babies. Alone with strangers. Her head tells her that Marty can handle that image, her heart says otherwise. And then there's the pact with Jack.

When the knock comes at the door, Lynn is glad that Beegee is fed and content even though she needs a clean diaper.

Hannah looks like she was blown here from her own house by a major gale. There's more hair fanning her face than secure in the braid, and her cheeks look like they've been scrubbed with sand.

"I think you need some tea," Lynn says. She settles Beegee on the couch, and heads for the stove before Hannah can get there and take over herself. The tea is still warm, but Lynn dumps it anyway, fills the kettle, clamps it onto the burner. She'll make a fresh pot. If only this headache would abate.

"Any idea where Einar would keep Tylenol? Advil? Aspirin?" Lynn asks.

"Jesus! It's just colic. You can't give drugs to a baby!"

Lynn rubs her eyes and taps her forehead. "For me. Headache. Very bad headache." Longingly, she's been thinking about the bottle of drops that was a mainstay in the medicine cabinet at home when Heather was this size. Sweet elixir in a dropper that the pediatrician told her would likely not make much difference to the baby but seemed to make the mother feel she was doing something about the problem. Not likely Hannah has an old bottle of Phenergan in her bathroom cabinet.

"Well," Hannah laughs, "why didn't you say so." She opens one of the kitchen drawers and fishes around, pulling out a tube of Bengay ointment, Buckley's cough medicine, a couple of prescription vials. "Nada," she says. "I can phone and get Destiny to bring some Advil down."

Lynn shakes her head. "I'll be okay until I get to the store. Don't bother her."

"It's not a bother. I have to keep her busy or she'd be down here wanting to hold the baby all day. But suit yourself. So." She looks around the room, everything in its place from Lynn's afternoon of restless tidying. "No sign of Heather yet?"

Lynn doubts that Einar has told Hannah what's going on, or that she's being coy—coy is not Hannah's nature, nor is it Lynn's—but she'll find out soon, so why not just answer. "She's on her way," Lynn says. "I ran away with the baby because Heather was going to give her up for adoption and I couldn't face that. But now she's found out where I am, and she's coming. By tomorrow, I guess." The kettle begins whistling. Lynn takes it off the burner and then turns back to face Hannah. "How the rest of it plays out…your guess is as good as mine." She hears the flatness in her voice, the same feeling of cold inevitability she had when she was imagining Beegee surrounded by cousins who looked like Donna and Grant.

Hannah sucks her teeth for a few minutes and looks at Lynn with neither surprise nor dismay. "So that's what brought you out here. I knew it had to be something big. Einar told me you never much liked this place. He was some surprised to hear you were coming." She sits down at the table, wipes away non-existent crumbs with her hand. "Well, what else could you do, I guess."

Lynn pours water onto the tea bags in the pot, leans against the counter. The cabin feels oppressively warm now, even though the rain has begun again. Maybe Hannah radiates this heat. "What would you have done," Lynn asks, "if your daughter was giving away a baby? To people who promised you could be part of your baby's life, but looked so scared you just knew that wasn't going to work? And with two other grandmas waiting all agog in the wings for you to hand her over."

Not a moment's hesitation. "Same thing. Although I would never let it get so far that a hi-jacking was necessary." Hannah stands up and takes two cups off the shelf. Lynn brings the teapot to the table and sits down across from Hannah's chair. "One of my girls give away a baby? Not a chance." Hannah opens the fridge, peers inside.

Oh, to be one of these resolute women, Lynn thinks. Able to speak her mind, right or not. But what on earth is Hannah doing now, hauling things out of the fridge?

"Have you eaten?" Hannah asks. "I didn't have an appetite when I fed the kids, but I'm hungry now."

"I'm fine," Lynn says. She watches, amazed, as Hannah opens the foil-wrapped pouch of leftover bacon, spreads a thick layer of margarine on a piece of bread, aligns three crisp rashers and folds the sandwich.

"Don't look so shocked," she says. "I wouldn't feed this poison to my kids. Or even to the dog come to think of it. But when I'm stressed I eat." She pats her well-padded hip. "What's a couple of pieces of bacon to a body like this?"

Suddenly Lynn imagines Hannah and Einar hunkered over plates, mopping up egg yolk with white bread. But where's Hank in these pictures? Even though she's met him at least a half dozen times, she has no recollection of the man. All that she can dredge up is an image of someone who looks a lot like Einar, but less substantial. A tall, slightly stooped, bearded man with wire-frame glasses. And overalls. Yes, she remembers Hank in overalls with one shoulder strap dangling, the tail of a plaid shirt rumpling at his waist. And a child on his arm.

Lynn pours the tea. Watches Hannah nibble her way daintily around the crust of the sandwich.

"So what are you going to do, now that they know where

you are?" Hannah asks. "It makes the whole exercise kind of pointless, doesn't it, if Heather drives out, picks up the baby and carries on as planned? What have you done except thoroughly piss off everyone involved?"

What indeed. How much comfort will it be to know that she's just prolonged the inevitable? Hannah, as she says, would never have let this go so far without least trying. She would have been proactive. One of the goals Heather had foisted on Lynn three years ago, before Jack moved out, after she saw Jack and Rhea walking arm-in-arm down a street offensively close to home. She'd stormed into the house and told Lynn it was time she opened her eyes and acted before she was acted upon. "Stop being so freakin' passive!" she screamed. "For once in your life be proactive!"

Hannah picks up the mug of tea, crosses the room, sets it on the table and puts a log in the fireplace.

"It's awfully warm in here already," Lynn says. She's longing to step outside for just two minutes and lift her face to the rain.

Hannah tosses the newspaper she was crumpling back into the kindling box. "Fine with me. I just thought it would cheer the place. Lord knows I could use some cheer." She waves away any concern before Lynn can even voice it. "Nothing new, just Sunny."

Lynn hesitates, trying to find the least intrusive way to ask about Sunny. Just in case Hannah does want to talk. After all, she's just loaned her own ears to Lynn's troubles. Hannah's face, though, is as closed as a cellar door. She turns away, and kicks the log to the back of the fireplace.

When Hannah sits down on the sofa next to the baby, Lynn drags the rocking chair across the room, ready to lift Beegee away if she begins to fuss. Head tilted, Hannah contemplates the sleeping baby. Looks up at Lynn. "What's the big deal here? Can't be money. I'm sure you guys can afford as many kids as you want, so why not help Heather keep this one?"

"You make it sound so simple. To Heather, being a single mother feels like quite a large deal."

Hannah sniffs. "So tell her it's not the end of the world." She tucks the corner of the afghan more securely around Beegee. "Look at her. How much trouble is this?" Then she laughs. "Okay, we both know this is about two percent of the time. Still, far as I can see, giving a baby away is a much bigger deal than keeping one."

Lynn nods. Funny how that got reversed in Heather's decision-making. How she seems to have assumed from the beginning that adoption was the easier choice. Lynn wants to put her head down and sleep. She is so tired of thinking about the impenetrability of Heather's choice. So afraid that no matter how much it hurts, Heather will grit her teeth and forge on just to prove she can do it.

Lynn is aware of Hannah watching her, waiting for her to say something. "On the other hand, the people she chose are lovely and will do a fine job of raising the baby. Heather has so much ahead of her."

"Yeah yeah yeah." Hannah flaps both hands. "I heard all that years ago from her proud father. Your kids are geniuses. The perfect family. One boy, one girl. He never said as much, but I could tell he thought my kids were one extended accident. With about half the combined brilliance of your two spread among the six of them. You can spare me the details of the brilliant future Heather's going to have to give up to raise this kid."

Lynn feels her cheeks reddening. Embarrassed for Jack, when she thought she was finally over that responsibility. He was scathing about Hannah's brood of kids. "That lifestyle," he'd said, "can barely support two adults and one child. How on earth do they think they can educate an endless number of children? Old Hank sure doesn't look as though he's thrilled with the population explosion. Kids all over him like barnacles." Lynn, though, had always thought that Hank looked perfectly comfortable, oblivious to the confusion and to Hannah's bossiness. Wherever he is, she wonders if he carries pictures of his children in his wallet and sits on the edge of a bed at night, contemplating their futures. For Jack, Heather's and Marty's futures were a given. They're bright, they have their parents behind them, they will do well. If anything gets in the way, he will help them find the solution.

"Sounds to me like you needed to kidnap the mother along with the baby and get her de-programmed. I could call my sister on Thetis if you want to take Heather and the baby there and hide out for a week and try to talk some sense into her. Is she coming alone?"

"Thanks," Lynn says, "but I think one kidnapping is plenty for my lifetime."

"Look, I'm serious. Not about holding her captive, but surely you can talk her into a week with just the two of you and the baby. Stay out here and thrash it out. That's what I'd do with my girls." She looks away, toward the window as though she's checking on her own house, her own girls.

Lynn won't bother to point out that she and Heather have already had three weeks together with the baby. That experiment is over as far as Heather's concerned. Lynn's daughter, Hannah's daughters, different mothers, different lives. But still…

"You have two daughters, right? Destiny and Sunny?"

"Right. Two girls, four boys. Thank God for Des. I don't know what I'd do without that sweet kid for company. We have to peel the boys off the ceiling at night, throw them in their beds, and by the time I get up in the morning they're swinging from the rafters again."

"And Sunny? She's not at home?"

Hannah's voice sounds scratchy, distant. As though this tape has been played too often. "She's been in Victoria for a couple of years. Finished high school there, as far as she was willing to go. Lived with my sister. Now she's in a house with a bunch of other people."

Lynn doesn't dare ask what, if anything, Sunny is doing with her life. "That must have been hard," she says, "having her away from home when she was still so young." Or maybe a relief, depending on the reasons for her leaving? Hannah does not look relieved in any way at the moment.

She suddenly stands up straight and yanks the leather tie off the end of her braid. She rakes her fingers from her scalp to the ends of the long hair until it crackles around her head. Then, all business, she begins to re-braid, feet planted like a couple of oak trees in front of the chair.

"Yeah. It was. She could be back anytime though. I hope so. She's sick, and they're being evicted from the house." She stands up suddenly, slides Beegee into Lynn's arms. "I'd better get back. My offer stands. Let me know if you need a hiding place."

Alone again, Lynn sits imagining Heather on the sofa, a real conversation between the two of them. Or is that as likely as a happy reunion for Hannah and Sunny?

10

According to Mapquest, Heather is supposed to roll into Horseshoe Bay eleven hours and twenty minutes after departure from Calgary.

Lynn might have made it in her car, or Heather and Marty in his, but the little Starfire starts to wheeze if she pushes too hard. Major delay in a white-out on the Coquihalla, and Heather had to stop an hour ago and walk up and down the highway because she was falling asleep. She would have gone for a real walk—there was a hiking trail at a rest area where she pulled over—but she's afraid of bears. Nothing else scares her, but as far back as she can remember, probably as far back as she knew there were such animals, she's been afraid.

Most of the drive she's been thinking about Beegee, wondering what she and Lynn are doing right now. Beegee goes ballistic about four o'clock every day, screaming so hard she turns a scary shade of red, stiff as a board. Morning is best. A long long feeding in the morning—another thing no one ever told Heather was that babies can suck for hours—a nap, then a bath, then more feeding. She was terrified of giving Beegee a bath. It was like holding a little seal who could slip under any second and be gone. Glub, just like that. And keeping the gross-looking stump of cord dry. Nothing was simple. Heather printed out a sheet of instructions for Donna. She knows Donna has a whole shelf of books and took a baby-care class, but Beegee isn't any generic baby. Heather knows what her baby likes and the things that piss her off. Also something she's learned. Babies get pissed off if you don't listen.

When she first decided she was giving the baby away, Heather imagined a bundle in a blanket. Don't even hold her, one of the women in the adoption agency support group had told her. This was the dumb bunny's second baby, and she'd seemed proud that she was giving it to the same family as the first. What, are you under contract to them? Heather asked. How many more do they want? Carmen told her later that she was being insensitive. That she either canned the sarcasm or quit the group. Heather quit. She didn't need a bunch of women who'd made the same mistake as she had telling her what to do. What kind of expert advice was that?

She forces herself to think about something, anything else. Her boobs leak, her eyes leak, she's a mess from thinking about Beegee. Think ahead, Carmen told her. Think six months from now, and what you hope to be doing then. So, next spring. Next spring she will have finished another semester of school, be looking for a good summer job. A couple of her friends were tree-planting this summer and have been trying to convince her she should come with them next year. But she won't. Bears. And she'd be too far away for monthly visits with Beegee.

Heather arrives in Horseshoe Bay two hours behind schedule. Starving again, and desperate to pee by the time she leaps out of the car at a service station, she's stopped by the smell of the sea. She leans against the car for a minute in the grey drizzle and sucks wet salt into her lungs. This is the same smell that gushed out of her body when Beegee was born. The same scent she picks up when she nuzzles the baby's head.

She looks around at the wet street, the huge BC Ferries sign that points the way to Nanaimo. Now, she finally feels as though she's closing in. All day, even though the miles have been sliding by, she's felt like the car was barely moving, that she wasn't getting any closer to Beegee. In fact, on that stretch of the Coquihalla where she was pretty much convinced she was going to die, it seemed she was moving away from her baby instead of toward her.

She dashes into the service station, grabs the key to the Ladies. Before she leaves the chilly toilet, she runs cold water over her wrists. It helps, but she's going to need coffee, lots of coffee to get her across to the island. That's her goal. To get onto Vancouver Island. Then she'll find somewhere to park, sleep for a couple of hours.

She decides to skip food, go straight to the ferry terminal. She can eat and drink on the way over. She has a flashback to a choppy crossing when she was about ten. Marty, scarfing down his bowl of clam chowder and Lynn's too, because Lynn was feeling queasy. Marty running out of the dining room and not quite making it to the railing before he puked. Heather and Jack are never seasick. She's inherited his strong stomach, his ability to put mind over matter when everyone else is caving in. Heather, Jack insisted for years, would be an astronaut. That was her dream, at fourteen, after Robert Thirsk, Calgary's contribution to space, made a guest appearance at her junior high school, his own junior alma mater. She considered changing her name to

Rob. Robert Thirsk, Roberta Bondar, there had to be a connection. Whoever heard of a Heather accomplishing anything earth-shaking? She realized in high school, when Jack was hiring tutors to keep her chemistry and physics marks in the honour zone, that she'd lost interest. The whole thing seemed childish. Marty's the one with the passion for science and math. And now? Winston told her she'd be a good lawyer, and that's stuck in her mind. She won't dare mention it to Jack, though, or he'll be imagining her a Supreme Court judge by next week. She won't hear the end of it. When she gets home, though, she'll talk to Marty, ask him what he thinks. She wishes he was with her, wonders if he still gets seasick. She's sure Lynn does. Imagines Lynn pacing the deck of the ferry with Beegee in her arms, taking deep breaths, her eyes locked on the land.

Bad news at the dock. The nine o'clock ferry is full. And it's the last one of the day. Heather spends five minutes cleaning out the car. She flings water bottles so they fly end over end into the trash barrel three metres away. Two kids on skateboards whistle and cheer each basket. Then Heather gets back into the car, crosses her arms and sits staring across the water. Well fuck it. If the plan's going to fall apart because of something as stupid as a ferry schedule, she's not waiting out here in the cold for morning. She'll find somewhere to sleep.

The one motel she passed on the way in was flashing a No Vacancy sign. Even though the last thing she wants is to spend the night in someone else's house, the thought of driving any further to find a hotel is even more gruesome. She stops the car in front of a cottage style house with a B&B sign in the window, and grabs her jacket and the small overnight bag from the back seat.

The young woman who opens the door shows her a bedroom and bathroom at the back of the house.

"There isn't a private entrance," she says, "but you can come in through the kitchen. I'll give you a key to the back door."

Heather shakes her head. "I don't need a key. I'm going to bed now, and I'll be gone early in the morning. What time's the first ferry?"

"Oh, gosh." The woman rolls her eyes. "Six-thirty. That's going to mean breakfast before six o'clock."

Six-thirty. Why? Why does she need to be on the island before the sun comes up? She shakes her head. "Forget it. That's too early." She wants to be well-rested for tomorrow.

"The next one's eight-thirty," the woman says, "and then there isn't another one for two hours. You want breakfast at 7:30?"

Heather's never stayed in one of these places. She has no idea what to expect. A minute ago, a baby started to wail in one of the rooms at the front of the house. She presses her elbows tight against her breasts to stop her nipples from answering.

"Whatever," she says. She forgot, in the frustration of missing the last ferry, that she's hungry. All this talking about breakfast. "Maybe I will take that key," she says, "and go out for something to eat before I go to bed. Anything close by?"

The baby's quiet now, and Heather can hear a man's voice. Low, crooning, then singing. She imagines him swooping round and round the room with the baby clamped to his shoulder. Two wet circles the size of loonies are spreading on the front of her shirt. And the woman is staring. "Food?" Heather asks again.

"Sure." The woman blinks like crazy as though she's trying to focus on Heather's face and not on the leaky breasts. "There's a great fish and chip place just up the road. You're welcome to bring your food back here and eat in the kitchen." She flaps her hand toward the room beyond. "Help yourself to something to drink. There's juice in the fridge, milk…" She glances again and then quickly back to Heather's face. "Kettle on the stove, teapot and teabags on the counter right beside it. Really. Make yourself at home. I'll go get the key."

God, how can they do this? She could be anyone, and they're going to give her a key to the house. Tell her to make herself at home. Is it because she's dripping milk? Someone who's just had a baby couldn't possibly be a threat? She could be one of those girls who gives birth in the basement while her parents are asleep upstairs, takes the baby out into the alley and dumps it into a neighbour's trash can.

Heather digs through her bag, and shrugs into an old flannel shirt of Winston's. One of the two things he left her.

When the woman comes back into the room and hands her a key ring, just like that, Heather stares. "How long have you been doing this B&B thing?"

The woman looks embarrassed. "For a week. You're our first guest. We just had a baby—three months ago—and I decided I don't want to go back to work. We thought we'd make up a bit of lost income this way. It's quiet now, but in summer we should do pretty well."

Heather glances around the room. Everything looks new. The lacy covers on the pillows on the bed match the cushions on the small chair which match the frill over the window. "Nice place," she says.

"This used to be a family room, but we figure we don't really need it right now." She frowns. "Excuse me if I'm being rude, but you look like you're nursing a baby. You're not in some kind of trouble are you?" There are footsteps in the kitchen, then a man looms in the bedroom doorway.

"Hi," he says. "Jenny says you're taking the eight-thirty ferry. Got someone to stay with in Nanaimo?"

Oh, here we go again. Traveling alone? How far are you going? Heather shakes her head, slowly, mechanically. Mr. Jenny looks friendly, but he's measuring her up. "Campbell River," she says. No point in being too specific. "My mom and my baby are up there."

Both of their faces crease into smiles. Oh. She has a mother. It's okay.

"Look," Heather says. "I'm not in trouble." Ha! "No one's going to come banging on the door looking for me. But if you're worried, I'll go someplace else." She's thinking it might be easier to sleep in the car after all. She can take the early ferry.

"Nah," the guy says. He puts his arm around Jenny. "You go on out and get yourself some supper, and have a good sleep when you get back. Jenny makes a mean breakfast. She'll set you up real well before you leave in the morning."

Fleetingly, Heather thinks that they look like Donna and Grant, just a little younger. The way people with babies are supposed to look. Two people in the picture.

The two of them turn to leave the room, but Daddy looks back over his shoulder. "If you hear noise in the kitchen in the night, that'll be me warming the bottle. My turn to get up. I'll try to be quiet."

Heather shakes her head. "I won't hear a thing. I'm totally bagged."

"Yeah? Where'd you drive in from?"

"The east," she says. And before they can ask any more questions, she drops the key into her jacket pocket and slips past them to the kitchen. Turns and waves before she goes out the door.

At the fish and chip shop, two tables are crowded with people Heather's age. University or college kids? She wonders what's nearby. Orders, then leans against the wall to wait. She'll go back to the B&B place. The thought of eating here alone is depressing.

You can practically see globules of grease hanging in the air. God, fish and chips. Coleslaw dripping with mayo. And she's salivating. Hormones? When the guy at the counter pushes the bag toward her, she can hardly wait to get outside and start cramming fries into her mouth. She peers into the bag. Ketchup, malt vinegar, salt. Plastic fork. They must have assumed she was eating on the street. Good. She won't have to poke around in Jenny's kitchen looking for utensils.

She unlocks the back door at the B&B with her left hand because she's holding a piece of cod in the right. She's eaten most of the chips. The kitchen is quiet, but there's the muted sound of television from the front of the house. The only light flickers from a fluorescent bulb over the sink. She sits at the table and has swallowed the last greasy bite before she notices a place mat, plate, silverware and glass of water on the other side. How sweet. They set the table just for her. So the gesture doesn't go ignored, she carries plate and cutlery to the sink, rinses it and stacks it on the drainboard, then takes the glass of water to the bedroom with her and closes the door.

This is too weird. She's a guest in a house and she knows even less about the people who own the place than they do about her. Still, the place is probably a lot cleaner than the Best Western she might have found if she had driven back into Vancouver.

A few things have been added since Heather went out for food. On the bedside table, there's a glass and a carafe of water with ice cubes and a bit of lemon floating in it. An extra blanket is folded at the bottom of the bed, and when she wanders into the bathroom there's a fluffy yellow bath towel and face cloth beside the sink and a basket with mini bottles of toiletries. Heather fishes out a tube of green tea bath salts, and turns on the taps in the tub. She wrinkles her nose at the smell of the clothes she sheds on the floor. She has Lynn's sweater and a clean pair of leggings in the overnight bag. Her body's been oozing secretions from every pore and orifice since she gave birth. She suspects from the look on Jack's face the couple of times he's been near her that she smells as ripe as a stray cat. Everyone else is too polite to mention this to her, but Jack has a nose like a bloodhound and he can't hide his reaction to smells. It was never Lynn waiting at the door when Heather and Marty came home in the middle of the night. Jack, sniffing for booze and weed. Marty kept a bottle of Febreeze in the car and sprayed himself before he came in the door. He still smells like laundry.

Heather steps into the tub and stretches out in the deepening water. She lets the taps run until the waves are up to her chin, the overflow drain is gurgling and the water is dangerously close to the rim of the tub. Her breasts float like two young porpoises. Before she gets out of the water, she'll squeeze out every drop of milk so that she can go to sleep with a deflated chest. Milk bath.

Eyes closed, she takes deep cleansing breaths. Her arms and legs rise and flutter just below the surface. As soon as she's home again, she'll go back to her yoga class. The last two months she was pregnant, she was too tired to go anywhere. And for the three weeks with Beegee, she was even more tired, but couldn't bear the thought of leaving the baby even if she'd had the energy. Things will be different now. She'll be alone again. Without any warning at all, a sob leaps from her throat and her eyes sting with tears. She crams a fist into her mouth and bites hard. She does not want Jenny and husband rushing into the bathroom thinking she's slashing her wrists in the tub. What's with all this sniveling? Seven months ago, she told Winston she was not going to cry. Not because he was leaving, and definitely not when she gave up the baby. She hadn't cried since she was eight years old. She wasn't going to start now.

She bites her lip hard, thinks about Donna and Grant, the photo they'll send in a couple of weeks. The two of them side by side on the sofa in their pretty living room with baby Belinda in Donna's arms. Exactly the way it should be.

She lets a bit of water out of the tub, turns on the hot for another minute. Her nipples are puckering and extending as though they can sense a tiny mouth closing in. She reaches for both, and pulls gently. A deep shudder courses from the nerve endings on the swollen brown tips to that place deep in her belly. That uterus she didn't even think about until Beegee stretched it to the size of a watermelon.

But it's not Beegee's mouth she's imaging now. It's Winston's. Winston who has been on her mind through every mile of this day, because he is the one missing from the picture.

Again, she lets out a bit of water and warms the tub. Her fingertips are wrinkled, their steady pull on her nipples clouding the water around her breasts with milk.

Winston. She closes her eyes again, and tries to imagine that the man who will be creeping through the room beyond her bedroom door tonight to warm a bottle is Winston. That he's here now, beside the tub, his hand trailing in the water. Tracing a path down the soft mound of her belly.

The tears just won't stop.

11

Lynn is pacing again, even though Beegee is content. Awake, propped into the corner of the sofa, sucking on her fist, the baby seems to have decided this dark cabin is home. With each circuit of the room, each longing gaze out the window, Lynn is trying to define her own restlessness. After Hannah left, afternoon melted into evening, and the calm prevailed through a feeding and much internal dialogue—Lynn rehearsing what she will say to Heather when she arrives. But then she began to anticipate Einar's return and wonder how Heather would react to finding the two of them here together. Heather tends to look for drama on every stage. It was Heather, still a child, who put together the dates of Marty's birth and Lynn and Jack's anniversary and came up with far too many questions. Now Lynn has begun to worry again that she will say something too revealing, something that will lead to the next thing, and her daughter, the sleuth, will grab hold of some tiny clue and nip at Lynn's heels like a terrier until she spills out the story. And to what purpose? The more she thinks about it, the more Lynn knows that

Heather will find Lynn's story as irrelevant to her own as Jack does. Or as Jack would like it to be. But it will be too juicy a morsel for Heather to keep to herself. She will have to share it with Marty. So does Lynn get to Marty first? Is it really inevitable? The restlessness becomes anger. At Heather, at Jack, but mostly at herself for not having the guts to come clean years ago on the whole mess around Marty's birth. Secrets. Lynn loathes secrets, because they inevitably become lies.

The baby begins to whimper, sensing Grandma's agitation, Lynn thinks. She almost wishes the door would open and Hannah would come back and tell her once again that she's done the right thing. Hannah gets it. Hannah knows why Lynn threw the baby in the car and flew away. So would Marion if she'd been around the last few weeks. Bernie, no. She will be furious with Lynn when she finds out about this caper. Just as furious as she was when she heard Heather was pregnant. Disbelieving that people could mismanage their lives in this way. Jean, off in England, would find it all terribly interesting, and want Lynn to describe in depth why she's done what she's done. Neither Bernie nor Jean is a mother.

Hannah's advice is to hide somewhere else. Take this kidnapping to a new level. Maybe when it's over, after Beegee is back in Calgary, Lynn will run away from it all. She picks up the baby and smiles into her serious little face. "How about this," she says. "How about Grandma runs away to New Zealand. Just like in a cheesy romance." She swears the baby is listening to every word. Lynn tickles the roll of fat under Beegee's chin. "I appear mysteriously in a small town. The post-mistress—or no, maybe it's the owner of the boarding house where I find a small room—tells me there's no work around for a city woman like me. Unless I'm willing to consider a position as a housekeeper. There's this recently widowed sheep-rancher…" Lynn lets her eyes get wider, her grin expand, and she's rewarded finally, with a smile. Fleeting, but a smile for sure. She tries to coax another, but this time Beegee only yawns and stretches.

"Yeah, I know baby. It's a boring story. Been done too many times. I've pretty much decided life on the lam is not for me. And sadly, not for you either."

She carries the baby to the window and lifts her to see moonlight trickling through the boughs. "Look," she whispers, "so beautiful, and your grandma goes crazy because she can't see beyond the trees."

Then, headlights on the road curve and dip into the driveway, and there is Einar stepping out of his truck. And Loki with him. Lynn has wondered all day where the dog could be. She stays at the window, watches the two of them plod up the steps, the dog looking as weary as the man.

The door opens, and Loki wriggles past Einar. Well-trained, he stops on the rug, shakes off a strong scent of wet pooch.

"Hello, hello," Einar greets them. "What a nice welcome to see you at the window." He sits down heavily on one of the kitchen chairs to take off his boots. "Long day. Everything okay here?" He looks around the room. Expecting to see someone else? "Sorry I didn't get back earlier."

Lynn glances at the baby, thinking she should put her down, offer to make some supper for Einar. But she's sure Beegee will fuss. "Don't mind my pacing," she says. "We're about five minutes from sleep with this one if I stay in motion."

"And Heather?"

"She's on her way."

He nods, satisfied, it seems, that things are moving forward. "So this is going as you planned it then?" Lynn has no answer. She thought after their conversation last night, it should be clear that she had no plan. If anything is clear.

Loki is sitting beside his food dish, whining. Einar stands up and scoops dog kibble from the sack beside the bowl. He takes the water dish to the sink, rinses and refills it. Scratches the dog's ears before he looks at Lynn again.

Lynn shakes her head. "I never really had a plan. I guess we'll proceed from here."

"Have you had anything to eat?" Einar asks. He opens the fridge and takes out eggs.

"Yes, thanks," she says, "you left me well-stocked. Can I make you something? An omelet?"

He already has the frying pan on the burner. "I don't need anything fancy." Finally he smiles. "A couple of eggs and a pile of toast. Some for you too?"

She's tempted, just to be gracious, to sit down and eat with her host and then do the clean-up afterward. A good guest. But she shakes her head. Watches him crack four eggs into the pan and peel four slices of bread from the loaf. Shakes her head again when he pours rye into a glass, and holds the bottle up.

He's silent, as sure-footed around the stove as he was re-finishing cabinets in her kitchen long ago. She remembers the way his hands moved with such confidence. After Lynn and Jack moved to Calgary, Jack recommended Einar for a position as a shop teacher in the school where he was teaching, and in exchange Einar insisted on doing some kitchen renovations for them. Lynn remembers drinking coffee at her own kitchen table, watching Einar's hands on the cabinets, stroking for slivers, rough spots, his nose almost touching the sandpaper he used for the final touch. The maple, stripped of two layers of paint and the original varnish, had gleamed like old bones. "Maybe we should leave them as they are," she'd said. "They really are quite lovely."

He looked her way with surprise, as though he'd forgotten she was sitting there. "No no," he said, "they'll never last this way."

Now he looks at her with an expression she can't quite read. He didn't have a beard twenty years ago. Was it there even two years ago? They didn't see Einar that last time they came to Quadra. The beard hides the lower half of his face, all but the shift of his jaw when he's about to speak. "How did Heather sound when you talked to her?"

"I didn't talk with her. I couldn't reach her, but Marty called this afternoon and told me she was on her way."

He nods. He's shoveled eggs between slices of toast and finishes a sandwich in three big bites. Then he sits back and rubs his chin. Lynn can almost feel the calluses on his palm rasping against the matt of grey. "And Jack? He knows where you are?"

The baby is limp in her arms, sound asleep, but Lynn doesn't want to let go of her. She's noticed, all day, that when she puts Beegee down, she feels a cold ache in her arms. "Yes," she says trying hard not to sound impatient. Every time she thinks about Jack, she becomes irritated, for no particular reason, and for everything. "Jack knows. I called."

"Good. He was probably worried sick." He looks at her sideways. "I almost called him myself."

She stifles the weary sigh that comes with imagining that conversation. The two of them talking in low voices about what could have come over Lynn, Jack asking Einar to please look out for her, keep him posted.

When the phone rings, Lynn is so sure it's Jack that she walks toward Einar with her hand outstretched, but he shakes his head. Yes, he tells the person who's calling, he'll be there in five.

"I won't be long," he says, pulling on his boots. "I'm just

going up to Hannah's for a minute." This time Loki stays behind.

Lynn sits down, her foot automatically setting the rocking chair in motion. She puts her head back, closes her eyes. She has Jack's voice echoing in her mind, and he will not go away. She's beginning to doubt that he'll ever truly go away, even though he's now married to someone else. It seems that from that day she met him in the Students' Union Cafeteria, she was fated to be tied to Jack Bishop for life.

For three months Lynn and Jack were together almost every day, and she felt as though she was changing into some other girl. It frightened her at times, the sense that she was losing her old self. Then one day, after Jack cancelled a date because he had to study for an exam the next day, she saw him arm-in-arm with one of those girls she would have expected him to date. She didn't take his calls, went home for Christmas and managed to avoid him when she got back. Two weeks after she confirmed that she was pregnant, she bumped into him in the hallway of the Tory Building and he grabbed her arm when she tried to squirm past.

She agreed to meet him after her class, and all through the lecture she worked the words around in her head. She hadn't intended to tell Jack. Not ever. But when he'd stopped her as though nothing had changed, she wanted him to know what he'd done. He linked his arm through hers. As soon as they exited the building, she pulled him off the path, and stood on tiptoes to look him in the eye. "I'm pregnant."

He looked genuinely puzzled. As though he didn't know the meaning of the word, or at least that it had no context in his life. "Oh, you can't be," he said. Remembering, she was sure, the great care he'd taken with condoms, the reassurance he'd given her that he had everything under control.

"There isn't any question about it, Jack. I had a pregnancy test and I am."

He grabbed her arm and steered her across the street, away from the campus and along the high bank of the North Saskatchewan River. Neither of them said a word until they began a twisty descent into Emily Murphy Park. Jack's face was as white as the birch bark trunks they skirted. "How the hell did that happen?" It was clear he didn't expect her to answer. He charged on ahead, kicking branches and last year's leaves from the path.

At a picnic table a stone's throw from the water, Jack dropped his books between them when he sat. Lynn clutched the edge of the bench and stared at the river, glancing every few seconds at his clenched jaw. Finally, he ran his hands through his hair and then clasped his head as though he was in pain.

"Oh God, Lynn, what are we going to do about it?"

The sharp little edges of the word bounced between them. "It?"

"The pregnancy."

"Oh. The pregnancy."

"What's wrong?" He turned and put his hands on her shoulders, reaching across the gulf. Two magpies scolded from a log a few feet away. Lynn glanced down at the remains of a hotdog bun under the table. Splash of yellow mustard against white bun, against black earth.

"I stopped thinking about 'it' when I found out 'it' was true, Jack. Since then I've been thinking about a baby."

"Stop. Don't think like that. I know someone who has some connections. We can get you an abortion."

Lynn was terrified at the thought of having a baby. But she'd already phoned home, and her mom and dad were coming to Edmonton in two days to help her "make plans." Even if she hadn't been more terrified at the thought of an abortion, it was too late.

"We can't get married, Lynn. You know that, don't you?"

Of course she knew that. She'd never expected to marry Jack Bishop. Nor anyone else for that matter. She thought she'd get her Arts degree, then join CUSO. That was what her mother kept pushing her to do—get an education, travel, stay out of the rut.

"I'll work it out," she said. "You don't need to be involved. I'm giving the baby up for adoption."

"I want to be involved," he said. "We can't get married, but I won't leave you to do this on your own. Besides, they'll need my permission too, won't they? I'll have to sign."

"No," she said, "they don't. We aren't married, and we weren't living together. I may not even put your name on the papers."

"That can't be right," he said. "I know you're upset, but I'm willing to take some responsibility. Won't you need money? Where will you live?"

She'd planned to stay at school, wear baggy sweaters, and finish the year. Then with luck, she could find a part-time job for May and June. The baby was due in July. She was sure her folks would agree that no one needed to know their business. She'd have the baby, sign the papers, and then go home for the rest of the summer. She had a plan.

Listen, she would like to say to Einar, whose boots are clumping back up the steps to the door. There was a time when I was able to plan. Only it didn't work out that way. The baby is beginning to stir, and hiccup. Einar stops just inside the room, and takes in the scene, Beegee twisting and snorting in Lynn's arms.

"Hannah's home," Einar says. "Should I ask her to come down and feed the baby?"

"No." Lynn tries not to sound snappish. She's had a vision of Heather's car chugging into the driveway while Hannah sits enthroned in the rocker with Beegee at her breast.

She works for a more civil tone. "I'll thaw some milk. She's getting better about taking a bottle."

Again the mulishness around his jaw. "That's not what Hannah said. According to her, Little Miss is all mixed up and shouldn't have any bottles at all."

Forget that Hannah understands all this. Lynn imagines that thick braid in her hands, how she will twist it like a giant corkscrew the next time Hannah comes through the door and will tell her to mind the business in her own house. Yet here she is, dependent on Hannah. And on Einar. "Little Miss and I are getting along fine," she says. She opens the freezer and pulls out a serving of Hannah's milk.

Einar watches while she juggles the fussing baby on her arm and tries to fit the plastic bag of milk into the tube. Lynn is prepared to hand him the baby when he crosses the room, but he takes the milk instead, fills a mug with hot water, sets the bottle into it.

"As a matter of fact," Lynn says, "she's taken the last two bottles so well it's probably best not to confuse her any longer by switching back and forth. That was the point, to get her to take the bottle."

"Small problems, eh? Feeding and colic and croup and all that nonsense. They keep getting bigger as you go along. Hannah phoned so I'd talk to Josh. He's got in some trouble with cars. Makes bottles and milk look easy."

"The oldest boy is still at home?"

"Still in school. When he shows up. Kids, eh?" He takes the bottle out of the hot water, shakes it, dries it carefully with a tea towel. Then he frowns.

"If Heather wanted to give the baby away, why the hang did they let her bring it home from the hospital?" he asks. "Surely it's easier if she doesn't even see it, just walks away."

"No," Lynn says carefully. "That was not an easy way. There is no easy way." She takes the bottle from him and sits down in the rocking chair, but this time Beegee has decided that the plastic nipple is not what she wants. There are signs this baby will be as obstreperous a child as her mother was.

"Maybe," Einar says with a shrug after watching for a minute, "she's just not hungry."

Lynn looks at the clock. "Good guess," she says. "It's only an hour and a bit since I fed her last. I think I'm losing all track of time as well as my common sense. There are other reasons for fussing." She holds the baby against her shoulder, rubbing and patting the arched back until slowly the tautness eases, and once again Beegee's eyes close. "Who knows what goes on in such a small brain."

Einar leans against the wall, presses his shoulders back, rolls his head from side to side. "Too much bending today," he says. "I think I need a day off. Maybe tomorrow."

Tomorrow Heather will arrive. Unless something slows her down, which Lynn can't imagine. Why, she wonders, is Heather coming at all? Why not phone and demand that Lynn come back? Immediately. That would have worked.

She looks up to find Einar watching her speculatively. "What you said a few minutes ago, about how that wasn't the easy way, just taking the baby, how can you be so sure?" he asks.

Yesterday Lynn would have said that Einar is straight as an arrow, says what he thinks, asks what he needs to know, never fishes around for tidbits of information. Since he's come back today, he seems as muddled as she is. For all Jack's cautions about telling no one, could it be that Einar knows they gave Marty away?

"Did you know Marty was born before Jack and I got married?"

"Yes, I think I knew that. But you were together, and you got married right after he was born, right?" He waves an arm and winces at the awkward movement. "All I'm asking is why you're so absolute about this. One way is right for everybody? So you kept your baby, does that mean Heather should be a mother if she doesn't want to be?" He pushes away and begins to put on his boots. "Forget I said all that. What do I know about having babies and holding it all together? Totally messed that up myself. Get a good sleep, Lynn."

"Einar, I'll move out here onto the sofa, so you can have your bed back. Sleeping on the sofa is not going to help that back problem."

"No, no, I'll sleep in the truck. I'm used to that. You need the bed more than I do."

"I almost went home yesterday," Lynn says. "I was so close to doing that and…I guess it's a good thing I didn't, because Heather and I would have crossed paths." She feels the headache returning. "I shouldn't have come here in the first place."

"Don't," he says. "What's the point in thinking about what you should have done? You're here. I'm not going to throw you out. Not with a baby, or without a baby, or with ten babies. Stay as long as you need. I'll try not to be noisy in the morning." He yawns, stretches, and he and the dog slouch out into the night.

Lynn tucks into Einar's bed with Beegee, but lies awake wondering where Heather is now. How far she's traveled and if she'll have the sense to stop and rest. She tries to calculate an arrival time, but has no idea exactly when Heather left. Can't even remember how long she and Beegee were in the car. She tells herself that Heather must be asleep somewhere safe. This girl is not the type to pull over in a picnic ground and curl up in the back seat. Then she begins thinking about adoption, about Donna and Grant. About how one girl's big problem should be the perfect solution to someone else's sorrow. She thinks, for the first time in a long while, about the family with whom Marty might have grown up. According to the social worker they'd been selected but not contacted. A safeguard to wait until after the ten days had passed even though the consent was rarely revoked. Marty was in a foster home. Why couldn't Heather wait until the baby was born to choose a family, Lynn asked Carmen, so that someone wasn't set up for a huge disappointment if she changed her mind? But that's not the way it's done.

After a visit to Donna and Grant's house before Beegee was born, Heather described the nursery. The walls painted in soft pastel stripes. The canopied crib with its Disney figure mobile, chirping "It's a Small World."

Lynn wonders how Donna will be able to put the baby to sleep in that big crib after years of waiting. Won't she cling to her day and night? Carmen told Heather that she has to put aside the McDonalds' needs and focus only on what's best for her and the baby. That someone else's childlessness is not her problem. Yet how can anyone who meets these people not feel empathy for their empty arms?

Lynn takes a deep breath, slides her arm out from under the warmth of the baby, and slips over the edge of the bed.

She creeps quietly into the kitchen, opens the fridge. After contemplating eggs, cheese, butter, she settles for a piece of thickly buttered bread topped with a slab of cheddar. Einar has left the bottle of rye on the counter. Lynn swirls a glug of it into an equal amount of water, then carries bread and drink outside. She's closing the door behind her when a shadow bounds onto the porch.

Balancing plate and glass on the porch railing, she kneels and scratches behind Loki's ears. He lifts his chin and makes a gurgly sound as she rubs her knuckles on his bottom jaw. He looks as though he'd sit there forever if she kept massaging.

She stands and opens the door. "Go on in. Do your job."

The dog woofs softly in agreement and trots tail-wagging into the cabin, straight to the bedroom.

After the last bite of bread, sip of rye, Lynn sits on the top step of the porch, carefully leans back. She presses her spine into the damp wood, slowly curling and uncurling, vertebra by vertebra. Overhead, the trees frame a pane of night sky studded with stars. Any minute now, headlights might appear on the road, Heather's car coast down the driveway. Stop it! she tells herself. Heather is asleep, she's safe. She will arrive late tomorrow.

Toes curled around the bottom step, Lynn does a slow sit-up, scrubs at her face with the hem of her t-shirt. She had washed the shirt in the bathtub with Beegee's clothes, put it up back on when it was still damp, and once again it feels like a second skin. One that needs to be shed. The jeans are worse.

There is the sound of a scuttled stone. Lynn stands, instinctively pulls far back into the shadows against the house. On the road, a figure flashes between the trees. Pauses at the driveway. Hannah. A froth of hair on her shoulders, a long pale garment swaying under a dark sweater. Lynn starts to raise an arm, hesitates, and Hannah walks on. Glides really. What on earth is she doing? Looking for Hank? One of the boys out late in the night? Sleepwalking?

Lynn tiptoes down the step, around the side of the cabin. She cups her hands to the window and peers into the dark bedroom. The lump under the quilts is still. But there's a flicker below. Loki stretched full length beside the bed lifts his head, then springs up and stares at the window. Lynn steps away.

She is about to walk up to the road, to see where Hannah is going, when she hears footsteps again. Einar, aroused from his sleep in the back of the truck? But no, the sound is still coming from the road, Hannah returning, arms swinging, nightgown flapping around her legs.

Lynn sits on the bottom step, watching. Two minutes later, Hannah slides by again, and then yet again. Pacing. Hannah is pacing the road in the middle of the night. Lynn would never have guessed her to be an insomniac. She would expect Hannah to sleep as efficiently as she does everything else.

On the next pass, a gust of wind lifts Hannah's hair; the skirt of her nightgown billows around her so that she looks as though she's floated down from the tops of the trees.

Minutes tick by, and there is no movement, no sound except for the soft scrape of cedar boughs on the roof. Lynn eases the front door open, listens, then finally steps inside. The cabin is cold. She considers a fire, but does not want to commit herself to sitting awake until the embers have died. Now that she's back inside, her eyes are heavy, even though the squirrels are still running in wheels inside her head. She wraps herself in the knitted afghan on the couch and lies back, feet on the coffee table. Where was she again in that New Zealand fantasy? Maybe she needs to go back to the beginning. To the trip to the airport, and her fear of flying.

In those years that she dreamed about joining CUSO, of traveling to the places her mother had wanted to see—don't miss Paris, my girl, she'd said, please go for me—Lynn had no inkling that the first time she stepped into a plane she'd feel as though she'd crawled into a coffin. When Marty was a year old, Jack's parents gave Jack and Lynn a trip to Las Vegas as an anniversary gift. Lynn was sure Alice simply wanted to have the baby to herself for four days, and she'd balked at going. They could wait until he was a little older, she told Jack. But he insisted, and in the pattern that would persist for twenty-four years, she gave in. She stepped onto the plane, could not find the air she needed for even a shallow breath, and tried to step back. Jack grabbed her arm and propelled her forward. He strapped her in, assured her that once they were in the air she would be fine, and then settled into the newspaper. By the time they were in the air, Lynn was hyperventilating, needed the flight attendant to stand beside her, a reassuring hand on her back and a paper bag over her nose. She embarrassed her young husband so badly he could hardly speak to her through the three hour flight. And Lynn, once she could breathe, did not calm down, but instead began to think about Baby Martin and what would become of him if this flimsy plane went down in the Nevada desert.

She has flown twice since that first nightmare flight, and neither experience was less than terrifying. Does anyone take a boat to New Zealand? Anyone except the adventure-loving families who plan sailing trips around the world with three school-aged children, and all their savings poured into a boat. Jack would have been that adventurous dad if he'd married the right woman. Marty and Heather would have been the kids in the magazine photos. Their mother, the right mother, would have been a journalist who posted travel diaries to her editor from each port of call.

Sadly, it has turned out that Lynn, Jack's wife—she realizes that she still doesn't think of herself as an ex-wife—Heather and Marty's mother, has allowed that fear of flying to leach away all sense of adventure. So how is it that she is also most recently a kidnapper? Blame Beegee. This baby has bewitched her in the same way as Heather did as an infant. Marty was so easy after the first week of turmoil. Lynn and Jack smiled smugly when their friends whined about sleepless nights and wearing out the floor with howling infants. Took credit for the cherub who ate and slept and cooed on schedule. Then came Heather, and a huge load of humility. Still, even on the days when Lynn prayed for a passing band of gypsies to whom she could sell the squalling baby, she knew that she'd fight her way to the roof of a burning building to save that bit of baggage.

Lynn sighs and realizes that her demeanour has become fraught with sighing. Stop it, she tells herself. Stop it! This time, you are right. Carmen the social worker, Jack, even Marty, have all righteously maintained that they are standing back to allow Heather to make this decision. To do what's best for her and for Beegee. Bullshit. Not one of them has uttered the obvious. Mothers do not give up their babies unless they have no choice. The very fact that Heather has a choice should be the only thing she needs to know.

"Bullshit," Lynn says out loud. And is not surprised when Beegee answers with a whimper. Lynn unravels herself from the quilt and stomps into the bedroom. She scoops up the baby and holds her tight to her heart. "No no, little girl," she says. "You do not have to cry. You are not alone."

12

When Heather opens the bedroom door, the first thing she sees in the kitchen is a fat baby strapped into a high chair. Jenny straightens up from the oven with a pan of muffins in her hand. "Good morning! I hope you don't mind if Owen keeps you company. His daddy had to get up twice in the night with him, so we're letting him sleep." She shakes her finger at the kid.

He's staring at Heather, so she stares back. He's a bland-faced bald little dude. An old-man baby. The way she imagined all babies looked until she saw Beegee's perfect face.

She's barely into the chair, reaching for the glass of orange juice, when Jenny shoves a plate in front of her. Eggs Benedict? It's barely eight o'clock in the morning. Heather wants to eat the bowlful of grapefruit sections, and maybe ask for granola, but she's heard Jenny pounding around in the kitchen for almost an hour. She should have come out and stopped the cooking frenzy instead of dozing until the last minute.

She considers scraping away the sauce, trying to eat the

egg. Her stomach is still churning from last night's mass of chips and deep fried fish. Just the smell of hollandaise brings back the sloshing waves of sickness.

"I don't normally eat anything before ten in the morning." She stares at the bit of ham protruding from under the poached egg. "You went to a lot of trouble. I should have mentioned that I'm a vegetarian." A lie, and she realizes as soon as it's out of her mouth that Jenny sent her out for fish and chips last night, but the woman is standing there looking like a puppy dog desperate for a pat and an attaboy.

"Oh." She frowns. "Well, what would you like?"

Heather points to the muffins steaming on the counter. "One of those would be good." She glances at her watch. "Maybe just wrap it in a napkin and I'll take it with me."

"Don't you even want coffee?"

The baby's lost interest. His head is lolling, the whites of his eyes rolling grossly under droopy eyelids. "Sure." Heather settles into the chair. Okay, she's not the guest Jenny's been imagining while she prettied up that bedroom and hung the sign in the window, but she doesn't have to be an asshole. "Coffee would be great." She reaches for the grapefruit. "Fruit's perfect."

Jenny pours a mug of coffee, hesitates, then takes another cup out of the cupboard. "Mind if I sit with you?"

"Jeez, no. It's your kitchen. Look, I'm sorry. I've never stayed in a bed and breakfast. I should have told you not to cook."

"Hey, we're a pair." Jenny grins, brings the cups to the table. "I've never done this before, but a woman up the street told me Eggs Benedict impresses the heck out of her guests. My guy'll eat it when he wakes up."

"Your baby's head is kind of..." Heather points at the chubby cheek that's now resting on the kid's shoulder. "Shouldn't you put something there for his neck?"

"No way!" Jenny laughs. "If I touch him he'll wake up. The only break I get is when he's sleeping. He's fine." She studies Heather. "How old is your baby?"

Tell her Beegee is only three weeks old and already Heather's had a break from her? "A bit younger than him," she says vaguely. While she stares at the sleeping baby, she feels the rush of milk in her breasts. She takes a long drink of coffee, looks out the window beyond Jenny. The morning is a filthy grey. Without looking down, she knows new circles are forming under her jacket. Like rings on a tree, the flannel shirt is going to record the number of times today she should have been feeding Beegee.

"Actually," she says, "my baby is only three weeks old and things are a bit of a mess." She glances at her watch again. "Which is why I'd better get moving."

In spite of a wind that feels like it's blowing straight down from Alaska, Heather stays out on the ferry deck. She's glad now that she didn't turn up her nose at the huge olive green sweatshirt Jenny insisted she borrow.

"You'll freeze," she said. "And besides I never wear this." Jeez, wonder why, Jenny. It's the colour of something you'd scrape off the side of the fish tank. Still, Heather had pulled on the sweatshirt, looking like the Michelin man with her jacket zipped over top. "You can drop it off on your way back. Stop and show us your baby." Like Beegee and pudding-head Owen can play together? Or like Jenny doesn't believe Heather will get her baby back?

Heather feels her hair wriggling up around her face from the damp. Those sweetsy curls she's been trying to straighten since she was six years old. And Beegee? Donna's already said she has a friend from Trinidad who's promised to show her how to do gazillions of cute things with Beegee's hair, but Heather hopes the kid is spunky enough to want to wear it wild.

How long has it been now since Lynn ran off with Beegee? Four days. A long time when you're only three weeks
old. The baby changed so much in the first week. Although
she never had that scary look that Heather remembers from
other babies. Scrunch-faced aliens with huge heads and
scrawny, twisted legs. Not that she's spent much time in her
life looking at babies. Lynn tried to talk her into babysitting
for a neighbour when she was twelve, and Heather told her
she'd rather walk dogs. That turned out to be a pretty decent
business, along with delivering flyers. She bought a skate-
board that summer. Maybe she'll buy one for Beegee some
day. Send it on her twelfth birthday. She imagines Belinda,
with black wings of hair, flying on a skate.

Every bit of Beegee is perfect. Fingernails like tiny seashells. Hair that towels dry like dandelion fluff. Heather felt
such a strong jolt every time she pressed her face into the
folds of the baby's neck, she was terrified. She screamed at
Lynn when Beegee was only two days old. "Why didn't you
tell me! How could you not warn me about this?"

"I thought I had," Lynn said. And then while Heather
rocked and crooned, there was a look of slow dawning on
her mother's face. "Oh, Heather," she said, "there's part of it
no one can describe."

Okay, so there were some secrets. Heather wasn't joining
any sisterhood, or magical circle of motherhood. Apparently
there were women who drown in their hormones, but she
wasn't one of them.

"Thanks a lot, Mother," she said. "But it doesn't make a
bit of difference." She handed Beegee to Lynn and walked
out of the room. In the bathroom, she leaned on the sink
and studied her puffy face in the mirror. Even while she was
gritting her teeth, determined that the tears were going to
stop, they gushed out of her eyes with the same stubborn
insistence as the milk that kept welling in her breasts.

Now, the memory of it makes her clamp her elbows to her chest. She imagines this same jackknife reflex months from now whenever she thinks about Beegee. Maybe Carmen is right; the once-a-month visits she's insisted on will only make it harder for the first year. Maybe a year from now, Heather won't even recognize the kid they carry into the living room when she comes to call. She'll be Belinda, Donna and Grant's little girl by then. Not a baby anymore, but a dusky-skinned, curly-haired, big-eyed girl. They won't have to carry her. She'll walk in all on her own. Is that possible?

The first words out of Donna's mouth after Heather finally agreed to let them come to the hospital for a quick peek were, "Oh, but she's so fair!" Carmen had looked as though she wanted to shove a sock in poor Donna's mouth, but Heather felt sorry for her. She was up to the ass herself with all the things Carmen warned her about saying and doing, and she was glad that for once Donna had said what flashed into her mind. Yeah, they would be happy to raise a mixed-race child, any child, but if the baby looked like them, wouldn't that be even better? Who could blame her for feeling that way?

Heather hunches forward in the deck chair, elbows on her knees. The ferry is gliding through fog so thick that she's lost sight of both the mainland and the island toward which she's moving.

An hour later, Heather is in Nanaimo. She finds a cyber café that looks more interesting than the donut shop down the street, orders a large latté and a spinach and feta scone. It's ten-thirty. A civilized time for breakfast. On impulse, she pays for internet time, sits down at a computer. Logs on to her webmail, scans the Inbox. Oh joy. Carmen@lovingarms.

ab.ca has sent her a message: HEATHER. WHERE ARE YOU?? WE MUST TALK.

Yeah, yeah. She'll phone Carmen as soon as she has the plan figured out. For now, Carmen can wait just like everyone else. Heather might call Jack when she gets to Quadra. He's likely talked to Marty, and he'll have phoned Lynn at Einar's place, and bullied her into coming back. Maybe she'll pass Lynn on the highway going the other way.

She opens emails from a couple of friends who obviously think she's gone ahead with the adoption already. Lots of "Ohmigod you must be wrecked. Call me. We'll talk." About what? The Experience? She wants to crawl into a hole when she remembers mouthing off about wanting the experience but not the responsibility. Lynn, with her lips thin, told her that it might be best she didn't put that in writing, in case Beegee happened upon those papers some day.

She logs off, carries her coffee and scone to a table by the window.

"How's the latté?" The guy behind the counter wanders out and collects cups from one of the other tables. If he asks if she's traveling alone and wants to know where she's going, she's going to throw the scone at him.

"It's cold," she says, and clunks the cup down hard.

He grins. "No problemo! I'll make you a new one." He whisks the cup off the table, and hovers over the plate. "You want me to nuke this and bring you some more butter?"

Heather shrugs, and while he's messing around with a fresh coffee, she hangs her jacket on the chair and wanders to the washroom at the back of the room. The toilet is clean but it stinks. She glances down at the wastepaper basket, at the crinkly plastic of a disposable diaper. Imagines someone changing their baby on the floor in the tiny room.

After she's washed her hands, dragged a comb out of her

bag and raked the tangle of curls behind her ears, she opens the door and calls to the barrista.

"When you get a minute you might want to empty the trash. There's a diaper in here."

"Aw jeez!" He slips out from behind the counter with a green garbage bag. "My girlfriend. She comes in with our kid every morning. I keep telling her to change him at home."

He looks like he should still be in high school. Does everyone have to have a baby? She's probably going to arrive at Einar's cabin and find out that he's had one too. Or for sure that woman down the road. Every summer they went out to Quadra there was another baby at her place.

The new latté isn't any hotter than the first one, but she gives the guy a break. Drinks about half of it, munches her way through the scone, makes another trip to the can. On the way out, she points to the phone on the counter. "Mind if I use that? It's long distance, but I'll charge it to a calling card. You can listen if you want, to make sure I do."

"Nah, I trust you. Go ahead." He laughs. Heather can see how the girlfriend got snagged. The guy has a heartbreaker smile. "Besides, tomorrow's my last day. I won't be around when the boss gets the bill for your call to Thailand."

Marty answers all businesslike. She pictures him sitting in his cubicle at work. Some day he'll have a real office, he tells her, and will have found the woman of his dreams. He's on a quest, her brother, that sometimes makes her downright scared for him.

"Hey, I'm in Nanaimo, should be at Einar's by this afternoon. What's up?"

"Finally! Why the hell didn't you call me last night? You didn't drive all night, did you?"

"Nope. Stayed with my new friends. Remind me to tell you about them some day. Did you talk to Lynn?"

"Well, yeah. I told her you were on your way."

"How about Jack?"

"He already knew. Lynn phoned him."

"That's a switch."

"Listen, when do you think you'll be back?"

"Just as quick as I can make it," she says. "I may even leave tonight as soon as I pick up Beegee. Stop somewhere to sleep and then drive the rest of the way tomorrow.

"Alone with the baby?"

The coffee guy has wandered outside and is leaning against the wall talking to someone. "Lynn came out here alone, didn't she?"

"Sure, but she knows what to do with a baby." His voice drops off the cliff. "Listen," he says more quietly. "Call me as soon as you get there. I've been thinking about all this Heather. We need to talk."

She hangs up the phone, gets into the car and the coffee guy waves goodbye. She's making so many friends along the way she may have to come back again.

At the first red light, she glances at the map. It's going to take her at least two-and-a-half hours to get to Campbell River. Maybe another half hour waiting for the ferry. Half, three-quarters of an hour to get over and find her way to Einar's place. By then it'll be the middle of the afternoon. Maybe leaving tonight isn't such a good idea. She'll figure it out when she gets there. But she knows for sure that she's going home in Lynn's car. Lynn can drive this one to Calgary.

Just before Parksville, Heather passes a hitchhiker. Female this time. A bedraggled-looking bird. It's been raining for the past half hour, and the girl is drenched. Blonde hair plastered against her skull, a saggy sweater that must weigh more than she does. At the next intersection, Heather loops back and cruises up at the same time as a rusty truck with two guys in the cab. She pulls in front and watches. The girl stops beside the truck, the door opens, then she looks up and sees Heather's car. Heather turns in her seat and waves. The girl begins to run toward her. The truck roars past on the gravel shoulder, spinning rocks at the side of the car.

The girl wrenches the door open and slides in. "Shit-heads!" She shakes her hair, spraying wet onto the windshield. "Hey, thanks! I've been freezing my buns off for like hours. I kissed off at least four other creeps before these last two." She looks familiar. Her voice has a slight twang to it that Heather's sure she remembers.

"Where you going?"

"Quadra. Dump me in CR. Oh please don't tell me you're turning off in another five minutes."

"I wouldn't have stopped if I was only going ten kilometres." Heather reaches into the back of the car and throws the girl the pukey green sweatshirt. "There's a muffin in the pouch if you're hungry." She looks like she'd eat right through the plastic if she had any more trouble getting it unwrapped. Her lips are blue, and she's shaking so badly she can hardly get the crumbling bran muffin to her mouth. Big brown eyes and blond hair that used to be braided so tight she could stick feathers into the criss-cross plaits and turn herself into a bird. "So what do you have to do on Quadra?"

"I live there. Used to anyway. I need to talk to my mom."

Heather slows down, signals to turn into a Husky station that's coming up fast. "Me too, Sunny," she says. "But let's stop and buy you a real breakfast first."

The girl stares at her, then claps her hands together like a little kid. "Hey! You're the girl from Calgary. Einar's snooty friends." One hand flies to cover her mouth. "Oops."

"Yeah," Heather says. "That would be us."

Inside, Sunny orders pancakes, spreads on three pats of butter, drenches them in syrup, but after the first mouthful she puts the fork down. She looks as though she'd like to spit the food into the napkin she's holding in her hand, but she finally swallows. "I guess I'm not that hungry." She leans back. "Man, is this ever weird, you coming back to Quadra. A couple of years ago, I almost hitched out to Calgary. I thought I'd give you a call when I got there, maybe crash at your place for a few days."

Wouldn't that have been swell? Jack would have called the child welfare people and had Sunny shipped home faster than you could say "runaway juvenile."

"So what are you doing out here now? You're coming to visit Einar?" Even as spaced-out as Sunny seems to be, she looks puzzled.

"It's a little more complicated than that," Heather says. "My mom's already here, with my baby."

"You've got a baby?" Sunny rolls her eyes. "Well that sucks." Then she shakes her head. "Excuse me if you wanted one, but there's no way I'm ever having kids."

Good thing, Heather thinks. If Sunny was any skinnier, or sicker-looking, it would probably kill her to have a baby. "Where have you been?" Heather asks. "You still live at home?"

"No." She drums her fingers on the table and looks around the room. "I really need a smoke."

"No luck here," Heather says. Or in my car, she'd like to add. She'll pay for food on Jack's credit card but damned if she's buying cigarettes. In this light, Sunny really does look sick. Her skin has a mottled look, scaly patches on her forehead and cheekbones, brown splotches under her eyes. She picks at the edges of the pancake with her fork. When the waitress brings her tea, she pours it when it's barely coloured, and stirs in three packets of sugar. Her hand shakes when she lifts the cup, slopping tea into the saucer. They sit there watching the other customers for a while.

"So how have you been anyway?" Sunny asks suddenly, blinking at Heather as though she's just noticed her sitting there.

Compared to you, Heather thinks, pretty freakin' wonderful. Even though I didn't want a baby either. "Not bad," she says. "You about finished with that?"

Sunny nods and stands immediately, but detours to the washroom.

As soon as they're back in the car, Sunny gives Heather directions for the faster inland road, then curls up against the door to sleep. Heather glances at her every now and again, wondering what the story is. Sunny's a year or two younger than Heather. She looks like a kid who's been on the streets for years. And yet Heather remembers her as regular kind of lippy girl who liked riding her bike and jumping over waves until she was blue with cold. She had a bossy mother, but the kind who looks after everyone and makes sure they eat their granola.

Traffic is light, and the scenery just more of the same forest except for the occasional shrine at the side of the road. Heather hates these wooden crosses, plastic flowers, sad-looking mementoes of traffic fatalities. What if she and Sunny got wiped out right here on this next bend? Eighteen years from now Beegee might get curious about her past and come looking for where her real mother died. Except who'd tell her about the accident? And if Heather dies on the way to Quadra, without signing the adoption papers, that probably makes Lynn and Jack Beegee's legal guardians. Lynn would keep her? That's an interesting twist. Lynn doesn't want Heather to give Beegee away, but would she raise her? Or maybe Winston would have custody and take her back to Jamaica. His mom would raise her along with the other grandkids. That was already Winston's contribution to the plan.

Just outside Campbell River, Sunny wakes up but she's too groggy to be of any help with directions. Heather's surprised when she can remember all the turns to get to the ferry dock. It's been about five years since she made this trip and she never paid much attention from the back seat. When they pull into the line-up at the ticket booth behind a flashy red sports car, Sunny leaps out and zigzags between cars to a building on the other side of the parking lot. Washrooms.

With the windows rolled up, the car is muggy. The smell of Sunny's damp clothing has stayed behind. After a decent night's sleep, caffeine, Heather should be wide awake, but she would love to take her cue from Sunny, and curl up in her own corner. She opens the window and lets the rain cool her face.

The rain on Quadra always made Lynn crazy. She couldn't stand being closed in by the tall trees, and when the clouds hung down to the ground for more than one day, she'd start packing and rag at Jack to go home early. Heather's sure there were more sunny than rainy days, because whenever she thinks of Quadra, she remembers bikes and the beach and wandering back from the store with Popsicles dripping down their arms faster than they could eat them. Lynn, though, when anyone mentioned Quadra, would mutter about the rain and the interminably long drive to sit in a damp cabin until it was time to turn around and drive home again. And then Jack would calmly suggest they could fly out, rent a car and avoid all that driving if she'd get over her silly fear of flying. The fear, Heather knows, is not silly. They've been to Disneyland twice. The first trip, the drive down took up more of their Easter vacation than the fun spots of California. She was only four years old, and she barely remembers Mickey and Minnie from that visit, but she remembers the arguments about it that went on for years afterwards. The AC quit and they almost fried, they spent a whole day waiting in some pokey little town to get something else fixed, Jack bitched all the way about the driving but wouldn't let Lynn take the wheel. Marty rolls his eyes whenever anyone mentions Disneyland. The second trip, he was sixteen and did not want to spend his Easter vacation at Disneyland with his family, but Jack insisted that it would probably be the last trip they took as a family. He got that right. Marty spent the whole time looking for internet access so he could email his girlfriend. A couple of weeks before their trip, a plane had gone down in the ocean near Los Angeles, and Lynn went hysterical trying to convince Jack to cancel. They weren't flying Alaska Air, he argued, and the fact that there'd just been a major air disaster actually decreased the probability for a while. There was nothing, though, that could decrease the terror on Lynn's face from the minute she stepped onto the plane. She recovered from the flight down just in time for the flight back. Both were wild rides, seat belts on the whole time and Heather, who was sitting next to Lynn, was sure she'd be scarred for life by her mother's fingernails digging into her arm. At the same time she was trying to pretend she didn't know Lynn, the only person on the plane puking into one of those paper sacks that Heather was sure were only for display. So far as she knows, Lynn hasn't flown anywhere since. And she'd have bet money against Lynn ever coming to Quadra again. For any reason.

The cars are starting to load but there's no sign of Sunny. Just when Heather's decided she's not going to look for her whacked-out old playmate, here she is getting back into the car as though she's wafted up from under it. Heather doesn't even want to think about what Sunny might have been up to in the washroom. They end up parked next to the red

Porshe. The blonde who slides out of it looks like she was ordered to match the car.

"I'm going to stretch," Heather tells Sunny. "You getting out?"

Sunny's eyes are closed again and she's breathing like poor old Nana Bishop with her oxygen tank. A good thing, Jack told Heather, that Nana was too far gone to realize that her favourite granddaughter had screwed up.

Up in the lounge, Heather sits in front of the rain-streaked window. The blonde is pacing, arms folded, looking like she's being forced to hang around this tacky old boat. Heather would kill for the butter-coloured leather jacket, but the streaks in the woman's hair are too brassy. The hairdo must have cost her bundle though. Too bad Marty's not here. A little old for him, but this is the type of woman he's been trying to hook up with for the last year or so.

When Quadra appears through the rain, Heather makes her way down to the car. Sunny is sitting up, looking like a new girl. She's pinned her hair up on top of her head in a crazy topknot, her cheeks have pinked up a bit, and the wet sweater is in the back seat. She actually looks good in the B&B sweatshirt.

As soon as Heather's back in her seat, Sunny starts talking. "So this is like some weird reunion, the two of us meeting up and now both of us going home to our mommies. I couldn't wait to move away from home, our house was such a circus, but your mom seemed like a really nice lady." She frowns. "Your dad was kind of a turd though, wasn't he? Is he still around?"

"Sure." Heather's not sure why she answered that snoopy question even though it was with a half-truth. She asks one of her own. "So why are you going home?"

"To see my mom. I've been in Victoria for a while. We got kicked out of the place I was living in and everybody

184

else took off for Seattle, but I couldn't get across the border because somebody stole my ID. Hey, I could ride to Calgary with you. I know these guys who were supposed to be moving out there last month for some really good jobs. Maybe I could stay with you until I hook up with them."

"How about I get back to you on that?" Heather says.

13

Lynn picks up the New Zealand copy of *National Geographic,* studies a photo of a pair of royal albatrosses. Eighty-five per cent of their life spent at sea, they only come back to land to breed. Monogamous birds. She tosses the magazine aside.

Since morning, she's contemplated fashioning a sling out of one of Einar's shirts and taking Beegee for a long walk. But she's afraid Heather will arrive while they're out, and panic at the empty cabin, her mother's car covered in needles and cones as though it's been abandoned for weeks. Lynn knows she should have the coffee on, be sitting up straight with a coherent explanation of the kidnapping of Beegee at the ready. She should be anxious, both on Heather's behalf, and about the outcome of this day, but she is so weary from the long night of lying awake, listening, that even worry takes too much energy. Beegee is sound asleep in the bedroom after a morning of surprising alertness. Loki is asleep on the floor beside the bed. So seize this moment of calm, Lynn tells herself, and she stretches out on the sofa, the old blanket wrapped around her feet.

She dozes, floats, and dreams that she is standing on a beach, Beegee in her arms, waves lapping her toes. Then a rogue wave rises out of the sea, curls toward her, and rushes for shore. Her feet turn to cement in the soft sand. All she can do is clutch the baby in her crossed arms and wait to feel her torn away. But waiting with the strange detachment that a daytime dream brings. Only a dream, but still, when she opens her eyes her mouth is dry, and her feet tangle in the loopy afghan as she tries to kick free.

She sits up, ears tuned for the sound of Heather's car. Or Einar's truck. This morning the rain was lashing down in such heavy curtains she couldn't see to the end of the driveway to check if he was still there. True to his word, he's been quiet, so quiet she didn't hear him come inside at all. When she got up there was a pot of lukewarm coffee on the stove. By early afternoon, the rain let up and she looked out to find the driveway empty.

Lynn stares at the door, wondering who will be the first one through. Heather will knock. Or will she remember that this cabin door is never locked and rush in, angry and with every right to be so? At home Lynn locks her doors, but refuses to use the security system Jack installed before he moved out. As though he was leaving a bit of himself behind to ensure that no one trespassed.

Lynn plans to sell the house if she can take the last step and sign the listing that has already been drawn up. The paint is bought, and sometime soon she'll ask Marty to spend a few weekends helping her spruce the place up. The house isn't shabby enough to list as a "handyman's special", but a bit too faded to be appealing. A quick cosmetic fix, she's been told, will guarantee a good price and a quick sale.

Lynn never imagined moving until she spent a month

working as a temp in a real estate office. She thought she might take the course, get her license, sell houses. One of a dozen ideas she'd tossed around when she decided that she would not ever again under any circumstances, work in a school. Not as a clerical worker, library assistant, special classroom aide, or lunchroom supervisor. Those were the jobs Jack found for her, and in his twenty-year career, he has taught in so many schools that it is impossible for Lynn to be anything but Jack Bishop's ex-wife.

After listening to the realtors in the office, Lynn knew within a week that she would never make a living in sales. But house prices have gone wild, and now is the time to make a move. At first she only flirted with the idea, the "what if", but then she began looking at listings for condos with clean walls and shiny floors, tiny patios that would require only two lush pots of flowers to make a garden, outdoor maintenance provided. Surely a person would feel liberated in such a space. She was on the verge of signing when Beegee was born, and then Heather announced that she was coming home.

Into the third week, Lynn began to think that it would be best to keep the house. She dared to imagine Heather and Beegee in their own apartment, but frequent visitors so that the space, especially the fenced back yard would be a good thing. She dared to imagine being a grandmother in her house. Heather will be gone soon.

Lynn walks across the room to put away the few dishes she left to drain earlier. Housekeeping is easy in this small home. In fact this is all the space she needs in a new place. She shudders when she thinks of emptying her house. Both Marty and Heather moved out but left their childhoods behind. Everything outgrown remains archived in Lynn's house. Even Jack left old clothes, books, boxes of papers related to his father's dying and his mother's senility. All these things she's crammed to the back of her mind for the past few months because she's been preoccupied with Heather. Heather's pregnancy, Heather's adoption plan, Heather's labour and delivery, Heather's baby.

She tiptoes back to the bedroom, and sits on the edge of the bed. Loki hears the car before Lynn does, and races to the door. The muffled thud of a car door closing, then light footsteps on the porch. Lynn takes a shaky breath and follows the dog.

Heather stands in the doorway. For a few seconds she looks unsure of herself, but as soon as she sees Lynn she plants her hands on her hips, and pulls up tall. This is not the Heather of last week with swollen eyes and a lifeless mat of hair. This is Heather with eyes flashing, curls bouncing. Heather in the ubiquitous black leggings and Winston's shirt. She goes from hands on hips to arms crossed, making it very clear that she does not want her mother to rush across the room with an embrace. Loki stands guard in front of her, a low growl issuing from his throat.

"Hey, Loki." Silly dog gives a woof of welcome and then flops back down in front of the stove. "Where's Beegee?"

"She's fine, Heather," Lynn says as her daughter makes a beeline for the bedroom. Lynn's knees feel so weak she's afraid she won't be able to follow, but after another deep breath, she finds a stride as sure as Heather's. Watches her fall on her knees beside the bed and pull the baby into her arms. Lynn has played this moment so many times in her mind, but of course none of it will go as she imagined. She walks across the creaking floor into the bedroom, sits on the edge of the bed, rests her hand on Heather's hair.

"I'm sorry, Heather. So very sorry." She expects the hand to be pushed away, and is relieved that it's not. "I didn't know what else to do."

"You could have done what I asked you to do." She can barely talk through the great gulping sobs. "Jeez, Lynn!"

The baby is still asleep, but won't be for long, Lynn thinks. She lowers her voice to a whisper. "We'll talk in a bit. I'll leave you alone for now."

When Heather kicks off her shoes, and curls around Beegee on the bed, Lynn pulls the quilt over both of them. She stands in the doorway, almost dizzy with relief. But when she pulls the door quietly closed, she remembers, like a quick slap to the side of her head, that she is out of this picture. The young woman asleep on the bed with her baby, is back in charge.

Lynn begins with the bathroom. She scrubs sink, tub, toilet. Ties up the top of the bag that holds the dirty diapers, sets it outside next to another one full of towels and the items she's borrowed from Einar, the baby clothes from Hannah. Before she leaves, she'll find the laundromat.

Magazines tidied into a pile, blanket folded on the sofa, ashes swept from the hearth, she puts on a fresh pot of coffee, wishes she had the ingredients to make broccoli cheddar soup. Heather has likely not eaten in hours.

Oddly, the cabin seems even quieter now with the three of them than it did with just two. Lynn tiptoes around the room, hoping Heather will sleep for a good long time, wishing she would wake up now so that finally this waiting will be over. She sinks onto the sofa with a pillow in her arms. Thinks about Heather holding Beegee as though raging wolves couldn't tear her away. If nothing else, this foolish thing Lynn has done has given Heather the chance to take Beegee back one more time before she gives her away for good. Like one more taste at the end of the best meal ever. Beyond this moment, though, Lynn has no expectations.

She wishes Einar were here so she could say, "See. This is why the old way was wrong." Except he would argue that this proved his point. That Lynn, holding Marty two weeks after he was born, with no prior knowledge of the warm weight of him in her arms, was better off. If things hadn't worked out, if her request to have consent revoked had been refused, she would never really have known what she was missing. She would argue back that she would indeed. That when Heather was born, the flood of tears that had so astounded everyone was not just Lynn's joy over her baby girl, but real grief that she had missed the first two weeks of Marty's life. She has never stopped mourning that loss. The one comfort all this time is that Marty doesn't know she'd set him aside even so briefly. Then why, she asks herself, is she wrestling with this need to tell? She squeezes the pillow even tighter. Because she feels as though it's made a liar of her, that's why.

Lynn smoothes the wrinkled pillow case and looks around the room. There is nothing to do. When Heather wakes up, Lynn will apologize again, try to explain, and they will talk.

The coffee has been burbling for some time now. Lynn gives herself a shake and gets up off the sofa. She feels as though she's the one who's just arrived after a fourteen-hour drive. The energy she so optimistically felt returning yesterday, blew out the door when Heather came in. While she's filling her cup, she hears the sound of someone else arriving. Kind man that he is, Einar knocks, giving warning before he opens the door. He'll have seen Heather's car in the driveway. He hesitates on the threshold.

"She's asleep," Lynn says. "Both of them are. Come in, Einar. You live here. I'm so sorry for all this."

He pulls off his boots. "What can you do? It'll sort itself out soon, I guess. Have you talked?"

"Not at all. She only got here half an hour ago. The baby will be awake soon, though. It's been a long time since she was fed." She takes another mug from the cupboard and pours coffee for him. "Not nearly as strong as you like it, I'm afraid. Can I make you something to eat?" He must wonder if that's her answer to everything. She's always trying to feed someone. It won't be long until she's trying to get Heather to eat.

He shakes his head, sits down at the table and stirs sugar into the coffee. "And you?" he asks. "How are you holding up?"

She isn't even tempted to lie. "Not well. I have the horrible feeling that all this has been a huge mistake on my part. For a little while yesterday, I was convinced I did the right thing, but as soon as I saw Heather's face…"

She sips her coffee and looks out the window. At the driveway. Einar's car is parked directly behind Heather's car, which is parked in front of the step. The parking spot next to the woodpile is empty. She feels the coffee hit her stomach like a water balloon. "Where's my car?" she says.

Einar clomps to the window beside her. He looks out into the wet, then at Lynn, then into the yard again. He opens the door and they step outside together. There is no sign of Lynn's navy blue 1999 Honda Accord. Lynn put the bag of diapers out not more than twenty minutes ago, but she's sure she barely registered what was beyond the step, she was so intent on the scene in the bedroom. Back and forth, they try to remember who last saw the car, and when. Was it there last night when the ghost of Hannah was walking the road? Lynn remembers seeing the truck, imagining Einar asleep in the small camper unit on the back. But her own car? How long since she even looked at it? Einar's sure it was there this morning when he left. But maybe not.

"Okay," he says, "we don't know how long it's been gone, but it's gone. I'd better call the boys." He knows the RCMP officers on Quadra well, he assures her. The car is likely still on the island. Some kid took it for a joyride.

192

"Happens all the time?" She's trying to keep her voice calm, but her throat is so tight her words come out an octave higher than usual. The coffee cup slips from her hands and cracks in two on the step. Her hands shake when she picks up the pieces, coffee dripping from her fingers. It's a car, she tells herself. Don't you dare cry about a stupid car! She wipes her hand on her jeans.

Einar puts on his boots, walks up to the road, then comes back and drives his truck a couple of kilometers in every direction. To be sure, he says, the whole thing wasn't just a prank, the car left sitting in the ditch spitting-distance from home, rather than an actual theft. After he's come back and they've gone inside and Einar's phoned the RCMP, given them all the details about the car, he turns to Lynn.

"Don't worry," he says. "They'll find it."

He looks out the window again and tugs at his beard. "Maybe I have a clue." Then he picks up the phone again. "Hannah!" His voice booms.

Lynn finally drops the broken mug into the garbage. Not a sound from behind the bedroom door, but she feels as though it's bulging, so much trapped behind it. Forget the car. The car is nothing. What's the worst thing that could possibly happen? The car will either never be found or it will be a write-off when it is. And what will she have to do because of it? Drive back with Heather—is that so terrible? As Einar says, no big deal. Worst-case scenario. Something her dad taught her to imagine when she was a kid. A worrier.

Now she remembers that when she was no longer a kid, but Heather's age and pregnant and sobbing her eyes out, her dad asked the same thing. What's the worst thing that could possibly happen, Lynn? She'd thought a long time. My baby will die? she finally whispered. After she'd gone home from the hospital without even holding the baby, left him behind for the social worker, she'd felt as though he had died.

But he did not die, she tells herself sternly. Marty is alive and well, Beegee and Heather are alive and well. For God's sake, pull yourself together.

Einar hangs up the phone. "So, we'll find it. Don't worry. I thought maybe one of Hannah's kids might have seen something. She's going to ask the boys."

In the length of time it takes Einar to pour Lynn another cup of coffee, Hannah must have flown out her front door, because she barges in, coatless, sandals flapping.

"That little shit!"

"Shhh!" Einar jumps up and puts his finger to his lips, points to the bedroom door.

Hannah looks from him, to Lynn, to the door. "Heather's here?"

"Sleeping," Einar says. "Maybe we should go outside."

Hannah lowers her voice. She sags against the kitchen counter, rubbing her temples with her fingertips. "Your car," she says to Lynn. "It was probably Josh. Goddamn, I'm going to kill that kid. Or better yet, send him to live with his dad. He took off again last night and didn't come home."

And his mother paced the road, waiting for him, Lynn thinks. Or walking off her frustration?

"You'd better call the cops and tell them to look for Josh. It's about time he got a serious shake-up." Hannah's brushing away tears. Lynn can hear sounds from the bedroom now, Heather's voice.

Einar takes Hannah's arm and steers her toward the door. "If it was Josh, he'll bring it back. We don't need to tell the police. They've got all the information, let them work on it. They'll take their time, like always." He turns back to Lynn. "I'm going up to Hannah's for a minute, and then I'll take off for a couple of hours."

Poor man. Turfed out of his house yet again. Beegee is crying, and Lynn is afraid that it might be Heather's sobbing she's hearing as well. She taps on the bedroom door before she opens it.

"She doesn't want me anymore," Heather says, calm and dry-eyed. She's at the window, holding the flailing baby in her arms. She lifts Beegee to her shoulder. The nightgown has come untied, and the baby's back is bare, as mottled with anger as her face. "I tried to get her to nurse, but she acts like I'm killing her. I guess that problem's solved."

"No," Lynn says, close enough now to smell the problem. "I doubt it. Until this morning she was fussing so much at the bottle…" Well, never mind what she had to do. This is not the time—there may never be a time—that Heather needs to know about her baby at her mother's breast, or the neighbour's. Beegee's crying has reached a volume that makes it impossible to talk anyway. Cloth diapers do not hermetically seal the baby's bum the way Pampers do. Heather's shirt sleeve is at risk. "Come," Lynn says, and leads Heather to the bathroom. She fills the sink with water, drapes the last dry towel in the room over the toilet seat. All of Einar's threadbare towels are now co-opted for baby use. She folds a clean diaper, lays a fresh nightgown beside it. Afraid that Heather is going to hand the baby to her, she leaves and closes the door behind her. Goes straight across the room, and out onto the porch. In the wet, the rusted fender on Heather's car looks like a freshly scabbed wound. But if the car brought Heather here with no difficulty, then it will get the three of them back to Calgary. Lynn tilts her head. The treetops are shrouded in mist. With luck, once they're off these islands the clouds will lift, and the road home will be dry. All those hours, whatever talking does not get finished here will be done in the car. Surely by Banff, Lynn will have been able to steer Heather down all those side roads she's refused to travel. Even if the decision is the same, every bit of territory will have been explored.

The air is so drenched, Lynn feels as though she'll drown if she takes the next breath. She goes inside, contemplates the clock on the kitchen wall. Too late in the day to leave now. It will be dark in another hour. Still, they could at least get off this island by nighttime, sleep somewhere else. She looks around the now so familiar room. No, best to stay until morning. Babies, she knows from long ago experience, even babies as small as Beegee, sleep best in the places they know. Marty wailed inconsolably the first three nights at home. Lynn was allowed, finally, to talk on the phone to the foster mother who'd had him. They always do, for at least a couple of days, she said. Hang in there, and best of luck to you, dear.

All is quiet in the bathroom now. Lynn knocks again, waits. "Come in," Heather says softly. She's on the floor, leaning against the wall, Beegee nursing in her arms. If Lynn was inclined to pray, she would offer a prayer of thanks for this kind mercy. She was afraid the nipple confusion that made Hannah scowl might now have reversed itself, Beegee deciding the plastic was her surest bet.

"Good," Lynn says. "Do you want to come out to the rocking chair?"

"No. I don't want to move until she's done."

"Okay. When you're ready, come sit by the fire. I'll make you something to eat."

While she scrambles eggs, makes toast, puts the kettle on for tea, Lynn keeps an eye on the two framed in the bathroom doorway. She wants to hear soft murmuring, see the baby's cheek stroked while she nurses, but Heather has her head against the wall, her eyes closed. When Lynn looks back again after she's poured the boiling water over the tea, Heather is in front of the mirror, Beegee in the crook of one arm, the other hand splashing water on her face.

She walks into the room as stony-faced and appraising as

she was when she first came through the door. Carries the baby to the sofa, and settles her into the nest that's become part of the décor, then picks up the plate of scrambled eggs from the table and returns to sit beside Beegee. Lynn tucks kindling around the embers in the fireplace and fans them back to life.

"Looks like you've settled in really well," Heather says.

"I'm sorry," Lynn says, and wonders how many times she will utter these two words before it's over. To how many different people.

Heather puts the plate down, and folds her arms over the plaid shirt. "Yeah, me too, because you have really fucked up my plan, Lynn." She stops with her lips parted, tongue between her teeth. "Aw, man, I am so angry, I don't think we should talk for a while." She stands up and pounds across the room to the window.

Lynn wishes she had a cup of tea in her hands, but the coffee has already made her jittery. "No, Heather, that's the problem, I think. I've had all this time to think and it seems to me the problem is that we don't talk. None of us. We keep leaving the room, and closing the door behind us. I shouldn't have left. I should have opened your bedroom door and come in and told you why I couldn't be the delivery girl." Now her own anger is rising. The baby asleep, the crackle of the fire, the warmth spreading through the room, does she tell Heather how heartless it was to ask that of her mother? She knows the way this girl reacts. A misstep and Heather could easily bundle Beegee into the car and fly away. The back of Lynn's throat is beginning to ache again. That three-week-old pain that she suddenly realizes has subsided in the past two days.

Heather doesn't turn from the window. "Okay, let's talk then. I suppose it's been raining since you got here. Maybe a good place to start is by telling me why the hell you came here, of all places."

"I don't know. That's the God-honest truth, kiddo. I don't know." She would like to walk up behind Heather, put her hands on her shoulders, turn her around. But that stance holds her back. The baby is fretting, squirming in her blanket. If she was on her stomach, she would probably have gotten rid of the gas on her own. Lynn hesitates, then picks her up. "When I got in the car, I knew I couldn't take Beegee to Donna...Heather, do you realize I don't even know their last name?"

"McDonald," she says. "How could you forget that after Grant's bad jokes about naming the baby Ronald if it was a boy?"

Lynn doesn't think Heather ever told her the adopting couple's surname. She certainly wasn't there for the bad jokes about names. But that's not the point. "What I mean is that I felt like I was being asked to put my beautiful granddaughter into the arms of total strangers. And then walk away."

Heather finally turns from the window. She lets her hands drop to her sides. "Why did you pick her up? She was quiet."

"No. She needed a burp." Beegee is asleep again, but obstinately, Lynn hangs on to her. When the phone rings, she gestures to Heather to answer it.

She could have guessed that it was Jack.

"I'm fine," Heather says. "Yeah, she is too." Lynn doesn't know if it's the baby or her Jack would ask about first. Is the baby okay? Has your mother lost her mind? With the quick sense that she needs to stop whatever Jack has in his mind, she jumps up with the baby in her arms, tries to get Heather to give her the phone, but Heather shakes her head. "Sure," she says. "That'll work. See you in the morning." She hangs up the phone.

"Heather, call him back. He doesn't need to come."

"Too late. He's in Victoria."

"Why didn't you let me talk to him?" She could call. She has Jack's cell number. Tell him what? To turn around and go home, they don't need him? Precisely. But that won't sit well with Heather.

"Because I didn't want to listen to the two of you ragging at each other even if I only got half the conversation. It's a good thing he's coming. He flew out. You can flip to see who gets to drive my car back. I'm going home in yours, but this way I won't have to drive."

Somehow they have to chip through this wall of anger before Jack arrives. Lynn hands the baby to Heather. "I think she needs a few more burps before sleep. Why don't you rock her." She pours a cup of tea, stirs in milk and sugar and carries it to Heather. The baby's blanket has fallen open. Lynn reaches in and tucks the ends of the nightgown around Beegee. "You've probably never even seen a baby in one of these," she says. "The ties go in the back."

"Whatever."

"What did you tell Carmen?"

Heather looks up at the ceiling. "I told her my mother was even more of a crazy woman than she feared. But that I'd be back in Calgary with the baby in a couple of days. To tell Donna and Grant to hang in there."

Heather has always been so blunt and to-the-bone, she lies badly. "Heather, have you talked with her?"

"Of course I have. Now I can phone back and tell her that I'll be home by—the day after tomorrow—I don't even know what day it is anymore. And she can tell the McDonalds." She looks down at the baby. "She's asleep. Can you put her back on the sofa? I need to go for a walk. I feel like every muscle in my body has turned into lard."

Lynn knows this is pay-back. After that first clutching

of Beegee to her breast, Heather is determined not to show any attachment in front of Lynn. All those hours in the car, this girl has had too much time to fume and foment. Maybe she's had so much time away from the baby that she's going to use this as preparation for the first time she visits Beegee as "the birthmother." Lynn is tired of being simultaneously shut out and dragged in. She shakes her head. "A walk is a good idea, but you need to take Beegee with you. I'm going to the laundromat to wash the things Hannah lent us, and it's too hard to take her along." She looks out the window. "It's not raining anymore. You can tuck her into your coat. I don't imagine you'll go far, will you?" Lynn's inward cringing at the hardness in her own voice is even greater than the look of surprise on Heather's face.

"Sure. Fine. You go do laundry." Heather's out of the chair so fast, and into her jacket and shoes, Lynn doesn't have time to offer to hold the baby. Out the door, down the steps and in a minute the two of them have disappeared into the trees.

Lynn sinks into the rocking chair, still warm from Heather and Beegee. She's said she was going, so now she must, even though the last thing she wants to do is step outside into the dusk. Damp towels, baby clothes, and the t-shirts she's borrowed from Einar crammed into a plastic bag, she's out on the step, reaching down for the dirty diapers before she remembers that there is no ignition into which to fit the key in her hand. Nothing but a patch of darkness next to the woodpile.

14

Heather stops under the dripping trees and looks back at the house. All the way out here, she's been imagining Lynn and Beegee alone in a dark cabin. She'd almost forgotten about Einar sliding around in his woolen socks. She remembers watching Einar knit, poking Marty until he was about to explode from holding back the giggles. Lynn grabbing Marty and Heather, fingers digging into their armpits, hauling them onto the porch until they could behave "like human beings instead of turkeys." As soon as she allowed them back inside, they cracked up again and went running into the rain where they gobbled until they ached. Heather wishes that something, anything, would make her laugh like that again. She's been trying to quietly snort back tears ever since she came out of the bedroom with Beegee. Probably what Lynn wants to see, a whole lot of messy emoting. No way.

She thought she'd just stand out here until Lynn leaves, and then go right back in again. Where the heck is Lynn's car, though? Heather peeks into her jacket, still trying to absorb the shock of that warm weight in her arms once again.

Beegee's wound up tight in a blanket-towel. Even in this light, her face is a surprising dusky rose against the faded blue towel. Fringe of black hair soft as cat's fur dips into a peak over her crinkled-up brow. Eyes the colour of deep water on a dark night, pupils huge. "Smile," Heather whispers, but Beegee's eyes stay intently fixed on hers.

"So what do we do, little Miss Trouble? Drive down to Victoria with Jack tomorrow—oh spare me the lecture on what a great future I have without you—and then fly home. Call Carmen and get her to meet us at the airport. Nah, I'm not having her deliver you to Donna wrapped in a towel. We have to go home first, find something pretty and pink." Heather had noticed the Peter Rabbit sleeper hanging over the edge of the tub. Donna and Grant had brought the outfit to the hospital—sleeper, stupid little hat with ears that Heather buried somewhere at home, and a matching bunting bag to stuff Beegee into. The baby could probably survive an Arctic winter in that sack. Also stuffed away in a drawer.

When Heather finally told Carmen the adopters could come to the hospital, they brought her an obscenely huge bouquet of pink roses and a book of inspirational reading for Lynn—where the hell they'd gotten the notion Lynn was going to pray her way through, Heather had no idea. She wanted to behave decently, let them hold the baby, but instead she'd clung to Beegee for the full ten minutes they stood by the bed looking like famine victims. Told them she was taking Beegee home for a few days, not because she'd changed her mind, but because she'd decided she was too emotional to give her up just yet. She'd wait until she could be rational. Not weeping and wailing. That was not her style.

"No screamin' meemies allowed," she says to the baby now. "Keep reminding me, okay? Or maybe we should choose option number two. Drive back in Lynn's car, listen to her talking to herself for about ten minutes out of every hour. I'm almost curious enough to do that, to hear what she's going to say. Because something's weird here, Beegee. Your grandma's turned into somebody I don't quite recognize. Some island woman?

"Or..." she touches the tip of her finger to the end of the baby's nose, smiles at the way it wrinkles in response... "we find our own way back, leave tonight, and enjoy thinking about the fireworks when Jack gets here tomorrow. Mean, but I'm tempted."

She trudges through the tunnel of cedars that forms the shortcut to the neighbours' cabin, memory tugging at her the whole way. She can almost hear Marty and Sunny's bratty brothers whooping and snorting the way they did when they pelted the girls with pine cones and chased them through the rain. Their goal, hers and Sunny's, was always to ditch the boys. Every time they got away, Sunny's mom would come charging down to Einar's yard and haul Sunny back to babysit.

Lights are on in the house ahead. As always. Heather can't imagine anyone wanting to live on this island. A place where the houses are so dark you need electricity even on a sunny day. She's about to turn around and go back, when Sunny's mom and Einar come out of the house, get into Einar's truck, and drive away toward town.

"C'mon, babe," Heather say. "Let's go visiting."

She gives her feet a half-hearted swipe on the scratchy mat, knocks once, then again. She's about to walk away when a little girl opens the door.

Two boys are sitting on the floor in front of the television. Heather doubts they can see anything, even up close. The screen is a scratchy blur of colour, lightning flashes of interference zigging across the centre every five seconds or so. Television? Who let that in the house? Sunny, all those years ago, was totally ignorant about all the best shows. Her parents were fanatics about things like television, and junk food. Everything was made by hand. No wonder Sunny took off to join the real world.

Now she's back, sprawled on the couch, staring at the ceiling. She rolls onto her side when Heather walks into the room ducking a line of laundry.

"Hey," she says. "You're not leaving already, are you?" She yawns, and curls into fetal position.

The room feels like a sauna. There's a yeasty aura. It mingles with the smell of the wet clothes on the line, and the sharper scent of burnt tomato sauce. The few times Heather was inside this house, there was always something burbling on the stove.

Sunny seems to have slipped back into her coma. Heather hesitates, unties her shoes and goes barefoot over the braided rugs thrown like giant footprints across the floor. The wood floor has the creamy look of maple fudge. Sunny's dad is a carpenter, like Einar. A quiet guy. Heather remembers him hunched over furniture under the lean-to at the side of the cabin, sanding and polishing and fondling the curved legs of a table as though he was building himself a woman. One as sturdy and serviceable as Hannah. She doesn't remember his name, or his voice.

The little girl, arms folded across her chest, is scowling at Heather. What's her problem? She was barely walking around the last time Heather saw her, the baby Sunny was so excited about because there was finally another girl.

Heather taps Sunny on the shoulder, and blue eyes open. "I'm not driving back to Calgary after all," Heather says. "I'm going to drive down to Victoria and fly home."

Sunny pulls herself up, shivering inside the quilt she has wrapped around her shoulders. "Like tomorrow?"

"No, like as soon as I make a couple of phone calls. That's kind of why I'm here. Can I use your phone?" There must be an evening flight to Calgary, still time if she hustles. Phone for a reservation? Lots of room left on Jack's credit card. Three hours, maybe more, in the car with Beegee? Better than two days. She'll get Marty to pick her up at the airport. No way is she letting Lynn take off with her car, and no way she's staying to hear the collision of Lynn and Jack.

Sunny points toward a phone on the wall by the door. The biggest boy in front of the television looks up. "You can fly from Comox you know. You don't have to go to Victoria."

Comox? Yes! Heather remembers passing Comox just before Campbell River. She gives the kid a thumbs-up. But when she gets Westjet on the phone, the last plane from Comox is already in the sky. Same story on the last flight from Victoria. Tomorrow morning from Comox, nine-fifteen. Reservation? She hesitates. She'll call back.

"Hey, Heather." Sunny rubs her eyes. "If you can lend me the cash for a few weeks until I get a job, I could fly to Calgary with you. That would still work."

"Didn't you come home because you wanted to see your folks for a while? Your mom isn't going to be thrilled if you take off again tomorrow morning."

Sunny yawns. "She won't even notice I'm gone, she's so busy chasing after my brother. She thinks he stole somebody's car. She's nuts. Josh wouldn't do that."

"You feeling any better?"

"A bit. I'm just going to sleep all day. So when are you going?"

Heather scuffs back into her running shoes, then opens the door. "Looks like I'll be around at least until tomorrow morning. Maybe I'll see you later."

Outside a fine mist is falling. She tries to protect Beegee's face from the damp but as soon as the towel covers her face, the baby starts that crazy snorty hiccup thing she does. One fuzzy arm fights its way out of the wrappings.

"What?" Heather whispers. "Don't get excited. We're going home." But whose home is the question. Heather realizes that she should have made one more phone call while she was at it. She likes Carmen, she really does, and this isn't fair. As soon as she goes back to Einar's. It doesn't matter if Lynn's there, and maybe it's better if she hears Heather tell Carmen that the deal is still on. That way she'll stop asking.

She treads carefully from the slippery steps to the needle-soft carpet below. Sunny is probably snoring again by now. Stay here, Heather would tell her if she thought it was any use. Just stay on Hannah's sofa, eat her soup, and come up with a real plan. Do something with your life. Good God, she sounds like Jack. When did she turn into a career counselor? Sunny should do whatever makes her happy, except Heather's afraid for her that the thing that makes her happy comes in a chemical form.

She sucks up a deep breath of moist evergreen air. Not a sound but the drip drip drip from the low roof onto Hannah's verandah. Then the foghorn call of an approaching ferry. Heather shudders. She's starting to feel like Lynn. She wants to get off this island and go home.

The ground is soft under her feet, her footsteps muffled by silence. She glances down. Beegee is as still as the forest. But not asleep. Her mouth has found her free fist and she gnaws with fierce concentration. Heather strokes the plush cheek, smiles at her daughter, and the sucking stops. The fist is abandoned in a gummy grin. All over in a few seconds, but no mistaking. Beegee has smiled.

Heather stops beside her car. Comox is less than an hour away. In the morning…she looks down at the baby again, imagines driving alone. How will she know if Beegee's okay in the backseat? Those creepy roadside crosses. How many are there because someone took their eyes off the road to check the baby? What if the mother survives but the baby dies?

Instead of taking the short cut through the trees, Heather trudges up the driveway to the main road. She turns up the collar on her shirt, braces her arm even more securely under the sturdy weight of her baby, and strides down the road, away from the cabin. The sound of sucking and her own pounding heart are all she hears.

When Heather is finally deliciously physically tired from loping down the road and returns to the cabin, Lynn is still there. She gets up to help Heather off with her jacket, takes the baby while Heather slips off her shoes and goes to pee.

"I forgot that my car's been stolen," she says, when Heather is back. "It just disappeared last night. So no laundry today."

"You can take mine," Heather says. "The key's in my jacket pocket." She lifts Beegee from Lynn's arms and stands in front of the fire. So many memories are coming back about this cosy place. She wishes Marty was here. They could play hearts and drink hot chocolate.

"So no car," Heather says, "how are you going to get home? Or are you planning on staying for a while?"

"Good grief, Heather, of course not. Why would I do that?"

"Beats me, but so does why you came out here in the first place."

"Then maybe it's time we sat down and talked about it?"

Heather glances at the clock. "I have to call Carmen first. It's an hour later there. I don't want to leave it too long." She intends to put Beegee down on the sofa again, but Lynn comes and takes the baby out of her arms, carries her into the bedroom, and closes the door.

Heather stares into the fire. Whatever it was that fuelled her mom for the trip out here is still in good supply. She has the feeling they're headed for a showdown.

Meanwhile, there's Carmen and this nasty big lump in Heather's throat when she thinks about calling. No choice. She walks across the room, picks up the phone, dials?—the phone must be even older than Einar—the too-familiar number for Loving Arms, and hopes that Carmen is out, her voice mail left to tend the shop. No such luck. Oddly, though, she doesn't seem all that relieved to hear Heather's voice.

"Heather, finally," she says. "You seem to have disappeared."

"Yeah, well, things were a little more complicated than I told you. My mom kind of panicked and took off with Beegee but we'll be back tomorrow sometime. Everything's good." She bites her lip.

Carmen is silent for a few seconds. "That's good," she says, "good that you'll be back, because we need to get together."

Yes, they do, and Heather waits for Carmen to tell her how pleased Donna and Grant will be, and how they'll sign the papers first, and then blah blah blah. But there is no blah blah blah. Just another lag in the conversation. "We need to get together," Carmen says, "to come up with a new plan. The McDonalds are no longer in the picture."

It takes Heather a few beats to remember who the McDonalds are, and what picture it is that Carmen's looking at that's not in Heather's line of vision. "What do you mean?"

"I warned you," Carmen says quietly, but with that stern note, "that they wouldn't wait forever in such an indefinite situation. Pulling out that way, you really did destroy their trust."

"Forever?" Heather says. "It's only been a few days! I didn't pull out. It was my mother."

"Your mother feels like a threat to them, and I doubt they could get over that."

"What if she talks to them?" Heather feels like ripping the damn phone cord out of the wall. Stupid phone. Why doesn't he get a cordless?

"It's too late," Carmen says. "Someone at their church heard about what happened, and they've had another young woman approach them. She's due any day, and they say they know for sure that she's not going to change her mind. Heather, there are other families. You know this. We'll talk tomorrow when you get back, and everything will work out. I've been doing this long enough to know that when an adoption doesn't go, it wasn't meant to go. The next one will work."

"Right," she says. She fits the phone carefully back into the bracket, and stares at the wall.

"What happened? What were you shouting about?" Lynn is behind her, Beegee whimpering in her arms.

"Donna and Grant are getting someone else's baby. Everything's totally screwed up now. Thanks, Lynn." Heather leaves Beegee with Lynn and slams into the bedroom. This is such hard work, and now she has to do it all over again.

15

Heather refuses to speak to Lynn after the phone call. About anything. She comes out of the bedroom an hour later as soon as she hears Beegee crying, glowers from the rocking chair while she feeds her, then hands the baby back, and returns to the bedroom.

All Lynn knows is that the McDonalds are no longer in the picture. A week ago, Lynn would have been relieved, hopeful at this news. Now it feels like one more blow that Heather has to absorb, and Lynn finds herself perversely angry. Irrationally offended that they could so easily walk away from Beegee, their Belinda. Easily? Come now, she tells herself. They haven't been allowed to make her their Belinda, and Heather is probably turning into their worst nightmare of a birthmother.

The baby is fussy tonight, refusing to settle when Lynn puts her down. Although she doubts that Heather is asleep in the next room, Lynn moves quietly, speaks in a whisper to Beegee.

"Don't worry. This has nothing to do with you." No one,

she thinks, will ever tell this little girl that she was rejected. Then Lynn feels an abrupt halt in her breathing, a few quick beats to catch up. Another secret they'll have to carry around forever? She and Heather have never talked about this, about what Beegee will know. That, they assumed would be up to Donna and Grant. There must be a standard text for explaining away a young woman's need to be free to pursue her life unencumbered. Heather will visit, tell Belinda repeatedly how hard this was, but how much better for all of them.

Beegee is fighting to get her arms out of the blanket. She seems happiest with one fist in her mouth and the other free to punch the air. Maybe Lynn can hope that none of Carmen's carefully screened families will find this pugnacious behaviour appealing. But what if someone takes her, and finds out later that they can't love this little girl because she's come to them too late?

The basket is on the floor beside the chair. Lynn brings a pillow and fashions a lounger so she can put Beegee on the kitchen table while she finds something to eat. Tomorrow, she'll stop somewhere for salad. Eggs and cheese and bacon and bread have lost all appeal. Deep in the cupboards she finds more canned goods. The baby's eyes seem to be tracking her around the kitchen. Lynn stops each time she brings something to the table, and touches her finger to the tip of Beegee's nose. Four touches, one smile. She's stingy with her graces, this little one.

Beegee's contentment lasts while Lynn eats a salmon sandwich and drinks a glass of milk. But not long enough to make a pot of tea. Back in the chair, they rock and rock, Lynn's eyes on the bedroom door, counting down ten minutes more and then she will go in and put this responsibility back in Heather's arms. Yes, she is sorry. Sorry about everything, but this is not the way to fix it. It's becoming clearer and clearer to Lynn that she does not have the answer for Heather. Only the questions.

A new question flies down the chimney and sits on her shoulder now. What if the miracle happens and Heather does keep Beegee? How much of this mess will they tell her? When? Or will there be a pact to seal it all away, just as Lynn and Jack have done. But there were only two of them, and they are tight-lipped. Heather, keep secrets?

They rock and rock. When Lynn awakes with a start, it's because her arms have gone limp and the baby is sliding toward the floor. She grabs Beegee back, clutches her to her chest, and then dares to breathe. The baby's eyes are widely startled, her chin beginning to work its way into outrage. "Sorry," Lynn whispers. "Wow. That was very bad."

Almost ten o'clock. The bedroom door opens. Heather crosses the room to the bathroom, and emerges in a few minutes with hair combed, faced scrubbed. When she leans down to take the wailing baby, it's with gentler arms.

"Does she need to be changed first?"

"That would be good. Then you can settle her for the night. She's been sleeping a good stretch at night." Lynn expects an angry retort, but Heather looks thoughtful instead, wounded. The baby has gone quiet in her arms. "You could bathe her, seeing as she's calm for the moment." She knows she's pushing her luck, all this advice. Surprisingly, Heather heads for the bathroom. Lynn, too tired to move from the rocking chair, tries not to watch, but is mesmerized by the sight of Heather arranging towels, undressing the baby, each action as though she's done it a hundred times, knows precisely what the baby needs.

She resists the urge to make more tea or prepare more food for Heather. This time she'll wait until she's asked. She gets the fire going again, and pulls a chair close to rest her feet on the stone face of the fireplace while she thumbs through another magazine.

Heather is so quiet coming back into the room, Lynn doesn't realize she's there until she hears the creak of the rockers, then the baby snuffling while she nurses. She waits until the feeding seems to be over, then pulls her chair across the room, near enough to put her hand on Heather's shoulder. "One more time? I'm sorry." Heather shrugs, her lips twitch. "What did Carmen say, exactly?"

"They found another baby. I have to choose someone else." Heather wipes away a bit of drool at the corner of Beegee's mouth with the tail of her shirt. Looks up at Lynn. "Yeah, I know it's not all your fault. Maybe it's mostly mine. They've been holding their breath ever since she was born, those poor McDonalds."

"Then there isn't any urgency, is there? At least there's that, Heather."

"More time is exactly what I didn't want," Heather says. "I hate the way this will go. The next people will have to meet Beegee and decide if they want her? How sick is that, as though they're shopping and trying her on for size?"

"I'm sure it's not that way, Heather. You can trust Carmen to handle this well." She almost stops there, same as always. But there has to be some purpose to these past four days. "If that's what you want."

They stare at each other, then, as though they've been stage-directed, down at Beegee. "What if no one wants her?" Heather says finally, ignoring Lynn's invitation for more. "Maybe the only people who'll want her will be the desperate ones who haven't been picked because...of whatever."

Lynn looks down at the baby and almost laughs at the absurdity of it all, but oddly, the phrase "older child" pops into her mind. Just before Marty was born, Lynn asked the social worker what would happen if she kept her baby but found it too hard in a few months, and wanted to give him up. That would involve a different process, Mrs. McKinnon said, and it might take at least a year before the baby was legally free for adoption. He would be in a foster home until then, and considered an "older child" in the adoption vocabulary. Harder to find a family, because everyone wanted a newborn. So much easier to bond.

Lynn wishes she was treacherous enough to feed this fear, use it to try and shift Heather's course, but that was then and this is now. She shakes her head. "We know that's not so. Carmen's told you how many people are waiting for babies and how few babies there are. Someone, many people likely, will want her." The backs of her eyes are stinging. "Why don't you want her?"

This is the wrong question, the tears it unleashes washing away any possibility of real talk for now. All Heather can manage, over and over again is, "Because…because…because…" and just as she is wrestling for control, there's a knock and Einar's face peeking cautiously around the door.

"Sorry," he says. "I'll come back in a bit. I was going to use the washroom before I turn in." Heather gulps, and shakes her head. "Better still, I'll go up to Hannah's and use theirs."

"No," Heather says. "It's okay. We're finished here. It's your bathroom." He looks back and forth between the two of them, both nodding at him, and finally comes inside. When he's closed the bathroom door, Heather asks, "Where is he sleeping?"

"Out in his truck. There's kind of a bed in the back, I think." Lynn shakes her head. "We'll leave in the morning, give him his house back."

"Are you sure?" Heather asks. "I feel like I'm going to be stuck here forever." She stands up. "Wake me early, please. There's a flight from Comox in the morning."

Lynn doesn't even remember where Comox is. How does Heather know about flights home? Before she can ask, Heather and Beegee are on their way to bed. Maybe, Lynn thinks, after Einar too has passed quietly through the kitchen and out the door to his bed, Comox is in Jack's plan.

Lynn lies awake on the sofa wondering why Marty hasn't called again. She dreads Jack's arrival in the morning. But by the time the fire has burned its way down to the faintest of embers, she has decided that no matter what, she is not going to run off and leave capable Jack as Heather's guide home.

Lynn has just tiptoed into the bedroom to see if Heather is awake when Jack and Einar come through the door. She's been awake herself since six o'clock, lying there as the room lightened, trying to remember when the first ferry arrives. She was sure Jack would be on it. But she stayed in the crumpled blanket, leafing through magazines, ignoring the yearning for the coffee that would jumpstart her brain. Now she'd like to run to the bedroom door and slam it shut as soon as she hears the men's voices.

Heather is sitting up in bed, nursing the baby. "What time is it?" she whispers.

"Just after eight-thirty."

She groans. "I asked you to wake me early. Like six-thirty."

"You said early, not six-thirty," Lynn tells her.

"Can I come in?" Jack steps into the room and turns on the light. He looks disheveled, as though he's spent the night in his clothes. Unusual for Jack to go anywhere without showering, shaving, checking himself in the mirror.

He hesitates. But for the nursing baby, Lynn thinks, he'd sit on the edge of the bed to talk to Heather. "How is she?" he asks.

Lynn wishes she could take Jack by the arm and lead him

to a chair in the kitchen, sit him down and ask what he's really wondering, feeling about this baby. She would like to remind him of the proud words he'd used to describe Heather from the time she was a tiny girl. She's a tough little nut, she'd say of Beegee. Just like her mother.

"She's fine," Heather says. "She doesn't know what's going on. I'm the one who's had everything totally screwed."

"We'll have you back on track before you know it." He doesn't even look at Lynn. "Should I make a plane reservation for this afternoon? We'll have to leave pronto. Or would you rather drive to Victoria today, and take the first flight out in the morning?"

Heather lifts the baby to her shoulder. "At the moment I just want everyone to go away. I'm barely awake here."

"Heather, I had to take time off work at a very bad time to come here." Still not looking at Lynn. "Asking everyone to go away is hardly a reasonable request when you're in someone else's home. His bed, in fact. You need to get dressed, and we'll sort this out."

He turns and walks out of the room.

"Take your time," Lynn says softly to Heather. "If you want to have a bath when you're done nursing, I'll change Beegee and keep her happy."

Heather rolls her eyes. "Close the door, okay? Maybe I'll escape through the window."

In the kitchen, Einar has lined up four mugs and pours coffee into three of them. He hands one to Jack. "Sit down. You look terrible. Do you two want me to leave so you can have it out?"

They shake their heads at the same time, Lynn a little more vehemently, and surprised that Jack doesn't choose to have privacy for what he must surely be dying to say.

"If we don't get away soon, we could end up wasting another day. You never know what delays you're going to run into." He needs a shave. He used to wear a shadow well, in a sleepy sexy way, but since his hair's gone grey, it only makes him look tired.

"You didn't need to come out here," Lynn says.

"Neither did you."

Touché, she thinks, and remembers that he doesn't know about the McDonalds. He might have been gentler with Heather if he did. She should tell him. But her tongue is stuck.

"Westjet flies to Comox now," Einar says. "But I suppose you have to take the car back to Victoria?"

Jack frowns. Lynn knows the look well. No matter how reasonable an alternative anyone comes up with, he hates changing course. His own plan is always the best. "It's probably even harder to get a reservation out of here," he says. "We'll fly from Victoria." He finally makes eye contact with Lynn. "Einar told me the car's been stolen. You'll have to drive Heather's back. I'll take it over to the garage and have it checked this morning just to be sure it's safe. There's a puddle of oil under it." He glances at his watch, taps his wrist, time running out, and keeps on talking. "I'm coming back for spring break, and if your car turns up by then, I'll drive it home. Otherwise we'll let the insurance deal with it."

Plan, plan, plan. Lynn is trying to interrupt to tell him to halt, desist until Heather comes out and can be part of the discussion, when the phone rings.

The RCMP. For Lynn. "Mrs. Bishop," the cheery voice says, "we found your car just north of Campbell River. Looks like it's had a rough ride, a couple of flat tires and some dents, but no serious damage."

Then there's work to be done, and Einar and Jack act like two boys setting off on bikes on a summer day. The urgency to get home seems to drain right out of Jack. He and Einar agree it would be better for Jack to go to Campbell River and deal with the RCMP.

"Why? He said the only damage is the tires. You think I don't know my way around a tire shop?"

"You don't need to go, Lynn. My name's still on the registration, isn't it? I'll take care of it." The same way he keeps taking care of things at home. Two months ago someone appeared to clean the furnace ducts. Booked by Jack, paid for by Jack. She thought, after she shouted at him on the phone to stop managing her house, that he'd gotten the message. Einar watches with a bemused look. He has nothing pressing for the day, he says, and he'll be happy to drive Jack over and have a visit along the way.

When the two of them finally drive away, Lynn raps on the bedroom door. Heather is dressed, just buttoning the plaid shirt. "They found my car," Lynn says. "Your dad's gone to retrieve it."

Heather scoops Beegee off the bed. "See. I knew I was going to be stuck here. Unless you want to drive me to Comox. In my car."

"No," Lynn says. "That's not necessary. Come have some coffee, and…"

"This is working out exactly the way it always does, isn't it?" Heather brushes past into the kitchen. There she turns and faces Lynn. "Jack's here giving orders, and you're making breakfast. You still haven't told me why you ran away. I know it was a shitty thing to ask, but I thought you'd understand that I have to do this. God, Lynn, of all people you should understand."

Lynn feels the blood leave her brain, rush through her heart and pool in her feet. Left with her mouth open, she can't close it and still catch the breath that's also been sucked away.

"I mean after giving up everything you planned to do

with your life to marry Jack and look after us, aren't you hoping I'll have the guts to make some different choices?"

All that blood comes back in a rage. Lynn takes the trembling steps necessary to get her to a chair so she can hold onto the back. "I'm hoping you'll have the guts to not give away your daughter in favour of some plan you haven't even made yet. Heather, from what I can tell—and God knows I may be wrong, forgive me if I am—you have not seriously considered at all the possibility of keeping Beegee." She wants to grab Beegee and put her safely to bed in Einar's room, close the door, so the baby doesn't have to be party to this conversation.

"I didn't need to sit and daydream about what it would be like to marry someone I barely know—and yes, Winston did suggest that—because I've seen you and Jack in that trap all my life. It's a no-brainer, Lynn. One look at that questionnaire listing everything I'd need to do if I was a single mother told me I wouldn't be good at it. I don't know how to be a mother!" The baby is wailing now, her voice rising above her mother's.

"Nobody knows how to be a mother, Heather. You muddle along—with the help of your own mother if she's lucky enough to be included—and you never find out if you were right or wrong. I think that's the way it's supposed to be." She swallows and swallows and will not succumb to tears or to this terrible instinct that wants her to run from the room. "Is it my sad example that's guiding you? Because if it is, you'd better rethink. I have never regretted keeping Marty. Never." She has to shout to be heard over her fractious granddaughter. Lynn stands up straight, walks to Heather and takes the baby out of her arms. She puts her finger to her lips, turns her back on Heather and walks up and down the room, back and forth until the baby is calm enough to settle on the bed. But she doesn't close the door. They need to keep an eye on Beegee.

Heather has poured coffee and sits at the table, eyes down, fingers drumming the worn arborite. Lynn takes the chair across from her and reaches over to put her own hand on the agitated one. "Funny," she says, "but it seems that what I've been telling myself all along is what I should have been saying to you. This is not about me and Jack and what we did in our life, Heather. This is about you and Beegee. You can use your brain to come up with a plan for your life, and I know you'll be a success. But unless you listen to your heart about this baby…" Heather is getting angrier, Lynn can tell by the long exhaling of breath and the tension in the hand under her own. Lynn tries to manage a smile. "If I hadn't listened to my heart about Marty, I wouldn't have had you either." Or Beegee, she wants to say but doesn't dare, even if it's only these weeks, I wouldn't have had Beegee.

Heather looks up. "God, this sounds so mean—please don't ever tell Marty I said this—but maybe you really would have been happier if you'd given him away. You don't know how it would have been."

Lynn thinks so long and hard before she answers, she's afraid Heather will be able to read her mind. "I think it would be a good thing if we could drive home together. With two of us, Beegee will be fine in the car. She'll sleep and we'll stop to feed her and she'll sleep again. Really, that's the way it was on the way here."

"Why would I want to be in the car for two days when I can fly home from Victoria in an hour?"

"For more time to talk, Heather. Before you go back and see Carmen again." She steels herself for an outright refusal.

"It's all pretty much irrelevant until Jack gets back with your car, isn't it? I'll decide later. I don't want to talk about it now. I'll let you know when I do." She stands up and looks out the window. "I'm going crazy in here. What is there to eat? I think I'll have breakfast and then go for a walk."

Lynn knows better than to ask if she can come along. She feels pathetic even considering the question. That's what this new feeling is, that's creeping over her. Pathetic desperation. "A walk is a good idea," she says. "I need fresh air too. I'm going out now. There's eggs and bread. Cheese. Help yourself. I'll replenish Einar's fridge before I leave."

Then she puts on her jacket and shoes, and walks up to the end of the driveway from where she can at least see the road that will take her away from this place. She wonders what Heather is imagining for herself once she's home again. Originally, Jack promised a trip to Vegas, or Mexico or wherever she wanted to go for an interlude before getting back to her old life. What if Lynn had had such an option when she walked out of the hospital? A trip to Mexico instead of the return to her dingy apartment. Heather would probably argue that she could have, would have, gotten over it all if she'd had a plan.

The day Lynn left Marty in the hospital, she took a deliberate wrong turn from the nurses' station. Instead of going down the elevator, she walked down the hallway to the nursery. All she wanted was a peek through the glass, but she couldn't find his name on the row of babies next to the window. She tapped on the glass, held up her wrist band, and the nurse inside smiled and began looking for a match. Suddenly, she glanced from Lynn to a bassinette against the wall. She shook her head, then looked as though she might give in, but another nurse wandered over and after a quick conference the two of them came out into the hall. Lynn turned and fled before they reached her.

Mrs. McKinnon had asked if Lynn wanted her there, if she could drive her home, but she couldn't imagine leaning on someone who was almost a stranger. She'd asked her mom and dad not to come. She was afraid of their tears, afraid it would be even harder. Something she had to do on her own, she was convinced of that, probably as stubborn as Heather. Her mother had phoned so many times the nurses finally told her they couldn't take her calls anymore, they were too busy to be fetching people to the phone. Funny how each time Lynn's allowed herself to revisit these moments in the past few days, they've become sharper. She can see her young self in the eye of her mind, still remember the maternity top she wore to the hospital and home again, a soft brushed cotton shirt in a plaid one of the nurses told her was Gallagher, as though the tartan was of any consequence to a young girl giving away her baby.

16

Heather is afraid, when Lynn walks out the door, that she won't come back. But she doesn't have a car, so where would she go? And why should Heather be afraid? Since she got here, everything about Beegee seems easier. At home, she rarely put the baby down because Beegee would howl as soon as she felt the arms let go. Or maybe Heather hung on because she knew she only had a bit of time. Now, maybe it's knowing that it won't go on forever that makes this seem easier. Or maybe it's because Beegee is in the next room and Heather isn't looking down at her grumpy little face.

Heather pokes around in the fridge. What she'd really like is a tall glass of orange juice and some yogurt, but Einar's kitchen is stocked with the things most people take along on a camping trip. She walks to the bedroom door. Lynn has propped Beegee on one pillow, fenced her in from the edge with the other. Beegee looks as though she could be supervising the action in the main room, except that her eyes are closed. Amazing. She's gone to sleep with no one carrying her.

Heather pulls a strand of hair across her face and sniffs. If Lynn would just get back here, she could have a bath. She hesitates, then picks up her bag and carries it to the bathroom. Who told her you couldn't leave a baby alone in a room? She'll only be a dozen steps away and she can leave the bathroom door open. Well, no. What if Jack and Einar come back?

While the water rumbles into the tub Heather stares at herself in the mirror. You'd think she'd have a new face by now. A grown-up mother face. But with these damn curls, and the freckles on her nose even though it's been weeks since she's seen the sun, she looks about as old and as capable as that kid sister of Sunny's. Faith? Something like that, some virtue. The boys, she thinks, should have been named after the seven deadly sins.

She slides down the sloping back of the tub, all but her shoulders and head submerged in the deliciously hot water. Eyes turned to the skylight, she remembers lying on the cedar shakes with Marty, peeking down at Lynn in her bath. Just Heather peeking, Marty with his hands over his eyes, his face crimson. Trying to talk her down.

No shampoo in reach, so she tilts back to let her hair drift, swishing in the clear water. She wraps her head in a towel before she begins to soap, standing to scrub every inch of skin, then down again in the froth. She floats, thinking about her apartment, the glass shower cubicle. Maybe she needs to find another place. The top floor of an old house near the campus. One with a claw-footed tub and some big windows. Wood floors. She can see herself in this new place. Two bedrooms.

Right. She stands up in the tub, grabs a towel. How the hell did that dream sneak in. Lynn must have left it behind, because there's a crib in the second bedroom, the smaller one tucked under the sloped roof, and a butterfly mobile dancing from the ceiling. Dreams. Wake up, Heather.

Beegee is still asleep. Heather turns the heat on under a pot of coffee on the back burner. It pours thick and gritty. She dumps half of it back into the pot, tops her cup up with milk and microwaves it. Two teaspoons of sugar and it's not bad at all. There's bread and real butter. She's too hungry now to bother with cooking. Toast will do.

Finally, the door opens, and there's Lynn, back again. "Not a bad day," she says, hanging her jacket on the wall by the door as though it belongs there next to the flannel shirt and green raincoat on the other two pegs. "I think the sun may even shine."

She peeks into the bedroom at Beegee, then pours coffee and sits down at the table. She shudders after the first sip. "Should I make a fresh pot? This tastes like it's been boiling over a campfire for about a week."

"Only if you need it. I've had enough." Heather hands Lynn a piece of toast off the stack on her own plate. The toast and jam tastes so good she could eat another four slices. But she hates the way her bum hangs over the seat of this hard wooden chair, and she can feel the flab on her belly over the waist band on her tights. She looks at her slim mother, licking butter off her fingers. "How long did you stay fat after you had us?" she asks.

"Fat? Heather, you're not fat. You'll tighten up all those muscles again in a couple of months and look even better than you did before."

"Yeah, right? That's what happened to you?"

"I don't remember. That was twenty years ago."

"Well I hate this. The jiggling and the leaking. It's gross. I'm not doing this again. Ever. Just so you know."

"Well just so you know, I don't think you've ever been prettier."

Heather wishes she could say the same to her mom, but Lynn has never looked this old. There are puffy little pillows under her eyes, and new lines that run from her nose to the corners of her mouth. "Ha! That's what Marty said too. He came over the night I figured out you were gone." Heather doesn't want to tell Lynn how long it took them to even realize she was missing. It seems so horrible that she was asleep the whole time Lynn and Beegee were driving. "He has a new woman. Did he tell you the last one—that weird chick who looked anorexic, Maggie or something—dumped him?"

Her mom winces. Heather knows Lynn worries about Marty in his quest for the perfect woman. He keeps setting himself up. She wishes Marty would walk through the door right now. That she could go home with him instead of either Lynn or Jack.

But when there's a knock a minute later, it's Sunny's mom who sticks her big face into the room. "I'm walking down to the store," she says from the doorway. "Do you need anything?"

Heather is astonished when Lynn stands up immediately. "Yes. I'll come with you." She thought Lynn wanted to talk.

"But I was going to go for a walk," Heather says. "You just got back."

Lynn pauses in pulling on her jacket. "Do you want to come with us?"

Of course she doesn't want to go down to the store with Hannah. She wants to go for a long quiet walk, maybe even a run. She can't do that with the baby. "No," she says. "I don't want to go shopping." The two women are waiting, looking at her. "At least leave me a key, so if I get back before you do, I can get in."

"Oh," Lynn says. "That's what I keep forgetting to ask

Einar. I had to break in through the window when I got here because I couldn't remember where he keeps the key. Yes, we should lock the door if we're all going out."

Hannah opens the door wide, points to a spot on the outside. "Up there. There's a nail at the top of the frame on the right side. Key's there."

Well, then. Heather shrugs. "Okay, but if my car's gone when you get back, it's because I've decided to fly home this afternoon. I'll park it at the airport at Comox. I guess you can get Jack to drop you there." Why is she doing this? She has no intention of leaving on her own, and she hopes Lynn knows this. That look on her face. "But I probably won't," she says.

Lynn looks at her for a long time, then nods. "Your dad says there's a puddle of oil under your car. I won't be long," she says. "Is there anything you want me to buy you for the trip home?"

"No thanks. I don't even know yet how I'm going back." There she goes again! Why doesn't she just tell her mother that she's leaning toward flying home because she's tired! Not because she wants to cut Lynn out of the action. She'll wait for Lynn to come back before she calls Carmen.

Heather sits on the edge of the bed, watching Beegee sleep. The baby's eyelids flicker. Dreaming? What could a three-week-old—no wait, Beegee is four weeks old now—baby dream of? Even though it feels selfish, Heather hopes that Beegee will dream about her. But if she does and Heather's not there anymore...Quit it, she tells herself. Enough shit to worry about already without making up anything new.

She has to get out of here or she'll go crazy, waiting. She finds Beegee's own blanket on the towel rack in the bathroom, wraps her tight, and then slips on jacket and shoes. She's halfway up the driveway when she remembers the key, trudges back down, locks the door, hangs the key again. She considers walking up to Sunny's house and asking her if she wants to come along. Just like the old days. Not for company, but because she's a bit nervous about walking alone. She never worries about making her way around the city even at night, but here you can't see for all these trees and she doesn't remember ever being outside alone on Quadra. So quiet she can hear Beegee's soft snoring, chittery-chirping from up on the roof, the sigh of her feet on the mossy ground. At least there are no bears. She's sure she remembers Jack telling her there are no bears on Quadra. She'll stick to the road. There's a bit of a breeze, but the sun is shining and the air feels warm as bathwater.

She stands at the top of the driveway, town in one direction, the only thing she can remember in the other, Rebecca Spit. Those long beaches, ocean in every direction. "Hey, want to see the beach, Beegee? Where Uncle Marty and I built a fort out of driftwood?" Man, does she wish he was here. Uncle Marty. Beegee will be able to call him that, even if she's someone else's kid, but what will she call Heather? Even though Heather's called her mom and dad Lynn and Jack since she was a snotty teenager, she doesn't know how she'll feel about being Heather to a little girl. Weird. Other people's kids call her Heather. And Beegee will be somebody else's kid. Unless.

Yes, she needs to walk the whole length of Rebecca Spit because "unless" is swimming around in the front of her brain and she has to think it through. Before Lynn and Jack start in on her. Lynn already has. Totally uncorked this morning, like she's been fizzing away for weeks, afraid to say what she thought.

Heather's been walking for about ten minutes, about to turn around because she's decided that the spit is a lot farther away than she remembers, when a red sports car pulls over just ahead of her and the woman leans out and waves.

Heather bends down to look in the passenger window. How dangerous can this be? It's the woman from the ferry, and it looks as though she's just come from the store at the cove. There's a bag of groceries on the seat. She swings it onto the floor. "Want a lift?"

Why not? Heather eases awkwardly into the car, one hand on the back of Beegee's head, the other steadying herself on the seat.

"Where are you going?" the woman asks.

"Out to the spit," Heather says without a moment's pause. If she gets a ride there, she's sure she can handle the walk back. It really can't be that far. She remembers biking the distance with Sunny. On hot days they took water bottles to empty over their heads while they pedaled, and drank from a pump in the picnic grounds. Today is just pleasantly warm, easy walking.

"Cute baby. Is she yours?"

Why else would she be carrying around a new baby? Kidnapping? Heather nods.

"Married?"

She shakes her head. "Why do you ask?" She tries not to sound belligerent. It's not as though she didn't hear the question a dozen times when she was pregnant. It freaks her that people think they can ask personal questions just because someone's pregnant. And not wearing a ring. Beegee's feet are kicking against the blanket. She can't be hungry already. Of course she can, because all she does is eat, and it's been a couple of hours now.

"Didn't mean to pry," the woman says. "Are you okay out here alone? You're meeting someone at Rebecca?"

Heather feels a prickle of apprehension. Too many questions. Why wouldn't she be okay out here? "Just rambling and re-visiting. We used to come here on holidays when I was a kid." And then, "Yeah, I'm meeting someone. A couple of my friends are there already, and someone else should be catching up any minute." We're surrounded, she's trying to say with the lies. Sounds stupid even to herself.

"Sure." The woman grins at her. "You're smart enough that you wouldn't have gotten into the car with me if there was any chance I was a pervert. Relax."

"Do you live here?" Heather asks. This is not the kind of island girl Heather has met on any of the trips to Quadra. The clothes, the car, everything about her is polished to a rich shine.

"Nope." She turns to Heather, shakes her head, looks back at the road. "I stopped coming on family holidays a long time ago. My dad has a place at Heriot Bay. Everyone uses it. Fortunately, all my sibs are in their respective homes at the moment so I came here for some solitude." She glances at Heather again. "How about you? How long are you here?"

"I'm leaving later today, I think."

"That was fast. Where are you from?"

"Calgary." Hey, maybe Porsche Girl comes to Calgary occasionally, and Heather can introduce her to Marty. A sister-in-law with a sports car might be fine. She feels Beegee's mouth rooting against her shirt. She eases the baby away from the smell of her body, can't bring herself to haul out her breast in this car.

At the entrance to the park, the woman signals to turn in.

"I can walk from here," Heather says.

"I'm in no hurry. I can save you a few steps. I don't imagine that bundle is very heavy, but still..." The park looks empty. Picnic season is past. And this is...Wednesday? Heather's lost track. Not the weekend, anyway.

They drive the narrow strip of land that stretches like a finger into the bay. The road winds through the trees with glimpses of beach on either side. At the final parking lot, the woman pulls in and turns off the car. She shifts sideways in her seat and watches Heather lay Beegee on her lap to tighten the blanket around her. "She looks pretty new."

"Four weeks," Heather says.

"What's your name?" the woman asks.

"Heather."

"And the baby?"

Heather hesitates, lifts Beegee to her shoulder and puts her hand on the door. "Belinda." Is that still Beegee's name, now that Donna and Grant don't want her anymore? Maybe they'll give that name to their new baby. Something to ask Carmen. Does she fill in a new form now, or are they stuck with Belinda Janice Marie until the next new parents put their own name on the next set of papers?

"I'm Kate Duncan. What do you do when you're not wandering around with your baby?"

She wants to get out of the car now; too much snoopiness. "University. I'm in third year."

She looks surprised. She thought Heather was a cocktail waitress? "Good. So you'll be able to carry on even with a baby to look after?"

Enough questions, no more answers. Beegee is gnawing on her shoulder. She slips her knuckle against the wet lips and feels the baby's gums clamp on. Heather throws the door open and slides out. "Thanks for the lift."

"Oh hey! I didn't mean to pry. Well, I did, but I'm sorry it offended you. It's not safe for you to be out here alone. Honest. Go have a walk on the beach if that's what you need, but I'm going to wait for you."

Heather looks out at the rocky stretch of beach, the piles of driftwood, the dazzling water. Far in the distance, the hazy backdrop of mountains on the mainland. Not a soul in sight. Beegee will be wailing in another minute. It's a long walk back. What the hell is wrong with her, thinking this was a good idea? "We'll be fine," she says. She turns and walks along the grassy verge until she comes to a path that cuts down to the water. At the first pile of logs, she settles into a convenient niche, opens her shirt, and nestles Beegee to her breast without any thought to strategy. They seem to be getting better at this. The baby burrows into her and feeds like a hungry pup.

Someone built a nest in this place. Along one of the logs, seashells have been set out like plates at a dinner party, bits of seaweed and pebbles served up on each one. A bit of blue pokes out from under the carpet of leathery brown kelp. Heather reaches down and pulls out a small canvas shoe. Imagines someone's dad searching the beach while mom and the kids are already back at the car, the picnic basket loaded into the trunk. Imagines Jack crouched down beside Marty, his arm raised to point across to the mainland. Always with his field glasses at the ready in case a seal poked its head up in the waves. Or some seagull he thought he knew screeched past. Imagines Jack and Lynn holding Beegee's hands and walking her down this stretch of sand. Except there is no more Jack and Lynn. There's just a stranger who for some reason has decided Heather isn't safe out here alone.

She can't see the car from here, but she hasn't heard a motor starting, wheels on gravel. She half expects to see Kate come wandering down the path toward her, but there's no sound and no movement but the slurp of the waves a few feet away. From the look of the sand, the piles of weed, the tide is going out. She closes her eyes, takes a deep breath. The smell reminds her of the hours after Beegee was born. The air in the birthing room was oddly unlike the rest of the medicinal smell of the hospital.

Salt. That's what it was. Salt and fish and weeds all warmed to body temperature. She dips her head so her nose brushes the soft spot on Beegee's head. The faint throbbing of that bit of scalp totally spooked her in the first few days. It will take months to close, months in which it will not be her concern. The smell is still there, but ever so faint. With a shaky finger, she traces the spot at the top of the skull, lifts the fine hair and fashions the curl. Way more information stored in Heather's brain now. Did she know what a fontanelle was last year? All that pregnancy and childbirth vocabulary? Yeah, it was a learning experience. Good thing she did it. She scrunches her eyes tight. She will not cry.

Beegee stops sucking, lets the nipple fall from her lips and lies content on Heather's arm. She should be upright so she can burp. Oh well. Heather kicks off her shoes, and digs her toes into the sand. She swings her arms side to side, rocking her baby.

The wind is picking up, tangling her hair. Someone crunching across the stones behind her. Kate stops a few feet away. "Tide's coming in," she says. "Are you about ready?"

Heather slips back into the gritty sneakers, and climbs cautiously over logs. Follows Kate to her car.

"So what do you do?" she asks, when she's settled into the deep bucket seat of the red car.

"I'm an investment analyst." Kate wrinkles her nose. "Sounds boring? It is."

"If it's boring, why don't you do something else?"

"Because it's lucrative and the other things I'm interested in are not. Simple as that. I enjoy a nice life. Where are we taking you?"

"Back the same way we came," Heather says. "I'll tell you where to turn."

The rushing wind is cold now. Heather holds Beegee tight to her chest. Kate glances her way, then presses a button that slowly raises the top of the car. Instantly the air feels trapped, suffocating.

"At the risk of prying yet again," Kate says, "I'm going to ask a really personal question for a very personal reason. I'll explain in a minute, but only if you decide to answer. Ignore me if I'm over the line here."

So what is she waiting for, if Heather's free to ignore her? Nothing pisses her off more than someone telling her they hate to ask, but... She stares back at Kate, raises her eyebrows.

"Did you ever consider letting someone adopt your baby, someone you met and liked and you knew could give her a great future so that you could go on and have a great future too?"

She sounds like a television commercial for mutual funds. Is this the kind of investment she works at? Finding babies and trading them around? Heather shakes her head to tell Kate that no, she does not want to have this discussion, but Kate seems to take this as a negative on the question, like no, Heather's never considered this amazing option, because she keeps right on talking.

"Heather, there is nothing noble about being a single mother. And for sure nothing romantic about being poor, I can tell you that from experience. My dad's a financial wizard. He's wheeled and dealed our fortunes all my life. Wins big, loses big. We've been filthy rich and filthy poor and not a lot of in-between. But I've never wanted in-between and I have the feeling you're a very smart girl who doesn't want it either, not for you or for your little girl." She pauses, but Heather knows there's more to come. Oh there is a lot more.

Under her hand, Heather feels a slow spread of damp. Which means it's through the diaper, through the sleeper, through the blanket. Those damn cloth diapers Lynn borrowed. She's afraid to look down to see what's leaking. Takes a deep breath, but can't smell poop. Kate doesn't seem to be aware of any smell. She's waiting now for some kind of response.

"Yeah, actually, I have considered that option and I have found some people I really like, and when I get back to Calgary if I decide that's what I want to do, they'll be taking the baby. So wherever you're going with this, I don't think I'm interested."

She waves her hand toward a house approaching on the right. "You can pull over here."

"Good for you. I'm glad to hear that." Kate cranks the wheel and stops at the top of the driveway. "But let me just finish what I have to say, okay? In case your other arrangement doesn't work out." She pulls a card out of her pocket, hands it to Heather.

Well, her name is Kate Duncan all right. But anyone can have a business card printed. Heather could have some done for Beegee. Baby at Large.

"My sister and her husband have been trying to have a baby for ten years. They're fantastic people, and they have the resources to give their child anything in the world. They're willing to give the baby's mom a nice start in her new life too." Well, well. Who would have thought? "Funny, isn't it?" Kate's face is grim, no sign that she finds any of this amusing in the least. "They have everything to offer, but can't get pregnant, and you probably hadn't planned on having a kid for at least another ten years and you got caught. If you need them, they can help you, Heather. And even more important, they can give your little girl a fairytale life."

Heather leans back in the seat, tightens her arms around Beegee, not caring that the yellow stain is going to soak right through Winston's shirt. "How much?"

"Pardon?"

"How much will they pay for Belinda?"

"Oh no no! That's not what I'm suggesting. My god, they don't want to buy a baby!"

"Then what are we talking about?"

"A private adoption arrangement, probably just like the one you're already thinking about, but they'll pay all of your pregnancy and post-pregnancy expenses. That's only reasonable, right? Just the expenses that were involved in having the baby?"

"Jeez, they haven't even met me. How do you know they'd want my baby? Her father is Jamaican," Heather says. "Black."

Kate's smile strains, but she hangs on to it. "Hey, they'd be cool with that." She leans over to peek at Beegee, but only for a second. "Would you meet them?" Heather starts to shake her head, and so does Kate. She puts a hand on Heather's arm. "Look, this is my sister, and I care a lot about her. They've been through ten years of hell, wanting a baby so badly. I know this probably feels really creepy, but keep it in mind, okay? My cell number's on the card. I'm only twenty minutes away if you want to talk."

Heather stares at her, wondering if the sister looks like Kate. Wonders how long it will take before they find someone willing to deal. Why they haven't just taken their purse full of money to some third-world country and bought a baby. She swings her legs out of the car. "I'll let you know if I decide to sell her. But don't hold your breath."

"Oh, Heather, I'm sorry I upset you. Think about it," Kate says. "Please. I know it sounds awful to you right now, but it's not. Give yourself some space to change your mind."

Then she puts her snazzy car in gear, tosses her hair back, and drives free as a bird, off to her daddy's luxury vacation home. Well...she did say her job was boring. Heather's heart is pounding so hard she's afraid to hold Beegee to her breasts. "You want an Aunty Kate, kiddo? Sounds like you can have her even without Uncle Marty. As if."

She kicks gravel as she trudges the half-mile to Einar's cabin, and she can't quite bring herself to toss that card into the weeds at the side of the road. She walks slowly. Lynn is out shopping with bloody Hannah who should be at home feeding soup to Sunny and trying to talk some sense into her.

17

Lynn wanders into the coffee shop in Quathiaski Cove while she waits for Hannah, who's making slow progress around the grocery store. An espresso machine discharges a blast of steam as she comes through the door. The air in the room is so thick with the smell of coffee she can almost feel a rush of caffeine with the deep breath she inhales. She orders a large dark roast and a blackberry muffin, and chooses a table next to the window. She's never minded sitting in restaurants or coffee houses by herself, but usually she carries a book. Here, where everyone seems to know everyone else, where she has so many reasons to feel that she's visiting without an invitation, she finds herself faking. Looking out at the window as though she's waiting for a friend.

She blows at the steam rising from the coffee, sips, stares out at the quiet street, and wonders if she'll see her own car go by, Jack at the wheel. There will have to be a conversation before today is over. She knows what he's going to say to her and the tone of his voice. He will say she's acting out of loneliness. If she had some purpose to her life, she would not be clinging to Heather's baby. There is no point in telling Jack to get lost, because this will not be resolved without talking. She also knows that before this is over, she and Jack will talk about Marty. Those first few days of his life they have not spoken of in twenty-five years, by mutual consent. Well, she is revoking her consent. And asking for a renegotiation of that contract.

Lynn should feel lighter today, she thinks. No more weight of baby in her arms, but when she and Hannah set out, the empty road stretching ahead, she felt the absence of Beegee like the violent loss of a tooth. Her arms wanted to cross over her breasts to enfold the empty space in the same way her tongue would search a bloody socket.

She made a list in her head as they trudged along, Hannah oddly silent, her jaw set. Eggs and bacon and bread to replace Einar's food and bottled water and a cache of junk food for the drive home. Red licorice, Cadbury's Fruit'n Nut bars, dry-roasted peanuts. Heather's favourites.

A red sports car flew past when they were just a few houses down the road. Hannah snorted. "I used to tell Hank I'd look good in one of those. These days I'd be willing to look good in anything besides that rusty old truck he left me." This was the first acknowledgement Hannah had made that Hank wasn't due back any minute. She waved her hand at the car. "There you go. That's the picture Jack has in mind for Heather, right? Sporty convertible, a thousand dollars worth of clothes on her back, and not a thing to worry about but little old selfish her?"

Lynn wasn't in the mood for dissent, so she shrugged, even though she knew this wasn't true. Jack never wanted Heather to be glamorous. He wanted her to be successful. He'd be more likely to imagine her flying first class to a medical conference in Geneva to deliver a ground-breaking paper than driving a sports car around a sleepy island.

As they walked, Lynn glanced back over her shoulder, expecting to see Heather's car nosing up out of the wet green burrow of Einar's driveway. There was a vehicle coming toward them, but it was a truck that drifted to the wrong side of the road and stopped beside Hannah. A bearded man leaned across the seat, opened the passenger door.

Hannah hopped in, bounced over to the middle of the seat right up close to the gearshift. "Come on," she said, waving Lynn in beside her. "Fred. Lynn." Introduction finished. She launched immediately into a conversation with the driver. Apparently he was supposed to have replaced a hot water heater at Hannah's house some time ago. Days, maybe weeks, from the haranguing Hannah gave him, but he seemed oblivious. Kind of spaced-out and likely been that way for years. Hank sometimes had that look about him. Another of Jack's rants. Dopers. He was sure of it, and the kids were being subjected to second-hand weed. Even their clothes smelled of it, he said. Lynn had never seen Jack close enough to any of Hannah's kids for him to have picked up a scent, but she just rolled her eyes and shook her head. Einar, on the other hand, had shown a rare flash of anger.

"What's it to you, Jack?" he said. "Even if it was true, they're minding their own business, living their lives on their own small piece of the planet. Do they come to Calgary and look over your shoulder?"

Jack mumbled a defensive apology, and never brought the subject up again. Not when Einar was around.

But the scent in the truck, the cigarette bobbing in the corner of the water-heater man's lip was a fat and tidy roll of plain tobacco. If another substance had mellowed him it had not come along for the ride. And a slow ride it was. The truck crept along, the guy's wrist dangling limply over the top of the steering wheel, his attention on Hannah, the two of them talking about someone named Flash, whose wife had taken off for the mainland and left him with the kids. Lynn could have walked faster than they were traveling. When they finally pulled into the parking lot at the grocery store, Lynn leapt out leaving Hannah still gossiping.

"I'll be back in a few minutes," she said. She took the road that led away from the shopping plaza, down to the water, where a long line of cars awaited the next ferry. Unlikely that Jack and Einar would be arriving anytime soon. She was sure the paperwork and the tires would take the better part of the day. She was still puzzled that Jack had chosen the retrieval of the car over bundling Heather and Beegee into his rental and getting them back to Calgary, back to Carmen, as quickly as possible.

She walked out onto one of the docks and looked across the water to the hazy skyline of Campbell River. Jack had pulled them through every museum and historical site, stood the kids in front of every totem pole for pictures, had taken them whale-watching, made sure each trip was packed with teaching and, yes, she grudgingly admitted, the stuff that family holidays were meant to be. She was the rock strapped to their ankles, the one who wanted to be somewhere else. Did she let that show enough to ruin it for them? Something else for which she should apologize someday. She did remember picnics and chasing the kids into the waves, poking through seaweed for shells to take home. There were boxes of shells in the closet in Heather's bedroom.

A tugboat was chugging past in the channel towing three huge barges stacked with containers. Cheerful little boat, with a bright yellow wheelhouse. But all that cargo.

"That would be me," she whispered, "with a baby." She glanced around to make sure no one was listening to the crazy woman talking to herself. "And those barges would get bigger and bigger as the years went on."

The ferry was in now, the arrivals making their way onto

the dock and on to their business. Some of them, she knew, heading straight across the island to Heriot Bay for yet another ferry to another island. No sign of her car, nor of Einar's truck. Relieved, she turned and walked back up the road to the store.

Inside, she grabbed a carry basket and wandered down the aisles. Stopped at the baby supplies. Heather would need diapers for the trip home and enough for at least a day afterward. She took the basket back, and got a cart. Loaded in the largest box of Pampers. Swaddlers for New Baby. Stood a minute looking at the array of formula that was no longer required. How would she have decided what to buy if Hannah hadn't come to the rescue? She knew of people switching from one formula to another to another with the infant howling all the while because nothing agreed. Grant and Donna seemed to have taken every baby care course available. They would have known what to do if Beegee was allergic to milk. Or peanuts. Or bee stings. All the things out there to endanger a little girl.

When a woman pushed her cart past, then stopped, dug in her pocket and handed Lynn a tissue, she realized that she was crying. A quiet flood of tears coursing down her cheeks, dripping down the front of her jacket.

She mopped her face and turned away from the pictures of smiling babies on every single item on the shelf, went to look for Hannah in the produce aisle.

"I'm going to park this for a minute," she said, "and get some coffee. I need…I'll be back before you're done."

"You okay? You look a little feverish."

For a few seconds Lynn thought Hannah was going to reach out and put a hand on her forehead. "Fine," she said. "I only had a few bites of toast before we left and I feel a bit wobbly. Blood sugar, nothing more."

Now she finishes her coffee and the last bites of the muffin and she does feel better. She buys a half dozen muffins to take with her, and finds Hannah outside on a chair. She looks as comfortable on this verandah that stretches across the front of the mini-mall as if she owned it. "I'll be a few minutes," Lynn says. "Can I buy you a coffee to drink while I go get my diapers?"

"No thanks. Already had a quick one. I met one of Hank's pals on the way into the grocery store and he treated."

Lynn goes back into the store and throws ground beef, spaghetti sauce, French bread into the buggy as well. No matter whether Jack and Heather leave together before this day is over, she doesn't think she'll have the energy to get behind the wheel until morning. She'll make dinner for Einar. Then sleep, and an early start.

She pays for the groceries, pops back into the coffee shop to buy a pound of good dark roast for Einar. Outside, Hannah is beside Fred's truck, her grocery bags stowed in the box next to coils of rope and tool boxes. "Fred's in the bar, but he promised me he'd come down in an hour and fix that heater. He can bring all this. You want to throw yours in too?"

Lynn slips the sack of muffins into one of Hannah's bags. They likely won't pass muster on the organic test, but maybe the kids will find them first. She shakes her head. "You're a trusting soul."

"What's he going to do with a pound of pinto beans and a bunch of veg? He knows I'll feed him if he carts the stuff home for me."

Okay, but Lynn may need the food before Fred's indeterminate time of arrival. Hannah takes one of the two sacks from her and they cross to the road.

The bit of mist that had clung to the tops of the trees earlier has burned off. Shafts of slanting sunlight tinge the ferns in the ditches with gold. Lynn looks up into cerulean

243

blue and has a quick flash forward to the moment when her car will cruise past Lac Des Arcs, out of the mountains, and the landscape will open up around her, the sky stretch miles high. She wants to leave now. But won't. Can't.

The birds seem to have awoken with the sunshine, and flit between the trees, dark silhouettes that she can't identify. Jack would stand here on the road with his binoculars to his eyes until he'd put a name to every one of them.

Lynn chugs along beside Hannah, trying not to think about the blisters on her heels. Her feet bare, because Einar's socks are too thick to fit her wet shoes. "It must be nice," Hannah says suddenly, as though she's been holding back the words for some time, "to be able to just run away like you did. Nothing at home you need to do? Don't you work?"

Lynn's sure Einar's told Hannah about the divorce. "Yes," she says, "I work. I need to eat." She wonders how the money Hank sends home stretches to feed all those kids. "How about you? Do you work?"

"During the summer," Hannah says, "I waitress here and there if anyone needs me. Nothing permanent, but it helps buy school clothes and all the other stuff they need in the fall. So what do you do?"

"I work for a temp agency. Receptionist here, file clerk there."

"No kidding. I thought you were a teacher."

"Nope," says Lynn. "Never was. I can barely remember what I started out to do. I had Marty at the end of my first year of university and never went back."

"So you're going to keep doing that? Temping?"

No, probably not. But she doesn't feel like telling Hannah that she'd like to go back to university, piddle around with a General Studies program. She suspects her reaction would be somewhat like Jack's. Although, who knows what aspirations Hannah's got filed away.

"I'm not sure what I'll do," Lynn says. "I may go back to school." She can afford tuition if she sells the house. She got the house, Jack got their investments. Her lawyer said it was a decent settlement. If Jack had known how dramatically house prices were going to continue to climb, he might have worked it out a little differently, but it's a done deal now. As soon as Jack's mother dies, he'll have his share of the Bishop fortunes, more money than he'll ever need.

"What about you?" Lynn asks. "Your kids are growing up. One's gone already, and the boys will soon be finished school, won't they?"

Hannah shrugs. "Will they ever be gone? Sunny's back. Didn't Heather tell you she picked her up somewhere out there on the road?"

"No," Lynn says, surprised, because amidst all the things Heather has refused to talk about, this would have been a distraction. "Is she going to stay?"

"That would be the question, all right." Hannah pauses in the middle of the road, bends down to adjust the strap on her sandal. She squints off into the trees and then looks at Lynn, shrugs. "I doubt it. Sunny hates living here, too messy, no privacy. So what does she do but go off and live in a filthy house with a bunch of bright lights just like herself, all figuring they've got the answer to everything. Can I tell her she's wasting her life? Not a chance. She has to muddle through, same as I did." She starts walking again, shoulders back. "I can't even tell her how much it hurts that she uses me as the reason for all this. My life sucks so much in her estimation that she has to get away from here so she doesn't end up with a bunch of kids and a lousy existence like mine."

They walk along in their own silences, Lynn wishing there was something she could say to the tall woman with whom she's trying to keep step. There is so much moisture in the air, everything shimmers, even the stones on the road look as though they've been licked clean.

"Don't get me wrong," Hannah says finally. "We'll figure it out. I was a lot like Sunny at her age. If she doesn't stay this time, she'll be back. So long as she's only one island away I can keep tabs on her until she grows up." Einar's driftwood sign is visible now. "What are you going to do about the baby?"

Lynn shakes her head. "That was never my decision. I'm hoping Heather will drive home with me so I can get her to at least look at all the options."

"See, that's the problem with you people," Hannah says. "You have too many options. Too many places to go. You're not grounded. If you lived on a small island like this one, you'd know that there are limits to where you can go and what you can do. You have to rely on yourself."

"Don't you think that's a tad over-simplified? We can't all live on your island."

"God, no! We don't want you!" Hannah cackles, puts her hand on Lynn's sleeve. "I didn't mean that literally. Each to his own island, y'know? Are you thinking about raising that little girl yourself?"

Finally someone asking the question. "No," Lynn says. "I have been thinking about it, even though no one has ever asked if I'd keep her. If something happened to Heather—God forbid!—of course I'd raise her. But if you knew my daughter well, you'd know how thorny this would be. Maybe that's why she's never suggested it herself. She wouldn't be able to stand back and let me do the job. She'd be supervising. I'd be the nanny. And I would be so tired." Hannah is grinning and nodding. "Then there's Jack, who'd probably be directing things from his corner as well." As she talks, Lynn realizes it's just now that she finally sees this clearly. "Of course I'll help Heather if she keeps Beegee. I'm the grandma. That's what grandmas do. But, Hannah, I'm only forty-five years old. There are some things I want to do."

"Good!" They're at the driveway now. Hannah claps her hands on Lynn's shoulders. "You get on with whatever you want to do. One little baby girl won't be in the way. Not for anyone."

Lynn sighs. "Ah, but that's the part Heather has to be sure of. One little baby girl grows into a bigger girl, and she's with you for good." Lynn looks into this woman's face and is surprised to feel regret that they're not likely to meet again. She would like to drink herbal tea with Hannah a few months from now. To be sure that Sunny is safe, that Josh is staying out of trouble, that Destiny is still her sweet self. "In case I don't see you before we leave, I want to say thanks, Hannah. For feeding the baby, and for the clothes, and everything else. Tell Destiny she was good company, and a big help"

"Oh for gawd sake, you can't give up that easily. She'll keep her if you just slow her down a bit." Hannah nods sagely. "Just watch her with that kid. Even in the couple of glimpses I had, she's hanging on like a mama grizzly with her cub." She starts down the driveway with Lynn and for a minute Lynn is afraid she's going to come inside for tea. Give Heather all this advice as well. But Hannah stops at the woodpile. "I'd better get back. If Fred shows up and I'm not there, he'll dump off the food and bugger off without fixing the heater." She hands Lynn the bag of groceries. "Don't you leave here without coming up to tell me how things turn out."

Her sandals slap against the soles of her feet as she walks across the wet ground, through the trees, up the path toward her house.

18

Lynn comes striding through the door on a mission. Heather knows this from the way her mom's long neck is stretched just as high as it will go, her chin up, eyes zooming right in on Heather. This is the Lynn that Heather and Marty were slightly scared of when they were kids. The mom who'd just found the bad mark on the ripped-up essay in the garbage, just got the phone call from the neighbour about the slingshot water balloon that went right through an upstairs bedroom window. Who knew those things were more than a toy? The Lynn who rolled her eyes at their lame excuses, but after the restitution was made didn't think it was necessary to pull Jack into the discussion.

Oh yeah. Heather can tell that Lynn wants to talk. Will insist that they talk. Which is good, because Heather thinks she might be ready to listen.

"Beegee asleep?" Lynn asks.

"Yeah, I took her to the spit and wore her right out playing on the beach."

Lynn doesn't blink, doesn't know Heather's serious.

"Good, because we need to talk, and no distractions this time." She drops a couple of bags of groceries onto the counter, takes off her jacket, hangs it on the wall, lines her shoes up on the mat. All business.

"Can we at least eat while we talk?"

"I had a muffin and coffee," Lynn says. "Here." She digs around in one of the bags and throws Heather a pack of red licorice.

"Thanks, I guess." Heather tears the bag open with her teeth, and peels out two twisters. Could be tricky. How can you talk earnestly when you're chomping on licorice?

Lynn sits down across the table. "Did you really go to Rebecca Spit?" Heather nods. "That's quite a hike, isn't it?" Lynn glances at her watch. "Was I gone that long?"

"I got a ride."

"With who?"

"A woman I saw yesterday on the ferry over. Just this person who recognized me."

"A total stranger?"

Oh gawd, is she going to get a recycled lecture on the dangers of strangers? "Not total, Lynn. I just said I met her on the ferry." A bit of a stretch, but parking next to someone could possibly be described as a meeting.

Lynn frowns. "Hannah said you picked up her daughter somewhere along the way too."

"Yeah, a whole carload of company."

"How did you recognize her after all these years?"

Okay, she is not going to admit that she didn't recognize Sunny until she'd been in the car for at least five minutes, which means that she did pick up a total stranger. Come to think of it, that was as dumb as wandering around on a deserted beach with a baby. "I dunno. She hasn't changed much, I guess. What do you want to talk about?" She fishes out another piece of licorice. "Apart from telling me again that you've never regretted having us, which I find hard to believe." Heather knows she sounds "chippy"—the word Nana Bishop always used for her when she was rude—but she can't stop herself. She feels chippy.

"I said I never regretted keeping Marty, which is quite different from the generic question of whether people regret having had kids. There are times when everyone does, I think. Ann Landers asked that question years ago. Would people have children if they were given the chance to live their lives over again, and you know thousands of them wrote letters saying they wouldn't." She smoothes the hair off her forehead and leaves her hand there as though she suddenly has a headache. "I wouldn't answer that way, though. I'd say yes, I'd do it again. With some better planning. Knowing that every now and again there'd be a time when I wished I hadn't."

"Like what kind of times?"

"Oh really, Heather. Use your imagination. Did I want to get called into the school when you were in kindergarten because you bit that little boy so hard you left a dental imprint in his arm? Did I want to come home early from a New Year's party and find Marty and his friends smoking dope in my living room? Did I want all the other moments that were embarrassing, or infuriating, or downright scary?"

"You want me to buy into all that? You won't come right out and say it, but you think I should keep Beegee, don't you?"

She's surprised by how long it takes Lynn to answer. She was sure this was the mission, to tell Heather she needs to keep Beegee so her heart won't break, and all that other sad stuff Lynn has been hinting at but never coming right out and saying, just going around in circles.

"Yes," Lynn says finally, and Heather has to chew hard to get her teeth unstuck from the licorice. "Or maybe it would be more correct to say that I don't really know if you should, because how could I make that judgment, but that I hope you will for reasons that are purely selfish. I've avoided telling you this was what I hoped because I'm afraid you'll say, 'Okay, then I will, but you're the one who wanted me to do this, so when it's really hard, it's going to be your fault, and you're going to have to help me.'"

"What's so wrong with that? Didn't you and Daddy tell me that you'd be there to help me whatever I decided?" Daddy? She can't believe she said that.

"Of course we did. Of course we'll help you. All new mothers need help, and that's what families do. But assuring you of our support isn't the same as trying to sway you by promising to make it easy. You can't hold us ransom for your decision. You're an adult, Heather."

"It's hard!"

"I know it is, sweetheart. I do."

"You don't! You had Jack. You didn't have to decide."

Lynn knocks her chair over, she stands up so quickly. Comes around the table, and puts her hands on Heather's cheeks. "Heather it was twenty-five years ago. You think it's tough now?" Heather feels like her face is in a vice, Lynn is squeezing so tight. "Don't make the same mistake I did by assuming you only have one choice. Sure, this new kind of adoption is enlightened. You can choose a family, stay in touch. No more secrets or lies. Is that enough? Is that all you want from Beegee? A crayon picture they'll stick in the envelope with the Christmas card every year? A Belinda masterpiece of a house with a bright yellow sun, a stick family, probably a little brother added in a couple of years? Well no, you might get to see her a couple of times a year. Take her to the park if she isn't too shy with you, but likely her mom or dad will come along. I'm the one who'll get the card and the crayon picture. That's why I ran away." Lynn's face

251

is wet, but she just keeps on talking. "I didn't want to be a grandma, Heather. But you've made me one and I honest to God couldn't do anything last Friday except grab Beegee and run. So make this decision yourself. I know that Carmen is right. You have to decide, but please don't forget that you are not alone in this. You're not the only one who has a stake." Her hands fall away and she stands up. "That's it. My selfish rationale for what I've done."

Heather's head is so full of Lynn's words, she can't find her own. Lynn puts a hand on her shoulder. "Don't answer. There's time to talk later." She rubs her eyes. "I'm sorry, but I think I need to sleep or I'm going to be sick. Just for a half hour or so."

Lynn almost runs to the bedroom, but she pauses at the bed. Heather watches her circle around to the other side and curl up facing Beegee, but with an expanse of blanket between them.

Heather is sitting in the same spot twenty minutes later when she hears cars in the driveway; still sitting there when Jack drops two sets of keys on the kitchen table. He rubs his hands, looks around the room, and this time he comes to Heather with his arms wide.

"Okay, both cars are good to go. Marty says he'll come out and drive yours back some time in the next couple of weeks. I'll fly him out here to Comox, and Einar will pick him up. Sorry, sweetheart, but you'll have to be without wheels until then."

Heather stands and allows him the hug that's meant to re-assure her all is well. He's wearing a blue anorak she doesn't recognize. The jacket smells of fresh air, as though Jack's spent the day outdoors. His cheeks are pink, and his eyes are bright. He looks a hell of a lot better than when she last saw him at home, or this morning when he barged into the bedroom. That must be on his mind too, because when he stands back, he takes her hands. His feel cold. "I'm sorry I was so testy this morning, Heather. I was short of sleep and worried sick. I had a decent nap in the truck while we waited at the tire shop, and now we can get back on the rails."

Heather puts her finger to her lips, points to the bedroom. *Shhhhh.*

He looks at his watch, purses his lips, but speaks quietly. Einar's gone into the bathroom, and will probably stay there a tactfully long time. "Have you called the social worker? She'll need to get things organized for you at the other end, I imagine."

Heather crosses the room and closes the bedroom door before she comes back to stand in front of him again. "Donna and Grant changed their minds. They're getting a baby from someone else instead."

He pounds his fist on the table. After a deep breath, "So you'll choose another family?" She supposes she should say, yes, that's what Carmen's suggested, that's the reasonable course of action here. Then she could tell him to please just go away for a while, come back in a couple of hours when the baby's awake, because there's no point in rushing away now. Already, it's getting dim inside these rooms. It'll be night before they know it, and why drive at night? She would sound just like Lynn if she said all this.

Jack's not waiting for her to offer any plans. "I guess you broke the contract," he says. "If you'd gone ahead right after she was born, instead of dragging things out. They probably feel like they've been on thin ice all along. Yes, I guess I see their point of view."

"What about my point of view?" Heather asks. She wishes her voice didn't sound so small. She steps away, because he looks like he's going to put his arm around her again and she really can't handle another meltdown. "What's your point of view, Jack?"

"I understand why it hurts, Heather…"

"You don't understand that part at all. You never gave birth to anyone, and you never gave anyone away. But what about being a grandpa?"

Oddly, that shuts him right down. He looks as though every bit of wind just left his sails. The bedroom door opens. Heather wonders if Lynn's had her ear to the thin wood. She has Beegee in her arms. Beegee squirming and getting ready to squall. "She needs to be fed, Heather."

The sight of Lynn seems to puff Jack up again. "So," he says, "Heather just told me about her first adoption plan falling through."

None of them can possibly miss the ranking of Donna and Grant, as though there are nine more families lined up on the tarmac at the Calgary airport. Now Einar finally comes out and stands awkwardly in the middle of the room. "I think I'd best go…"

"No," Lynn says. "Don't go anywhere. Heather needs to bathe and feed the baby, and I'm going to start dinner for all of us. It's early, but Heather had licorice for lunch, and I've only had a muffin, and even if the two of you stopped for something, you can probably eat again, can't you, Einar?" Heather wonders if Jack notices that Lynn doesn't seem concerned about feeding him. "Jack and I have plenty of time to talk later. Unless of course you're still determined to get home tonight," she says. "In which case, you'd better get on the road now. Heather can drive home with me." She puts Beegee into Heather's arms and nods toward the bathroom. Okay, so much for any discussion on who's leaving when with whom. Lynn's already in the kitchen, hauling out the frying pan. She's right about Beegee needing to be bathed even before she's fed.

Heather looks around the bathroom, trying to remember what she'll need. There's a box of Pampers on the floor. The damp towel on the edge of the tub from her own bath will have to do because it was the last one in the pile. A couple of those weird little nightgowns and some cloth diapers big enough to be blankets. Beegee's eyes seem drawn to the reflection of lights in the window, but then her gaze skitters around the room. Heather can't remember how much a baby can actually see by now. She glanced at the pamphlets from the public health nurse, but never thought she'd be the one checking off milestones. Leaning close, she brushes her cheek against Beegee's, then slowly pulls away, smiling. A grimace wriggles its way across the baby's brow, her mouth opens as though to yawn and then the corners turn up. Gone as quickly as it dawned, but for sure that was another smile. Heather loosens the towel, peels off the wet clothes, and holds Beegee in the air.

"Yay, baby! Big accomplishment." She lowers the baby into the sink on her bent arm, and notices that the ugly stump of cord is finally gone. Only a pink nub left to show where they were joined. So relaxed in the warm water, Heather thinks that if she eased away her arm, Beegee would float there, wisps of hair drifting around her ears, hands curled. With the corner of a facecloth, Heather gently wipes the pouchy cheeks, the folds under Beegee's chin. She cups her hand and scoops water over the black hair, works a bit of lather off the bar of soap and washes the baby's head. Hair slicked back, eyes huge and round, Beegee looks like a little seal.

A knock on the door. Lynn's voice. "Can I come in?"

"Just a minute," she says.

She soaps and rinses and wipes in all the folds and creases of her daughter's skin. She lets the water drain, lifts Beegee onto a towel. Wraps her so that only her face is showing. When she opens the door, Lynn is back in the kitchen. She nods at a pile of towels on the rocking chair. "I guess Einar took my laundry bags up to Hannah's last night. She just sent Destiny down with those."

Jack and Einar seem to have disappeared again. "Where'd they go now?" Heather asks.

"To get your dad a room at the Heriot Bay Inn. Apparently he's decided it's not so urgent after all that he get back by tonight."

Heather moves the towels, sits down in the chair and opens her shirt to the baby. Sweet little face looking up at her. She thinks, suddenly, of the big baby at the B&B, snoozing away in his high chair. "I didn't tell you I spent the night at a bed and breakfast in Horseshoe Bay, did I?"

"No," Lynn says. "I'm glad to hear you stopped." She's frying ground beef, the smell of onions and garlic billowing across the room.

"It felt kind of weird," Heather says, "like I was a house guest in this place where I didn't even know the hosts. They had a baby. But not cute like the Beej. Did you stop anywhere on the way out here?"

Lynn just keeps stirring and frowning and Heather knows that she did not. That she drove right through, and any minute now she's going to be saying she's sorry she did that. She's spared by the ringing of the phone.

"Marty!"

Heather wants to jump out of the chair and grab the phone from her mom's hand, but there's this problem of the baby glommed onto her breast. So she waves frantically, and in a few seconds Lynn says, "Just a minute, Marty. Your sister's going to fling the baby through the air if I don't give her the phone first." The cord doesn't stretch far enough, so they push the rocker across the room and Heather is able to attend to both Beegee and Marty.

"Hey," she says, "I know I was supposed to phone you, but why didn't you call sooner, you big doofus."

"Ha! After talking to Jack, I figured I'd stay out of this. Like Nana Bishop would say—sounds like a real Donnybrook. How's it going?"

"It's not," she says. "I talked to Carmen last night and I have to find a new family." She's aware of Lynn at the stove, suddenly still, her hand poised over the skillet with a can of tomatoes. "My people got tired of waiting."

"Well, that sucks, Heather. You didn't need this to get any worse than it was."

Lynn's picked up a cloth now and is wiping splashes of tomato off the top of the stove. She heaves the rag into the sink when she's done, keeps stirring, stirring.

"Yeah, well. I'll figure it out. Hey, are you picking us up at the airport?" She grits her teeth, wishing Lynn would at least turn around and glare at her or something, but no, she just stands with her back so straight she looks as if she'd topple like a tree if you touched her.

"I can. But I think Jack said Rhea was lined up already. Is that a problem?"

"No, it's swell. I completely forgot about her. Listen, I'll call you tomorrow, when I know for sure what's going on. Just stand by."

"Tomorrow fine, but Friday I'm leaving town. Kaylee's folks have a condo at Invermere. We're going up there for the weekend, and I'm thinkin', Heather, if things move fast, maybe you want to come with us? Get away for a couple of days?"

No wonder he's still looking for a woman. "Give her a break, Marty! Jeez, what kind of a guy asks his hot new woman if he can bring his weeping sister along on a dirty weekend?"

He laughs. "Well, I haven't asked her yet, but I know she'd say yes. You're going to love Kaylee. Really. If I don't see you tomorrow, I'll call you when we're back and you can meet us somewhere for dinner next week. Now let me talk to Lynn."

Heather waves the phone around until Lynn finally looks her way. Then Heather stands up, Beegee braced on one arm, and tries to drag the chair back into the centre of the room with the other.

"Just a sec," Lynn says into the phone and gently steers Heather out of the way so she can carry the chair back to its spot. She pats Heather's arm before she goes back to Marty.

Beegee's fussed by all the up and down, and won't latch on again, doesn't want to be on Heather's shoulder to burp, doesn't want the other breast. So now they'll pace until she settles, and then she'll sleep a while, and then she'll nurse again. And again and again. There are no martini bars, nice restaurants, trips to someone's lakeside condo in this picture.

19

Lynn wishes she'd ignored Heather's frantic waving and talked with Marty first. Then she could have left the room after
their conversation to give Heather some privacy, and saved
herself the aggravation of hearing yet again about the quest
for a new family, the plane trip home, all the things Lynn
is so fervently hoping will not come to pass. Or is it all just
Heather, and this need of hers to push buttons and will she
never grow out of it?

"Marty," she's finally able to say, "it is so good to hear
your voice. Although I'm sure the thought of being out here
with us is as appealing as…well, as being out here with us
ever was, I wish you were."

"Good old Quadra. Thanks, but it sounds like a bit of
a shmozzle. Everything getting sorted out? I told Dad I'd
fly out maybe next weekend, or as soon as I can, and drive
Heather's car back." Lynn knows from years of standing behind Marty, pushing, that the car is quite likely to stay out
here until Jack flies out in March, even though Marty's in-
tentions are good.

"I think Einar will be happy to see you, so try to figure it out, okay?"

"Sure," he says. "I have a couple of pals in Vancouver I wouldn't mind stopping to see."

Marty has pals everywhere. Unlike Heather, he has huge patience, can suffer fools, and friends stuck to him like barnacles when he was growing up. "What are you up to?" Lynn asks him now.

"On my way to Kaylee's place. We're cooking dinner together. I want you to meet her when you get back. I think she's a keeper."

Lynn smiles. "You deserve a keeper, Martin. I'd love to meet her."

"So you're driving back alone?"

Lynn stares at the bedroom door. "I'm not sure. I'd like Heather to come with me."

"Isn't it easier for her to fly? With the baby, I mean."

"Maybe," Lynn says. Although it's just occurred to her that if Heather flies home with Jack, she'll arrive back at Lynn's alone, and until she came here, to Quadra, she wasn't willing to be alone with the baby for more than an hour at a time. Two days?

"I guess she'll go to Jack's then, until she gets this next adoption set up?" he asks, as though he's inside Lynn's head, nudging her in the direction she would otherwise have ignored.

"I guess that's an option," she says. Heather and Beegee and Jack and Rhea? "But I'm still hoping she'll drive back with me. We can take it slow, have lots of time to talk. I finally figured out that this must be the whole point of what I've done."

He's quiet, and she imagines him with his eyes closed, brows creeping together over that long Bishop nose. "Okay,

I understand. I guess. But about the baby? I think it'll be okay, Mom. Whichever way it goes."

"It has to be, doesn't it? I love you, kiddo. See you in a couple of days. We need to talk too."

Lynn hangs the phone back on its hook ever so carefully, her eyes on the window where, once again, Jack and Einar are climbing out of Einar's truck. The half hour of sleep helped. She's ready for Jack now. She opens the door for them, but Einar waves and heads up the path toward Hannah's. Jack stands outside, hands in his pockets, and she knows that if she was a little closer, she'd hear his keys and the loose change jingling.

"Einar says not to hold up supper for him," he says when he's inside. "He's going up to talk to Hannah for a minute and then down to the pub to meet somebody for a beer."

"Well you'd better come in," Lynn says. "I guess we need to sort out a few things before morning."

"A few things?" He takes off his shoes, but leaves the jacket on, sits down in the rocking chair, and runs his hands through his hair. The day is catching up on him. If he was at home, she knows he'd sit down to read and within five minutes his head would be lolling, the book hanging from his hand. She wonders if Rhea marks his place before she sets his book aside. If she brings a pillow to slip onto his shoulder, to ease his neck. "You've made a real balls-up of this one, Lynn."

"I have. But I can't say I'm sorry. Not for the way it turned out, even though I am sorry for causing a lot of worry. I've apologized to Heather, and I guess I owe you an apology too."

"Those adopting people? You don't feel sorry for the way this has gone for them?"

"Oh for God's sake, Jack! Of course I feel for them. But is it Heather's job to make them happy?"

261

The bedroom door opens and Heather comes out with the sleeping baby in her arms. "Sorry, sweetheart," Jack says. "Did we wake you?" Heather shakes her head, and wanders to the window. "I almost booked a room at the inn for you as well. We'll get away early. I've arranged to leave the car at the Comox airport so we can fly from there. We have reservations on the noon flight." Heather turns around and Jack smiles, pleased with himself, Lynn can tell, that he has tidily knotted up the loose ends.

"You didn't ask me if I was flying home. You just made the reservations." Oddly, Heather doesn't look angry, just puzzled.

"I can cancel your reservation if you're not ready," Jack says quickly. "I was just covering the bases, Heather. In fact we got the last two seats on that plane. There was nothing on the earlier flight."

Lynn is hungry. Suddenly ravenous. She fills a dented pot with water, sets it on to boil and opens the box of spaghetti. "Marty called," she says. "If he was here, this would be just like the old days, wouldn't it? Seems to me we had spaghetti every time."

"I don't want to eat with you." Jack's voice is so cold, Lynn reacts with a flare of heat to her face. You'd think she'd have extinguished that response by now. "I'd like to talk with Heather alone if you don't mind."

"I do mind," she says, willing that damn flush to leave her cheeks. But why? She used to try and hide the hurt and the anger too, but she doesn't need to do that anymore. "I'm cooking. If you need to talk, then you go somewhere else." He hasn't taken his jacket off, but she doesn't want Heather to stand out under the dripping trees. "You can talk in the bedroom."

"Jeez, you guys!" Heather stamps her foot. "Yeah, just like old times, with the two of you sniping at each other. Lynn, I

262

don't want you to cook supper for me. Jack, I don't want to talk right now. I need to think. I can't find a minute to think without someone yanking at me." She looks at the baby in her arms, and a sob, just one sob, breaks through. "Even you, Beegee. Just give a minute."

Lynn heaves a handful of spaghetti into the pot, and crosses the floor to Heather. She lifts Beegee from her arms. Takes Heather's jacket from the hook by the door, hangs it on her shoulders. "There will always be someone who can give you a minute for yourself," she says. "Go. Get in the car and drive to the beach and watch the waves. That works for me. Just remember to keep the doors locked." Then she shakes her head. "No, just do whatever you want." She glances at her watch. "You just fed her?" Heather nods. "Well there you go. You have at least two hours. Go."

When the door closes, Lynn holds out the swaddled baby to Jack. "I think it's finally your turn," she says. He is contemplating leaving. She can tell. She'll be left here alone with the baby once more, and nothing accomplished. "All right, then," she says. "I'll put her down if you won't hold her. But please don't go yet. Jack, we must talk." She pretends to adjust Beegee's blanket, wipe away an imaginary trace of milk from the baby's lips. She won't let Jack see that she could be provoked to tears by a single word.

Finally, he takes off his jacket and hangs it on the back of one of the kitchen chairs. "I don't know what it is you want from me, Lynn, but okay, we'll talk. Give me the baby and go rescue that pot before it boils over."

While Lynn blows on the foaming pot of pasta, adjusts the heat, turns the flame on under the sauce, Jack moves to the rocking chair. "Strange to be here again. This is the last place on the planet I would have expected you to hide. Clever."

"No," she says, glancing back at him from the fridge

where she's looking for Parmesan cheese, overly optimistic, she's sure. "I didn't think about it that way at all. I was running, Jack, not hiding. Automatic pilot, I guess. I doubt that I'll ever be back."

"We're coming back in the spring," he says. "I've missed this place."

There is Parmesan cheese in the little bin on the door of the fridge. Not the shaker of grated cheese Lynn thought she might find, but a lump, tightly wrapped in plastic, so hard that she suspects she may have left it behind herself. Jack is looking at Beegee, his head tilting this way and that as though he's trying to bring her into focus.

Lynn unwraps the cheese, smells it, tries to remember if they ate spaghetti on their last stay here. She has difficulty imagining Rhea in this cabin. Imagining her at all, because she's only seen Rhea twice, and she avoids attaching an actual physical presence to the name. Not that she hates Rhea; it's not the woman's fault that she fell in love with Jack, nor Jack's fault that he fell out with Lynn and in with Rhea. It seemed to surprise everyone else that he'd go so far as to marry Rhea, but Lynn was not surprised. Not in the least. There is completion to everything Jack does.

Rhea on the old sofa in front of the fire, her shiny head on Jack's shoulder? Rhea standing under the trees with raindrops sparkling around her? Rhea with the sad serious look she had when she came with Jack to the hospital after Beegee was born. That was a surprise. It took Lynn a minute to realize that the woman who came into the room behind Jack was Rhea. She could tell they expected her to leave, but she'd stayed stubbornly in her chair, leafing through a silly book of prayers the adopting parents had brought for her.

As though he's reading her mind, can see Rhea there, Jack says, "We won't be staying here. I think Einar's had enough of this family for a while."

So they'll stay at the Heriot Bay Inn. In one of the rooms with an ocean view, a view to the Discovery Islands. Maybe the same room Lynn and Jack had several years ago when Einar insisted on taking Marty and Heather to Campbell River for fish and chips and a movie so their parents could have a night alone.

For at least five minutes, they are perfectly quiet together. Lynn chips away at the cheese with the edge of a knife, tests the spaghetti, drains it.

Then Beegee gives one of her warm-up squawks. Lynn walks across the room and looks down at the baby. "See any resemblances?" she finally asks.

"No," Jack says abruptly. Not happy with the scrutiny, the lack of motion, the absence of a breast—who knows what makes a baby grieve?—Beegee's face is screwed into a look of abject misery. She twists and arches her back in her grandfather's arms.

"She's like Marty when he was tiny," Lynn says. "Doesn't like to be wet." This isn't true, but Lynn wants Jack to have to change a diaper. "Everything you need is in the bathroom."

He opens his mouth as though he's going to refuse, then shakes his head.

He leaves the bathroom door open, kneels on the bathmat with his back to Lynn, spreads a towel, lays Beegee on it. She's worked into full frenzy now, high frequency wailing, knees tight to her chest.

"Talk to her," Lynn calls. "Or sing. That sometimes works."

When Heather had colic, Jack would hold her across his arm with her head resting in the crook of his elbow, the top of her legs in his hand, and walk slowly, calmly around the house. Now he comes out of the bathroom with Beegee in the same hold. Magic. The baby is still. Lynn wishes it wasn't so. She does not want Jack to demonstrate competence with his granddaughter.

He takes the rocking chair, shifts Beegee to his shoulder. A short bleat of protest, then silence.

Lynn prepares a plate of spaghetti and carries it to the table. He said he didn't want to eat with her, but she may offer to feed him when she's done. Depending on how the next ten minutes go. The creak creak of the rocking chair, a few crackles from the dying fire the only sounds in the room, Jack's one arm hanging slack, the other holding the baby securely to his chest.

"You can probably put her down soon," she says. "If you prop her against a pillow on the couch, she'll be content for a while."

He shifts Beegee slightly, tucks her head under his chin. Lynn imagines cheeks pressed to his shirt, milk-blistered lips sucking even as Beegee dreams, the warmth of the baby. "She's a beauty, isn't she?" he says so quietly she can barely hear him. Wonders if she really did hear him.

If she looks at him, if she says a word, if he says another single word, she will cry.

He saves her that moment of weakness. "Well, you sure did make a mess of things. Although maybe it's all for the best if those people were so desperate they ran out to find another baby as soon as there was a delay. There are thousands of other good families waiting for babies." He takes off his glasses and cleans them carefully with the corner of Beegee's blanket.

"Aren't we a good family?" Lynn plays with the spaghetti on her plate, arranging the strands into a tidy mound with her fork. "Carmen told me that we should be very proud because when she asked Heather what sort of parents she wanted for her baby, Heather said she wanted people like us. Carmen said that wasn't so very common. So many young women are looking for their own notion of a perfect family that's in another universe from what they knew when they were growing up."

Jack's head flies up. "Good God, Lynn, you didn't do this because you want to raise another child yourself, did you?"

"No." She breaks a piece of bread from the loaf still peeking out of its paper sleeve. "I did it because I'm her grandmother, not because I want to be a mother again. Once was plenty." Jack's gaze returns to the baby. "What about you?" she asks, automatically. "How would you feel about raising another child?" Funny it's never occurred to her to wonder this before. He's married a woman at least ten years younger. Rhea's likely younger than Donna, the adopting mother.

He's silent so long, Lynn thinks he hasn't heard the question.

"I've thought about it," he says. "Rhea would love to have a baby, but she's not able. She had a tubal pregnancy in her first marriage." This is way more information than Lynn wanted or needs to know. Rhea was married before? "We talked about adopting Heather's baby when we first found out she was pregnant."

The spaghetti in front of Lynn has turned into a plateful of snakes. She pushes it away.

"The truth is, I really don't want to start all over again, and adopting Heather's baby would be far more complicated than adopting someone else's."

Lynn impresses herself with a calm voice. "Jack, why would you even have considered this?"

"Because there are two of us. You would have to do this alone."

She should not have ignored the headache that began hours ago. The taste of the one strand of spaghetti she's managed to swallow rises in her throat. "Excuse me," she says, as though she's leaving a table full of guests, and stands up.

"I feel a bit ill." She walks outside, leans on the railing, and takes deep breaths. She'll be okay. So long as she stops thinking about this. About Rhea raising Beegee. Rhea has Jack. That's why she'd be more suitable.

On a winter's day, when Heather was about a year old, Lynn left Marty with a neighbour late in the afternoon, bundled her daughter's demanding little body into a snowsuit and strapped her into the stroller. Heather had been awake since four in the morning, nodding off in little catnaps and howling every time Lynn's head touched a pillow. The sink was piled high with dishes, the living room carpeted in Marty's toys, cracker crumbs and unfolded laundry, and the house stank of an overflowing diaper pail and the tomato soup that had bubbled over onto the red hot burner of the stove at lunch time. Lynn's mother had phoned in tears that morning before she left for the cancer clinic for a round of chemotherapy. The kids were noisy; Lynn wasn't able to talk over the din, so she promised to call that night. The one sure way to settle Heather was to push the stroller for at least an hour, so they plowed along drifted sidewalks and finally ended up on the snow-packed bike path beside the river. When Heather was finally quiet, Lynn sat down on the blanket of snow, looked at that blessedly sleeping little face, and wept because she feared that if Heather had, at that moment, arched her back and begun screaming again, she would have had the urge to heave her, stroller and all into the icy river. It was dark by the time she pushed Heather up the front walk, so tired she leaned on the buggy for the last few steps, the momentum dragging her feet to the door. Marty was building with Lego, the laundry was folded and sorted into neat piles on the corduroy couch and the smell of omelets and fried potatoes wafted from the kitchen. In the hour since he'd come home from school, Jack had shoveled the walks, reclaimed Marty from next door, and accomplished all that Lynn had failed to do since eight o'clock that morning. The house was in order and supper was on the table—the least, the look on his face said, that he would have expected to find at the end of the day.

After dinner, Jack pulled on his sheepskin jacket. "I need to get out of here for a while. Don't wait up."

Lynn nodded, put both children to bed without argument, and phoned her mother. Her mom was tired, but calm. Lynn burst into tears. "I appreciate the help," she sobbed, "but does he have to take over and make me feel like a failure. Just a little help would have been enough."

Her mother sighed. "He's the hardest kind of all, babe. Sweetheart half the time, asshole the other half. No in-between."

Lynn's head has cleared now, the waves of nausea receded. She steps back inside, where Jack is nodding in the rocking chair, both he and Beegee asleep.

"Jack," she says, loud enough to be sure that he hears. "You can be such an asshole."

He shakes himself awake. "What?"

"No, I'm not in a situation where I want to raise a baby, and it's not because I'm alone, but because I have a life ahead of me that could well include someone else some day." She feels like carrying the plate of cold spaghetti across the room and dumping it on his head. "And while a baby might be a bit of an obstacle in Heather's social life, there are young men who like babies. But not so many middle-aged men daft enough to want to start over again, I think."

20

Heather opens the door to the pub and steps inside. She always wanted a peek in here when she was a kid. Her dad and Mr. Haugland came for beers, and her mom stayed at the cabin with her and Marty and played Monopoly.

Well, there's no mellow Monopoly-playing Mom tonight. Holy shit! Heather is still reeling from being hustled out the door by Lynn. When she couldn't resist a peek through the window while she was standing outside trying to decide where to go, she saw Lynn hand Beegee to Jack. All this time he's avoided even looking at the baby, and there he is right now, holding her. Although Heather's not sure what purpose Lynn thinks that's going to serve. Jack will fall in love with the baby, and insist that Heather keep her? Not likely when all along he's been telling her to keep her eye on the future. A future cluttered up with a baby is not what he has in mind.

Heather scans the dim room. The red sports car is parked out front, but it's hard to imagine Kate at the neighbourhood pub. More likely a martini bar. No sign of her. Someone else on the island, one of the bearded guys at the bar with Einar drives a Porsche? There's a young dude all alone at a table by the window. Maybe he's the one. A big, good-looking guy in a plaid shirt with hair falling in his eyes. He doesn't look much older than Heather.

Heather considered going up to Sunny's place and seeing if she wanted a night out, but that idea lasted about a minute and a half. She's afraid Sunny really will want to come back to Calgary with her, and even though there's no way either Jack or Lynn would take her along, Heather doesn't want to hurt Sunny's feelings by even getting into the discussion. No, Sunny's better off here, she's sure of it. Funny, though. Six months ago she would probably have dragged her old summer friend home and tried to set her up in a job. Maybe she should rethink her career. Be a social worker. Yeah, right. She could lead Carmen's support group.

While she stands there, feeling a bit shy about walking up to Einar and asking if she can have a beer with him, she catches sight of Kate making her way from the back of the room to the table by the window. Heather turns and pretends to read the posters on the wall next to the door. And now that she's facing the other direction who does she see but Hannah, sitting with two other women, eating a basketful of wings. Hannah barely looks at Heather as she passes, just kind of frowns and goes on talking to the other women.

Heather taps Einar on the shoulder. From the corner of her eye, she sees Kate watching her. "Can I sit with you?"

"Jeez! Heather! You shouldn't be in here."

"Why not? Isn't the legal age nineteen out here?"

"Yeah." He shrugs. "I guess it is. How old are you now?"

"Twenty." She slides onto the stool next to his, and points to his drink when the bartender looks her way. "What he's having." Heather's not much of a drinker. A beer usually lasts her as long as she's willing to sit in a bar, and she can't tell one kind from the other.

"Your mom and dad looking after the baby?"

That sounds so weird. She has to think about it for a minute. "I guess they are. I'll go back before she wakes up."

"Everything okay over there?"

"Totally." She takes a sip from the glass that's appeared in front of her. "What is this stuff? It tastes like you should pour it down clogged drains."

Einar laughs. "Guinness. I should have warned you." He pulls the drink away. Beckons to the bartender. "Bring the young lady a coke."

"Einar!" But that will probably be fine.

"You want something to eat?" he asks. "The fish and chips are good."

Twice in a week? Sounds better than scrambled eggs. Lynn was cooking spaghetti when Heather left. She's sure there'll be leftovers. Still… "Sounds good," she says. "Are you hanging out here so we can fight in private at your place?"

"Something like that, but I'm hoping not too much fighting." He takes a drink, licks his lips, waves the bartender over to order the food for her. "So you're going to go home and give the baby to those folks you picked out?"

"No. They got tired of waiting."

Einar nods like this is totally reasonable. She glances over her shoulder at Kate. "Einar, do you know that woman by the window?"

He turns around, stares full at the two people at the table. Raises his hand, and the guy waves back. "I've seen the girl around, but I don't know who she is. Troy looks like he fell in the butter with that one. He's an old boyfriend of Sunny's. Hannah's girl."

Fell in the butter? Einar is full of quaint expressions, but this is a new one. She doesn't want to know.

272

"So?" he says. "Do I dare ask the sixty-four thousand dollar question?"

For a minute Heather thinks Einar knows that Kate's offered money for the baby, but where did he get sixty-four grand as a price? She shakes her head.

"What are you going to do, Heather? As if you're not tired of everyone asking."

She picks up the glass of coke and pokes a straw through the ice. "I guess I have to decide soon if I want to be a mother."

"Is that it?" he says. "Seems to me you're already a mother. You have to decide what you're going to do with that little girl, no? Find another family?"

Heather runs that one around in her head for a minute, and thinks she should probably blush. "Guess that sounded pretty selfish."

"Aw no, when it comes down to it, it's just a different way of saying it's a helluva tough choice."

Heather and Einar sit quietly sipping. The waiter slides a platter of fish and chips in front of Heather. She moves it so it's within Einar's reach too. "You'd better help me with this."

"I already had mine with extra chips," he says. "Eat up."

He's right about the fish and chips. Even better than the greasy fix in Horseshoe Bay. When she starts to douse it all with ketchup, Einar pinches a chip off the plate and holds it up. "See now if you gave that a good soaking of vinegar and salt instead, the Guinness would taste a real treat. Heather, don't be too hard on your mom."

She stops with a forkful of fish halfway to her mouth. What did he just say? "Pardon me?"

"She had her reasons." He folds the French fry into his mouth. "That's all I'll say."

Heather nibbles. "No, don't quit," she says. "I'd like you to say more. Seriously. Tell me what you think I should do.

Everybody keeps telling me I have to make this decision myself." Now she really should blush. If Marty was here, he'd whoop at that one. As if she was willing to listen to anyone's opinion? She wipes her greasy fingers on the paper napkin. "You know what?" He shrugs. "I feel like a kid. How am I supposed to know what to do with a baby?"

Einar shakes and shakes his head. "I don't have a clue. You're asking the wrong man."

"You have kids, right?"

There's a little flicker behind his eyes like he's not real pleased with the question. "Yeah."

"Are you glad you had them?" If she's going to do that survey she may as well broaden the sampling. She glances across at Hannah. Wonders what her answer would be.

Einar folds his arms and lowers his voice so she has to lean closer to hear. "No, I'm not glad about that. I supported them all the time they were growing up, and I sent as much as I could when they were going to school, and they think it all came from their mother. What do they think of me? Not much, I guess, because I haven't heard from any of the three of them in years. The littlest one, Ingen, used to send me a Christmas card, but nothing from her since she was sixteen. She'd be twenty-nine years old now. So you see, I don't know much about raising kids."

Heather doesn't know what to say. She's got a lump in her throat and she wonders why they never knew any of this. Jeez, what a sad story.

"Don't look so serious, little girl." He claps her on the shoulder. "I wasn't cut out to be a school teacher living in the suburbs and taking the kids to soccer. Things turn out the way they turn out. Shouldn't you eat, and get back to the baby?"

Someone sits down on the other side of Einar and starts asking about cupboards for his kitchen. Heather munches her way through the food, every bit of it. Is this a good sign that her appetite is back, or does it just mean she's still eating for two? You need fish and chips to make milk?

There's a clatter from the kitchen, loud voices, the sound of a door slamming, more voices outside. A couple of the men at the counter rush out. "What's that about?" Heather stands up and tries to peer beyond the bar, into the kitchen.

Einar waves his hand and laughs. "Aw, it's that damn bear again. They should just let him in, he could be the mascot."

"Bear?" Heather grips the edge of the counter. "There are no bears on Quadra!"

"Of course there are," Einar says. "Where the heck did you get that idea?"

"My dad told me there are no bears on Quadra!"

Einar seems to ponder for a minute. "Ah well, he probably said there are no grizzlies, just black bears here." He puts his hand on her arm. "Don't look so worried. We haven't lost a girl to a bear so long as I can remember. This one outside is a garbage bear. He's loping off to someone else's trash can by now."

Einar turns to answer a question on the other side of him, and Heather sits there swallowing. Thinking she might need to have a beer before she leaves, after all. Okay, so there are bears. What else did they tell her that isn't true?

The pub is getting busier, noisier. The men who went outside have come back, chuckling, shaking their heads. Heather can hear Kate's voice, laughter. Sounds like she's having a good time. Why not? Good job, lots of money, fancy car, and a hot guy. Heather's always thought she'd be able to corner the first three, but guys are a bit of a problem. Marty says it's because she's too mouthy. Winston's the first guy she's met who just laughs when she can't stop the sarcasm. So does she want to be Kate? Or Kate's sister?

Finally, Heather gets out her wallet, but Jack's credit card is saved another hit by Einar's big hand. "Put it away, Heather. My treat." She stands up, is surprised when Einar does the same. "I'll probably park up at Hannah's tonight, and use her facilities in the morning so I don't disturb you and your mom. So…" He sticks out his hand, and they shake solemnly. "Good luck to you and the little one."

Now Kate is watching and waving and trying to catch Heather's eye. Heather doesn't want to talk with Kate here, in front of Einar. Doesn't want to talk to her at all. Or does she? "I'll be back in a minute," she tells Einar. "I met that woman on the deck of the ferry yesterday, and I just want to ask her about something she said."

Standing beside the table, Kate and the guy smiling at her, Heather feels like a little kid, all gangly arms and wrists not quite knowing where to go. "Hey," she says. "I didn't expect to see you again." Just to let Kate know that she's not really looking for her, not rethinking the proposition.

"Glad to see you got a night off. Found a babysitter?" Kate says. The guy looks surprised. Kate lowers her voice. "Heather, I phoned my sister after I talked with you…"

No, this is not where she wants to go, not now, not at all. Heather turns to walk away, but Kate stands up and grabs her arm. "Just listen, please! I'm not trying to harass you." She frowns. "Yes, I guess that's exactly what I'm doing even if I don't want to. But give me a minute. Danielle and Phil live in West Van. They can get here in a heartbeat, and she said to tell you that if you have any inclination at all to meet them—no commitment, nothing but friendly curiosity— they can be out here tomorrow morning. Or they'll meet you somewhere else on your way home. They'll fly to Calgary if you want them to. Fly you to Vancouver. Whatever. Aren't you even slightly interested?" She pulls out a chair, motions for Heather to sit down. And Heather does, simply because she's aware of Hannah watching, and Einar looking her way. Create a scene in the Quathiaski bar? There's a story to tell Marty when she gets home.

She leaves the chair a good distance from the table, and perches on the edge of the seat. "Look. I'm impressed that you love your sister so much that you're trying to find her a kid. But." She remembers that she lied to Kate yesterday, told her there was a family waiting in Calgary. Well, theoretically, there probably is, but they don't know they're in the running for Beegee, so they aren't set up to be undercut by this rich sister of Kate's. If Heather drives back instead of flying with Jack, she could stop in Vancouver. Would it hurt to meet these people? Alone, of course. No way she'd let them see Beegee until she checked them out. She could leave Beegee in the car with Lynn.

Whoa! Heather can almost hear Lynn's voice in her head, telling her that this is exactly what she's done. Dragged Lynn along, but left her sitting outside because this is only about her, Heather, and the baby, Beegee. As Lynn reminded her this afternoon, so bluntly that Heather should still be reeling, this is about Lynn as well. And about Jack. And probably Marty too. So what the hell is she doing talking with Kate when she couldn't wait to get out of the car earlier today? Is it just because Beegee is safely tucked away, out of sight? Heather feels a surge of milk as soon as she lets her arms imagine the baby.

She shakes her head, stands up. Kate has leaned back in her chair, toying with the empty glass in front of her, moving it this way and that to fit on the little paper mat. She shrugs. "Okay, I tried. I enjoyed meeting you, Heather. I really did. Good luck with the kid."

"Thanks." Heather shoves her hands in her pockets. "Good luck to your sister too." If she had one of Carmen's cards, she'd hand it to Kate, but she doesn't and this is another province and surely they have adoption agencies here. "There must be someone for her."

Kate looks down at the table. "I hope so. But it's a little complicated."

Right. She knew there had to be more. "Yeah, that's the thing, isn't it? It's so complicated," Heather says, and she turns and walks away, back to Einar.

He interrupts the conversation he's having with the man beside him. "What was that about? Looked like she was giving you a hard time."

"Nah, just a misunderstanding. It's all good now. Hey, thanks for everything," she tells him. "All this last couple of days, and all those holidays and…" She looks him in the eye. "Were we a pain in the ass, coming here every summer and crowding your space? I know Jack's your pal and everything, but that was a bit much."

Einar throws his head back and laughs. "Never," he says. "Correct. Your dad is my pal." He winks. "But it was your mom I always looked forward to seeing." He grabs her then in a big hug and gives her a smacking kiss on the cheek. "And you kids. Behave yourself back in the city, and tell Marty you two are welcome any time."

At the door, Heather watches until someone gets out of a car in the parking lot and starts toward the pub, then runs to her own car in their wake.

Bears! But then she smiles at Einar's parting invitation, the thought of coming back some day with Marty. He'll probably be dragging a Kaylee along with him, but it might be fun. And what about that crack about looking forward to seeing Lynn? Something going on between her mom and Einar? Now that's a creepy thought. But it can't be. Lynn's not like that. Heather's sure of it.

She looks in the rear view mirror, and there's the empty baby seat. The food, the warm pub, the hug from Einar dissolve in the rainy night. No. There's no way she's coming back to Quadra Island.

21

When Lynn fled the hospital nursery without a glimpse of Marty, one of the delivery room nurses caught up with her at the elevator. She took Lynn by the arm and led her into a small waiting room. Probably the place where fathers paced, this being the days before they were expected to participate in the delivery. She handed Lynn a box of tissues, and patted her shoulder.

"What is this, honey, the fifth day?"

Lynn nodded, embarrassed that she was crying so hard her nose was streaming. She scrubbed at her face. "I just wanted to have a peek before I leave him."

"Aw come on," the nurse put her arm around Lynn, "that's only going to make you feel worse. You wait here a minute." Lynn sat and blew her nose, tried to staunch the tears, and the woman was back in a few minutes with an envelope. "Don't you dare tell anyone I did this. The photographer who takes pictures for the new parents always takes one of the babies who are going for adoption. He thinks we can give them to the people who are getting the baby and he might get an order. I never remember to pass them on to social workers. They'd probably just file them anyway. You take this little picture and put it somewhere safe." She slipped the envelope into the pocket of Lynn's maternity top. "Don't worry about the tears. Heck, on the fifth day everyone cries. It's just new baby blues. You'll get over it." Then she wished Lynn good luck and bustled her onto the elevator.

Lynn didn't take out the photo until she was back in the dark basement suite she'd rented after she moved out of the dorm. She didn't cry when she looked at the blurry picture of a puffy-eyed baby. There was no magic moment of recognition, no easing of the need to see her son. She picked up the phone and called home. "I want him back," she told her mother.

Her mom and dad were there by the next morning, and they sat in the dingy kitchen drinking instant coffee, eating the cinnamon buns her mom had made during a sleepless night. Yes, they said, whatever you want. We'll help. It will be fine.

"Does *he* get a say in this?" her dad asked. He'd never met Jack, and never referred to him by name, only as *he* or *him* or *the father*. Didn't ever want to meet *him*, he said. Jack hadn't signed the adoption papers, but he was named on the baby's birth certificate.

"You don't want your baby to grow up thinking you didn't know who his father was, do you?" the social worker had said. What her baby would think about it all someday didn't become the subject of discussion until after he was born and there were all these fine points to consider.

Lynn shook her head. If he didn't get a say in giving the baby away, surely her keeping the baby was not Jack's business either. Even though Lynn had told Jack that day in the park, that she did not want to see him, he'd continued to call. To see how she was doing, he said, to stand by in case she needed him. Lynn called him from the hospital the day after the baby was born, told him nothing had changed.

"Please let me come see you. Both of you."

She refused. Told him the nurses wouldn't let him in because she hadn't put him on the list of allowed visitors. She made that up. The part about the nurses and the social worker not wanting her to see the baby was true.

It was Friday when Lynn, with her mom and dad standing beside her, phoned Mrs. McKinnon to say she'd changed her mind. The social worker was gone for the weekend. She'd get the message first thing Monday morning. On Monday morning, she was in a meeting. Monday afternoon, she still hadn't called back. Lynn kept counting the days on her fingers. She had ten days after the signing to change her mind. This she remembered, but if anyone had explained how she would do that, she'd closed her ears.

On Monday evening, while Lynn was asleep, her dad answered the phone and finally met Jack. Her dad came quietly into the bedroom and sat on the edge of the bed. "That young man just called. He wants to come over."

She struggled up out of a dream. She'd been trying to feed a baby who grew in her arms until he was taller than she was. In spite of the pills to dry up her milk, her breasts were still swollen, the nipples sore to her touch and dripping. "Why? Did you tell him I've changed my mind?"

He nodded. "I figured he'd have to know eventually."

Lynn's mother had followed him into the room. "Dad says he sounded pretty upset, Lynn. He said he was glad you changed your mind. Surely it wouldn't hurt to talk to him."

Jack won over Lynn's parents in the first half hour of the visit. He sealed their admiration the next morning when he got hold of the social worker on his first try. Lynn needed to write a letter giving her reasons for changing her mind and outlining her plans for the baby. Jack came over with a typewriter under his arm.

And here are Jack and Lynn, for the first time in twenty-five years, about to revisit that campaign to have Marty returned to them, because Lynn is not taking "no" from Jack again. She is determined that he will remember exactly how it felt to have someone else in charge of Marty's future.

"Do you intend to ever see your granddaughter again if Heather gives her away?" she asks.

He's still holding the sleeping baby, has ignored Lynn's suggestion that she would be fine on the sofa, has refused the offer of food. "They promised to give us pictures, and to give Heather access. I think that's enough, isn't it? I'm sure that if we want to see her again Heather can arrange that."

"Really? That will be enough? Jack, don't you remember how furious it made you, the hoops we had to jump through to get Marty back?"

"How many times do I have to tell you that I do not want to drag myself through the useless exercise of what might have been, Lynn? We figured it out, and if we hadn't, well then we would probably have survived as well. Harsh though that sounds. At least Heather gets to choose the family herself. Although I'm not sure it's a good idea for her to stay in contact." He's staring fixedly at Lynn now. She wishes she could force him to look at Beegee and say all this. "Maybe they were right," he says, "when we had Marty, in discouraging the girls who were serious about adoption from seeing their babies. If Heather hadn't seen Belinda, or held her, she might not be in this mess."

Lynn is so tired she's beginning to doubt that she can stand up to Jack. She's beginning to feel like she's twenty years old again. "You're forgetting that I didn't see Martin? All I had was a lousy photo, and it occurred to me that it might not even be him, just some left-behind picture the nurse gave me to get me out of the hospital. Nothing has changed in spite of the changes, Jack. When did we become the kind of people who can give babies away?"

He stands up with Beegee in his arms. "For at least the tenth time—don't confuse your own decision with Heather's! We have to keep our experience out of this, Lynn. It was pretty clear that you wouldn't be able to give Marty away, even though at the time it probably was the best decision. That's why I kept calling. I hoped that with some support you'd get through it."

Jack lifts the afghan on the couch, and then tosses it aside. "Bring something to put under her," he orders. "The dog has probably left hair and fleas and God-knows-what on this sofa."

When Lynn ignores him, sits rooted to the chair, he stalks to the kitchen chair, grabs his jacket, and spreads it carefully before he settles Beegee. Face down. He kneels there a minute with his hand on the baby's back before he stands up again.

Any warmth Lynn felt toward Jack, watching him with his granddaughter, has been doused as surely as if she had a handful of snow flung in her face. "There's a big gap here," she says, finally.

The afternoon Jack brought over the typewriter to help Lynn document her plan for the Minister of Social Services, he suggested to her mom and dad that they go out for coffee while he and Lynn had a serious talk. As soon as they were out the door he wrapped his arms around Lynn.

"Marry me," he said into her hair. He was holding the hospital photo of Marty.

Lynn pulled away. Her instinct was to shout at him, to shove him out the door. She wanted her mother to come back. No! Her head wouldn't stop shaking. "We barely know each other."

He grabbed her hands. "Lynn, we have a son. Isn't that a good reason to get to know each other? I knew the day I met you in the cafeteria line that I could love you."

Could love her. How reassuring. What was with this guy? Anyone else would have run for the hills by now. Or so Lynn's dad had said the night before, after Jack left. A real fine chap after all, young Bishop. Even her mom, who was a little less excited about Jack, seemed to see him as Lynn's saviour. "We believe you could do this on your own, Lynn," she said, "and Dad and I will help. Still, Jack seems a nice boy, responsible, and it would be easier for the baby if there were two of you." Would anyone have thought she could do it on her own if they'd foreseen that a few years later, she and little Marty would have to muddle through the death of first her mom, then her dad, left with only vague promises of help from the handful of relatives who thought she should have given her baby up for adoption. No, that's not quite it. Relatives who thought she should have been a good girl and never gotten pregnant in the first place.

By the time Lynn held Marty in her arms ten days later, Jack had convinced her that the three of them were meant to be together. Had worn her down with all that he could offer, and the inadequacies of her single-parent plan. They went to Social Services with their intent to marry, continue their university education, an exemplary young family. Who could turn down such a plan? Then the two of them decided that Marty should never know that they'd abandoned him, even for those twelve days it took to get him back. Lynn's parents agreed, and promised to keep the secret. Jack's parents didn't know Marty existed until Jack told them he and Lynn were getting married. If his mother knew what had happened, he said, some day she would undoubtedly tell her grandson that his parents had been on the verge of giving him away, but she had rushed in to save the little family. The story of the first days of Marty's life would remain securely sealed.

Lynn has wondered, over the years, if she would have agreed to marry Jack if she'd met his mother first, there was that much animosity between them from the very beginning. Now Alice is barely in this world, and doesn't even know that the marriage is finally over.

Jack has stood up now, is walking away from the baby, across the room toward the door.

"Did you hear me, Jack? Which version of that drama are you watching in your head? You practically got down on your knees and begged me to marry you, because you wanted to be Martin's dad," Lynn says. "You forgot all that?"

Jack stops to leans on one of the kitchen chairs and closes his eyes. "There's even less point in revisiting our marriage than there is in rehashing Marty's birth. None of this has anything to do with Heather and her baby." He's gone dangerously white around the lips. Probably taking blood pressure meds again. The calcium blocker makes him sick to his stomach.

He straightens up and walks a cautious beeline to the bathroom. Lynn watches him at the sink, splashing water on his face. Then his wrists. He comes back with colour in his face. "Okay?" she asks. The recovery is so quick, she suspects this is not medical, just pure white anger and once again he has it under control.

He nods, glances toward the door, then at the clock. "I'm going in a minute. We have a flight at noon, so we'll have to be away from here by nine."

"So you've told us," Lynn says. "But don't count on Heather coming with you." He sighs. "Yes, I know," she says. "You're as weary as I am. Go get some rest, Jack."

"Lynn, you're not planning on telling Heather, are you? About your giving up Marty, and getting him back again?"

She is about to sigh, and tell him, no, a promise is a promise, when she unaccountably remembers Heather on the phone with Marty earlier in the evening. Heather, refusing to provide relief from the worry, hinting one way, then the other, pushing all the buttons. Not letting Lynn off the hook for a minute. "Not unless I tell Martin first," Lynn says, and watches Jack's face go white again. "Don't you think it's amazing that we've managed to keep the secret all these years? Do you remember why we turned that into such a big issue, Jack?"

"Of course I can. We wanted to be sure that Martin never ever doubted that we wanted him. Or thought that he somehow forced us to get married. It's too difficult to explain all that away."

Lynn stares at him. Has he totally forgotten that she would have kept Marty whether she married Jack or not? The keeping had nothing to do with Jack…has he forgotten that?

Another glance at the clock. He's likely thinking that he needs to get back to the hotel and call Rhea. When Jack went away to conferences, he always phoned home at 11:00 PM sharp. He won't want to make the call from Einar's driveway. He'll phone from his bed, tell her he'll go to sleep thinking about her. I love you, goodnight now

He looks over at Beegee, asleep on his jacket.

"I can move her to the bed," Lynn says. "She won't wake up until she's hungry again."

"I don't need my jacket. I think the rain has stopped."

"The rain never stops here, Jack. Don't you remember that either?" Lynn doesn't realize she's said the words aloud until she sees the look of bewilderment on Jack's face. She shakes her head. "Marty knows we didn't get married until after he was born," she says. "That didn't seem to ruffle his sense of security, did it?"

"Lynn, please. Enough already."

"Go," she says. "Get some sleep. I'll see you in the morning. I won't be leaving early." She turns away from him. On the other side of the room, she stares into the cold fireplace and contemplates starting another blaze. The room is warm enough, though, and there are only a few pieces of wood remaining. She would have to go out in the dark, dig into the pile to find dry logs. When the door opens, then closes behind Jack, she doesn't turn around until she hears his car begin the ascent up the driveway.

So what did she accomplish by keeping Jack here? The way he holds Beegee is as familiar and comfortable as watching one of the old home movies Jack's dad took to chronicle the life of the Bishop dynasty. Jack, in those wobbly old films, handling fatherhood with the same ease and success he handles everything else. The pride of his parents. Howard, at least, was friendly to Lynn, but gave her the sense that he felt the same about her as he did about his employees. Lynn was instrumental in the production of the grandchildren he worshipped, worthy of decent compensation, but if he'd been alive when they separated, Howard wouldn't have questioned Jack's leaving. Lynn suspects, from dark hints from Jack's youngest sister, that Jack's roving eye was part of the genetic package, and that Alice had good cause for her fierce protectionism.

When Jack told his parents that he was marrying a girl they'd never met, and that he was the father of a baby already born, Alice demanded blood tests to prove that the baby was not Jack's. Jack had actually suggested to Lynn that this would be a way to gain Alice's approval and Alice's approval would make their life much easier. Lynn refused. She allows herself to smile at the thought of her young self with that much gorm. Where did it go? Does she really think it's retrievable?

22

Heather can hear Beegee wailing as soon as she gets out of the car. When she opens the door, Lynn practically tackles her from across the room.

"Give me a minute." She shakes drops of water from her hair. "All it ever does in this place is rain. God, how can people live here?" She drops her jacket on the floor and rubs her hands to warm them before she takes the baby. "Why didn't you feed her if she was this upset?"

"I tried." Lynn points to the bottle on the floor beside the rocking chair.

"I thought you said she was taking the bottle now."

"Apparently she forgot. Or she thinks she gets to choose."

Beegee's red in the face, her mouth stretched into a howl. "Yipes! Scarey, Beegee. You look like Demon Baby." Heather sinks into the rocking chair, and within seconds she has the baby sucking as though she's been abandoned overnight in the forest. So much for being able to walk away for an hour or two.

Lynn droops against the counter. Long evening for everybody apparently. "How long did Jack stay?" Heather asks.

"He left half an hour ago. He'll be back in the morning, and he wants to get away by nine." Lynn waves her hand at the cluttered counter. "There's spaghetti," she says. "Do you want some?"

"I had fish and chips at the pub. Einar treated."

"Ah, so you went to the pub." Lynn seems distracted, like she's trying to keep her mind on the conversation, but her eyes keep roving to the window. She picks up a plate, scrapes food into the garbage.

Heather brushes a crumb of sleep from the corner of Beegee's eye. "I saw that woman again. The one who gave me the ride this afternoon." She has to tell someone. "She has a sister who wants to adopt a baby. She offered to set up a meeting."

"Heather!" Lynn's lips turn down, quivering as though she's going to either burst into tears or puke. "You don't even know who she is!"

"Relax. I didn't say I was going to do it. She offered money, and you know how creepy that felt?" She runs her hand over the sticking-up tufts of hair on the baby' head, then gently cups the soft spot, feels Beegee's heart beat against her palm. "Kind of mind-bending isn't it, how many people are out there looking for babies?"

Lynn begins to slam dishes into the sink and turns on the water. "Fascinating. But it's a subject I'd rather not have had the chance to explore."

"Hannah was at the pub too," Heather says to her mother's back. "With a couple of other women. Why don't you go down?"

Her mom dumps food into a recycled container from the pile on the counter and stashes it in the fridge. She moves around the kitchen like it belongs to her. She looks up, finally. "When did I start going to pubs?"

"I don't know. Maybe you did when you were my age."

"When I was your age I was married and had a new baby." She rests her elbows on the edge of the sink and stares out the window. What is she looking at? Rain and more rain. Lights in Hannah's windows. Heather looks down at Beegee. One hand has worked its way out of the blanket—why does Lynn insist on wrapping her up like a spring roll? Heather tickles Beegee's hand; it closes around her finger.

"Why didn't you ever want to talk about that? About having Marty before you and Jack got married. Did you even think about having an abortion, or giving him up? You were in the same boat, so why haven't you told me how you felt?"

Lynn turns around slowly. "You've said all along that you weren't interested in hearing from any of us, Heather."

Heather looks down at Beegee's fingers, still clutched around her own. "Okay, I feel kind of embarrassed about that. I was wrong. Obviously."

Lynn's eyes are huge, like she's just walked into a surprise party. "Thank you," she says, in barely a whisper. "I suspect that was hard to admit."

Heather shrugs. "Not really. I know I can be a pain in the ass, but mostly I don't get bothered about it."

"And tomorrow? Do you know what you're going to do?" Lynn looks like she's crawling toward the edge of a cliff. Afraid to look over.

"I wish." Heather tilts her head, lets her hair fall across her face, and looks down at the baby. "Look at her," she says. "She's smaller than…that stupid dog." She nods at Loki, asleep on his mat. "And she's totally turned things upside down. How can I give her away? How can I keep her?

Would you please tell me how you decided?" She's managed to keep her voice steady. Proud of that.

Lynn's mouth opens and closes and opens and closes but no words come out. "I can't," she finally says, "maybe some day, but right now I can't." She watches Heather for a moment. "But I can tell you that I was just as scared as you are. What on earth did I know about babies?"

"I'm not…" Oh, but she is. So scared, her throat gets dry just thinking about cutting herself loose from Carmen and the adoption plan. "If I decide to fly home with Jack tomorrow, will you be terribly hurt?"

"Hurt?" Lynn's cheeks flush. She brushes a wave of hair off her forehead. "I don't think 'hurt' is enough of a word to describe how I'm going to feel, Heather. But I'll live with it, won't I, if that's what you've decided?"

"No, no," Heather says. "It won't mean I've made up my mind. Just that flying would be so much easier. I won't decide until you get home. I promise."

Lynn laughs, one sad little harrumph of a laugh. "Don't tell me that or I'll come home by way of Alaska. Don't promise anything, Heather," she says, far more seriously now. "What if you get back and Carmen phones and has the perfect family and you can't wait for me? But you've made this promise."

"Okay," she says slowly. The baby has stopped nursing, her mouth open, a drop of milk still trembling from Heather's nipple. "The other thing," she says, and takes a deep breath, because she knows that it will hurt, "is that I think I need to give Jack equal time, you know? If I'm going to turn into this ridiculously reasonable person, shouldn't he get to have his say?" Silence. She looks at the clock. It's too early for the two of them to go to bed, to pretend they're asleep. She can't take another two hours. "Hey, Lynn," she says. "Why don't you go to the pub and have a beer with Einar and Hannah."

She tries to sound jokey. "Make up for the ones you missed because you had Marty."

Heather doesn't remember ever seeing her mom look this muddled. But damn it, Jack's the one who pays all her bills. And he is her dad, and she does care about how he feels. And Heather loves flying.

Lynn moves to the coats on the wall, takes hers down and stands there brushing the folds. "He will certainly have his say. He's convincing, isn't he, your dad? Always able to quote chapter and verse to back up his convictions." She shakes out the coat and slips in one arm, hesitates as though she's going to change her mind, but then slides in the other arm and does up the zipper with an angry snap of her wrist.

Heather lifts the baby to her shoulder and stands up. "That doesn't mean I'm going to do what he wants me to do." She'd walk across the room so that she was closer to Lynn, but she doesn't want to feel tall. For years she's used that trick when she was having an argument with Lynn. Stand close to her, so that her mother felt smaller. What a brat. "Haven't you ever noticed that Marty and I both deal with Jack the same way you do, Lynn? I think we learned it from you." She holds up her hand. "Don't get defensive, because it's not a bad thing. When I was old enough to notice, it always blew me away the way you could be so quiet and dignified when Nana Bishop was being a bully. You just ignored them all." Okay, she has to get Lynn out of here, because her eyes are burning with a whole new set of tears, and she's about to go all sudsy. "Get out of here, Mom," she says softly and now she does take the few steps to the door and gives Lynn a quick hug. "Go have some fun for a change."

After Lynn is gone, Heather tucks Beegee into the big bed and roams the cabin, packing her few belongings. The breast pump is still in her bag, completely forgotten now that she's back with Beegee's demanding little mouth. She should be pumping between feedings, same as she did at home, freezing milk for....She fills the sink with soapy water, drops the pump in to soak, sets a kettle of water on to boil so she can clean it properly. There is no formula in the cabin, she realizes suddenly. Great timing if the thermos bag of milk lasted until she got here, but how was that possible? She opens the freezer compartment of the fridge and stares at a pile of plastic bags full of white. Not the Playtex bags she uses, but what other liquid exactly like this would Einar be storing? Whose breast milk? Hannah's? Heather didn't see a baby in the house when she went up to use the phone, but there could have been one tucked into a corner somewhere. There was always a baby at Sunny's house.

She sits down at the kitchen table. So maybe this place was exactly where Lynn needed to come? It's almost spooky. Like a Stephen King movie and the scariest is still to come. Oh man, she needs to talk to Marty. She picks up the phone, but once again he's got his voice mail handling calls. Of course. He's with Kaylee. If she knew the number, she'd call Sunny and ask her to come down for...a cup of tea? She snorts, and suddenly the cabin isn't scary at all, just the friendly place they've known for years.

Kitchen table and three chairs, rocking chair, sofa, coffee table. In the bedroom there's a bed and a chest of drawers. Heather's one-bedroom apartment is crammed with television, desk, bookshelves, computer, sound system, cappuccino maker, bean bag chairs, lamps, futon, exercise bike, queen-sized bed, two chests of drawers. Overflowing with books, CDs, papers, sports bags, backpacks, clothes that don't fit into the tiny closet. Her bike is parked inside the door, her inline skates, boots, running shoes in a jumble.

Imagine Beegee in the bean bag while Heather checks her email, updates Facebook, whirls up a protein smoothie in the blender. Heather shakes her head, still that tight knot in her throat.

Heather lies down on the sofa and stares at a blackened log in the fireplace. She pulls the afghan off the back of the couch. Her leggings are damp from tripping through the rain to the pub. She presses her face to the sleeve of Winston's shirt. For a long time it had his scent, but now there's a mix of Heather's sweat, milk, and Beegee.

Winston's phone number is on a scrap of paper in her wallet. Not fair to stick Einar with a call to Jamaica. She'll get some cash from Jack in the morning and leave it beside the phone.

A woman answers on the first ring, sleepy sounding and Heather remembers that it's two hours later in Kingston. Or maybe three from here. She hasn't bothered to reset her watch. This is the same voice that answered when she called to tell Winston about Beegee. His mother, if what he told her is true, and she's never had any reason to think Winston lied to her. He's not there, the woman says, friendly now. "Where you calling from, dearie?"

"Canada," Heather says. "Can you tell me when he'll be back?"

A rich laugh that sounds so much like Winston, Heather's throat aches. "He's in Canada. Went back last week."

"To Calgary?"

"No no. Toronto, where his brother lives. You get a pencil, I have the number right here."

"It's okay," Heather says. "Thanks anyway. Sorry to wake you." She hangs up the phone, turns out the lights, and joins Beegee in the cold bed.

23

This is not a night for walking, even though that was what Lynn had in mind when she stepped outside. Or as much as her crowded mind could manage with all of Heather's words swirling. In the short dash to the car, her hair is soaked to her skull. Her shoes are still damp, and will probably not dry out until she's back in Calgary. Shoes, jeans, t-shirt. All into the recycling bag when she gets home.

When she backs slowly up the driveway, she has the feeling she's steering someone else's car. Something slightly wobbly, too much play in the wheel. Of course. Her car has been borrowed and driven, and Jack no longer in tune with this "dandy little car" he bought for her ten years ago, so pleased because he'd done hours of research and had finally settled on the one that would keep her safe, last forever. Once she's on the main road, she barely notices that softening. It will be fine. So she'll go home on a wobbly wheel.

Einar's truck is in the parking lot at the pub. A few cars lined up at the dock, awaiting the next ferry. Lynn has a fleeting urge to hop out and buy a ticket, get herself on the road without any more conversation, because everything is in place. This drama now has the momentum to play out on its own. But what has changed is that Lynn feels consequential, and running out on Heather once was enough.

Still, she's tired of talking, and while Heather's urging her to the pub makes her smile—have some fun—there is nothing she needs to say to either Einar or Hannah tonight. She parks the car, fishes her umbrella out from under the seat, and walks to the pier. Across the channel, the lights of Campbell River look far more inviting than those behind her. But there's open sea on the other side of that bigger island. And what she wants is her endless mass of land. She leans against a post, wishes she smoked. Like an old movie. The woman waiting.

A carnival looms up out of the mist. Four stories of lights, a burst of fireworks. A cruise ship sliding through the channel. On one of their first trips to Quadra, Lynn and Jack stood in this very spot and promised one another that for their twenty-fifth wedding anniversary they would cruise to Alaska. Lynn is sure that she still has old cruise brochures under the phone book and the take-out menus in a kitchen drawer.

The damp is getting to her. Her legs feel as though they're wrapped in wet towels, her hair drags icicles against her cheeks, the hand clutching the umbrella aches with cold. Still, she's relieved to feel the outline of her body again. When Beegee was constantly in her arms she took on a clumsy, fuzzy shape. All that juggling and jiggling. She wonders if Heather is pacing, or if she's snuggled up to Beegee in the dark bedroom, listening to the drip of the cedar boughs on the roof. Or asleep, dreaming about the miles of road she's driven. It seems so long ago, but it was only yesterday that Heather arrived. Maybe it's the thought of the blue skies she'll be flying tomorrow that will put her to sleep.

The ferry is approaching now, the blast of the whistle. Lynn folds the umbrella, hunches into her jacket and dashes back to the car. The first car off the ferry signals and turns into the motel across the road. Lynn stares at the Vacancy sign, at a lamp in a window, the silhouette of someone looking down at the harbour. There will be a coffee maker on a table in the corner of the room, packets of tea, sugar, coffee whitener, a television with a bad movie. The sheets will be crisp, the room warm and dry, a rack of fluffy towels in the bathroom, a good shower, tiny bottles of shampoo and conditioner. Her clothes hung over the shower rail will dry in the night. The rooms face east. In the morning, the sun will shine on her face, and she will wake languorously from a restorative sleep. There will be a complimentary basket of breads downstairs in the lobby with coffee. She'll take a blueberry muffin outside on a napkin, a coffee in her other hand, and sit at one of the tables beside the pool watching the commuters file onto the ferry.

Someone knocks on the passenger door. Hannah peering in at her. Lynn unlocks the door and like a very large wet dog, Hannah scrambles into the seat.

"What are you doing out here?" she says.

Lynn shrugs. "Thinking. Watching the rain. You?"

"I came out to meet Josh. He ran to his dad. Hank phoned this afternoon and said he was sending him back tonight." They both peer into the rain as the last of the foot passengers straggle past. No teenagers. Hannah shrugs. "Hey, I was wrong about your car. That wasn't Josh. He knows who took it, but he's not saying."

Lynn nods. "You're going to wait for the next ferry?"

"Nope. If Hank couldn't talk him onto the last two, there's not much chance he's coming tonight. So, how did things shake down with you and old Jack? I saw Heather come in and sit a while with Einar. You ended up babysitting?"

298

"No, I let Jack do this one. I don't know what shook down, Hannah. I wanted him to hold the baby. So far, I think she's only been a name on a piece of paper to him. And the name was one someone else chose. He does have a soft heart, and I guess I wanted it to be as wounded as my own."

"Can't blame you for that," Hannah says. "I'm hoping that if Josh is still with Hank, he'll give him some of the grief I've had to put up with." She sighs. "No, I'm not hoping that at all. I'm hoping Hank will talk some sense into him. Isn't that the kicker?" she says. "That we have to stand around sucking our thumbs while our kids make the stupid mistakes we made? Hank quit school when he was sixteen and buggered off to California. He says he's never regretted that experience, but I know he has. He's a smart man, and he's stuck doing hard physical jobs. I tried to get him back to school for years, but he's too damned stubborn. That'll be Josh in thirty years. Sunny too if she survives." She blows her nose, looks for somewhere to deposit the tissue, and finally shoves it into her pocket. "Would you do me a favour," she says, "and try to divert Heather if she decides to come up and see Sunny again? My girl has some half-assed plan to drive back to Calgary with yours and find a job out there."

"There's not much danger of that. I think Heather's going to fly home with Jack."

"Awww!" Hannah slaps her knee. "Now why the hell is she doing that after all the trouble you took? Why don't you leave your car and go with them, so at least he doesn't have her alone for the whole flight?"

"The flight's only an hour, Hannah, and even though Jack is very convincing, Heather is his daughter in every way. She will make her own decision."

"Don't they all? Can I get a ride home with you?" Hannah asks. "We both look like hell. I think sleep is the answer."

In the ten minutes it takes to get back, Lynn wonders if Hannah's dozed off, she's so quiet in her corner. But as they pull into the driveway, she comes to life with a shake. Turns in the seat, and sits there nodding at Lynn. Holds out her hand, which, when Lynn takes it, feels surprisingly warm. Dry and calloused, like the sun-warmed bark of a tree.

"Good luck with the kid," Hannah says. Lynn doesn't ask which one she means, just nods back. "I always thought you were a bit of a dishrag," Hannah continues. "The store-bought kind that's pretty damned useless. But you have gumption, even though you don't know it. That kid will thank you someday."

And still Lynn doesn't ask which kid.

Lynn lies awake, watching a dance of shadows on the cabin wall. She sits up to tuck the blanket around her icy feet, pulls it high under her chin. She's cold, has been since she came inside, and couldn't bear the thought of pulling off her jeans, even though they're damp and probably stealing away her body heat. She'd run a hot bath, but doesn't want to wake Heather. Marooned out here on the couch, she has a view through the open bedroom door. The rain must have stopped, the curtain of clouds receded to let the moon flood the room. Dark shape of the bed, Beegee and Heather floating on that silver light.

Lynn heard Einar's truck about an hour ago, imagines it now, washed in moonlight, the man asleep in the camper on the back amidst toolboxes and sweet-smelling wood. She's tempted to peek out the window, to check for Hannah on the road, but feels certain that Hannah, too, is tucked into her bed. And Sunny? Does she still have a bed in that house, or did one of the boys claim hers when she left? Once, when Heather was about twelve, she ran back from playing with Sunny to ask if she could sleep over at Sunny's house. Lynn shrugged, ready to give permission, but Jack sent Heather back, sulking, to tell Sunny that she was not allowed. "My God, Lynn! We have no idea what goes on over there, and where on earth would she sleep? There are so many kids in that house, they probably stack them like firewood." Bunks, Heather snarled when she came back. They slept in bunks and there was room in Sunny's bunk for both of them.

Jack is tucked into a king-sized bed at the Inn with an eiderdown and God only knows what dreams. In another eight hours, he'll come through the door, rubbing his hands, ready for the journey home. Beegee's first flight. What if she's inherited Lynn's phobia, and is terrified, screaming the whole way home? What will Heather do? And Jack? Will he hide behind his paper, or recognize the fear?

Lynn shivers. Her feet are not going to warm up ever. She unwraps, tiptoes into the bedroom, slides open a dresser drawer.

"Mom?" Heather's voice is thick with sleep.

"Shhh. Just getting socks. My feet are cold." Lynn fumbles in the drawer for a pair of Einar's socks. She sits on the edge of the bed to pull them on, then tucks the quilt securely around Heather and Beegee before she leaves the room. In the kitchen, she reaches the bottle of rye out of the cupboard. Just enough to warm her for sleep.

It seems only minutes later that Lynn is startled awake. She sits up in the tangle of wool and lets her feet thud to the floor.

"Did I wake you? I was sure you'd be up already." Einar strides across the room with a mug in his hand. "Here," he says. "It's camper coffee but you look like you need it."

Lynn rubs her eyes. Maybe she can make all this go away. She feels as though a fire alarm has gone off in her head. "Just a minute," she says, to ward off the cup Einar is hold-

ing in front of her. Then, "Thanks," to make up for her lack
of enthusiasm.

He sits down beside her on the couch. Making her far
too aware of her morning breath and the funky smell of her
t-shirt. His t-shirt. He looks, for a minute, as though he's
going to put his arm around her. "I'm worried about you,"
he says. "Why didn't you come into the pub last night? I saw
your car over in the parking lot when I stepped out to see
where Hannah had disappeared to."

She takes a deep breath, exhales, finally accepts the cup
and raises it to her lips. He's stirred in a glug of cream. The
real stuff, not milk or edible oil product and even though it's
barely tinted the black black coffee, there's a sheen of grease
on the surface. And hot. So hot she swallows fast, puffs out
her cheeks, and blows. "Yipes. That's killer coffee, Einar."
She hands the cup back to him, and brushes the hair off her
forehead. "I needed a bit of time alone to think. Why are
you worried?"

The eyebrows and beard are twitching so much they
could knit themselves into a rug. "Oh, this baby business.
I'm afraid you're going to be badly hurt."

She tries to pull the blanket around her shoulders, and he
takes the cup again while she rearranges herself. "No matter
which way it goes, I think the worst of the hurt might be
over. I've had some time to ponder my own motives, and
prepare a bit more, I think."

He lifts her chin with his thumb. "Why don't you stay
out here for a few more days. Let the dust settle where it
will, back home, and give yourself a real rest." She considers
him carefully. The lined face, thinning hair, lopsided beard.
The huge hand that holds out the coffee mug to her like he's
offering far more than a hot drink.

"Einar, you're one of the kindest men I've ever met, and
I appreciate that so much, but I'm ready to go home." She

takes the cup again, another drink. Already she can feel the caffeine stirring her blood. "We'll keep in touch, right?"

He smiles at her, mustache curling over his lip, hiding his teeth. "Of course."

"You come to Calgary," Lynn say. "I'll send you my new address. I'll be in a spiffy new place close to a park where I can walk my dog." She does her best to smile, but the muscles in her cheeks feel stiff. "Are you in a hurry? Can I at least make you breakfast this one time?"

He shakes his head. "I went up to the Inn bright and early and ate with Jack."

The bedroom door opens and there's Heather, gym bag in one hand, baby in the crook of the other arm. Wet hair combed straight back from her face, she's fresh and pink-cheeked. Dressed in leggings, and a yellow sweater. Lynn's favourite sweater. Heather has been up, splashing water in the bathroom, and Lynn has slept through it all? How is this possible?

Heather pads across the room in bare feet and settles into the rocking chair, but apparently not to feed. She holds Beegee on her lap facing Lynn and Einar. The baby's chin slumps, but she's holding her head up admirably. Her hair stands up in tufts, and over the Peter Rabbit sleeper Heather has layered one of the nightgowns from Hannah's kids. Beegee looks like Hallowe'en with the hair, the cape, the fierce concentration that means she's getting ready to poop.

"Sorry if I interrupted something."

Einar looks at his watch. "I only came in to say good-bye. I want to get the next ferry." He crosses the room to Heather, hand outstretched, and she solemnly shakes. It always amused the kids that even when they were small he'd shake their hands in welcome and farewell. Lynn's too, but this time, he comes to her with a hug. A long, tight, embrace. "And you," he says so quietly that only she can hear, "remember what I said about being welcome if you decide to stay on. I'll be back tonight."

Then he's gone, and she's left watching Heather and the baby. Beegee, so small, so silly in that get-up. "Interesting outfit she's wearing," Lynn says.

"The bunny sleeper shrunk," Heather says. "The back won't close."

"The clothes didn't shrink. The baby grew."

Heather's eyes widen. "Hey, I guess she did! Well, anyway, I like the cape. It suits her." She glances at the clock. "Jack will be here any minute, I guess."

Beegee squirms, goes red, and even across the room, Lynn can hear the diaper filling. Well said, little girl, she thinks. "You're flying back?" she asks.

Heather lifts the baby, holds her at arms' length with a crinkled nose. "Yeah. I can't face the idea of all those hours in the car. It's okay, right?"

"Of course it is," Lynn says. "I'll be right behind you. By the time your plane takes off, I may even be back on the mainland." She packed her meager belongings last night, the bag is at the door. "I need to get cleaned up. There isn't any coffee ready. Einar brought this in from the truck."

Heather sticks out her tongue. "Thanks, but I'll pass. Jack'll buy breakfast at the airport. Let me use the bathroom for this diaper first."

Lynn finishes the coffee even though she knows it will roil mercilessly in her empty stomach. She'll stop somewhere for toast and fruit. Which reminds her of the bag of junk food. She fishes out the red licorice and lays it on top of Heather's bag before she goes to the window.

Still too dim outside to tell if the clouds have lifted, but she imagines a clear sky. Headlights appear at the top of the driveway and Jack's rental car makes its cautious descent to park behind Heather's.

He knocks before he opens the door. He looks well this morning. Good colour, a clean crisp shirt showing under his corduroy jacket, even a sharp press in his jeans. Something in the way he enters, a little more tentative than usual, the way he darts his eyes around the room. "Where's Heather?" He spies his anorak draped across the coffee table and crosses the room to retrieve it.

Lynn waves at the bathroom door. "Changing the baby. She won't be long. I guess you have company for the trip back."

"Good." But still he's tightly wound. Casts his gaze around the room again. "We need to talk for a minute before we go, Lynn."

"You want me to hide in the bedroom? You'll have hours to talk."

"No, you and I need to talk."

"Well then talk."

"In private."

Could he have re-considered, decided that it was okay to come clean with Marty on his near-abandonment? Or maybe another pep talk to ensure that she keeps her promise? He grabs her jacket and brings it to her. "Let's go outside for a minute. It's not cold, just damp." Then he takes her arm and hustles her out onto the step.

"When are you leaving?" he asks.

"I'm ready to go," she says. "I'll be right behind you." She decided last night that she wanted to drive away at the same time, to be on the same ferry, to let Heather know that she was still with her, even though they'd part ways at Comox. She may even drive into the town, wave when they turn at the airport, and then find her way back to the highway. She does a quick calculation in her head. This time it will be a civilized trip. She'll stop somewhere late in the day, have a decent meal, find a place to sleep, get a very early start. "I should be home by early tomorrow afternoon. You can take Heather to my place. She's doing so well with the baby, I'm sure she'll feel comfortable on her own." She leans against the railing with her arms folded. Jack still has his hand on the doorknob, the jacket draped over his shoulder. There's a crackling in the bushes and Loki woofs up onto the step, stands looking from one to the other.

Lynn crouches down and scratches the dog's chin. "Hey, I was wondering if you'd come to say goodbye." She keeps meaning to ask Einar where the dog hangs out all day.

When Lynn stands up again, the dog leaning against her shins, Jack hasn't moved. He clears his throat. "Lynn, Rhea and I had a long talk last night after I left you. We're going to offer Heather the option of leaving the baby with us for a month while she decides what she wants to do. A chance to see if she can get through a month with no contact."

"What?" She can't hide her incredulity. Rhea babysitting for Heather? For a whole month? While Beegee turns into one of those older babies. Then Lynn catches up with him, and feels the bitter coffee threatening to rise up into her throat. "And then?"

"If she still wants to go through with an adoption, we'll offer another option. She can give us Belinda. By then, the baby should be well settled. If she wants her back, then so be it."

Is this what she's been waiting for since yesterday's spaghetti? The reason for the sodden lump in her chest ever since Jack told her that he and Rhea had "considered" adopting Heather's baby. She has been unbelievably slow, and yet this is unbelievable.

"I think this option could turn out to be the one that will take everyone's needs into account. Of course there will have to be some very definite guidelines. Lots of negotiation to get through and a firm contract."

So this is why Einar was worried. Dear man must have been privy to Jack's planning. Lynn sits down on the top step, facing away from Jack. He keeps on talking, dredging up every argument he's already made against Heather keeping the baby, adding now every advantage he and Rhea are able to offer. Lynn nods and nods at the wet trees, the woodpile, the cars, the path to Hannah's house, looking for the answer out there. What can she possibly say to Jack? She just nods, Bobblehead Grandma. She stands up to face him, her bum cold and wet from the wood, shivering, but she will not huddle into her coat. She lets her arms hang straight at her sides and stares him down. "That's not a good plan. Can you really imagine Heather staying out of the way? It's like giving Beegee two mothers, three parents." And what about the grandmother, where would she fit? She doesn't want to know. "This is a recipe for trouble, Jack. Huge conflict."

"Okay, Lynn," he says, and finally moves away from the door. He looks as though he might even try to take her arm, but she will use physical force to keep him away if she has to. "I knew this wouldn't sit well with you."

"Sit well!" She may swing at him even if it's not in self defense. "Good God, Jack! Surely you don't expect me to rejoice over the woman who stole my husband taking the next step and stealing my granddaughter." She pushes him aside on her way to the door. "There is nothing more for us to discuss. I'm going inside for my own private moment with Heather, and then I'm leaving. Don't look so alarmed. I'm not going to run to Heather with this just-in news of yours. You can do that yourself."

Heather is standing just inside the door, baby in her arms. "What's all the shouting about?"

"Come sit down a minute," Lynn says and leads the way to the couch. She folds up the crumpled blankets, sits down, and pats the cushion beside her. With incredible effort, she keeps a calm voice. "I'm going to leave now, Heather. We'll talk at home. Please go home when you get to Calgary. Call Marty and get him to pick you up. That would be a good thing, wouldn't it?"

The baby is bundled, ready for the trip. "I guess," she says. "You won't be back until tomorrow, will you?"

"I will be home as soon as humanly possible," Lynn says.

Then Heather looks away, around the room. "I phoned Winston last night," she says. Lynn feels as though she's being rocked by the aftershock of the earlier quake. "Except I didn't talk to him, just to his mom. He's back in Canada, in Toronto but he hasn't called."

Lynn grabs Heather's shoulders. "You don't need him! Listen to me, Heather. You don't need Winston. I didn't need Jack. I could have been a good mother to Marty all on my own. I married Jack because he wore me down, but I didn't need him. My mother even told me so, but I didn't believe her." She pulls Heather close, Beegee sandwiched between them. "Whatever you do, look at all the possibilities, but ask yourself if any of them, any single one of them, can give Beegee what you have to give." She wipes her eyes. "That's all. That's all I'm asking you to do. Now, I'm going to leave, because you were right yesterday. Your dad does deserve equal time with you and Beegee."

She peels off the wet socks and leaves them on the sofa. Einar won't mind. There is nothing else she needs to do. Bag in hand, she opens the door, steps past Jack without a word, and doesn't look back even when she's on the road.

So early in the day, the proprietor at the motel at Quathiaski Cove is surprised that she wants to check in. Just for a few hours, she tells him. She needs a shower and a bed, but she'll likely be away by two o'clock. Not the usual arrangement, but he has vacancies galore and shrugs and hands her a key.

Offers a complimentary cup of coffee, a blueberry muffin which she carries up to her room. When she's stowed the bag, she takes a pillow from the bed. Her back is sore. She settles in front of the window in a wing chair with floral print covering. But instead of using the pillow to ease her back, she finds herself, instead, holding it in her arms.

Einar is long gone. Disappeared into the mist. Already a line-up is forming for the next boat. It's not too late to change her mind. But she is so tired, and she wants to make this journey safely. She closes her eyes, presses her face to the pillow. When she opens them again, that vaguely familiar car is approaching the dock. There they go in Jack's rental, all lined up and ready to board. Lynn squints, but can't see into the back seat, just the outline of two heads in the front. She should not be watching. She should get up out of this chair, walk to the bathroom, close the door. Sit on the edge of the tub until the scene below is played out and the stage is empty again. She desperately needs to pee. But she can't leave. The room is stuffy, even her bare feet are hot against the industrial-looking grey carpet. She settles back in her chair, the pillow clenched so tight she can feel the prickle of feather shafts through the cover. Now the baby must be crying, because Heather appears at the side of the car and opens the back door. She leans in, then stands with Beegee in her arms, swaying, looking out across the water. The line-up behind them is growing, the ferry in sight now, surging across the narrow channel.

Lynn reaches for the coffee, sips at a tepid facsimile of Einar's stiff brew, then carefully puts the cup down and leans toward the window. Heather is staring across the road. Into the parking lot where Lynn's blue car is the only inhabitant. She disappears behind Jack's car, then pops up again. Now Jack's door opens and he stands. So tall. Arms akimbo, he looks up at the motel on the hill. Then he walks around to

Heather's side, puts his hands on her shoulders, his back to Lynn.

Finally, Lynn closes her eyes, freezes the two of them as they were. No, she reminds herself. Not two. There are three. She clenches her toes to keep herself rooted into the chair. So easy to walk out onto the balcony and wave. She waits.

When she opens her eyes again, Heather is threading her way across the two lanes of waiting cars, her hand up to halt the traffic coming off the ferry. Jack standing beside his door, calling to her. On the other side of the road, she turns and waves at him, waves her hand toward the ferry, head shaking. Waves until he gets back into the car. Lynn holds her breath, sure that he will turn that car around, out of the line, into the parking lot. But when the cars in front of his begin to creep forward, so does Jack's.

Lynn picks up the muffin and carefully peels away the paper on the bottom, her eyes everywhere but on the sweep of road up to the motel. She puts the muffin down. How can she swallow when she can't exhale?

She watches Heather's slow trudge up the road until she's next to Lynn's car. Heather raises her hand to shade her eyes and scans the windows.

As soon as Lynn slides the balcony door open, she can hear Beegee's squall. She steps out onto cold concrete. The salt air clogs her throat. "Two ten," she calls. "Come on up." The ferry slides away from the dock with two long mournful pulls of the whistle.

Acknowledgements

I have written about these characters, allowed them to haul their baggage from story to story for so long, that the number of readers along the way is too long to list. To all on whom I've inflicted early drafts of my fiction, warmest thanks for your sharp eyes and insight. Particular thanks are due, as always, to Dave Margoshes for years of friendship and mentorship of the highest order.

I am grateful to the UBC Creative Writing program for providing the rich ground in which this story finally set down roots. Special thanks to Catherine Bush for guiding me through the thesis with such generosity of time and attention. Her knowledge and passion for the novel form kept me reaching ever higher, and for this I am deeply grateful.

As always, my gratitude and love to my family—Robert, Elisabeth, Stefan, and Eric—for endless support and all they have taught me.

And once again, my thanks to Oolichan for putting the story on the page.

Betty Jane Hegerat has been a social worker, a teacher, and a serious student of fiction. She has studied at the University of Alberta, University of Calgary, Sage Hill, the Banff Centre, and the University of British Columbia, where she completed an MFA in Creative Writing. An avid gardener, she has learned that the challenges of growing food and flowers in an unpredictable climate bear striking resemblance to those of raising children.

Domesticity, the messy dynamics of family, the search for "home", and a deep-rooted love of the Alberta landscape underpin her stories and her obsession with finding truth through examining the secrets and lies in ordinary lives.

Betty Jane Hegerat teaches creative writing for Continuing Education at the University of Calgary, and the Alexandra Writers Centre and is the 2009 Writer in Residence at the Memorial Park Library.